Lon watched.

The tall woman with hair of gold stood out from the rest. Her skin was darker tanned than most, her body lean. Clearly a gifted carver, she did any necessary work, setting up forms for the wet sand, carrying buckets.

Secure in his hiding place, Lon felt a tightness in his chest whenever the woman rested her hand on someone's shoulder and smiled at them. He wanted to be that someone. He wanted to bask in the brilliance of her approving smile and feel the touch of that marvelous hand.

If only he could be close to her. . . .

There had to be a way.

SANDMAN

LINDA CROCKETT

TOR®

A TOM DOHERTY ASSOCIATES BOOK
NEW YORK

SANDMAN

Copyright © 1990 by Linda Crockett Gray

A Tor Book
Published by Tom Doherty Associates, Inc.
49 West 24th Street
New York, N.Y. 10010

Cover art by Joe DeVito

ISBN: 0-812-51878-0

First edition: October 1990

Printed in the United States of America

0 9 8 7 6 5 4 3 2 1

Contents

Chapter 1

"**O**KAY. LET'S GET TO IT." STAN JACOBSON SHADED HIS eyes with one pale, well-manicured hand and with the other waved at the fellow down below by the Dunes entrance. Instantly, the guy nodded and passed on the signal. The stillness of the spring morning ended abruptly. In erratic sequence, the drivers in the convoy of trucks lined up a few hundred yards away along the highway started their engines. The massive machines hacked and grumbled in response like bulldogs peeved at being prodded from slumber.

Jack Button shifted his stance, touched the front rim of the hard hat he'd been issued so it no longer rested on his wire-rim sunglasses, and tried not to appear as uncomfortable as he felt. He didn't like heights. He was hot. It was only nine o'clock. The morning mist that had cloaked the grounds earlier as they assembled for the shooting had burned off. Already the sun was intense enough to make Button's backside prickle with perspiration.

"Ready to roll, Mike?" Stan yelled below to the tall frizzy-haired guy with the video camera propped on his shoulder.

"Ready," Mike yelled back, giving him a thumbs-up. While Mike aimed the camera at the two of them, zooming in for the opening shot, Button stiffened and discreetly drew in his slight paunch.

"Here we go." Stan Jacobson waved again toward the convoy, this time for the camera. The dump trucks ground into motion. One after the other, they began lumbering forward between the massive obelisks framing the entrance to the Dunes, central Florida's newest luxury community.

"Pretty goddamn impressive," Jacobson muttered as he watched the procession approach. The ground vibrated beneath his feet as the weighted trucks picked up speed and rolled by. "Pretty goddamn impressive." He patted Button's shoulder appreciatively. "Looks good."

Button simply smiled. Visually it was better than goddamn impressive; it was magnificent. And it was going to get better. Jack Button was orchestrating a public relations dream-come-true, and he intended to milk it for all it was worth. For now, Jacobson's pat was enough. But once he had the sales figures to back him up, Stan Jacobson and Flordel would have to deliver far more than a slap on the back.

Jack Button wanted a vice-presidency and he wanted it now, before the firm mushroomed. And it would. The Dunes was just the first of a series of similar installations that Flordel planned for the Southeast. While Flordel expanded, Button wanted a new title and a bigger part of the take. And he was about to prove he deserved it. He'd been the one to come up with the concept and initiate the event now under way. He thought up the name: Dunesfest. And he'd been sharp enough to insist they hire a professional videotape crew to document every phase of the operation. When the annual review came around, he'd simply replay the footage then sit back and wait for the accolades. The Flordel board knew sheer brilliance when they saw it, and Button knew this promotion campaign was just that. Brilliant.

Two years earlier, standing on the beach with his camera dangling from one shoulder and a cold beer clasped in his fist, Jack Button had seen his future in a castle of sand. The previous year, Bluebeard's Castle, the world's largest sandcastle, had drawn national interest and over three hundred thousand sightseers to the pristine white shoreline of Treasure Island, just off St. Petersburg on Flordia's west coast. That thirty-seven foot record was broken by the castle Button 'had come halfway cross the state to see, the fifty-three-foot-tall Lost City of Atlantis. The number of sightseers this time was almost double the previous year. Besides bringing an influx of tourists, Atlantis made the *Guinness Book* and every top paper and television network nationwide. Foreign publications ran photo stories.

When Atlantis was underway, Button had only recently joined the public relations staff of Flordel. He had left his job as events coordinator at a mall complex in Lakeland and relocated to Tampa. He'd been working on his first assignment, a promotion for an executive complex in Tampa. But he knew that the critical campaign would be for the next development—tentatively called the Dunes—a resort community that would be located near Crystal Springs, sixty miles north of the bay area.

Sand. Dunes. Castles. As he stared at Atlantis that afternoon, it all suddenly came together. Button could feel the magic. The onlookers, of all ages and sizes, came alone, like he had, or by the carload, with kids or friends. Button had watched them hurrying along between the motels, still caught up in their own affairs until they'd make the turn onto the open beach and see the castle before them. That's when the magic happened.

Confronted by the masterwork, they stopped. Suddenly they were all kids again. In face after face, he'd see it. Wonder. Delight. Enchantment. Childlike and instantaneous. The castle cut through any veneer of sophistication to some still-surviving capacity for make-believe.

"Oh, my God."

"Check it out."

"Mom!"

They all had the look Button lived for. He'd built a career in public relations eliciting that look. All it took was joining the right connections to the right vehicle.

Indisputably, the castle of sand had an elusive charm. Everyone wanted to believe in fairy tales made real. Whether they spoke or not, Button knew as he studied the onlookers at Atlantis that they were all drawn into the magic. Behind their thoughtful glances, they were imagining all manner of mermen and fantastic sea creatures inhabiting the silent structure. They marveled. They took photos. And they stayed. They bought souvenir T-shirts and visors. Some picked up shells and stuffed them in a pocket. Mementos. Anything to make the magic linger. That peculiar blend of fascination and longing in their faces convinced Jack Button to pull out all the stops. The Dunes. The biggest sandcastle ever. Button couldn't stop smiling.

The only drawback Button saw to Atlantis was the severity of the design. Architecturally, it was impressive, a blend of classical Greek and Egyptian, but it wasn't really the style of structure he'd associated with the word "sandcastle." It was too angular, too stark, too Eastern, too remote. There were some nice aquatic touches, fish shapes and shells, but Button noticed that the children, the real ones, lost interest too rapidly after their initial gawking at the size. The youngsters needed something more, a dragon or a wolf or an elf or better yet, some ferocious sea monster to help the fantasy along.

Even the light show at night, projected on a flat surface on one side of Atlantis, was primarily geared for the teen crowd. Like the sand structure itself, the high-tech laser show and rock music missed captivating the middle-aged, the retirees, and the young kids. That was an unwise oversight, particularly since it was the adults who had the crucial financial clout. And he really liked kids. Hook the kids, and they'd get their parents or grandparents involved.

Sitting in the dark late that night, watching the crowd on the beach dwindle, Button started putting it all together. He grabbed his legal pad and started jotting notes and making sketches for a castle that would have something for everyone. Especially the kids. For the grand opening of the Dunes, he'd build the definitive storybook castle and build it bigger and better than its predecessors. The Dunes. The greatest sandcastle ever. The concept had the right electricity to advance him into an executive slot, and Jack Button intended to pitch himself as emphatically as he did his campaign.

The proposal Button put together was a stunner. He studied the news clippings and interviewed the promoters of the Treasure Island event. He flew out to two national competitions, one in Vancouver and one in San Diego, and talked with the team members there. With the help of the Treasure Island veterans, an architect who did sandcastling competitively, and a couple of civil engineers who'd been working on the new stadium in St. Pete, he'd put together an architectural rendering, lined up the equipment, and recruited the supervisory talent to construct "Once upon a Time. . . ." The spectacular fairy-tale city was to be topped by Rapunzel's Tower, Prince Charming's Palace, and a ferocious fire-breathing dragon. The sandcastle would dwarf all previous attempts, with spires peaking as close to seventy feet as they could get, hundreds of storybook characters, winding pathways for tours, and lighting effects that would hold any audience spellbound. The topper was that Button planned to build this inland, at the Dunes, near Crystal Springs, where no beach existed at all. Every grain of the estimated ninety thousand tons needed would have to be trucked in.

"Once upon a time . . ." Button began his spiel in a low, dramatic voice, in one executive conference room after another. He'd flip open the large drawing pad with the architect's sketch of the castle and continue. The Dunes management was not his only target. Just bringing in the sand meant permits, scheduling, routing, and money. Staffing the event would be costly. Underwriting the expenses meant getting backers. Button took his packaged presentation, complete with slides and statistics, to corporate sponsors to coax them into bankrolling the event.

He succeeded. Articulate, persuasive, and adept at slanting each pitch to the special interests of a given company, Button drew them into the fantasy. An excavation and a construction company, a brewery, a tanning-products company, Kodak film, a soft-drink company, and a landscaping and horticulture firm all agreed to underwrite the initial costs. Souvenir and refreshment concession sales, T-shirt sales, and tour admissions would bring in additional monies later.

"What's in it for you?" Button would state in his matter-of-fact delivery. "Plenty." For the sponsors, the promised payback would come in widespread publicity and promotional privileges. The media would grab at a good story and give it plenty of free coverage. Button always stressed this to potential backers. Besides the direct acknowledgment sponsors would get in the news stories, their logos and products would in some way be conspicuous in interviews with the sandsculpting artists. From every camera angle there would be T-shirts and visors, concession tents with sponsors' credits, barricades with billboards.

"Visibility," Button would reiterate, flashing feature articles about Bluebeard's Castle and Atlantis. His castle would command even more coverage. The local, national, and international impact would be inestimable.

"We can't lose," Button had told his own firm. For the Dunes, the event would be an undeniably slick marketing tool. As public attention focused on the site, the sales team would gear up for the influx of visitors. Models of projected office complexes, town houses, condominiums, single-family dwellings, specialty shops, a golf resort, spring-fed lakes, and waterways, and a nature trail would be on display in the information center for potential buyers and investors. Buildings already constructed would be open for inspection. By mid-March, when the event commenced, the newly completed Grand Nile Resort would welcome guests and visitors. Its three luxurious dining facilities and bars would be in full operation throughout Dunesfest.

Button speculated that the spillover of guests unable to afford the Grand Nile rates, would cause a boom in tourism in the adjacent community. That appealed to the Flordel board. They were counting on the positive financial impact to placate disgruntled Crystal Springs citizens who had opposed the development. The locals hadn't wanted a mini-city thrust into their rural, citrus-growing area. But Flordel courted a few influential citizens and bureaucrats, and the development won out. By the time their intentions were made public, Flordel had bought up huge packets of acreage under an assortment of subsidiary names. Before the opposition could get organized, the Dunes existed. Stan Jacobson said it was time for Crystal Springs to wake up and accommodate itself to the future. Button could see that future, and his own, crystallizing in a vision of white.

Timing had been crucial. Organizing the spectacle turned into an enormously complicated procedure, which had consumed Button's full attention for the past six months. Flordel had to take on two additional staff members in the PR department to handle the routine work while Button concentrated on details. He booked everything with an eye to drawing maximum traffic. The next-to-last week of this monthlong operation would coincide with spring break in Florida schools and would overlap the Easter holidays. With balmy, clear weather predicted, Button was counting on attracting at least half a million visitors. The major television networks and a movie company were requesting permission to film. Four requests to have weddings performed on the heights were being considered.

Afterward, when the crowds were gone and bulldozers

leveled the structure, the Dunes would have a waiting list
of contracted occupants, the board of Flordel would be
pleased, and Button would have his promotion. Beyond
that, the pure spring waters of the lake that was being
dredged in the recreation area at the western end of the
development would have a breathtaking white sand beach.
Inland. That was the kicker. A tropical paradise with a
spectacular beach in the middle of nowhere.

"Formerly nowhere," Jack Button was adept at stressing in his pursuit of sponsors. The Dunes clearly would
become a somewhere, an oasis within commuting distance of Tampa Bay. Corporations looking to relocate or
expand would find the setting ideal. The sandcastle would
be the hook, a very spectacular hook.

Right now, however, while he stood watching the
trucks almost three stories below filled with sand, his
stomach lurched at the height and his balls itched. Between the humidity and plain nervousness, his boxer
shorts had become soaked with perspiration. The crotch
seam was wedged into the crack in his rear end. Button
knew better than to scratch or tug at it. Mike was still
down there filming. A vice-president-to-be didn't want
to be caught pulling at his balls or tugging at his butt on
videotape. Button had a new image to refine. Since he'd
relocated to Crystal Springs, he'd been dieting. He'd cut
down on drinks, and he'd grown a mustache and a trim,
dark beard to make his baby face appear more mature
and serious. He was still self-conscious about his weight,
and this on-camera participation, particularly the wearing of a hard hat, struck him as unnecessarily theatrical.
Nothing—other than perhaps bird shit—was going to drop
on them up there, but if Flordel wanted him and Jacobson in hard hats, he'd deliver. His job was to give 'em
what they wanted.

So here he was with Stan, both of them in their business suits, peering down into the valley like Egyptian overlords at a pyramid-construction site. Unlike the original, the Great Sphinx of central Florida on which they stood enclosed the fountain and pool plumbing system for the Grand Nile Resort. Its noseless visage peered eastward, its enigmatic smile carefully crafted and more complete than the original at Giza, the Sphinx turned its leonine shoulder toward the proposed castle site.

The action taking place in its shadow on the flatlands below Button and his boss was no massing of laborers or caravan passage. It was a convoy of another sort. Throughout the weekend and for the next full week, twenty twelve-ton Mack trucks with their dumps mounded high with pale white sand would be coming and going between the Dunes and the gravel plant in Arcola, bringing over ninety thousand tons of fine sand. From that pile, at least three hundred feet in length and width, a paid team of twenty-two sandsculptors and over a thousand volunteers were going to construct the largest, most spectacular sandcastle in the world.

The trucks halted, bumper to bumper, idled, then one after another fell silent. A few drivers climbed out, lit cigarettes, and clustered in the shade of the Sphinx.

"Well, Jack, I guess we should get back to the office." Attempting to remove his hard hat without disturbing his hair, Stan Jacobson pulled out his handkerchief and mopped his brow. The dark wisps that he'd earlier managed to spread out over his bald spot were now plastered in isolated wet curlicues. When his fingertips discovered one of them, Jacobson's affable smile dissolved into its standard tight line as he glanced over to see if Button was looking. But despite his slight case of vertigo, Button pretended to be contemplating the scene below. Already the trucks were backed up onto the highway while the lead truck deposited its load at a destination farther on.

"Sure. I think they can handle the rest of this without us," Button replied a bit sardonically, eyeing the standstill. Other than waving to start the procession, Button was well aware that neither he nor Jacobson had performed any vital function this morning, but Jacobson missed the underlying humor in Button's words.

"I'd like to see what there is on tape as it comes in." Jacobson gave his tophairs a few desperate pats with the handkerchief. They clung together in babylike spirals and collapsed haphazardly again. "Have Mike bring today's footage to the weekend conference in the morning. I'll have the VCR set up in my office." He looked around uncertainly, trying to remember his earlier path. "You think you should have them bring up a ladder or something?"

Their moment of glory had obviously passed. Button pursed his lips, repressing his possible responses. Whatever camaraderie had existed between him and Jacobson was gone. It was back to business. Jacobson, Vice-President and Director of Expansion, had resumed his executive persona.

"I think we can backtrack safely," Button replied. "Turn around and go down like you would a ladder." He pointed to the steplike indentations that led down the chest of the crouched figure.

Jacobson patted his head one last time, then gave up on the hair. Since he was clearly closer to the steps, he turned, almost getting onto his knees before starting to make his way down the chest of the Sphinx. Parked below near the four-toed paw of the creature was the company golf cart that would take them back across the resort

grounds to the Dunes headquarters on the second floor
of the Grand Nile Hotel.

"Don't forget the tape," Jacobson noted. "I wouldn't
want to have to go through this again."

"Will do. I'd like to see the videotapes myself," Button responded efficiently. He'd been through this back-
to-rank reversal before. Not just with Stan Jacobson, but
with countless other executives a rung or two above him.
Like a court jester, he'd set up events to please and amuse
them and their customers, and for a while he'd gain en-
tree to their realm. As long as Button kept the show
going, some illusion of friendship and equality prevailed,
however superficial. But once the entertainment ended,
the old order returned. The jester was supposed to bow
out. Only this time, Button knew the show wasn't over.
This time, it had all been recorded, and Button wouldn't
be pushed off stage as readily as he'd been before.

"Sure is turning into a beautiful day," Button commented stubbornly, deliberately moving into place so he'd
rush Jacobson a bit. "Nice change of pace to get out in
the fresh air and enjoy the scenery."

Awkwardly reaching a foot out toward a flat space and
steadying himself on the bulge of the lowest step, Jacobson didn't even nod. Button could see the beads of perspiration glistening like dewdrops between the sparse
tophairs on Jacobson's head. He hadn't really noticed before how Jacobson's ears stuck out beneath the remaining
fringe of black hair. The outer edges were already reddened either from exertion or from exposure to the sun.

Jacobson moved to the midsection of the beast and
reached for another foothold. Button fixed his customary
accommodating expression on his face and tried not to
appear too amused at Jacobson's ineptitude. "Maybe we

should recommend this as part of the company's physical-fitness program,'' Button remarked lightly.

Jacobson glanced up, managing a smile of sorts before his eyes glazed over again. He stepped onto the next flat landing, the top of the pedestallike wall that supported the Sphinx and surrounded the pool and several lagoon-style spas. The wall was a foot taller than Jacobson. There were only a few toeholds up its steep side. He still had to negotiate them. He looked up to check Button's progress.

''Let's get going,'' he said unnecessarily, then looked away.

''Prick,'' Button muttered silently, fleetingly recalling the first time he'd really understood the glazed look that meant he'd been demoted to underling, shut out again. It happened a lot after he'd moved to Florida in junior high, a chubby, shy boy who tried to cover his self-consciousness by acting the clown. He studied magic. He memorized put-downs and jokes from books and magazines. He listened to stand-up comics and disc jockeys and stole their material. And he practiced his delivery in the shower until he got it down smooth. He was clean, compulsively clean, but he also was funny.

In high school, Button linked up with another guy, who was good in electronics, and the two of them went into the DJ business. Sometimes he earned extra money wearing clown makeup, doing magic tricks, and creating puppies and giraffes out of skinny balloons for kids' birthday parties. Even then, Button especially liked kids. But he was always on. He was always trying to please. He loved having an audience begging for more.

Inevitably, when the party was over or the dance ended, Button may as well have been invisible. No one hung around to wait for him to go out for a Coke or a late burger. No one paid him any attention. Except maybe a kid. Usually whoever was in charge would pay him and say thanks. Then they'd get that glazed look that meant his usefulness had ended. And Button was left with an emptiness that was more humiliating because for a while, he'd let himself believe that he belonged, that they really saw him, Jack Button, behind all that glib talk and flashy delivery.

Still, he was a pushover. Occasionally he'd get invited along for an evening with a few school chums. But even then there was usually a payoff. "Bring some of those balloons," a fellow would add as he tossed out an invitation. "My girl is really into giraffes. You can make one, can't you?" Then Button would go home and practice doing a giraffe. He'd give 'em what they wanted so he'd be one of the group, so he wouldn't feel alone. Eventually, he stopped kidding himself. But he kept up the good-natured facade and tucked his secrets behind it.

Now, as Button followed Stan Jacobson down the incline, he didn't feel the pain that glazed look once gave him. Users. That's what they were. And Jacobson was just another one. Just a cretin in an expensive suit. And clumsy besides. Even at his top weight, Button had been agile. Thinner now by fifty pounds, he was making the descent far more smoothly than Jacobson, who was a few years younger than Button's forty-one and probably twenty pounds lighter.

"Clumsy cretin." Button chuckled silently. Jacobson skidded slightly on the flat surface of the privacy wall then flapped his arms to regain his balance. Button sniffed both in satisfaction and contempt. "Cretin." His narrowed gaze shifted lower toward the lagoon-type swimming pool, where a bunch of youngsters were squealing and splashing under one of the waterfalls. He liked kids.

Only the kids cared without strings attached. And there would be thousands of kids coming to see his sandcastle. For an instant, Button felt that familiar rush of anticipation. Then he shook it off.

"Say, Stan, do you know what's in the air that keeps making women pregnant?" Button launched into a joke just to get on course again. Stan Jacobson liked jokes. The younger man was really sweating now as he inched off the last ledge, backward. Finding the toeholds on the way up had been relatively simple. Down, especially with the rocks damp from the dew, was another feat altogether. Button repeated the line, louder this time. "What's in the air . . ." He liked making the cretins dance while he pulled the strings.

He waited until Jacobson stopped, glanced up at him, and asked. "Okay. What?"

"Their feet," Button replied.

He saw Jacobson's eyebrows arch. Then the quick smug smile.

"What can women put behind their ears to make them more attractive?"

"What?"

"Their ankles."

Jacobson wouldn't laugh outright. But if he liked it, he'd memorize the joke so he could tell it in the executive john. Or in the limo.

"Tell me the first one again," Jacobson demanded, clinging like a cockroach to the side.

Button repeated the lead-in. Jacobson nodded. Cretin. Then the punch line. The eyebrows arched again.

"And the other one?"

Button repeated it.

Jacobson nodded. "Their ankles," he murmured,

nodding again. Then he altered his position and scuttled downward.

Asshole, Button mused. Jacobson would probably screw up the jokes. He often did. But he did enjoy having a new one to pass around, the cruder the better. Maggot . . . Button found himself wishing the slick soles of Jacobson's expensive shoes would glance off the uneven surface and send the senior executive plummeting onto the rocks below. Preferably headfirst. Then those kewpie curls would really stay put.

"Got another other one." Button broke the momentary silence.

Again Jacobson stopped and looked up at him expectantly, eagerly, with the hooked-fish expression Button liked to see.

"Why is it that brunettes have the best orgasms?" He saw Jacobson's thin lips stiffen with interest. He waited for the cretin to ask for the punch line.

"Why?"

Half-smiling, Button pretended to be engrossed in his own descent while Jacobson clung there, unmoving, bound by anticipation.

"Hustle it up a bit, Zach." Kitty didn't like to pressure him, but she'd already changed clothes and checked the mail, and he was still in the bathroom, undoubtedly reading one of his X-Men comic books and waiting for nature to take its course. Granted, the kid deserved his privacy, but sometimes Zach got so absorbed in the TV or comics that he'd forget there were other things on the schedule. Under normal circumstances, she would have been more philosophical. "Zach, remember I have a meeting in Crystal Springs. We needed to be on the road soon to miss the rush-hour traffic.

"Come on, Zach," she called from downstairs, keeping the exasperation she felt from creeping into her voice. "Bring the books. You can read in the car. Please. Let's go." She kept the tone firm but still good-natured. Zach couldn't handle anything that sounded like anger. The few times that Kitty had snapped at him, he'd pulled back into himself and hid in his room. Generally under the bed. Sometimes he'd cower there, singing to himself, usually "Jesus Loves Me," comforting himself. Then it would take fifteen minutes or more to reassure him that she wasn't really that upset, she wouldn't hit him, and she did love him. Really. While she coaxed him, whatever memories triggered his flight reaction would gradually lose their hold on the present, and he'd finally come wriggling out and get a hug.

"Zach, we'll have just enough time to stop at McDonald's if you hurry up," Kitty tried again. Positive motivation. The HRS counselor who'd helped her in the placement and adoption process had said that Zach had been given plenty of the negative kind of motivation. Throughout the first eight of his eleven years, the kid had been bounced about between an alcoholic mother and one foster home or another. Along the way he'd been neglected and beaten, occasionally by an older foster child sharing the same home, more than once by the mother's current live-in boyfriend, and probably a few incidents that went unreported. At eight he was withdrawn, unwanted, undersized, and presumed unadoptable.

Zach was also assumed to be retarded. By then in certain respects he was emotionally and intellectually underdeveloped. For years he'd been underestimated, miscategorized, and treated inappropriately. However, when Kitty insisted on complete physical and psychological testing, the evaluation indicated that Zach's alleged retardation was not a birth defect but a result of the emotional battering he'd suffered. Linking up with Kitty was a turning point.

He'd come through the communications-equipment company on a tour with his special-ed class. She saw him pass by her office door, hanging back from the others a moment to scrutinize an interoffice security camera. With a halo of pale blond curly hair, slim and androgynous in form, the youngster reminded her of herself as a child, too often sidetracked by curiosity in directions not officially sanctioned. When he turned to face her, his sea blue eyes met hers with the somewhat startled expression of a furtive angel. For a few seconds they simply stared at each other in silence. Then from farther along the hallway the teacher's voice intruded, and with a sheepish shrug, he was gone.

But Kitty had followed. And while the tour of Biscom continued, she'd watched him and asked the chaperons questions. Every time she looked into those eyes, so much like her own, she felt as if she were seeing into a lost part of her own being. So she began wading through a bureaucratic maze, determined to adopt him. Now, after almost two years together, Zach and Kitty were still working out the kinks in their relationship. Emotionally and academically, Zach was gradually catching up with his age group. Often the progress was two steps forward and one step back; nevertheless, he was making advances.

But there were still short circuits. Zach could be stubborn. So could she. His ingrained dread of confrontations and outbursts could send them both into a tailspin. Then it took time to recoup. The counselors assured her that eventually Zach would learn to handle everyday tension better. It just would take patience, and reassurance, and time. Right now, all three were running out.

"Bring your homework. Do it on the way in case we get hung up," Kitty called through the bathroom door. There was a rustle inside, then Zach finally emerged from the bathroom, comics in hand.

"Sorry I took so long. You aren't mad, are you?" he asked timidly, just needing to hear her say no.

"I'm hungry, not mad. You're probably hungry, too. Let's move it. Don't forget the homework." She gave him a quick hug and sent him off in search of his school-bag. Lean and gawky, still a bit undersized for his age, he looked closer to nine than eleven. But that slow growth was diagnosed as a stress reaction to whatever dark trau-mas had haunted him before Kitty came along. But things were changing. His picky eating habits had improved, particularly over the past winter months. With spring ap-proaching, he had started to pack in food and down milk by the gallon. His feet had grown another shoe size. The doctor said these were all good signs. Sooner or later, Zach would hit a growth spurt, then puberty would be just around the corner.

"Nothing wrong with being a late bloomer," Kitty had comforted Zach after a bout earlier in the year with one of his less-sympathetic schoolmates. "Look at me. I was one," she had told him, flipping open an old photo album and pointing to the skinny kid with bony knees and a striped dress. "That's me. Twelve years old. Braces on my teeth. And that nose. Took me ten years to grow into it. What a beauty." She chuckled. "Shortest girl in my PE class. By my senior year, I was one of the tallest. I was through college before I developed enough of a chest to show I was female. Even then you had to look close," she added, nudging him and laughing. "Late bloomers run in our family," she had insisted. "Look at Buddy. He had feet just like yours." She poked a finger at the next photo, pointing to the tennis-shoe pontoons supporting her younger brother, then thirteen and short like Zach. "I called him Bigfoot." It helped that Zach knew Buddy was now six-two. "See, it's family tradition. You fit right in."

Zach had studied the pictures closely, flipping the pages as he saw the brother and sister dressed for proms, marching in the band, and graduating from high school. Then Zach had raised his puppydog eyes and grinned his goofy smile.

"Yeah. Late bloomers run in our family." He echoed her words, clearly delighted at last to be part of something that included an Uncle Bud, a grandma, a great-aunt and -uncle, some cousins, Kitty, and himself. "I fit right in."

At McDonald's drive-through Kitty called in the order. "Two fish fillets, two large fries, two medium Cokes." Zach made a lap tray out of his bookbag so he could eat comfortably while they drove the sixty miles north to Crystal Springs. "It will take us about an hour and a quarter to get there," she noted, "unless there's a traffic problem. So if you want to do some exploring, you'll have to start your homework on the way, right after you finish eating. I hear it's quite a place—Jacuzzis, a swimming pool with waterfalls, parks, waterways for canoeing. Lots of neat stuff. It's decorated with all kinds of Egyptian things, so I heard. But homework comes first." She paid the money at one window and pulled ahead to the next to pick up the food and drinks.

"I'll do my homework," Zach promised dutifully as he spread out some napkins and unpacked the sandwich and fries she passed him.

"And just because you're going with me to this meeting, don't get your hopes up that they'll let you sculpt with Vince or with me," she cautioned him. "This isn't going to be like any of the past sandsculpture events. They said they would make arrangements for our kids, but that did not include letting you work the mounds." She had said all this before, but Zach had a way of getting caught up in events, building unlikely scenarios, and forgetting the ground rules. Besides, he really couldn't anticipate what was involved in this kind of project. He hadn't been around when she worked Blackbeard or Atlantis.

Zach had not seen firsthand either of the previous record-breaking structures. He'd only looked at the newspaper clippings and a few videotaped segments Kitty had saved from the television coverage. His only direct contact with sandsculpting had come when he worked with Kitty for their own amusement or in local competitions at the St. Pete beaches. But when Kitty sculpted seriously, she didn't do castles. Instead, she created magnificent figures, larger-than-life-size and dramatic, and Zach mostly shoveled or sprayed or watched, afraid he'd mess them up.

Then Vince had volunteered to teach Zach to do castles. A professional architect, Vince Ammons had a flair for fine detail. He'd repeatedly won individual competitions with his exquisite miniature fortress-castles, complete with rose windows in the cathedrals and cannons on the parapets. Once he and Kitty had teamed up on a sculpture for a TV spot on tourism during the Superbowl coverage. But when the relationship turned romantic, they decided the sandsculpting partnership had to go. Kitty went back to her solo pieces. But Zach made the switch to castles.

Under Vince's tutelage, Zach had eventually turned out passable Gothic spires and Roman arches, but always on a small scale. The castle at the Dunes would be massive, and constructing it purely from sand would be a major architectural feat. Despite the festive atmosphere, Kitty knew working the mound could be dangerous. There were always accidents, from shovel cuts to sandslides to sunburn. The higher the mound, the more stringent the safety regulations. This was going over six stories. That meant no kids.

"I understand," Zach mumbled through a mouthful of fish and tartar sauce. "I only get to watch," he added sulkily.

"And to swim in the pools, play video games, and go canoeing and do whatever else comes along," Kitty stressed, not buying into his self-pity routine. "That's as long as you keep up with your schoolwork while we're there." For the two-week period from setting up the forms to completing the sandcastle village, she and Zach would stay in Crystal Springs, without having to battle the traffic on U.S. 19 to St. Pete and back each day. She was taking it off as vacation time. She'd made arrangements with Zach's teachers to prepare his assignments in advance, some on printed handouts, some from textbooks, and others on diskettes for an Apple computer. The Dunes staff would set up a study room for students and the Apples would be there for individual use. So if Zach did the schoolwork on schedule, the absences would be excused, and he'd get to stay in a luxury hotel for two weeks and be treated like an honored guest. That was the part of the Dunes package offer that made Kitty reschedule her vacation and promise to work overtime for the next two weekends at Biscom in preparation for her absence.

"I think we're there. . . ." she said softly. Zach had been leaning back, eyes closed, dozing the last few miles. Now he stirred and stared groggily out the window.

From a distance, the flaring headdress of the massive Sphinx dominated the far horizon. Wreathed by the adjacent trees, it seemed as if the six-story man-beast had simply settled in a wooded area to rest. But even before they pulled past the hundred-foot obelisks on either side of the Dunes entrance, the initial impact of the dull-eyed Sphinx had ebbed. Zach spotted the skeletal crisscross arms of the cranes, towering above the surrounding pine and oak trees. Like long-necked dinosaurs they stood with their dump buckets, openmouthed, in midair.

"Look at those things," he marveled. "Man, are they big."

The roadway, a sand-covered asphalt strip etched with broad diamond-patterned tire marks, veered off to the left, into the wilderness toward the castle construction site. It bypassed the pensive Sphinx, whose extended feet stretched out on a carpet of grass, artfully landscaped with a barrier of palm trees, papyrus, and clusters of meticulously groomed oleanders. To the right, beyond the Sphinx, the gleaming stepped roofline of the Grand Nile Hotel indicated that the heart of the Dunes complex was near. In the eerie gold of the sinking sun, the left-hand road was a sinuous trail into a prehistoric scene.

Kitty pulled to the right toward the booth where the security guard screened visitors. "When they get all the sand trucked in, you should be able to see the tops of the mounds from the highway. Sort of like the pyramids in Egypt."

Zach puckered his lips and said nothing, his pale eyes, narrowed somewhat, were taking it all in.

"Look, peacocks."

Zack lurched forward to get a better view of a parading male with tailfeathers elegantly outspread. "Wow. Look at that."

"There's supposed to be all kinds of wildlife here." Kitty tilted forward a bit, peering out the window like Zach. "Even alligators."

"Really?" Zach's eyes widened. "Walkin' around loose?"

"So I hear," Kitty replied. "This area used to be all overgrown, some parts orchard, other parts cypress swamp. There's lots of springs back in the woods. I read somewhere that the developers bought up about fifteen hundred acres. That's a whole lot of land. Some of it was a wildlife refuge. The whole place is designated a bird sanctuary." She slowed down at the booth as the attendant stepped out. "Kitty Westberg. I'm here for the sand-sculptors meeting."

The mustachioed fellow in the tan safari garb that was the Dunes official staff uniform checked his roster, his eyes hidden behind dark-lense sunglasses. "Westberg. Right." He smiled genially and handed her a parking permit and a map of the grounds. "Please follow Delta Drive to the right. The meeting is in the conference room at the Grand Nile East. Parking is reserved for you next to the building. The conference room is straight through the main door, then up the escalator to the mezzanine floor. Welcome to the Dunes."

At six o'clock, eighteen of the twenty-two chairs around the U-shaped conference table were occupied. Vince Ammons glanced at his watch, then at the door, then at the two individuals setting up three large easels at the front of the room. A reddish-haired woman arrived with an arm full of folders, spoke briefly with the Dunes

PR man, Jack Button, and began making a circuit of the room, placing in front of each participant a teal blue slipcase emblazoned in gold with the Dunes pyramid and lotus logo.

Button checked the time, pursed his lips, then looked over the group. "We're just handing out some information so you can glance it over while we wait for the remainder of the group. These orientation packets have your parking decals, room assignments, and the general schedule we'll be following during the two weeks of the event. If you have any questions about accommodations or schedules, Angie McLemore here is our liaison person." He waved one hand casually by way of introduction toward the auburn-haired woman. "Angie is here to make sure you have nothing to worry about while you're here, other than sculpting." The door at the rear of the room opened.

"Come on in, we're just getting started." Button beckoned to the young man who'd just walked through the doorway. "Nice to see you, Paul." He addressed the fellow by name as smoothly as he had each of the previous arrivals. "Pick up something cool at the bar and make yourself at home," he suggested, tilting his head toward the portable unit set up at the side of the conference room. The bartender glanced up expectantly as the newcomer ambled over and surveyed the array of gleaming bottles.

"You got mineral water? With a couple of wedges of lemon."

"Sure do."

Paul took the drink and headed for a vacant seat.

Vince Ammons tugged at his tie then loosened his collar, catching the newcomer's glance and nodding in greeting. Vince had taken off his jacket before as he drove to Crystal Springs from his office in St. Pete, but he'd yanked it back on when he got a close look at the elegant hotel. Until now, it had only been a photograph on a pamphlet Button had given him in St. Pete. Up close, the Dunes was breathtaking.

Like a chrome and glass descendant of the pyramid at Saqqara, it reached skyward, seventeen stories at the topmost point. Besides the arresting figures of the Great Sphinx and obelisks at the gate, the front entrance of the hotel itself, framed by a pair of two-story stylized granite statues of males with falcon heads, suggested a certain degree of formality was in order. Inside, halls and alcoves contained glass display cases housing remarkable reproductions of Egyptian art and artifacts. The central foyer was a multilayered garden with palm trees and fountains and lily ponds. Vince had been so impressed he even realigned his tie. But now, seeing that Paul Feneau, like most of the other sandsculptors in attendance, had come in casual clothes, Vince felt conspicuously overdressed. Except for Jack Button, Vince was the only one in a suit.

"You can move into the hotel anytime next weekend," Button went on. "The sand should all be in place by next Saturday evening. Heavy equipment will be set up that Sunday afternoon. Monday there'll be a meeting at eight and a site tour with Craig Stuart and Kevin Walters, the two gentlemen from Vancouver who are in charge of coordinating the overall construction." The two men who had been adjusting the easels glanced up and nodded, then went back to their labors.

Button looked at his watch again. "Craig and Kevin will be taking over in a few minutes to talk about the logistics of this creation. Sometime next weekend before we begin, you'll get your final blueprints. That first day out, we'll stake out individual sites and start setting the upper molds. Once the heights are started, we'll turn you loose with crews of volunteers to do the rest.''

Standing before the group of artists he'd personally recruited, Button felt an undeniable sense of pleasure as he tossed out terms like ''upper molds'' and spoke of logistics and blueprints with quiet confidence. He wanted them to know he'd done his homework. Whether he lifted a shovel or not, Button had diligently turned himself into an expert of sorts. Throughout the project, he didn't intend for his involvement to be underestimated by anyone. This castle was his.

''You can see from your schedule that during the event, breakfast will be served in the Courtyard restaurant from 6:30 to 7:30 each morning. There'll be coffee and juice available in a tented rest area near the castle site if you want to start light.'' Button went over a few more points. When the door opened this time, he looked up, smiled, and strode forward.

''Kitty Westberg, folks,'' he said aloud. ''Those of you who worked Bluebeard's Castle or Atlantis have undoubtedly met her. And you must be Zach.'' He lowered his voice. ''I hope you don't mind, but I figured Zach might find all this shoptalk boring, so I made arrangements for one of our staff to show him around the place.''

''Sound good to you?'' Kitty asked the boy.

''Sure.'' Zach was subdued, but curious.

''Angie, this is the young man I mentioned. Would you take him out and introduce him to Corey.''

The woman smiled and led Zach out again.

''Welcome.'' Button turned back to Kitty, shaking her hand then leading her to the bar. ''How about a drink,'' he offered. ''Orange juice?'' he suggested, subtly demonstrating how efficiently he'd absorbed the data he and

his staff had compiled on each participant. Westberg,
Kitty. 33. Divorced. One child. Adopted. Communications technician. Nonsmoker. Nondrinker. Button had it
all down. He didn't intend to miss a trick.

"Orange juice would be great," Kitty answered. While
the bartender filled the glass, she took a quick look at
the faces in the room, most of them familiar ones. Not
surprisingly, besides the red-haired woman handing out
folders, Kitty was the only female present. When she saw
Vince and the vacant chair he'd held for her, she took the
juice and headed in his direction.

"Make yourself at home," Button remarked as he returned to the front of the room. "Okay, now that we're
all here, I'm going to turn the meeting over to Craig and
Kevin. Don't forget, when we finish, there will be a buffet dinner in the Felucca Café just down the hall. The
location is marked on the map inside your folder. For
now we'll get down to the castle business. Craig. Kevin.
It's all yours." He stepped to the side, then took a vacant
chair at the conference table.

"Kevin, go ahead and start while I take a minute to
get these situated," the stockier of the two project leaders suggested, then hoisted a three-foot-square art pad
onto each easel, maneuvering so that everyone would
have a better view. The other fellow, blond and with a
reddish beard, stepped forward, tugging a bit nervously
at the single gold hoop in his right ear. Vince Ammons
looked him over then glanced at Kitty a little dubiously.

At thirty-eight, Kevin Walters still had the body of a
young man. Tan, broad-shouldered, and muscular, with
the large callused hands of a laborer, he looked like a
buccaneer with the addition of that earring. But when he
spoke, the voice was surprisingly soft, articulate, even
lyrical.

"We're here to join with you in bringing something remarkably beautiful into the world. I'm Kevin Walters and my genial colleague here is Craig Stuart," he began with a mischievous look in his dark, hooded eyes. "I cannot tell you how pleased we are to have each of you here. When I read over all of our credentials, I have to admit, we're quite an awesome assemblage." With several individual sandsculpting world championships to his credit, Kevin and his fellow Canadian Craig Stuart had moved into team competition and a few commercial ventures, then had dropped out of competition for a few years. But they had helped transform a casual pastime into an art form. At Button's urging, they'd agreed to take a leave of absence from their separate businesses in Vancouver and come out of sculpting retirement to head the Dunes Project.

"Each of us here is an artist, an architect of fantasy," Kevin began, his olive black eyes gentle and contemplative as he looked at each of his co-workers for the first time. Until now, their only communication had been in correspondence and sketches exchanged through Button's office.

"We each bring highly individual visions and talents to this project," Kevin continued. "Most of us have won prizes of one sort or another"—he smiled a slightly lopsided smile, tugging again at the earring—"but in this event, we have the luxury of having no competitors, no rivalry, and no prizes to concern us. The primary reward is the pure pleasure of participating in a remarkable experience." He rubbed his hands together and smiled again, his perfect teeth strikingly white against his darker skin. He glanced over his shoulder at the still-closed art pads that Craig Stuart now had set up and ready.

"And it will be remarkable," Kevin stressed in a voice low, soft, and strangely dramatic. "We have everything going for us. Talent and technology. With the combined imaginative powers and artistic abilities in this group and with the machinery and equipment Flordel is making available, together, we can push back the boundaries of possibility." A strange, faintly eager expression softened his features. "I think we all sense that. There is something irresistible about the sheer enormity of this undertaking. We're talking a storybook world seven stories tall. That's why we're willing to put the rest of our lives on hold for a couple of weeks while we come here to play in the sand. Of course, it's very nice to be accommodated so graciously by the Flordel Corporation," he added. "But I suspect the truth is, even if they weren't compensating us, we would probably be here, doing it for nothing. We all want to see how far we can push the art form and ourselves. Right?" He gave a conspiratorial nod, his thick curly red hair rippling with the motion.

Around the room slow smiles spread over the faces of most of the twenty participants. A few heads nodded in response.

"Thought so," Kevin said, grinning and wringing his hands delightedly. "I'm glad I'm not the only one in the group who loves a challenge." He glanced at Stuart, who was fidgeting with a pointer, eager to get on to the drawings. "Before we get too wound up," Kevin cautioned, "let's talk real straight." His expression suddenly became more serious.

"What we have here is a real opportunity to extend ourselves," he said emphatically, yet in little more than a whisper, cupping his hands as if he held some unseen, precious object. None of the occupants of the room could take their eyes off him as he moved back closer to the easels, turned, and let his gaze embrace them all. Then with near-mystical reverence, he lifted his invisible gift toward them, releasing it and setting it adrift in the space between them. No one stirred, not until Kevin himself chuckled and broke the spell. "We have here the opportunity to share. To learn. To create. To take what we imagine and make it exist in this realm. Together. Let's just keep that spirit when we start getting into this next week. No competeness. No prima donnas. We're in this for the beauty of it. Remember that, and we'll have a good time." He backed up, bobbing up and down as he retreated, bowing out of center stage.

"Now it's my turn," Craig Stuart began, his face clean shaven, his expression animated. "Kevin's our philosopher and visionary. I'm more the nuts-and-bolts man." Stuart flipped over the cover page on each of the three drawing boards. Each one presented a different view of the triple-peaked mound, complete with the projected fairy-tale structures.

"Let's go over the basic design and make sure everyone is happy with the proposal so far," Stuart suggested. At forty-one, with close-cropped steel gray hair and a restless energy about his movements, Stuart had been pacing during the last seconds of Kevin's opening remarks. "You have a duplicate of these preliminary plans in your folder. Let's pull them out and iron out any obvious problems." Owner of a general contracting company in Canada, Stuart had built more serviceable structures than castles. But he knew this undertaking required serious planning and that evaluating blueprints now would save hassles later. "Don't hesitate to speak out," he prodded them. "Nothing is definite yet. But once we get your feedback, we'll do a final revision. We all will start a week Monday with those blueprints in our hands.''

''Laminated, no less,'' Kevin interjected with a bemused smile.

''Yeah. We're going to laminate them so you can carry them with you on the mound and they won't get ruined,'' Stuart explained.

Vince Ammons glanced at Kitty, lifting one brow to show he was clearly impressed. They'd both seen their drawings disintegrate midway through their sandsculpting efforts. Occasionally they got buried or drenched and were illegible by the time they were recovered.

''Jack Button thought of the laminating idea,'' Stuart added. ''I tell you, this man has seen to it that we're going first class all the way,'' he declared. ''He's even supplying us with those little walkie-talkie headsets so we can all keep up with what's going on somewhere else on the mound. I know this won't be the only time I say this over the next few weeks, but I do want to thank Jack here for heading off a whole lot of problems. Appreciate it, Jack.'' He directed a nod at Button.

Button returned the gesture with a friendly grin.

''Let's go over the three peaks and the breakdown of work areas,'' Stuart proceeded. ''Pull 'em out.'' While the others located the tentative plans, Stuart lifted a clipboard holding several lists he'd made. ''Basically the flow is from south to north, from the urban mound to the countryside one, then to the seashore.'' He gave them a moment to look over the layout.

''We've set up three mound supervisors to keep things running smoothly,'' Stuart explained. ''Then we've designated some of you as resource people who'll step in wherever you're needed. Kevin is good with animals, particularly fantasy types, so he's heading up the dragon mound on the north end. I'm concentrating on the height, so I'm in charge of the initial construction on all three, but then I'll focus on the center mound, the country one with Rapunzel's Castle. Kitty will be supervising with me.''

He pointed to each blue-lined section in turn. ''We've got a guy named Dave Crockett who just happens to be the uncle of Jaisen here.'' He tilted the clipboard toward one of the younger members of the group. ''Crockett is a civil engineer with large-construction experience. He'll help us set up and pack the primary molds. He's also designing some scaffolding. And we've put Vince Ammons on the south mound, the city setting. He's in charge of Prince Charming's Castle and the town that surrounds it. But once he has the forms blocked out, he's going to be our overall architectural supervisor so the scale and proportions work throughout all three mounds.'' By now, each of the team members had their reduced-scale renderings spread out before them and were absorbed in studying the details.

''Make sure you're satisfied with your individual sites,'' Stuart directed them. ''We've tried to stick close to the sketches each of you drew out and sent to us. I know we've packed these tableaux real close together. Some of you have been given some additional characters to work on so one scene flows into the next. We all have to be flexible. Things will change as we get into the actual work. Some of this is pretty ambitious stuff and may not come off like we hope. The plans are simply guidelines. Like a wish list. But any major modifications you want should be brought up now.'' He and Kevin looked out over the group. ''Anyone spot a problem?''

Jack Button looked along the row of sculptors, contemplating the lot of them, intent, silent, studiously looking over the drawings. After several months of long-distance calls and late day conferences with construction men, his electronics foreman, and the team architect, Vince Ammons, then shipping everything back and forth to Vancouver for Kevin and Craig Stuart to go over, Button was pretty sure they'd come up with a workable design. He just wanted to hear it from them.

"Looks good to me." Chris Jones spoke up first. One of the younger sandsculptors, Jones was an art major who had come home from college for a few weeks to work on the castle.

"No problems here." One after another, heads bobbed in satisfaction.

"So far so good, then." Stuart grinned. "Now, besides doing your set pieces, we have some other jobs to delegate. Just in case you don't know each other, I suggest you learn who's who now. This may seem a bit like grade school, but raise your hand when I single you out." He shrugged apologetically. "Okay. Here goes. Paul Feneau is our beastmaster."

The young man with the lemony mineral water raised his hand. Slim and quiet mannered, he seemed an odd choice for a title like beastmaster.

"Doug will set up the big animal displays on the first two mounds. Horses for the carriages, swans in the pond, Little Red's wolf, Goldilocks' bears. That kind of thing. If you need animals in general, call Paul. But if you need monsters, call on Kevin. Get the drift?"

The nodding heads signaled no problems.

"Kitty Westberg is really good with faces, actually figures in general. Once she finishes Rapunzel, she'll be supervising or helping out on the remaining characters." He went on down the list.

"Chris Jones is good with vehicles—carriages, pushcarts, you name it. Jaisen Crockett does dramatic terrain, rocks, caves, crashing waves, and such. Myron Hansen is excellent with foliage—vines, trees, flowers," Stuart proceeded, clarifying particular specialties throughout the chain of command. "We've got a crew of high-school art students that Hansen has trained in fabric textures for the costumes. They'll be coming up the end of the first week when spring break begins."

Stuart paused and looked up. "We want you to let the volunteers get involved. Once you block out a design, delegate the labor. That's the key to getting this done. Delegate," he repeated earnestly, sawing the air with his clipboard. "We'll have lots of volunteers willing to haul water or shovel. There'll be trained ones who are willing to carve anywhere. What you have to do is use your energy where it's needed. Do the initial blocking, then delegate, and come back later and do the finishing details." He leaned forward as he spoke, punctuating his comments with emphatic gestures.

Kevin Walters, who had been studying the individuals around the conference table, his hands thrust deep in his pockets, stepped forward and placed his hand on Stuart's shoulder. "I guess it comes down to this," he observed. "The aim is to keep your workers busy and keep the overall vision consistent. If your problem is aesthetic, talk it over with a supervisor or another team member. If it is a specific figure that you need help with, call on the appropriate individual. You'll have list of our specialists and their mound position on the back of the final blueprint. That's the beauty of having the headsets. Assistance is a sentence away. We can communicate."

Craig Stuart nodded in agreement. "Right. Let your headset do the walking," he stressed, slicing through the air with his hands. "If it's manpower you need, Roseanne Petty will be handling the volunteers. Sandy Huff will run communications. If it's a construction issue, call me. This is a very big production. Time and energy are of the essence. Don't waste either. We have to be organized and we all have to be flexible."

Kevin chuckled and rubbed his hand through his thick hair. "Now that we're all committed to being organized, let me add one more thing. We all know that things will still go wrong. Murphy's law applies, especially with sandsculpture. We'll have our disasters. Pieces may collapse. Faces drop off. Whatever. But all we're hoping for is to come out of this with something that resembles what we've all imagined. Something absolutely enchanting." A childlike wistfulness crept into his expression as he turned once more and looked at the large drawings of castles and dragons and banner-topped towers and curving walkways.

"I have an idea," Craig Stuart proposed. "I don't know about you folks, but I'm hungry. Let's relax a bit and think this over while we have dinner." He eyed the group for a response. "Talk among yourselves. Then if you have suggestions or modifications, get them to Kevin or me. Or to Jack Button. Preferably before you leave tonight."

"Sounds good to me," Paul Feneau declared. "Let's eat."

"I'm ready."

"Where's this Felucca Café?"

"What the hell's a felucca?"

"One last comment," Stuart spoke over the shuffle of papers and chairs. "I want to thank each of you for the effort you've put in this already. Your proposals and sketches were really exciting. You're a sharp lot. Just keep in mind that even though we figure we'll enlist and train over a thousand volunteers, the ultimate responsibility is with each of us. Just twenty-two of us. Let's make the magic happen.''

Jack Button's smile stiffened perceptibly when Stuart tallied twenty-two of "us." Abruptly, the show was over, the circle was closed, and again he'd been left out of the count. Recovering quickly, he fell in step with Paul Feneau and struck up a conversation. He'd arranged dinner for twenty-three of them, twenty-four counting Westberg's kid. When they took their seats at the small tables, Button didn't intend to end up in the Felucca Café without a dinner partner.

"It sure is good to see you looking so fit, Paul," Button remarked.

"I'm really feeling good. I can't tell you how glad I am to be around for this," Feneau answered, munching on the lemon peel as they walked. "I'm glad to be around, period," he added. Two years before, when Paul had just turned twenty two and become engaged, he was told he had leukemia. After five months of chemotherapy, bald, painfully thin, and pale, he'd been released. The next summer, he took first place in a local sand-sculpture competition. When Button was recruiting, he'd gone after Paul for more than his expertise with sculpting animals. Button had seen the articles on Feneau. The press loved the leukemia angle. When the time came, Button would remind them to use it again. Jack Button had it all down. He'd done his homework. He didn't intend to miss a trick.

The forty-eight trainees for the Dunes adjunct security staff were conspicuously attractive, generally tanned, blond, and young. "They're makin' eighteen-year-olds a whole lot better lookin' than they were in my day," Bo

Shepherd said only half jokingly as he and Button watched a group of them file in and take their seats.

For the duration of the month, the larger staff meeting room of the Dunes business offices on the second floor of the Grand Nile Resort Hotel would be the security briefing room, but this was the first official adjunct staff gathering. Two young women in loose flower-print shorts and snug T-shirts strolled in front of the two men and headed toward the front of the room. "Sure is going to make coming to work each day a lot more interesting," Shepherd remarked.

"Makes one thankful for the wonders of nature," Button commented, staring after the bosomy twosome. Most of the trainees already in the room were males, not so subtly craning their necks to check out their female counterparts as they entered. A few nudges and whispers indicated approval of the latest two.

"Centerfold material," Shepherd professed. "Ain't seen a reject in the lot, female or male," he noted. "Matter of fact, most of those fellows in there look like they just stepped off the pages of one of those bodybuilding ads. We're talkin' suntans and muscles." The wiry, dapper fellow stood almost at attention as he spoke, partly a result of years in the army, and partly to make himself seem more formidable to these young and taller recruits.

"Real good-looking bunch," Button affirmed. "I told Roseanne we wanted wholesome and attractive. Looks like we got it." Even before they started screening applicants for the temporary positions, Button had set the guidelines. The emphasis was always promotional. He wanted the subliminal message of youth and vigor and good looks connected with the Dunes Project in every shot of media coverage. All the staff had to look good in the official Dunesfest uniform—safari outfits in teal and tan. He'd insisted they hire almost fifty-percent women, particularly for the highly visible posts of crowd management around the mound and for traffic control in the parking areas. The remaining twenty-three recruits were husky males, most of whom were area high-school and college athletes, but they'd also picked up some outdoor types from the orange groves inland and the marina and fisheries a few miles west on the Gulf. Mainly to avoid allegations of discriminatory practices, they had taken applications from a few older men and women, but only those with what Button called "camera appeal" were hired. Details. Button insisted they never overlook details.

"Good evening." Button exchanged a polite smile with a new arrival, this one bright and bubbly and radiant. "Cheerleader," he recalled, turning again toward Bo Shepherd.

"Nice . . ." Shepherd caught himself before he said "ass." As security chief, he had to exhibit discretion, especially with Button, whom he hadn't quite gotten a fix on. Until recently, they hadn't had any reason to deal with each other. Now Button was everywhere, and Bo Shepherd checked himself, playing it safe.

"We're going to have to cover a lot of territory fairly fast," Shepherd began after Button welcomed the adjunct employees then introduced him. "We have ten full-time security people on our permanent staff. Several will be helping with the daily briefings. But after that, you'll rarely notice them," he added almost in a whisper. "Other than the gatekeeper, they don't wear official uniforms. They don't stand out. Even the ones who are authorized to carry a weapon don't do it conspicuously. They dress just like regular guests. Well, maybe not so classy," he added with a wink. "But their job is to blend in and keep an eye on things. Your job is quite another matter." He nodded to an assistant at the back of the room, who promptly dimmed the lights and flashed a slide onto the screen beyond Shepherd's shoulder.

The first image was a copy of a photo of Atlantis, its shell-like spires and aquatic motifs descending in tiers. On ground level, a cascade of white sand waves and frolicking dolphins was surrounded by a moat, then a wide expanse of beach.

"This is how Atlantis looked at 6:30 in the morning," Shepherd commented, staring like the others at the image. Then a second shot flashed on the screen. The pale sand surrounding Atlantis had disappeared. It was now covered by a sea of people.

"This is at noon the same day." Shepherd spoke from the darkness. "Wall-to-wall people. All wanting a close-up look. This is why we need you on the site, and why we need you to be conspicuous." He flashed to an aerial shot that showed the pale mountain of Atlantis surrounded by an unbroken dark mass of people. Then in steady succession came pictures of congested traffic, sunburned tourists, long lines at the portable toilets, and littered grounds. "Let's talk a bit about crowd control. . . ." The lights went up again.

Jack Button deftly slipped out the door while Shepherd proceeded with the first part of the program. While they covered the general concerns of public drunkenness, overexposure, freeloading, pickpocketing, and miscellaneous safety procedures, he had thirty minutes to hit the john and the bar. Then he'd make sure the nonalcoholic beverages had been delivered and set up for the trainees before the first of the training segments ended. When the prebreak question-and-answer period began,

Button planned to be there to socialize. He'd use the opportunity to meet the new employees and put faces to the names on the list he'd been given.

"Any free show brings out the weirdos and wackos along with the peaceful and law abiding," Shepherd was reiterating when Button returned. "But keep in mind, you are not police officers. There will be a contingent of uniformed officers and a couple of plainclothesmen to step in where they're needed. Primarily your job is to be visible, to give out information and directions, to wake up anyone getting baked in the sun, watch for pickpockets and pilfering, track down little kids, and keep the bigger ones from getting overly intimate in public." He glanced at his watch then nodded at Button.

"So far this has been pretty simple." Shepherd began winding down. "However, when you get crowds the size we're expecting, there could be some real serious incidents. We'll get to the heavier stuff after the break. Meanwhile, if you have any questions so far, let's hear them." He narrowed his eyes, watching the group shift restlessly in their seats.

No questions.

"Okay. Rest rooms are down the hall to the right. There are soft drinks and snacks at the back of the room. Relax, get to know each other. We'll pick up again in fifteen minutes." The last few words were nearly drowned out by the rumble of conversation below.

When the meeting resumed, Bo Shepherd started in again. This time there was a sharper edge to his delivery. "Ron Avilla and Barry Mack." He introduced two of his permanent staff members, both fellows in their forties who had retired from regular police work before joining the staff of the Dunes. "We can't afford to be naive. Keep in mind that a lot of slugs creep out from under their rocks when there's a crowd to work. Let's talk real crime,'' Shepherd began. "That generally means drugs or sex."

Ron Avilla gave the first talk. Thick-necked and husky, he had worked vice for years. He told them flat out, there would be pushers and addicts and maybe a few cases of overdosing. Then he cited a few incidents from his on-duty experiences at public events. "You have headsets to connect you to security center,'' he reminded them. "If you see a deal going down or you spot drug paraphernalia, call in. If it's a medical situation, we've got paramedics on the site. Whatever it is, we'll get you assistance.'' Like Bo he cautioned the new staff to look but not touch. "Don't play cop."

Barry Mack, sandy-haired, bespectacled, and stoop-shouldered, spoke next. "I'm dealing with sex offenders.'' He pulled a notecard from his pocket and glanced at it. "Okay. Let's start with something simple. Indecent exposure.'' He peered over his reading glasses like a professor about to quote Chaucer. "Occasionally an exhibitionist or a flasher will decide to do his thing, or show it,'' he added dryly. "But other than creating a little excitement, exhibitionists aren't worth the time and manpower it takes to prosecute them. If we get one, we'll simply take face and evict.'' The group had picked up enough of the official slang from Avilla's cop stories to know that "take face'' meant photograph the person. These photos would be shown at each shift's briefing with copies on display in the communications tent by the site, at the entrance, and in the office. When such an individual was spotted on the grounds, he would be quietly evicted and told not to return. If the "undesirable'' came back, he'd be turned over to the police.

"In the office we'll have books of known sex offenders

residing in this general area. A few have warrants on them. Before the crowd builds, you all should browse through the warrants. Look over the books as well. These guys are repeaters. If they're here, they're looking for trouble. Sometimes you'll surprise yourself and pick up on a face in the crowd. Regardless, we'll handle things differently if anyone with a known history of sex offenses shows up," he explained. "They're turned over to the cops right away."

"Even if they don't actually do anything?" one young man asked.

"Right. We won't play wait-and-see with these guys. We don't have to. Some have probation restrictions excluding them from certain situations. Some are simply scum that we don't want around. The Dunes is private property, not public. We have the right to deny access to anyone who could be trouble. If they show, they're history. Any other questions?" Mack asked, adjusting his glasses.

There were none.

"Okay. Let's discuss prostitution." Mack glanced at a notecard then peered over his spectacles again. "With things the way they are these days, prostitutes aren't all that easy to ID. It's hard to tell sometimes if folks out there are selling it or giving it away. This Dunesfest event is pretty much out in the open. Not much privacy. Regardless, these transactions can happen in cars in the parking lot, concessions tents, behind trees and bushes, and even in hotel rooms for the well heeled. Don't go lookin' for trouble. If folks are discreet, it's their business. But if you get a complaint or if something catches your attention, deal with it." He leveled his stony gray eyes at them. "Just use your best judgment. You may not see money change hands, but if you spot grown folks using the portable john two at a time, I'd suggest you call in. Especially if one of them is a repeater and the partners keep changing. Trust your gut instincts. Male, female. Two guys. Two women. Whatever. Even if it's an older person and a kid, unless the kid is really too little to go himself, get suspicious. That may not be the kid's parent or whatever. By the same token, there are some real hardcases out hustling at eleven. Same policy. Don't do anything yourself, just call it in." Mack pulled out the notecard again and looked at it.

"Probably the lowest scum you'll meet are ones who prey on children." His gray eyes hardened. "When you have an event that attracts children like this is guaranteed to do, you'll have child molesters."

At this point Bo Shepherd moved up next to Mack, his own tight expression mirroring his colleague's. "We can't stress this problem enough. Because of the storybook characters used all over the mound and the widespread coverage of the event, this castle will draw families. Particularly ones with younger kids. And because of the parklike setting and all the concession stands and stuff, some folks will think this is a freebie Disney World. So they turn the kids loose. We're talking unsupervised kids. Molesters know that. They'll be cruising here like the big bad wolf stalking Red Riding Hood."

"And there will be thousands of Little Red's here," Mack picked up again. "Like Bo said, parents will just let em' roam around thinkin' it's safe." He arched his heavy eyebrows. "Let me tell you, it's never safe. Never." He paused and reshuffled his cards.

"We're going to spend a good bit of time on the subject of these pedophiles," Shepherd addressed the group again. Then he caught the uncertain expression on some of their faces. "Pedophile. *Pedo* means child. *Phile* means having a love or preference for something. That's what some of these degenerates consider themselves," he almost spat out the words. "Pedophile. Lover of children." He paused. "That's bullshit." He stared into the upturned faces. "Let me tell a little about these animals."

Jack Button glanced at his watch. Then he did a quick reconnaissance of the refreshment table. Bo Shepherd was supposed to conclude the session precisely at nine. Button ducked out and headed for the john and the bar while he still had time.

Even with the sliding-glass doors closed, from his town house in the Dunes Delta, Button could still hear the pulsing of the diesel pump belching eight hundred gallons of water a minute into the craters on top of the sand mound almost a mile away. All night long, through a snakelike pipeline leading into the underbrush, that pump would be sucking water from the canal and pouring it into the heart of the mound. Then the water would seep down through the sand, driving out the air so the loose sand would settle. Kevin Walters and Stuart had been at the site all week supervising the procedure and constructing segments of the wood frames that would serve as cribbing around individual scenes. Crockett, the engineer, had driven up from St. Pete a couple of times to confer with them. During the day, a continuous stream of trucks would dump the sand while a crew with bulldozers distributed it in three connecting piles. Then, late in the afternoon, the dozers would cut a volcanolike crater in the top of each pile and drag the water hoses into place.

"From the core out, the sand has to be hard-packed or it won't hold the height," Stuart had told Button. That meant wetting it down and forcing out the air. "If we don't get rid of the air all the way through, the whole thing will gradually give under the weight on top. It will start spreading and flattening out until it turns into a shapeless amoeba. Every bit has to be compressed." So until all the sand was in place and the sculptors were ready to begin, the pumps would throb all night.

At first Button had found their primitive cadence vaguely unnerving, but tonight that same tom-tom rhythm sounded somehow soothing and vaguely erotic. "Maybe it's just the liquor," Button mused, strolling toward the balcony again to stare out over the moonlit wetlands. Beyond a few surviving cypresses and a huge, mushroom-shaped moss-garlanded oak, the marsh spread out in the moonlight. Beyond that, where the grasses began, gleaming ribbons of spring-fed water wound back into the swamp buffer of bay and laurel and pine. The grounds crew had made these paths, trimming back roots and limbs to clear waterways for the rental boats to follow. But the marsh grasses, maidencane and spattersocks, and the fringe of rushes kept the boaters at a distance. Rarely did they intrude in Button's view. This portion of the Dunes development, an adults-only series of town houses, overlooked the main refuge area. Like the huge herons and snowy egrets that frequented the shoreline, the condos turned their backs to the gleaming heights of the Grand Nile Resort and civilization.

This illusion of absolute seclusion appealed to Button. The fact that he could drive to work or enjoy any of the Grand Nile amenities in four minutes pleased him even more.

Button drained the glass and poured himself another, determined to still the slight tremor in his hands. Then he pushed the hidden button in the base of the enameled liquor cabinet. With a barely audible hum, the shelf rose to shoulder level and a front panel folded forward, forming a serving table. The lower center section rose to display its contents. There was no cache of liquor bottles or glasses between its upright partitions. Instead, large photo albums were packed side by side. A stack of videotapes fit neatly into the final slot. A small drawer held a handgun, Button's grudging acknowledgment of the isolation of his particular town house. Button ignored the drawer, but he stared at the books thoughtfully then pulled out one album. His fingers still trembled slightly, but the mere contact with the book seemed to calm him.

Button loved to look at his books. He loved to see the pretty faces and smooth young bodies, all perfect, all trusting, all beautiful. He took a slow sip of scotch, letting it linger on his tongue. Gently touching only the top corner of each page, he leafed through the album. "So lovely . . ." he murmured as the scotch sent ripples of relaxing warmth through his limbs.

With the next sip, he stopped to gaze at one particular image. "Benjy . . ." he whispered reverently, not able to resist trailing his fingertips down over the color photo of a handsome, naked boy. Benjy had been one of the special ones. Bright, curious, eager to please, the boy had come to one of Button's magic classes at the library. The kid hung back at first, a bit shy, but taking in every move with his liquid ebony eyes. And his skin was like caramel candy. Button looked at him for a long time, remembering.

"Bastards . . ." Button mumbled suddenly, lifting one hand to wipe away the tear that had started to trail down the side of his nose. His hand was trembling again as Bo Shepherd and Barry Mack's words came to haunt him. "Degenerates . . ." Button took a quick swallow. "Animals . . . sodomists . . ." He had left the meeting hall, refusing to be assaulted by the words Shepherd and Mack had used.

"Pedophile. Lover of children." Button could relate to that, but not the way they had said it. Not how they described it. They made it dirty. The term should be spoken gently and caressingly, like the act of loving itself. Pedophile.

Button intimately knew the nuances of child love. And he despised the hypocrisy of the world around him. Children were inherently sexual. They possessed a playfulness and curiosity that society tried to suppress with rules, and labels, and lies. But Button had managed to free himself from those fictions. In turn he'd freed other innocents from society's lies, puritanical lies that taught only guilt, denial, and shame. He had led many children into a celebration of their bodies, a liberation that a neurotic society tried to deny to all but adults. Pedophile. He was one of them, and he was not alone.

Listing slightly, Button crossed to the cabinet for a refill. "I will send you beautiful children," he promised aloud, letting his fingers rest on the top of the ringed binder where he kept his special correspondence. There were others like him, other lovers of children who would exchange photos of their beloved ones or simply demonstrate their brotherhood by sending pictures that they hoped would please him. They, too, understood the truth of child love. And each one had his own personal preference.

Button preferred dark-eyed children with golden skin that hinted of mixed blood or some exotic ancestry. Perhaps it was the suggestion of the forbidden or the outcast that appealed to him. He had known too well that sense of being different and somewhat conspicuous. Through the newsletter he subscribed to, one he'd found years before in the personals column of a magazine for child lovers like himself, he'd made his preference known. And the responses convinced him that he was not the freak he'd feared he was. There were others, ones who would gladly exchange letters and photos. Under the code name Butler, he'd made some faithful contacts through the years. Even now he kept a postal box in Brooksville, twelve miles away, where those letters and photos could be sent. Never too close to home.

In return for pictures, he sent back pictures that those contacts would appreciate. But as the network of like-minded men expanded, there was always the need for more. This month, he'd amass a collection he'd never before dreamed possible. He'd already stockpiled fifteen rolls of film for the castle crowd. He'd bought several new lenses for his camera and had taken lessons. He could express-mail them to a Georgia lab where the contents would be processed without question.

At Dunesfest, there would be children everywhere, in the play areas or in the wading ponds, some very young and totally naked, others scantily clad. The surrounding border of tall shade trees and grass had limbs to invite the climbers and pine cones to gather. Concession stands and tents with souvenirs and snacks would attract children. And Button would be able to stroll around in his official Dunes shirt, taking all the pictures he pleased. Proud parents would smile indulgently, obliviously, delighted to have their child singled out from the crowd.

"Child lover. Bullshit." The assistant security chief's harsh words richocheted in Button's mind like a gunshot. Button hated the way Barry Mack and Bo Shepherd had approached the whole issue. They'd shoved all pedophiles into the same ugly category as child rapists and molesters. It wasn't right. Jack Button had never hurt one of them. He was good with kids. He loved them.

"Cretins . . ." Clasping the decanter of scotch, Button poured another hefty shot. He stopped, studied the liquid a moment, then carefully poured it back into the bottle. He'd sworn he could keep everything under control. He'd promised himself to lay off the liquor, or at least to cut back a bit. No self-indulgent lapses. He was on course, and no sawed-off beady-eyed sexually repressed sanctimonious rent-a-cop like Shepherd or Mack was going to get him sidetracked. "Someday I'll fire both their fucking asses," Button said tersely to no one there. "When I'm vice-president . . ." He placed the glass firmly on the bar.

Button went back to his pictures, finding comfort in the beautiful young boys frozen in time.

"Lovely . . ."

Gradually, the pulsing rhythm of the distant water pump seeped into his consciousness, primal, insistent, and seductive. More serene now, Button gradually felt his body respond. And as he touched himself, he smiled into the dark liquid eyes and breathed in the honeyed scent of yesterday. "Benjy . . ." he murmured. "Sweet dreams."

Chapter 2

"Exquisite." VINCE LEANED CLOSER AND BRUSHED HIS shoulder against Kitty's arm. Like nomads settling in at a desert campfire, sitting cross-legged atop the center mound, forming a half circle around the crater, they had gathered there for the sunset: Kitty and Vince, Craig Stuart and Kevin Walters, and Paul Feneau. While the sun began staging a spectacular exodus far off on the horizon, they watched the distant orchard and wetland hardwoods turn amber then darken into indigo outlined in tongues of orange. Immediately below the western slope spread the broad concave area of lowland that had been scraped bare by bulldozers months ago. Gradually it was filling with spring water. It lay like a puddle of deep crimson blood fed by channels cut into the wetlands all around.

Kitty had been almost motionless next to Vince. With high cheekbones bronzed by the sunset and eyes half-closed against the low fireball, she was bathed in light. Streaked by the sun and pressed back by the steady breeze coming inland from the Gulf, miles beyond their view, her chin length hair was transformed into a burnished headdress, like that of the exotic Egyptian goddesses whose serene presence watched over the guests from alcoves or among the gardens of the Grand Nile Resort.

"It is beautiful from up here," Kitty acknowledged softly, as if she didn't want to disturb the whisper of the wind with her words. Her gaze remained fixed on the horizon, taking in the shifting colors that transformed the wispy clouds into myriad hues. Vince smiled, realizing she was unaware his comment referred to her and not the scenery below.

"I sure hope I'm not disturbing you." The voice came from a tall angular fellow in the Dunes uniform, approaching from the south mound. "Are you folks having a conference up here or something?" He peered over his bifocals uncomfortably.

"We're just communing with nature," Stuart replied good-naturedly. "We came up to watch the sunset."

"Sure is a different view from any I'm used to," the older fellow noted, turning to glance behind him at the landscape below. "I was just wondering if it would bother you if I took a few pictures." The man had a camera dangling from a strap around his neck and was fidgeting uncertainly with the lens cap. "I have some grandkids up north who really would get on me if I didn't send them photos. I'm afraid this may be the only free time I'll have. Once this thing starts, I'll be up to my ears in automobiles."

"You're with security?" Stuart guessed.

"Usually. Name's Otto Breshears. I'm in charge of traffic control for this thing." His lanky frame leaned slightly against the pressure of the Gulf wind. "Can't say I'm ready for it."

"I'm not sure any of us is ready for this," Stuart admitted. "These events are like a roller coaster, easy at first, then they kind of pick up momentum and take your breath away."

"Stomping up that path just now took mine away for sure," Otto answered. "I'm too old for this kind of mountain climbing." He shifted a bit self-consciously as he eyed the group of them, seated shoulder to shoulder facing the sunset. "Say, I guess the light is too far gone to get much of a shot of anything down there. Would you mind if I took a shot of you folks? For the grandkids?" He didn't know any of them by name, but while he and his crew set up barricades during the day, he had seen them coming and going. The mere fact that they were up here at all, now that the place was roped off and patrolled by Dunes security, meant that somehow they were important. "The kids might get to see you folks on TV. They'd be pretty pleased if they had your picture."

"How about letting me take it?" Kevin suddenly scrambled to his feet. "You sit here in my place, and we'll really give you something to show those kids."

"You folks don't mind?"

"We need the practice," Stuart assured him. "We're going to be photographed from every angle possible over the next two weeks. We may as well get into the spirit."

"If you're sure it's all right." Otto Breshears's hesitant smile became a full-fledged grin. Eagerly he passed the camera to Kevin. Then he sat between Stuart and Paul Feneau, coloring visibly when they both draped an arm around his shoulders.

Kitty and Vince inched closer to the others, squeezing into the same frame.

"This is really nice of you folks," Otto kept repeating as Kevin took one flash shot then two backups. In the distance he caught the upper floors of the Grand Nile, its glass windows afire with the sunset glow.

"You come back up again when this thing's completed and we'll take some 'after' shots," Kevin insisted. "After all, traffic control is a big part of this event. You should get some of the glory. Don't forget. We'll give your grandkids something hot to show to their friends. We're all part of the same team." He helped the fellow to his feet and gave him a parting handshake. The older man was still grinning as he headed back down the mound, camera clutched to his chest.

"That was a nice thing to do," Kitty remarked as Kevin reclaimed his place on the side of the crater.

"My pleasure," Kevin answered sincerely, leaning back to contemplate the sun's finale. By now the sky was streaked in mauve and rose, and the wind temperature was dropping as darkness closed in.

Even when the last glow faded from the sky, the lake turned shiny black, and the surrounding woods became a velvety carpet of indigo, they lingered there, savoring the tranquillity. Tomorrow, construction would begin. The sense of intimacy they all shared this night would be gone.

Abruptly the generator below clicked on and the long hose leading into the crater stiffened then belched out a stream of clear water. Then it belched again and the flow became stronger.

"So much for communing with Mother Nature," Stuart remarked, poking the hose with his toe. "I guess we'd better get some dinner. We need to look over a few details before I fade out." He rested his hand on Kevin's shoulder.

"I'm coming," Kevin responded. "Soak it in, and we'll see you in the morning, babe," he said, patting the mound affectionately before he stood up.

Kitty stretched her legs then stood like the others. The spell was broken. It was time to go. "Let's drag Zach out of the swimming pool and feed him. He's probably waterlogged."

Vince took her outstretched hand and tugged himself up. Wordlessly, Paul Feneau followed.

In single file, they headed for the south walkway, which cut across the dark western slope of each mound. On the eastern side, the Grand Nile Hotel awaited them, with its glass-and-metal surface cloaked in an unnatural cocoon of light. Lotus-shaped globes throughout the landscaped grounds relieved the darkness there and marked the route back. Towering over the pool area, the shadowy presence of the Great Sphinx, spotlighted from below, summoned the wanderers home.

Gone to soak with the crocs. Meet you in the spa. The farthest one from the pool bar. Kitty. Kitty taped the message to Vince's door so he'd see it whenever he came back up to his room. Zach was already asleep, and she was too wound up to simply sit in the room and wait until a last-minute meeting between Vince and Stuart ended. So with towel in hand, she strode to the elevator and slipped out the side door.

At the Oasis Bar by poolside, several groups of the sandsculptors were still clustered about at the tables, laughing and exchanging stories. Kitty stopped to visit only for a few minutes. She ordered an orange juice and proceeded along the free-form pool and under the waterfall to the most secluded spa, one set off on a terrace overlooking the mound area.

"Couldn't resist takin' a last look either?" Paul Feneau was there in the bubbling water, stretched out so he could face the mound. "Sure is a big mama," he said in a voice etched with awe.

"My sentiments exactly," Kitty replied, shedding her shirt and quickly sliding into the warm water. "I hadn't realized until today just how much surface we were actually dealing with. There's a whole lot more than I imagined." Until she and Vince climbed the mound that afternoon, sixty-five feet was merely a dimension on a drawing. Up close, it had acquired texture and contour; it became real. And gradually the job of populating that entire expanse with fairy-tale figures had become more intimidating than she anticipated. From Feneau's solemn expression, she guessed she wasn't the only one who felt that way.

In the moonlight above the surrounding trees, the ridges of the mound rose like the curves of a sleeping giant, shoulder, hips, and legs exposed, graceful, pale, inviting. The water pump, wetting her down for the last time, pulsed like a heartbeat, a constant reminder of her presence.

"I was thinking about walking out there again just to look her over." Feneau spoke as much to himself as to Kitty. He slid up on the side and mopped himself off. "You want to go?"

"I'll pass. I'll be doing enough walking back and forth the next week or so. Right now I'll just soak and stare at her and hope I get sleepy.

"I tried that myself." Feneau laughed softly. "Didn't work. I've turned into a prune and I still can't get rid of that edgy feeling. I'd better walk out there and get it out of my system or I'll never get to sleep tonight." He was out and on his way down the path in a matter of seconds, whistling as he went. Gradually the whistling faded and the only sounds beyond the distant heartbeat were the gentle bubbling of the spa, the rush of the waterfall, and the occasional ripple of laughter from the pool area.

"Are you out here stargazing? Or couldn't you keep the wheels from spinning?" Vince came to join her.

"It's the wheels," Kitty admitted. "I'm feeling a little overwhelmed. There's so much area out there to be worked."

"True. A lot of surface." He threw his towel aside and slid in, wincing from the heat then emitting a sigh of contentment as the water enveloped him. Then he looked at Kitty's preoccupied expression. "We're not going to be doing all the work alone," he reminded her gently. "We've got some big-time pros, lots of experienced folks we already know, and some remarkable equipment. Plus we'll have all kinds of volunteers. We've got two weeks and good weather predicted. We'll get it all done."

"That's what I keep telling myself." For a moment they sat side by side, silently studying the hauntingly beautiful curves and peaks beyond the trees.

"Do you realize that we're putting a fifteen-foot tower on top of what's already there," Kitty spoke again. "That's eighty feet high." Sitting on the crater earlier that evening, feeling the force of the Gulf wind, she had tried to imagine what it would be like to work fifteen feet higher, balancing on scaffolding and trying to carve a tower, complete with balcony and Rapunzel, while the persistent wind pressed against her. Then she'd looked around at the rise and fall of the expanse of sand all around her, and the problems posed by the tower seemed insignificant in comparison to the desert stretching out on all sides.

"Just relax. It's going to be all right," Vince assured her. "Come on." He urged her to turn around so he could massage the tense muscles in her neck and shoulders. "Let's put this in perspective. First of all, imagine that we're all playing hooky. Button's giving us a chance to play in his very large sandbox." The calming rhythm of his hands was beginning to take effect. "Now, add to that the freebies. Good food, first-rate accommodations, no laundry, no housework, no cooking. Exceptional companionship. And remarkable recreational possibilities." He made the last comment with unmistakable seductiveness.

"Like stargazing?" Kitty teased.

"Close. If I were going to gaze at a heavenly body, it sure wouldn't be up there," Vince answered, all the while continuing the therapeutic magic of his hands.

"I could find that interesting."

He continued massaging unhurriedly until he could feel her relaxing. "Would you like to adjourn to my room so we can broaden the scope of this activity beyond the shoulders?"

Kitty turned to him. The way her mouth tilted up at one corner was all the answer he needed.

"Good. I'll hand you a towel," Vince replied, and sent the water swirling with his departure.

Hand in hand they walked through the lotus-lighted gardens past the falcon-headed sentinels carved into the columns by the doors. They strolled along the teal-carpeted corridor to the glass-walled elevators that would lift them to their floor. As the palms and lily ponds and fountains in the atrium gardens below diminished in the distance, Vince put his arm around her and leaned back against the cool metallic doors. He could tell by her expression that part of her was back at the sand mound again. "Turn it off. Leave it out there," he cautioned, still feeling tension in her body. "Let's take this one day at a time."

"I'm trying," Kitty answered. "But I sure don't want to let anyone down."

"Hey . . . this is going to be fun. Just give it your best shot. That's all we're expected to do. That, and have a good time in the process. I'll still love you if Rapunzel drops off her balcony or if Pinnochio's nose is too short. So will Zach. We're the real world. This is fairyland, and no one expects miracles. Besides, it's just temporary. Three weeks or so and it will be history. Ease off. Hooky. Freebies. Fun . . ."

Kitty let out a long breath. "There are so many characters. . . ."

"Priorities, lady, priorities. Concentrate on this character for now." Vince turned her toward him and kissed her on the nose. Then his lips dropped lower and the touch softened.

"Please, sir . . . we're in a fish bowl here." Kitty eased him away.

"We've never done it in a fish bowl." Vince wriggled his eyebrows lecherously.

"And we're not about to start."

"But the element of imminent discovery might get your mind off that sandpile out there," Vince teased. "Too late." He shrugged with mock disappointment as the elevator stopped and the doors whispered open. "You missed your chance."

"I prefer taking my chances in private." Kitty hooked her arm in his and marched off down the corridor. "Meet you in a minute. I just want to check on Zach." She stopped at her door.

"I'll open my side." Vince proceeded to the next room.

When she stepped through the adjoining doorway, Vince was out on the balcony. "How's he doing?"

"Asleep."

"How about you?"

"Better." She stepped out into the night air next to him.

Moments later, while the filmy curtains billowed in the wind and the pale moonlight flooded through the open window, they held each other. The distant, even pulsing of the water pump became only a counterpoint to the sighs and soft laughter and the beating of hearts pressed close. And finally they closed the doors and went inside, where it ceased to intrude at all. As their familiar dance of love began to build, the outside world lost its hold. In the near silence of the night, there was only each other, blending into one.

For a while afterward she simply lay next to him on the bed, her naked body curved against his. Then Vince's breath against her shoulder settled into a deeper, even rhythm, and she knew he was asleep. Quietly she slid out from under his arm, tugged on her oversized T-shirt, pulled a sheet over him, and padded through the double doors back to her room.

Instantly a wall of cold air swallowed her. "For Pete's sake . . ." She danced across to her bed, grabbed the heavy spread, and wrapped it around her. As soon as she checked the thermostat she guessed Zach must have found the meter too tempting to leave alone. He'd set it for fifty-five and turned the room into a refrigerator. Curled in his bedding, his cherubic features serene, Zach seemed oblivious to the cold. But she was shivering. Rapidly Kitty turned the dial up, opened a window, and let the breeze sweep in. She unwound Zach's wrappings and freed his arms then tucked the covers back around him more loosely. "Just because we're not paying the electric bill, let's not get carried away," she cautioned the sleeping boy. In the morning, they'd have this conversation again.

For the next few minutes, Kitty stood out on the balcony, waiting for the room to return to a normal temperature and her knees to stop trembling. The sand mound wasn't visible from this side of the hotel, but the distant heartbeat still pulsed.

Below, past the sculpted gardens, she could see the gleaming winding waterway and the bridge that led to the Nature Trail. Rows of small boats were lined up along the riverside. "Feluccas . . ." Kitty recognized them. One of these fully rigged small boats was mounted on one wall of the café downstairs. Zach had already signed up for lessons the next day, and the half-hour sessions, usually ten dollars a shot, came as part of the Dunes package. "Hooky with freebies." Kitty pondered Vince's appraisal of the situation. While she played hooky, Zach would have his air-conditioning, access to feluccas, and swimming, and friends.

"Can't beat that," Kitty said aloud, almost defiantly. She pulled closed the balcony doors, shutting out the sound, and quickly slid under the covers of the farther bed. "Feluccas . . ." she whispered, loving the way the sound floated on the air and made her smile.

"How do I look?" The tall fellow shook the creases out of the ivory and aqua T-shirt he'd been issued and yanked it on, smoothing it over his chest. Then he turned and flexed his biceps.

The young woman at the table glanced at him with

studied indifference and kept on working. "There's a packet for each of you. Visor, Velcro wristband, T-shirt, sunscreen, battery pack, and headset." Sandy Huff, one of the Dunes' regular staff members, was overseeing the issuing of equipment. Her shirt, aqua with an ivory logo, the opposite of the sandsculptors', didn't have her name printed across the shoulders. Or the large number, center back, like a football jersey. Only the twenty-two team members had that designation so they could be identified from a distance and readily located while anywhere on the mound.

"Hey, you should have put my room number on this," the young man with the biceps lamented, grinning all the while. "Chris Jones, Room 918. I wouldn't mind if that got out. Would you?" He turned to Jaisen Crockett, who was next in line.

"We'd like to keep the traffic problems outside the hotel," Sandy Huff replied, laughing at the pained look on Jones's face. "The Grand Nile doesn't want problems with groupies . . . or whatever."

Jaisen took his packet and shrugged apologetically. "You'll have to excuse him. He slipped out his high chair last week and suffered a head injury." His expression was deadpan.

"Did you say we're supposed to turn all this stuff in each night?" Jones leaned past Jaisen and asked.

"If you drop the shirts in the hamper here in the staff tent each night, we'll clean them for you and give them back. Regardless, you'll be issued a new one each morning. Headsets, battery packs, and wristbands should be dropped off at the tent, too," Sandy explained. "Beats you trying to keep up with them."

"Sounds fair to me." Jaisen looked at her and smiled. Paul Feneau came up next to collect his outfit.

Kitty and Vince started out to the site at 7:20. "Looks like we're not the only ones ready to get this underway," Vince noted as he and Kitty approached the castle site. No one was supposed to report officially until eight, but there was already a crowd of twenty or so gathered around the volunteer sign-in table and a smaller group by the staff tent where Sandy Huff was helping Feneau adjust his headset.

"Kitty . . . Vince." Sandy handed them each their packet.

"Just give me a few minutes to get organized and you can start signing in." Roseanne Petty was overseeing the activity at the volunteer table farther down. "You folks will be given a white wristband, a pair of work gloves, sunscreen, and a shovel."

There was some scattered grumbling in response, but Roseanne Petty only raised her voice and spoke over the noise. "I know shoveling isn't glamorous," she admitted. "Each of you will be assigned to one of the team members. After you have worked alongside one of them, they can recommend switching you to some other work. But everyone starts off shoveling. No exceptions. Please have your driver's license ready when you sign up."

"Driver's license?" Kitty gave Vince a quizzical look.

"Just to make sure they are who they say they are when they issue the bands," Vince explained as he shook out his shirt then tugged it over his head. "Stuart and Kevin and I discussed it a while back. We don't want any horsing around on the mound. If these folks want to work, then we have the right to get their names straight. Just in case there's trouble or an accident, we'll have something to go on."

Kitty shrugged approvingly, pulled her shirt on over

her shorts and halter, and trudged off toward the group gathering by the larger of the two cranes.

" 'Morning . . ." Kevin greeted them.

"Kitty, I'd like you to meet the heavy-equipment team. Ray . . . Eddie," Stuart introduced them. A husky, tall bearded fellow came toward them from the area where the molds were stacked. "This is Dave Crockett," Stuart added. "He's supervising the real tricky stuff."

"Like our tower?" Kitty guessed, shaking Crockett's hand.

"Definitely the tower," Crockett answered in a voice that rumbled like an offshore thunderstorm. "Should be a piece of cake."

"Okay, you guys," Stuart called out to the team members still hanging around back at the tent. "Listen up here."

Surrounded by his band of ivory-shirted co-workers, Stuart went through his list of opening instructions while Kevin handed out the laminated final drawings. "We're doing mostly heavy-construction work for the first couple of days, so we have to be real safety conscious," he cautioned them. "We'll have cranes and dozers moving around all the time. So keep alert. Keep your headsets on in case we need you. If you need us or anyone in particular, the call numbers are on the back of the diagram. Just press a button. Let your fingers do the walking," he insisted, making a tiptoeing design in the air. "When no one is calling, you'll get soft rock on the headset."

"What if we don't want rock?"

"Call Sandy and opt for something else."

"How about silence?" Paul Feneau asked hopefully. "I'm a purist. I like to hear nature sounds."

"No problem. Just tell Sandy. She's running communications from the tent back there." Paul Feneau's slight smiled showed definite relief.

Abruptly Stuart held up his Dunes-issued sunscreen. "This is a lifesaver," he proclaimed. "Besides being the product of one of our official sponsors, this is darn good block. Put it on. Wear it. Don't get burned. Don't get overheated. Drink lots of liquids. Gatorade and water will be on top under the pit-stop umbrellas. Take regular breaks. I know I must sound like your mother," he admitted, shaking his head good-naturedly, "but we want you healthy. And if Kevin or I think you're a bit overdone and you should come down and sit it out for a while, we'll be on you. We don't want any heroes or any arguments. Just take care of yourself and, in turn, watch out for anyone assigned to you."

Kevin had finished passing out the diagrams and had come back to stand next to Stuart. "Remember that we value the territory between your ears. Wear a hat. Keep your head covered, and while we're on the subject, don't forget to protect your ears. We had a guy cook the top of his ears once. Roasted. Oozing goo. So don't forget they're there, and don't let the nice breeze up there trick you into thinking that you're not being fried. By the time you hear the sizzle or see the pink turn red, it's too late. Grease up. And keep an eye on the next guy to see that he does the same."

"Okay, now let's get the main molds in place and banded," Stuart directed them. "Conserve your energy. You have to last two whole weeks. Use the volunteers wherever you can. But especially now that we've got this whole thing before us, don't use muscle where Ray or Eddie or the dozers can do the work." He took a deep breath and flipped the cover of his clip pad closed. "That's it for now." He looked up at them, shifting his feet restlessly. "Unless you guys have questions?" No one responded. "Okay, then pick up your volunteers and go to it. I'll be in touch."

By the time Sandy Huff made the general call for the lunch break, the smooth contours of the three mounds were drastically altered. The dozers had cross-cut the surface, making additional pathways and leveling sections into distinct plateaus. Large sections of wood cribbing, four feet tall, in widths of twelve feet or less, had been deposited in key positions, formed into squares or rectangles, then bolted or banded to hold that shape. While hopper loads of fine silica were dumped into those open mouths, volunteers and team members took turns soaking the sand and tamping it down with shovels and power compactors. Then another box form was stair-stepped on top of those and packed with more water and sand. Studded with these boxes, the mound was no longer smooth or beautiful.

"Copter's on the way. We can get the tower up next," Dave Crockett informed them as he stepped into the shade of the staff communications tent, munching a sandwich and ready to confer with Kevin and Stuart. "We'll only need about ten strong folks up there when we move it in. Other than them, I think we'd better keep everyone else off the mound while we're using the copter."

"I'll get the ten," Stuart agreed. He waved Kevin over. "While we're up to doing the tower, how 'bout you getting some of the others started on teaching this round of shovelers some rudimentary carving," he suggested. "Tomorrow, when we start uncrating these things, we'll need some backup carvers."

Kevin was already nodding in agreement. They'd set aside a training area off to the south end of the mountain of sand, a separate small pile with a few upended garbage cans, bottoms removed and packed full of the same fine silica, the prime carving sand they were using to fill the forms up top. Once the molds were lifted off, these smaller columns of sand could be used to demonstrate and practice basic sculpting techniques before turning anyone loose on the real thing. "Hanson and Jaisen Crockett can run a session on landscaping," Kevin replied. "Then we'll get Vince to go over some of his castle stuff, crenellations and guard towers and all that."

By now the copter Dave Crockett had requisitioned from his home office was visible in the distance, hovering about the Dunes golf club before circling and setting down in the parking lot north of the wooded area surrounding the mound site. A few minutes later, the pilot and his assistant were delivered to the tent in a golf cart driven by Jack Button. A curly-haired fellow with a video unit secured beside him rode on the back. Smiling genially, Button accompanied the copter pilot and the other fellow under the staff communications canopy while the cameraman unpacked his gear. The fact that Button was wearing a T-shirt, ivory with aqua logo, identical to the team members' except for the number on the back, drew a long, expressionless look from Stuart and a few others.

"Okay, here's how we'll handle this," Crockett resumed while the others looked on and finished eating. "This baby may kick up a lot of top sand. Cover up and keep your eyes protected. If you've got sunglasses, wear 'em. If you don't, squint."

"If it will help, we've got some Plexiglas goggles down by the main spring," Jack Button offered. "They're for snorkeling, but I'll call have them brought over if they'll help."

"They'll help," Crockett responded.

Button went over to Sandy Huff and had her forward the request.

Crockett continued with the instructions, then left the the others to finish their cool drinks while he went off with the copter pilot for a final check of the two-piece mold that would become Rapunzel's Tower. The heavy form had been bolted together and stood off the south end near the stockpile of construction materials. He and the duo from the copter circled the form, then separated, spreading out four cables that were connected to the rim.

A second golf car skipped across the grounds, this one carrying one of the Dunes staff delivering a box of clear swim goggles. Button took the box and plunked it down by Stuart's feet. "Help yourselves," he announced for anyone who needed eye covering.

"Okay, we're ready," Crockett announced when he returned. The copter team took off with the driver in the second golf cart, heading for their aircraft. "Don't forget work gloves or you can lose the meat on your hands," he warned the ten Stuart had recruited for the move. "And keep alert up there. All we have to do is line her up and make sure she's level. The copter team will do the rest. If anything doesn't look right, we'll clear out and leave it to them." While the others started up the mound, Button stopped Crockett and spoke briefly. Then he picked up a pair of work gloves and goggles. He and the cameraman fell in behind the others, following them to the top.

Lifting the cylinder proceeded smoothly. The copter hovered above, dropped four separate lines. Crockett connected the cables, the backup man in the aircraft wound the winches, then the copter rose with the mold dangling below.

"Just keep calling out your readings," Crockett told

the team members as the copter centered the cylinder over the circle Stuart and he had made. They'd drawn it like a target on the flat, graded surface. "Line her up with the circle, keep her in place, then start calling out those level readings as she settles in." With arms and gloved hands extended upward like a circle of suppliants, the ten team members, plus Crockett and Jack Button, waited for the copter to lower the mold.

"Jesus, look at the size of this mother!"

"Reminds me of the landing in *Close Encounters*."

"I think I've had this nightmare once before. . . ."

"Keep your feet back. Lean into it." Crockett's voice rose above the others.

The videocameraman caught it all.

"North. Push it north," Kevin called out as the mold descended in their midst, its lower rim only inches above the surface. The steady whoosh of the copter blades sent a blizzard of sand whipping against bare legs and arms.

"Too far east. Better. Better," Chris Jones called from his position.

"More north," Kevin insisted. "Push, you guys." They leaned into it. "Too far!"

"Come on south, push!"

"Better. A little more."

Then the fifteen-foot structure touched the surface directly on target and began digging in, squeezing a donut-shaped ring outside its lip.

"Okay, now we're talking vertical. Let's hear it," Crockett barked. He'd taped six-foot levels to four sides of the cylinder. He wanted to hear what they showed.

"Top needs to go south," Kevin called out.

"Top too far west," Paul Feneau yelled.

Standing back a few feet, Crockett used hand gestures to transfer the information to the winch operator above.

Like a puppeteer, the winch operator orchestrated its dance.

"Bring the top south," Vince shouted. "More. More." Crockett signaled upward again. The cylinder pressed deeper in the sand, compressing what it didn't push aside.

"Level on west side now," Paul Feneau reported.

"Level on north," Kevin yelled. "Looks good."

"Okay, let her rest." Crockett signaled to the winch operator.

The tension in the guidelines eased as he gave them additional slack and the cylinder stood on his own.

"How is she? Everyone got it?" Crockett double-checked.

"We got it." All four directions were straight up.

"Now back off and let this guy disconnect the lines. We don't want anyone hurt."

The copter sank lower, the lines slacked off more, then were disconnected from the winch, gliding to the ground like dark serpents, slashing deep trenches where they fell. The helicopter banked and swept off to the east, sending up one final blast of sand.

"Man, can you imagine if one of those things snapped while we were under it." Feneau stuck his foot into one of the cuts made by the cables.

"We're talking serious dismemberment here," Chris Jones said somberly.

"I don't take chances," Crockett spoke up, totally calm. "We could have hoisted one of those cranes up here with the strength cable we used."

Kevin simply peeled off his shirt and goggles and wiped the sand and sweat from his face. Then he yanked off his gloves and patted the side of the upright form. Only then did he realize that his hands were shaking. "I

think this was a tad more awesome than we expected,"
he confided to Stuart as his partner joined him in the
crescent of shade the empty cylinder cast. "This is one
big mama," he breathed. Stuart's gaze shifted from the
trenches to the mold to Kevin's somewhat pale countenance, which he suspected matched his own.

"Let's all take a break," Stuart called out to the scattered team members who stood staring at the monolith
in their midst. He started waving them off the mound
again. Behind him, the cameraman was still filming. Stuart turned to see Jack Button posing by the cylinder between Kitty Westberg and Vince. With a slight narrowing
of the eyes, Stuart shrugged, clapped Kevin on the shoulder, and headed down.

"Mom, you shoulda seen me!" Zach's pink cheeks
and even pinker nose framed in blond flyaway hair gave
him a kewpie-doll look as he bounded along the hallway
to meet her by the elevator. At 4:30, Stuart had proclaimed the first full day on the mound a triumph and
sent them all in early. No one protested. Hot and tired
and windblown, Kitty and Vince planned an early dinner
and time out in the pool.

"I was so good," Zach said said excitedly, grabbing
Kitty's arm and stepping in the elevator with them as the
two grown-ups smiled. "Corey took us down by the
springs this morning early to spot a few birds. Then on
the way back he taught us how to work one of those
boats. Man, you shoulda seen me. I can sail. I sailed a
felucca. I learned better than anybody." The elevator
stopped at their floor. Engulfed in this tidal wave of conversation, Kitty simply gestured over Zach's head, telling
Vince that they'd get ready for dinner and call him shortly.
He nodded and ambled off to his room ahead of them.

While Kitty unlocked the door, tossed the beach bag in a chair, and slipped out of her grit-filled tennis shoes, Zach kept on with his update, barely taking time to draw breath. "At lunch I met a kid named Chris. He's not one of our group. His mom is here for some convention. He can sail, too. We went out in the boats this afternoon and raced each other. It was great. And we're having a movie tonight. There's a theater downstairs—"

"Whoa, let me get a word in here," Kitty interrupted. "I keep hearing boating, birdwatching, and eating. What about schoolwork, bud?"

"Oh, we did that, too," Zach assured her. "Corey said it's best to do our classwork in the middle of the day when it's hottest outside. The room we use has air-conditioning and computers and a Coke machine. That Mr. Button came in. He took pictures of all of us. He's putting together a videotape show for all our folks. He does magic stuff. He even showed us how to make those wiener dogs out of balloons." Zach was literally glowing as he spoke, pacing after her as she moved about the room, setting out her clothes and getting ready for her shower. Zach was still in his bathing suit from a late-afternoon swim with his group.

"Could you possibly get dressed and find your shoes? We'll have plenty of time to talk over dinner. I'd like to go down early and enjoy being off my feet for a while. This old body had a pretty good workout today up there." She groaned, rubbing her upper arms, aching already.

"Oh, sure." Zach stood still a moment, trying to remember what he was going to tell her next. "Oh yeah." He grinned sheepishly. "There's a lady who's in charge of the girls, just like Corey is in charge of us guys. Melissa." Just the way he said her name made Kitty do a double take.

"Melissa. Sounds nice."

Zach's color deepened beneath his tan. "She's all right. She's some kind of art student at the junior college. And she's going to take us around the hotel and teach us about all this Egyptian stuff. She says this is like having a museum in your living room. This isn't the real stuff, but Melissa says they're good copies of things that are real. She says I can do a paper and turn it in for credit in my World Cultures class."

"Sounds like Melissa is smart."

"Not too smart," Zach said a bit defensively. "I can keep up with her."

"I bet you can," Kitty responded. "Once you set your mind to it, you're pretty swift. Now how about keeping up with me? Start getting dressed." She prodded him into action once more. "I have to shower. You have to change. So let's see some results when I come back." She left him standing in the room with one shoe in his hand.

Downstairs, while they waited for the hostess to seat them, Zach kept inching forward, peering into the Pharaoh's Chamber restaurant. "It's really fancy in there," he whispered when he came back to join them between the carved columns with stylized papyrus-and-lotus designs that lined the foyer. Inside, the gilded wall hangings and life-size carvings, all ornate reproductions of Egyptian art, were caught and reflected in the gleaming crystal and silver on the tables. The entire room shimmered in the candlelight.

"This is really impressive," Vince commented once they were seated. "Whoever set this up sure had some bucks. Those are gold leaf," he noted pointing to two carved female figures set on pedestals nearby.

"Is she an angel?" Zach asked, noting the one with outstretched winged arms.

"Sort of. She's a rank higher. She's a goddess," Vince explained. "The Egyptians had a lot of them. I'd bet that one is Isis. She's a fertility goddess. She caused the Nile to overflow each year and water all the lands so crops would grow. When her husband was killed, she brought the breath of life back to him by flapping her wings."

"Really?" Zach stared at the figure. "That's neat. How about the other one? Why does she have a snake's head?"

"That's the Egyptians' way of putting two ideas together. Snakes were dangerous, so they were used to protect things," Vince explained. "This snake goddess may look grim, but she's one of the good guys. She's just looking out for us."

Zach looked at the snake goddess a moment then turned to Vince. "Do you know her name?" He narrowed his eyes like he often did when he was up to something.

"I could probably find out."

"By tomorrow?"

"Why by tomorrow?"

Zach smiled slightly. "I figure Melissa would think I'm pretty smart if I could tell her some stuff about these things."

Now it was Vince's turn to smile. "I see. Well . . ." He sighed. "It's been a long time since I was into any of this. But I bet we could dig up a few postcards or something in the gift shop that would give up some information."

"Now?" Zach grabbed his chair as if he were ready to bolt.

"After dinner," Kitty said firmly, stopping him. "Eat first, shop later."

Zach pursed his lips and sat motionless for a few seconds.

"There's probably a decent library in Crystal Springs. Maybe we could pick up a couple of books so you could do a little research on the side," Vince suggested, trying to ease the tension. "Might even jog my memory. I haven't had much to do with this stuff since college. That's been a while," he added apologetically.

"Do you know anything else you can tell me now?" Zach asked plaintively. "Anything Egyptian?"

"Time out. Look at the menu. Let's get serious here, guys," Kitty interrupted them.

Zach opened his menu and glanced over the listings. Then he looked up, clearly dismayed. "This stuff is expensive, Mom. What's my limit?" he asked, knowing that Kitty usually set some kind of guideline when they ate out.

"The Dunes is picking up the tab," Vince informed him quietly. "Pick whatever you want, hotshot."

"Vince . . ." Kitty sighed. "That doesn't mean you go overboard," she cautioned Zach. "Just order what you really intend to eat. A regular dinner." She had visions of Zach ordering eighteen desserts as a first course.

"I'll handle it, Mom," Zach said, trying to sound very mature. "Melissa told us at lunch that we have to eat right. And Corey said that if we don't eat what we order, we'll be wearing it. But he was only kidding."

"He has a point," Kitty noted, nudging Zach gently as their waiter approached.

As soon as they were alone again, Zach started scrutinizing all the artwork in the room. "This stuff sure is weird. The statues are nice, but everything in the pictures is flat. And they all have weird stuff on their heads."

"A lot of the weird stuff in Egyptian art is symbolic," Vince offered, trying to come up with some information Zach could show off to Melissa. "Once you know a few of the symbols, it all begins to make sense. Like those columns out front and the pattern on the border of the wallpaper. The decoration symbolizes the union of the two parts of Egypt. The lotus flower represents upper Egypt that was called the Delta. That's where the Nile meets the Mediterranean Sea. The papyrus plant stands for lower Egypt, farther south. Papyrus used to grow in the marshes there and the Egyptians used to peel it and pound it flat to make paper."

"Which is the lotus?"

"The one that looks like a water lily. It has petals. The one that looks like a fan or an upside-down bell is the papyrus."

"Ah. I got it," Zach murmured with a sly smile. "Is that a lotus, too?" he asked, pointing to a carving on the pedestal supporting one of the female figures.

"You got it," Vince acknowledged.

"You know any more symbols?" Zach pumped him, obviously pleased with prospect of discussing plant imagery with Melissa.

"How about this one?" Vince tried again. "Let's talk about the sun." Their salads had arrived, and Kitty started eating, gesturing for Zach to do the same.

"Egyptians were fascinated by the sun. Their most powerful god was the sun god Ra. Sometimes he's called Ra Horakte. Because he was so important, you'll see sun symbols everywhere. Those obelisks out by the front gate represent a single shaft of sunlight or Ra himself. Even the pyramid shape is taken from the flow of sunshine onto the earth." Vince used his hands to demonstrate. "That guy over there is Ra Horakte." He pointed to a figure in one of the papyrus reproductions. "He's got the falcon head to show he's powerful and he's wearing a solar disk on his head. That means he's hot stuff." He saw a trace of a smile alter Zach's "show me" expression. "And since he's being carried across from one side of the picture to the other, that represents the movement of the sun each day across the sky. You can probably find him in a lot of other pictures around the hotel." With a satisfied shrug, Vince finally started his meal. Zach was still pondering the panel closest to them.

"Where does Ra go at night?" Zach caught him by surprise.

"Zach, let the man eat," Kitty protested. But Vince was nodding.

"Seems to me he goes by boat through a different realm. Some dark watery place. Then in the morning, he changes vehicles and begins his ride across the heavens again. That's how the cycle goes, on and on," Vince said patiently.

"What kind of boat?" Zach persisted.

Vince stared at the lad, dumbfounded.

"What kind of boat did Ra have?"

"Maybe it was a felucca," Kitty interjected. Zach looked at her, trying to decide if she were teasing.

"Maybe you and old Ra have something in common. You're both sailors, except the two of you signed on for different shifts. You sail days; Ra gets nights. Frankly I think you got the best deal. It's too easy to sail right off the end of the earth at night. And you wouldn't believe the big ugly things you bump into after midnight." Amusement flickered in the sea blue eyes that met his. Zach studied her expression then he smiled.

"Right."

"Now please," Kitty urged him. "Let's enjoy our dinner.

"Different shifts . . ." Zach whispered, chuckling to himself. "Big ugly things. Wait till I tell tell Chris."

By the time dessert was served, Zach had already abandoned them to meet "the guys" and see the movie.

"It's tough to be thrown over for part two of a film about a crime-fighting robot," Vince said, shrugging good-naturedly. "That leaves you and me, babe. What could we possibly do for the rest of the evening?" He eyed her hopefully. "I thought the part about bumping into things after midnight was pretty exciting."

"I'm going to be asleep by midnight. I'm exhausted. How about sublimating with hot chocolate-chip pecan pie and ice cream." Kitty sighed, imitating his petulant attitude. "We can stroll through the lobby and you can pretend I'm Melissa and point out the Egyptian goodies on display. Then we'll go upstairs, change into our suits, and sink up to our chins in the spa out by the pool. Sound good?"

"With or without room for improvisation along the way?"

"How long is that movie?" Kitty asked.

"Long enough," Vince assured her with a low chuckle. "Especially if you pass up the Egyptian goodies and concentrate on mine. I'll give you an Egyptian culture lesson on the way to breakfast tomorrow," he promised.

"Maybe the Egyptians can wait another day," Kitty replied in a velvet voice that made the hairs on his arms stand on end.

* * *

In the night, the silent bulldozers huddled against the foot of the mound while the long-necked cranes stood like sentinels in the moonlight, motionless, casting criss-crossed shadows against the pale expanse of sand. Like the prickly spines of a procession of porcupines, shovel handles poked up in clusters at intervals on the south mound where they'd been left when construction for the day finally ended.

Earlier in the evening, after the shovelers and crew of sandsculptors vacated the site for the day, another shift of experts had gone to work. Jack Button brought in the electricians, whose job was laying in, covering over, and marking the paths of heavy electrical cables that would eventually be needed to illuminate the mound. But once darkness had settled in and made further work on the heights unfeasible, the electrical crew had withdrawn to ground level. Before leaving, they aimed the periscope-like floodlights set in eight box-shaped molds around the periphery and tested them.

For a few minutes, these eight floodlights held back the night. They caught the dull flat sides and angled corners of the reinforced wood molds and sent deep irregular swatches of shadow across the mounds. Like a disorderly collage of squares and rectangles, the once-undulating triple peaks had become angular, a multilayered lopsided, cubistic birthday cake, topped by the majestic single column that would be Rapunzel's Tower. But to Button, it was coming along as spectacularly as he'd hoped.

"Looks good. Lock 'em in and shut 'em down," the job foreman had directed once the flow of light was evenly distributed. Button had told him just to get the basics set up tonight. They'd have a week to fine-tune before they'd start to illuminate the mound into the night. By the weekend, the crowds would be arriving. Most of the molds would have been broken down and carried away, and the sculptors would have finished at least a few of the uppermost buildings and tableaux. Cables already set inside some of those forms would have to be hooked up and equipped with individual lights. Footers set in near the bases would need smaller spots installed. The news coverage would increase. The momentum would build.

When there was something to look at, something to draw a crowd, then Button had said the lights would be left on. Otherwise it wouldn't be cost-effective. But now, only a solitary light pole installed by the volunteer sign-in tent remained on. A lone security guard stationed there poured a cup of coffee from his thermos and leaned back, propping his feet on a neighboring chair. Tool kits and flashlights in hand, the electricians filed past him. Then, except for the wind whispering through the leaves and rustling palm fronds, there was silence.

In the velvet darkness beyond the pale fringe of light from that single pole, the surrounding oaks spread their broad branches, keeping even the faintest trace of moonlight from filtering through to the grassy grounds below. But the two had come back again. The night before, the two had crouched farther off in the undergrowth, watching the few who walked up there, staring in wonder at the luminous monolith that had seemingly grown up in that spot like a pale-hued fungus. It had been pretty then.

Now it looked grotesque.

Tonight, the triple-humped mushroom form was zigzagged with pathways and littered with huge frames, hoses, shovels, and buckets. The two had come out at midday and had witnessed some of the destruction. They had seen the loud flying machine lift the cylinder and stab it into the topmost rise. They saw flat partitions hoisted onto steps cut in the sides then formed into four-sided shapes. Then workers poured sand and water in up to the rim. Finally, the loud machines that had dug and pushed and lifted all day were very still and silent, and the people went away into the buildings beyond the gardens.

But others came. This time in trucks with signs on the sides. The two watched the men with flat-nosed shovels hide the dark lines beneath the surface. They stared as the vicious lights made specters fly across the hillsides. None of it made any sense to them. But the many flat-nosed shovels and the dark lines that those men had secreted away remained to tempt them. And they wondered what was buried under the sand in those boxes. Then the lights went off and those men went away.

Except for one. They had smelled him and his coffee; they knew he was still there. But he didn't worry them. The dark of night was friendly to their eyes. They could travel unheard, their footsteps covered by the wind sounds. So the two moved in closer and circled to the opposite side of the area, staying under the protective shroud of the aged oaks.

But soon they were not content to simply look. Creeping on hands and knees, the two moved steadily across the clearing, heading toward the mound. Inching upward on the dark side, they hid behind one box frame, then another, then the next. Then Tommy scuttled up one level of the mold framing onto the smaller box on top of it. And with his bare hands, he started burrowing into the sand, trying to find whatever treasure was there. But the sand was hard-packed and difficult to move. With a soft owl hoot, he signaled to Lon. Shovel. He jerked his arms to show what he needed.

Lon went higher on the mound to get him one.

"Hey, Buddy? How's it going out there?" Bo Shepherd's voice came over the guard's headset, nudging him awake. Despite the coffee and the relative discomfort of the folding chairs, Buddy Pardo had dozed off. "Buddy? You there?"

"Sure. I'm here." Pardo adjusted the microphone, which had been tilted away from his chin drooped in sleep. "Everything's fine," he answered, trying to sound alert.

"You need anything? Skip is making his rounds in a while. He could bring you out a sandwich or a donut or something."

"A couple of donuts sounds good," Pardo replied, rubbing his thighs with his palms. "It's getting damp. I could use some more coffee. And a blanket."

"A blanket? What are you up to? Got a woman out there?" Shepherd sounded amused.

"Nah. It's just getting cool. If I'm stuck out here, I might as well be comfy, right? Tomorrow I'll wear my camping jacket. That sucker's quilted."

"I'll see what I can come up with," Shepherd promised. "Skip will bring the donuts by in a while."

"Don't forget the coffee. And thanks." Pardo refilled his thermos and scrunched down in the chair again. The damp air caught the steam and dissipated it.

At first Pardo thought it just was his eyes playing tricks on him. There was a shift in the shadow pattern near one cluster of shovels. The dark space split apart then merged with the next one. Pardo figured he was just tired. Or maybe a cloud passed over, altering the shaded forms cast across the sand by the moon. Then a part broke away and moved again.

Scarcely breathing, Pardo moved around to get a better angle on it, keeping back far enough so he'd blend in with the black beneath the trees. Every few feet, he'd stop, straining to catch some glimpse of movement again. He was a fourth of the way around when one shovel handle tilted to one side, then rose into the air and was swallowed in the adjacent shadow. Then a second shovel wriggled and dove into darkness. This time the hairs on the back of his neck pricked and stood on end. Someone was up there.

"Shepherd? Anyone there?" Pardo whispered his summons into his mike. "Assistance please."

"What's up?" A voice that was not Shepherd's came back to him.

"This is Pardo. I'm at the mound. There's something funny going on here. I think someone is up there. Might be trouble."

"Shepherd isn't here, he's on his way home. But Skip is already on the way out. I'll give him a call and hustle him up. How much help you think you need?"

"I don't know. It's probably just a kid out spookin' around. Is there any way we can get these lights on out here?"

"Dunno. Maybe. Let me call Button. He'll want to know about this anyhow. I'll try to catch Shepherd while I'm at it. Just wait for Skip and keep me posted."

"Will do." Pardo started back to the tent where Skip would expect to find him. He stood there a full ten minutes before he heard the hum of the golf cart that the security patrol used.

"Heard you had a prowler," Skip greeted him. "Still up there?" He handed Pardo some coffee and donuts. Pardo put them on the sign-in table and took the blanket Skip had clutched under his arm.

"Haven't seen anything for a few minutes." Pardo wrapped the blanket around his shoulders and then stood like Skip, staring at the mound, munching a donut. For a long while neither spoke.

"You want to check it out?" Skip sounded interested.

"Maybe we should set out in opposite directions. Meet on the other side around by the lake?" Pardo finished a second donut and licked his fingertips.

"You got a flashlight?" Skip asked, hauling out a long-handled one from its holder in the cart.

"Sure. But I wouldn't recommend using it right now. If you do, he'll know exactly where you are," Pardo warned him. "He'll just take off the other way."

"So what do we do? Keep circling until dawn?"

"I think we should pull in someone else. Two stake out below and let the third man go up there and look around. The man up top can use a light to flush him out."

"What does the office say?"

"I don't know. They're contacting Shepherd and Button now."

"Call and ask."

"What's the word from Shepherd?" Pardo called in.

"He's not too cheerful about it, but he's coming back. He'll be out there in a few minutes. And Jack Button is on his way. He's called the electrician about activating the lights. Just hang tight."

"Right," he muttered impatiently. "Until everyone and their grandma show up." Then he turned to Skip. "How about you going around there where the main path comes down." Pardo pointed to the left around the mound. "If all the action down here tips him off and he makes a run for it, you may be able to snag him on the backside."

"I'd like to give him a snag on his backside with this, all right." Brandishing his unlighted flashlight like a battle-ax, Skip headed around toward the opposite side. Draped in his blanket, Pardo remained behind, eyes riveted to the shadows on the center mound. But nothing moved up there.

Tommy was dug in up to his waist before Lon stopped him. Lon had seen headlights of an oncoming vehicle strafe the underbrush, so he knew it wasn't on the roadway. This one was coming straight for the foot of the mound. Lon hurried to the top and looked over.

"No more," Lon said, coming back and tugging at Tommy's shirt. But Tommy shrugged him off and took a couple more shovelfuls out of the form. Then he spat. Nothing there. Nothing but sand.

"Go home," Lon insisted. "Trouble." He thrust a finger in the direction of the guard and the newcomers.

Tommy spat again and shook his head. There had to be something there, but all he'd hit was layer after layer of sand.

"Like shovel. Take shovel," Tommy muttered, determined not to leave empty-handed. By now a second set of headlights had swerved into the area. A car door slammed. Tommy vaulted out of the half-empty form onto the surface. "Take two." He snatched Lon's shovel.

One after the other, they crept from object to object, heading around to the far end of the mound where they'd made their own route up. Hesitating a moment by a cache of shovels, Tommy switched one of his for a new one and pitched the one he'd snatched back to Lon. "Good shovels," he declared. Then he hoisted both of them, blade up, on his shoulder.

"Let's just spread out, cover the bottom. Tell Skip he can go up top and flush 'em out," Shepherd declared wearily. It was after one and he'd planned to be sinking into a hot tub with a cold beer about now. "Probably some kids just screwing around. I'll pull the bullhorn and order 'em down.'' He retrieved the hand-held amplifier and turned it on while Pardo and another backup guard took off around to dark side.

"Okay you up there.'' Shepherd's clear, clipped words pierced the night. "We want you down off the mound. There's a lot of equipment up there, and we don't want you hurt. Now there's a fellow with a light on the way to lead you off. Just give us a yell so we know where you are, then let him meet up with you. We want you down safely. No harm done. No trouble. Just come on down and let us all get some sleep.''

Jack Button stood next to Shepherd, staring up expectantly. No one answered. He shifted then tugged the zipper of his sweatsuit jacket higher, keeping the breeze out.

Shepherd repeated his request. Then he unbuttoned his jacket and checked his shoulder holster. "Wish to hell I'd brought my flare gun,'' he muttered.

By now the bright beam from Skip's flashlight was dancing over the top of the southern mound.

"Shit . . .'' Shepherd groaned, realizing that neither he nor Skip was wearing a headset. He'd have to yell. "Any luck?'' he bellowed over the horn, well aware than any hope of subtlety was gone.

"Not yet.'' Skip's thin reply was carried down by the wind. His light continued slashing and pausing as he headed toward the center mound. He circled the tower mold, then cut around to the dark side and dropped out of sight.

"Someone's been up here all right. He's torn up one of these forms,'' Skip yelled down to Buddy Pardo. "Wait a minute. The box is still intact but looks like they took the sand out.''

From below, Pardo could barely hear the details. He'd

been following the light pattern and occasionally could make out Skip's silhouette against the sky. But he caught the gleam of moonlight off metal behind Skip. And he saw the blade swoop down out of the dark. He heard the thud when it connected. Skip's flashlight ricocheted off one of the forms, bounced onto the sand, then went out.

"Skip? You hurt?" Pardo's voice cracked as he yelled into the pitch-dark space above. "Hey, heads up, you guys. Skip's been hit. We need help." His shrill sound brought Shepherd into view. "Up there," Pardo yelled. "Someone slammed Skip with a shovel."

"Okay," Shepherd called through the horn. "I'm comin' up and I'm comin' armed. We got a man down, and right now that's all that I'm interested in. Put your hands up and come out in the open. Now," Shepherd barked. "Mess with me and I'll blow your balls off."

No response.

"You take this," Shepherd ordered, shoving the bull-horn into Pardo's hand. "Call communications and get us some backup. I've got a shotgun in my truck. Circle around and get it. I'm going up." He yanked out his flashlight, reached for his handgun, and began climbing up the mound toward Skip.

"This is Buddy at the mound," Pardo started transmitting as he jogged around toward the truck. He heard it coming down on him before he cleared the dark side.

It sounded like a rhino charge, even though Pardo had never set eyes on a rhino outside Busch Gardens, but the snorting sound coming out of the dark cut right through to a place where thinking didn't help. All he knew was that there was a whole lot of bulk moving down the slope his way and a lot of heavy breathing coming with it. And when he spun around, flinging up the bullhorn like a shield, it looked as if the side of the mound was spraying down with it. Then it thundered onto the ground, spewing sand and bellowing, and in the little light available, he could tell there was more than one of them. Thick, dark, dirty, hulking male forms lunged at him. Then the handle of a shovel connected with the side of his head, and he was out.

"Get me some ice out here and call out the paramedics," Shepherd called in on Pardo's twisted headset. The wires were intact, but the blow had cracked the headband as well as Pardo's cheekbone.

"Tell them not to run their sirens," Button reminded him. "No need to get everyone upset."

"Try to get the fellas to keep it quiet," Shepherd accommodated him. "Looks like a concussion and a broken cheekbone. No real bleeding. Take a left inside the entrance. I'll have my truck headlights on by the mound. And get me the cops," he added. "Same routine. No sirens. We got trespassing. Assault. Theft. But the creeps took off. No reason to come charging in with the lights flashing."

"The electrician is here." The Dunes security man stepped into the light from Shepherd's truck. Jack Button looked at Shepherd and nodded.

"Tell him to get this place lit up," Shepherd ordered. "Let's see what the hell they've done up there."

The Crystal Springs police disregarded Button's desire for discretion. And they didn't need directions to locate the mound. Blazing white in the night, it loomed above the trees like a ghostly apparition. They could spot it almost a mile off. At 1:42, with tires squealing, they swerved into the Dunes entrance, veering left at the Great Sphinx as they headed for the eerie white ridges. Lights pulsing, the two units braked next to the orange and white medical van that had arrived five minutes before them.

Stiff-faced, Jack Button stepped forward and asked the officers to turn off their flashers.

Fifteen minutes later, Pardo and Skip were en route to Crystal Springs General. Shepherd, Button, and the officers examined the footprints left by the two and concluded the intruders had been wearing some kind of boots. "We're talkin' hikers, farmers, military, bikers. . . ." one officer said, shaking his head dubiously as they strode in single file back down the mound.

"Not a good print in the lot," another officer noted. "Every one of 'em slips or slides because of the sand. Looks like these guys were playing hide-and-seek for a while before you rousted them," he added, pointing out the erratic pattern the prints made over the surface.

"But no damage except for the one box—"

"We can refill that tomorrow," Button cut in, eager to resolve the matter quietly and quickly. "Other than a taking a couple of shovels, they really didn't do much damage."

"Except put a couple of guys in the hospital," Shepherd added tightly.

"Of course. That goes without saying," Button said. "What happened to them is very unfortunate, but they're in good hands now. I don't see how we can accomplish anything more tonight."

"Other than fill out and file a report," the officer said. "I'd bet these guys are transients. I'd bet they came in thinking they'd just browse around a bit, maybe pilfer some tools to swap off for food somewhere. Maybe even planned to sleep up there. They're probably scared shitless now. They won't stop running until they hit the Keys."

"Yeah, and unless they're carrying the shovels, we're going to have a heck of a time spotting them."

"Look, we can finish the paperwork without the flood-lights?" Button asked nervously as they reached ground level. So far the incident had only drawn a few onlook-ers, night-shift workers from the hotel laundry and grounds staff. But if anyone got up to take a leak at night and glanced out the window, there'd be questions. Button didn't want any rumors of crime associated with his idyl-lic Dunesfest. "It's pretty breezy out here," he noted, rubbing his hands together. "How about coming into the coffee shop and we'll get you guys something to eat while you do those reports?"

"Sounds good to me." The first officer moved toward his unit.

"Douse the lights," Button directed the bleary-eyed electrician who'd been summoned from a sound sleep and promised double overtime for a site call. A few sec-onds later, the floodlights were extinguished. Then the vehicles pulled off toward the hotel, leaving the backup guard behind in the volunteer tent with Pardo's blanket.

"This is Rob. Tell Shepherd and Button that we've got a couple more kids out here. Maybe three of 'em. Came in by car. Parked it in the north lot then came up through the back."

"Let me try to catch 'em before the cops leave."

Robbie Fiedler kept his eye on the shadows while he waited for a response.

"Don't try anything by yourself. They're coming."

The two police units, Shepherd's truck, and Jack But-ton's BMW came sweeping in, circling the mound like an assault force. Behind them, the electrician's van bobbed and skidded into place by the transformer unit. This time, when the lights went on, the bodies on the heights leaped for cover.

"You're wasting your time, boys." Shepherd spat the words into the bullhorn. "Get your butts down here. And follow the damn path. Don't mess up anything." For a moment, none of the youngsters appeared. Then a pair of arms appeared over one of the boxes, held up in surrender. Made even more pallid by the floodlights, the thin young man moved forward tentatively.

"Come on. The rest of you move it along. You won't like it if we have to send someone up after you."

Two more teenage boys came out of hiding. Hands up. Then the girl. Fifteen at best. Shoulder-length hair flung across her face by the wind. All of them were squinting, trying to peer beyond the barrier of lights at their captors.

"You can drop your hands," Shepherd said, softening his voice. "Just come on down. No one's going to hurt you. Nice and easy." He started forward to meet them.

"Will you be wanting these lights off again?" The electrician intercepted Button.

Button stopped and looked at the site. Between the sharp-edged shovels, the treacherous hose lines, the sudden drop-offs where paths cut across, and the poor visibility in the dark, the place was dangerous. "An attractive nuisance," the law could call it. A temptation for kids like these. That would put the liability on the Dunes. The insurance company would get hysterical. Any way Button tried to figure, it meant more money. Either he'd have to post more men on the perimeter or foot the bill for lighting the whole thing all night.

Button pursed his lips. If he had them set up a couple of concession stands with hot coffee and donuts and soft drinks, and if they had some sweatshirts printed up fast and charged plenty for them, that might offset some of the outlay. Besides, after they tidied it up a little, the mound wouldn't look so bad. "A work-in-progress," he told himself, already picking out a couple of places to post some appropriate signs and sketches. "An artistic feat-in-progress," he edited the PR release already spinning in his mind. There might be enough of a turnout to make it worthwhile.

"Leave the lights on," Button finally decided. "Set up a sensor to cut them off at the first sign of sunrise." There was no reason to go overboard. Dusk to dawn would do it. Besides sunrise would be spectacular, unaugmented by artificial light. And it would film well.

Chapter 3

"HEY. IT'S LUNCHTIME. MIND IF I COME UP FOR A look?'' Vince stood at the base of the pipe scaffolding that had been flown in and set down like a bird cage around the tower where Kitty was working. Crockett, Stuart, and the rest of them had popped off the mold first thing Tuesday morning. Unbolted, one half of the cylinder had been held steady by five workers while the copter lifted it up neatly and carried it away. Then they returned for the second half. Just as Crockett had predicted, the removal proceeded like a piece of cake. Then, just as neatly, the pipe scaffolding was lowered around the column of sand. For the rest of the morning, while Vince and the others uncrated a few forms on the heights, refilled the one the intruders had emptied, set up new molds, and cleaned up the clutter, Kitty and Craig Stuart had started sculpting. Stuart blocked in the general tower shape—roof, balcony, and bushes below—then they started out at the top together. Now Kitty was up there alone.

"Just let me finish this," Kitty called down to him. Perched like an aerialist on the ladderlike structure, Kitty leaned forward, using a stainless steel putty knife to backcut and define the shell-like pattern of tiles on the tower roof. "Before I break for lunch, I want to have this sprayed so when I come back I can finish with Rapunzel," she explained. Working at slightly less than full scale, Kitty had placed the pensive young princess with elbows resting on the balcony railing and a long braid curving down toward the base. The features of the face were already cut in, but the braid, arms and hands, and the dress needed work. "How's it look so far?"

"Good," Vince said simply. "You want me to get the spray now?"

"Please. Stuart was supposed to take care of this, but he keeps disappearing on me."

"I know. We had a few complications on the south mound, and Paul and I called him over to give us some input. Now he's on the north mound helping Kevin and Crockett lay out a few more sites. I'll tell you, things are really moving along. Let me get the spray and I'll be right back."

Minutes later, Vince was climbing up the scaffolding with a green spray tank strapped over one shoulder. Then Kitty gave the rooftop a final nod of approval, and he started misting the entire surface with the fixative, a transparent mixture of biodegradable glue and water. Without altering the color of the sand, it would coat the outer layer and hold the surface together like a thin, tough skin, strong enough to keep the details from being rubbed smooth by the wind. Once the skin was intact, that portion of the design couldn't be touched again. The sand inside would gradually become dry and powderlike, and if the outer skin were pierced, the inner skin would drizzle out like flour from a punctured bag. Then portion after portion of the outer skin could give way until the structure collapsed. So spraying meant hands off.

"Do her face, too. It's done."

Vince adjusted the nozzle, narrowing the mist so he could aim it accurately. Then he hesitated and looked eye to eye with Rapunzel. "Kitty, she's beautiful."

"I thought so, too."

"She looks like she's daydreaming. Quite an air about her. Kinda a cross between you and Zach."

"Any resemblance is purely coincidental. I was just after the on-the-verge look, just before her life got really complicated."

"She does have an innocent quality. It's nice work. really nice."

"Thank you, sir." Kitty bowed slightly. "Now spray her down. I'd like her to stay just like this."

"I'll do my best," Vince promised. "Maybe we should let this first coat dry and I'll come back and mist it again before you get back up here.

"I like that idea."

He gently sprayed the finished sections then swung the canister over his shoulder before backtracking down the scaffolding. "Come on. On the way to lunch, take a walk around with me. Come and see how things are going."

Kitty stretched and flexed her legs, rubbing the place where she'd been propped against the rung for almost four hours. "I could use something to drink first." She tucked her putty knife next to her other sculpting spatulas, slipped off the apron tool belt, and climbed down.

The world she stepped into had changed considerably

since she climbed up to her hilltop aerie that morning. "My goodness." Kitty brushed back her fair windblown hair and surveyed the action around the base of the mound. "Will you look at all the people down there. . . ." Totally absorbed in her work, she'd been oblivious to the peripheral activity. Several hundred people were below, some parked in lawn chairs, simply watching, others setting up concession stands and the press tent. Clusters of volunteers were signing up, shoveling, or being trained on the smaller forms that Kevin had set out. She followed Vince along one of the plateaus to a break site where an umbrella shaded an ice chest full of chilled drinks, water, and a cache of sunscreen and first-aid supplies.

"Button is down there with the video folks, his own and some from Tampa, filming the construction." Vince pointed out Button in his ivory shirt and pith helmet. "They've been shooting since we started lifting the molds. I'm sure we've all been repeatedly immortalized with the zoom lens. Especially you. You look real dramatic way up there on that scaffolding with nothing but sky behind you."

"I hope they can't tell how queasy I get when I shift weight and the whole cage shudders." Kitty dipped her hands in a bucket of water and washed off the layer of sand that clung to her arms. I'll be glad to get off that thing and onto solid ground."

"That may be a while." Vince popped open a can of soda and handed it to her.

"What do you mean by that?"

"Take a look." He pointed toward the series of new molds they'd framed in and filled while she was up top. There were almost a third again as many as the original plans required.

"What's all that?"

Vince tugged off his visor and ran his hand through his dark hair. "It means that you were right about this being a lot of area to cover. When we got a good look at it this morning, it was pretty apparent that there was going to be too much empty space, so we packed in a few more molds. We haven't figured out what they all will be, but we have Sandy Huff down below madly researching the Grimms and Hans Christian Andersen. All I know is that there will be lots of characters to rough out. And that means faces."

"And that means me," Kitty guessed.

"It also means using a portable scaffold," Vince added uneasily. "We figured that if we put together a smaller one, we can ship it around from place to place. Even if people have started on the body or whatever goes below, we can whisk you in and get you up high enough to do a face without worrying about disturbing the rest of it."

"You realize that my body will atrophy in a permanent right angle." Kitty groaned, arching her back to relieve the strain. "I'll have indelible lines in my thighs. My feet will have rung ruts."

Vince shrugged. "I'll get them to throw in a masseuse." He hugged her shoulders sympathetically. "And I'll rub your rung ruts myself," he promised, amused by her terminology.

"Maybe if we could rig up some kind of padding . . ." Kitty turned and looked back at her scaffolding. "Something to keep that top bar from digging into my legs."

"Come on." Vince took her hand and started leading her away. "Lunch. Shade. Cantaloupe. Pineapple. All that good healthy stuff you like. Then we'll think about padding your perch."

"Any sign of the kids?" Kitty asked, following him down the sloping walkway.

"That Corey fellow brought the boys out here in the shuttle about an hour ago, just to check things out. But until the heavy equipment is out of here, no kids are allowed near the mound. But they looked around. Button had them all meet the film crews and get their pictures taken. Then they headed back. Zach's fine," Vince assured her. "They're all having a great time. They were going to watch some National Geographic special about the pyramids on the VCR, then they were going sailing again."

"You think anyone would notice if I slipped away and went with them?"

"I'd miss you." Vince pulled her close and squeezed her affectionately. "Come on, sport. Lunch."

"Otto, we're up to our ass in old folks. Old farts don't have anything better to do than wander around out here like ducks lookin' for thunder. If we don't get a shuttle out here, we're going to have a few of these geezers dropping from the heat." The young man in safari garb radioed in his assessment midday Tuesday.

Otto Breshears came out to take a long look at the uneven procession of white-haired spectators making the trek from the north parking lot to the shade of the trees encircling the castle site. One nursing home had brought out a van with eight clients, all in wheelchairs. The driver had set up a picnic tent facing the center mound, and a female attendant had her elderly wards lined up like a reviewing committee, lunch trays propped across the armrests of their chairs, smiles of contentment on their faces. Jack Button and the film crew had spotted them and were on the way over.

"First of all, watch your mouth," Otto advised the younger man who was assigned traffic duty. "Or you won't have anything better to do either. Just stay calm and I'll get you another couple of fellas out here to keep things from getting snarled. But show some respect here. I'll have to ask Button about implementing the shuttle." He strode purposefully across the clearing, intercepting Button before he got to the wheelchair group.

"I know it's almost a week earlier that we scheduled it, but we're getting more traffic than we expected," Otto began. "How about starting up a shuttle run? I've got a couple of women I can pull in early for day duty."

Button narrowed his eyes and scanned the crowd. So far they were being cooperative about the signs and rope barriers around the action on the site, but the crowd was becoming large enough to require some kind of traffic management. Button had called in two of the Dunesfest special security staff already. While the cranes and dozers piled and hauled the fine silica up to the new molds, these early-bird spectators set up in the space under the shade trees where they could enjoy the progress unobstructed. But Button already could tell that whatever figures his staff had compiled about estimated crowd flow were no longer applicable. Ditto his budget for traffic and crowd control. Dunesfest was going to be a blockbuster. Beyond the knot of cold fear in his stomach at the prospect of things going out of control, Button felt the undeniable rush of adrenaline that came with success.

"Bring in one shuttle now. Run it on a half-hour schedule to start. Loop into the hotel each trip so we'll have a steady draw from the resort. When it looks like you need a second car, call me. We're playin' this by ear, so keep on it. This is a first-class show. Let's keep it that way." He patted Otto, then instantly relayed another message to the office, cupping one had over the earphone of the headset as he spoke. "We need a couple of those ice-cream carts out here. Get the concessionaire and have him set up right away. I don't care what his problems are. Let's get on it." Then without losing his genial smile, he continued toward the elderly visitors in wheelchairs.

"Welcome to the Dunesfest. You folks wouldn't mind if we put your picnic here on film, would you?" Button leaned down and smiled at each of them in turn. Behind him, the frizzy-haired camera operator had the video unit running. "You sure were smart to bring these contraptions. No matter where the action is, you can roll right up and have front-row seats." While he talked and patted and charmed the visitors, Mike kept filming.

"Get me Shepherd." Button took a break in the shade of the communications tent and called into security center by phone. "Bo, we're going to need to double the adjunct staff by the weekend," he said flatly. "Have Roseanne Petty pull all the applications, call them in, then notify the high school and junior college that we'll need more support people. Tell Roseanne to run a couple of radio spots. Set up a session tonight at seven for screening applicants and two back-to-back tomorrow night for screening and orientation."

"Who's going to run these sessions?" Shepherd asked, already sure he wasn't going to like the answer. "We've got a couple of men in the hospital. We're already running overtime." He'd only had three hours' sleep because of the trespassing incidents.

"We're just going to have to be flexible," Button replied evenly. "We've got three weeks of strangeness coming down on us. I think you'd better pass the word that overtime is going to be the norm. Have Roseanne check out the availability of rooms in the hotel. We might be smart to set up temporary quarters for some of our men for the next couple of weeks. You might have them pass the word to their families. That includes yours.''

"You mean you want the regular staff on the grounds round the clock?" Shepherd asked incredulously.

"Only if they want to still be here after the excitement dies down," Button answered coldly. "We need their help. They'll be compensated. Pass the word. And don't forget to set up those meetings.''

"Mr. Button, someone from Channel 10 is on the other line. Something about scheduling interviews.''

"Gotta go, Bo. Get Roseanne on that recruiting." Button clicked off then reached for the second line. "Jack Button here." There was only the faintest tremor in his hands.

"You cushioned it! Great!" Kitty braced herself on the rung and bent forward, testing Vince's addition to her scaffold. During their lunch break, Kitty and Sandy Huff and Kevin thumbed through the stack of children's books Stuart had one of the volunteers bring in from the Crystal Springs library, trying to pick out some additional characters for the latest mounds. Vince had found a sheet of foam rubber and some ducting tape and had gone back up to wrap the bars facing Rapunzel. "I thank you and my legs thank you." Kitty tested them, delighted with the results.

"It's only temporary," Vince qualified. "If it helps, then tomorrow we'll rig up a cushion that can be moved around. We could use something like Velcro bands to hold it on," he suggested.

"Then I could take it with me wherever I need it. But for now, it's a lifesaver," she said while he misted Rapunzel's face with the final coat of fixative. "You did good." She bent close and pressed a kiss on his cheek, leaving an oval of white zinc oxide from her coated lips on the spot.

"Watch out. They may be filming," Vince kidded, somewhat surprised at the public show of affection. Generally she was more reserved in public.

"Must be the altitude," Kitty proclaimed. "I guess I just lost control."

"Call me if you feel it coming on again," Vince replied. Then he sent a final shower of fixative over the tiles and switched off the sprayer. "If you're all set here, I'll get back to work. I've got a castle to put together." He dropped the spray tank and climbed after it. "When you take a break later, come and get me. And don't forget our meeting tonight. We have to brainstorm with Sandy and the others about the extra forms. Once in a while scope out those molds down below, and think fairy tales," he called up to her.

"Will do," Kitty promised, strapping on her tool belt and lining herself up in front of the enigmatic Rapunzel. "If Corey brings Zack out here again, have them call me. I asked Sandy to check on him. I'd just like an update."

"I'll keep an eye out for him. But I guarantee you, he's just fine."

"No doubt. But I'd like a glimpse of the kid now and then."

"He's promised us a little time at dinner," Vince said laughingly. "We're scheduled in between air hockey and some kind of ice-cream social with the girls."

"Well, it's nice to know he hasn't forgotten us completely," Kitty responded. "I've seen less of him here than I do at home."

"Get used to it, lady," Vince warned her. "First comes puberty, then a car and a part-time job, then college. Next thing you know, he's off on his own. But play your cards right, and you'll still be stuck with me. You could save years of uncertainty and marry me now." He broke into a wide-open grin. "I promise I won't tell anyone you're two years older than me. I'll grow a mustache. I'll act mature."

Kitty didn't answer. She just gave him a slightly bemused look.

"I know. Don't rush you." Vince chuckled. "Just want you to know the offer is always open. I'm not going to bail out on you, babe. I'll always be here. At least in spirit. In body, for now, I'll be over there. See you around." He strolled off toward the south mound, still grinning.

Kitty watched him a minute. There had been a time when she would have written off Vince Ammons in an instant. He was too brash, too casual, too undisciplined. She'd been on an executive career track in the Biscom marketing division with all the high-level conferences and expense accounts that went with her professional status. She'd even married an equally aggressive Biscom corporate attorney. But three years, two BMWs, and an ulcerated esophagus later, Kitty knew she couldn't stand the pressure or the pace, professionally or socially. She wanted off the track.

Her husband Richie wanted more. More money. More parties. More women. None of it was personal, he'd insisted. But Kitty couldn't get that idea to sink in. When he disappeared for an hour at a party or was off for a weekend on company business, she drank Maalox and churned. When their credit cards hit the maximum, she couldn't sleep. Then Richie was offered a promotion in the Atlanta office, and Kitty let him go, without her, as an act of survival. An attorney friend negotiated an uncontested divorce. She retrained in technical operations. She whittled away at the backlog of debts. She took up sandsculpting to relax. She didn't let anyone male get too close. Then two years later, she found another kind of love was possible when she met Zach.

Much later Vince showed up, digging in the sand one weekend. Younger. Funnier. Terribly unorganized. Highly creative. Habitually easygoing. As unlike Richie as he could be. There was something very solid about Vince, something that had slipped past all her defenses. And he said right out that he wanted to marry her.

"Hey, Kitty, are you able to listen?" Sandy Huff's voice came over the headset.

"Sure. Did you check on Zach?"

"Yep. He's fine. They're in class right now. That's not why I called."

"Okay. Why did you call?" She used the reverse end of an artist's brush to deepen the lines between Rapunzel's fingers.

"I have a story for you."

"Now?" Kitty switched ends of the brush and whisked away the loose sand that had fallen on the balcony railing.

"Sure. I'm still going through these fairy tales. Stuart wanted something big. How about this? Twelve Dancing Princesses. Do you remember the story?"

"Can't say I do." Kitty went back to her favorite tool, a narrow-bladed spatula, and dug out a column between each of the balcony supports. From a distance, the shadows would make it seem as if there was nothing between the railings at all.

"Okay. Here's the short version," Sandy began. "A

king had twelve daughters who wore out their shoes every night. He wanted to know what was going on, so he offered to marry off one of them to any man who could figure it out. A few princes tried, but the girls gave them wine and the princes fell asleep. They were killed for failing to come up with an answer."

"I'd say that was a little drastic," Kitty said dryly.

"It gets better," Sandy insisted, her husky voice full of enthusiasm. "A veteran soldier, with a limp no less, comes to give it a shot. Only he's met an old hag in the woods who told him to lay off the wine, pretend to sleep, then follow the girls and wear a special cloak she had that would make him invisible."

"Isn't that cheating?" Kitty teased.

"All's fair," Sandy answered her, not really amused by Kitty's cavalier attitude. Once Kevin and Stuart gave her the task of finding extra fairy tales between handing transmissions in the staff communications tent, she had become caught up in them. "Besides, the princesses cheated, too. They drugged the wine. Anyway, the soldier did what the hag said and followed them to an underground kingdom, where twelve princes brought boats to meet them. They sailed off to a castle, where they danced all night."

"And how does it end?" Kitty finished another rung of the balcony and started working on Rapunzel's heavy braid, which cascaded down over the edge.

"The soldier makes himself invisible and follows them three nights, takes back souvenirs, then shows the king and wins the princess of his choice," Sandy concluded triumphantly. "Isn't that marvelous. You've got boats and underground caverns and twelve princesses and twelve princes. And the soldier. That's a lot of possibilities to work with, isn't it?"

"And a heck of a lot of faces," Kitty observed.

"But isn't that what Kevin and Stuart asked for?" Sandy sounded disappointed in Kitty's reaction.

"That's exactly what they wanted," Kitty replied quickly. "You found a good one, all right. But twenty-four faces . . ." She drew in a deep breath and let it out slowly. "Let me think about it."

"You aren't upset with me, are you?" Sandy sounded childlike. Her question sounded like one Zach would ask.

"I'm not upset," Kitty said reassuringly. "I just need a little while to let the images float around in my head. But while they're floating," she added with a definite ring of amusement in her voice, "try looking for a story with a monster or another dragon or something big like that. Maybe a sea serpent. Let's spread this around a little."

"A dragon," Sandy repeated, eager to please. Kitty could imagine her thumbing earnestly through the books that Stuart had sent out to the communications tent below. "I'll look."

"Call me if you find something?" Kitty asked.

"Oh, I will, " Sandy promised. Then there was silence.

Under the twisted branches of the lone cypress tree that had survived the relentless crush of swamp hardwoods, the two of them sat together on the creek bank, whimpering as they peeled away the dried bits of dirt and blood and swept clean spring water into their wounds. In the night, they had been too exhausted to tend to themselves. Instead they had crawled around past the cypress roots and scrambled through the cavern opening, exposed now that the many changes had come. They had ducked their heads and groped their way along the underground ledge that opened into the sandy-floored great room and collapsed on the ground, moaning and shivering from the ordeal.

The breeder woman had been deeper in the cavern, sound asleep, lying on her side, hugging her large belly and snoring.

"Woman . . ." Tommy had called her. She hadn't stirred. "Woman," he growled, then poked his hand around in the darkness for something to throw at her.

Lon had stopped him. "Dummy," Lon gasped, still breathless from running. He knew that Tommy would beat her unless he reminded him that their breeder woman was not ignoring him. She just couldn't hear. "Woman deaf. Woman dummy," Lon squeezed out the words. Since the big blast two months ago that followed the start of the new development, the breeder had been deaf and mute. Then they had been in the old cavern, a winding subterranean chamber of many rooms with vaulted limestone ceilings. The entrance had been marked by fierce-looking totems chipped into the stone. Inside, they had been surrounded by all the treasures that the elder and his brothers and half brothers had made or salvaged and passed on for generations. There had been tools and fishing nets and animal traps. There were pelts and skins and marvelous knives. The healer had cooking pots and bundles of special plants and roots and clays that he kept to do his medicine. There was the old still that the elder used to make his brews. All of them had kept the dream sticks that they'd whittled over the years, magic sticks crafted into the likeness of whatever they desired. And there were ancient things rescued from the bottom of the deep spring caverns: tusks, and skulls, and spearheads. Then they kept two breeder women and the boy who served them all. But the treasures and that community of caves and brothers were gone.

First there had been the loud flying machine hovering just above the treetops like a hawk hunting prey. They had all hidden in the great cave then, lying about by day in the cool shade while the clop-clop sounded above, returning many times over the month. Then it went away, and the brotherhood of wetlanders had passed the summer undisturbed, gigging for fish, swimming in the springs, hunting gators, and harvesting fruits and berries.

Then the cool weather began. And the half brother they called Trapper came back from his wanderings and told them of the huge machines cutting down trees and scraping flat the ground off to the west. There were sloughs and shrub bogs, the marsh and swamps, and many small creeks between the wetlands and all the commotion, so they didn't worry at the time.

Then the men came closer, this time on foot. A party of fifteen men came overland, chewing though the underbrush with loud, evil smelling chain saws, baring wide strips and spraying them down with pale liquid, and scaring all the animals in their path. After that, the plants along those swatches turned brown and died. Snakes and lizards wouldn't cross those pathways. Possum and coon, gray squirrels and wild hogs were scarce for weeks. Birds lay rotting where they dropped. The deer never did come back.

Later, the men came overland again, following the dead routes they had marked earlier. This time, some of them brought suits of dark rubber and masks and air packs with tubes to let them breathe. Some of them went deep into the mother springs and stayed under for a long time. Other ones waded into the lesser streams and tributaries and poked little bundles into the dams that had been there since the before the healer's time. Then they all packed up and moved away.

But when the copter came over the next week, something frightful happened. Wherever it hovered, the water below erupted with a dull growl and the dams leaped up, burst apart, then were swept away in the onrush of freed water. Then the copter moved on, paused, and another roar shook the trees. After the blasting, everything changed. Some of the small spring-fed creeks dried up entirely. The fishing holes near the old dam sites were swept flat, their once-abundant deeps now filled with shells and white sand and littered with stinking, stranded dead fish.

That was when the river itself began to narrow and draw back down the bank. Despite the rainfall that usually made it swell and often overrun its banks, that year the river diminished. When the Trapper led the elder and the healer and Lon and Tommy beyond the shrub-bog buffer that was the dividing line between the outside world and the wetland territory that was theirs, they began to comprehend what was happening.

The men with saws and copters and hard hats had diverted the main spring and had built a dam of their own. They had redirected the flow to create a small lake. Around that lake, crews of men were harvesting the slash pine and bulldozing the remnants of the orange trees that had once been prime grove land. Then they cut in some sloughs to draw off the water, bulldozed the drier areas, and installed a huge pipe that drained away even more of the water so there would be more suitable dry land for the new development.

For a while, the men busied themselves with their loud machines. Then trucks and cranes were brought in and work crews erected buildings and paved roadways. But even then, they stayed on the far side of the shrinking river and the marshgrass basin. From time to time one of the wetlanders would venture close enough to watch their progress from the cover of undergrowth then move closer after nightfall so he could return and show off with some kind of souvenir. Sometimes it was a hammer or nails or other tool left behind on the construction site. Often it was a shirt or cap found hanging on an exposed beam. Meanwhile, the wetlanders rebuilt a couple of their old dams and chummed the fish into returning there. When they started spotting a few blunt-nosed dark-skinned gators, lying half-submerged by the water's edge, it seemed as if things were back to what they had been before, and the assault on their land was over.

With the onset of cooler weather, the wetlanders collected firewood, smoked fish and game, and moved deeper into their caverns. As was their custom, Lon and the elder took the logboat then poled and trekked downriver to the fishing camp to get new mantles for their lanterns and fuel to keep them burning. The old man there always took in trade whatever gator skins or pelts they offered, no questions asked. Usually he included a couple of bundles of old shirts and shoes and overalls he'd collected over the year.

Then the winter rainy season came and the storms paraded inland from the Gulf, grumbling and bellowing and spitting lightning across the sky. In the midst of those storms, the blasting started up again, louder than before. These blasts, often hidden by the thunder, made the network of caves vibrate and shook loose pieces of limestone from overhead. Then the Great Blasts tore up one of the mother springs. Another brought the limestone ceiling and tons of water and creek mud and jagged tree roots crashing down on them. The elder, the healer, Trapper, and the older breeder were killed. So was the young boy that they had taken with his sister when Tommy found them hiding out in an abandoned migrant-worker shack. They were runaways. And they had been the special pets of the colony of wetlanders.

Now there was just three of them. Lon and Tommy. And the sister, the dummy breeder, who did nothing but sleep and rock forward and back in her world of silence. There were no more treasures. No totems or dream sticks. They had stocked their new cave with what little they had salvaged when they dug with their bare hands into the debris of the old cave. Afterward, they had ventured farther out than usual from the wetlands, pilfering whatever they could find from the construction site, a few outlying farmhouses, the campgrounds by the larger lake a full day's hike to the east, and a couple of bedraggled trailer parks south where the creek still flowed strong.

But now they had something to add to their cache of acquisitions. Shovels. New ones. Once they recuperated from their harrowing escape from the men with the lights, they could go back to the old cave site and dig. Now they hurt too much. Last night, they'd been too frightened to remember all the newer pathways that they'd had to make since the Great Blasts. Instead, when the men with lights had come after them, they panicked and simply made a run for it. They had crashed into the underbrush and fought their way through the snarl of briars, buttonwood bushes, palmettos, creeper, and holly clumped between the taller trees. Only after they awoke, bruised and cut and aching, had they crept out into the daylight and started to wipe away the coagulated lumps coating their wounds.

Tommy was the worse off of the two. He'd led the

escape, swinging his shovels before him as he leaped for
the safety of the dark woods with Lon lumbering along
at his heels. Sharp thorns and vines full of nettles had
shredded their shirtsleeves and sliced into the skin beneath. Low limbs had thundered against their head and
shoulders like a hundred angry fists, waiting in ambush
then pummeling away at them. Roots caught their legs
and ankles and sent them hurtling onto the ground or
into the brush. Then there was the bog, swallowing and
sucking their boots with each step. Finally they'd untied
the sodden boots and let the bog have them. Their bare
feet ended up scraped and gouged and filthy.

Despite the pain, it had been exciting.

"Got 'im. Got 'im good." Tommy snickered, grimacing and lolling forward and back. While he bathed,
he'd been chewing mouthfuls of the bog plant that the
healer used to give them to dull their senses when they
were injured, then he'd spat the pulp onto his cuts. Between chaws, he'd take a long swig of "swamp likker,"
a brew he and Lon had concocted after the blasts, ap-
proximating the potent drink that the elder had been so
adept at distilling. "Jes' whomped 'im," Tommy said,
snorting deep in his throat.

Lon cleaned his cuts in silence, pausing from time to
time to look at Tommy uneasily. He'd awakened first and
simmered tobacco wood and rippleseed roots like the
healer had done over the years, only he couldn't wait for
it to seep and cool. He brought it with them to the bathing place. Once his scrapes were washed, he doused them
in the lukewarm potion. Then he took the cooked mush
from the bottom of the pan and used it for a poultice.
But Tommy preferred to numb his pain inside as well as
out, and that likker was making him mean.

"Coulda killed that fucker. Coulda take 'iz head off.

Wham. Just take it off." Tommy was drooling now, swinging the jug of likker backhand like an ax over his reflection in the stream. "Coulda killed that fucker." Then he made a series of short, raspy snorts like he made when he'd said or done something to amuse himself.

Lon didn't respond. He knew it wouldn't help.

Tommy drank some more. Then he said all of it over again. Only angrier. "Coulda killed that fucker." Finally he could hardly get the words out. And his frog eyes turned glassy. He started rubbing his crotch like he did when he was feeling no pain and wanted someone to mount. Then he downed the last mouthful of likker and struggled to his feet. Half walking, half crawling, he made his way back inside the cave. Lon went part of the way with him, but he didn't go inside. Instead, he leaned against the cool wall of the opening and covered his ears, trying not to listen to Tommy grunting as he humped away on the breeder woman inside. When there were no more sounds, Lon went in and found a cool place to lie down and tried to sleep.

Wednesday morning as the team of sandsculptors convened for breakfast, Jack Button and several camera crews were waiting on the deck of the courtyard behind the Felucca Café. Among the assortment of reporters, technicians, and lighting and makeup personnel, Kitty vaguely recognized one female interviewer from cable news.

"Some of these folks are doing background for an indepth report statewide, and some are working on profiles that may be packaged for the networks," Button explained as he greeted each of the arrivals. "Just give these folks your cooperation while you enjoy your breakfast, and we'll let you get on with your work as soon as possible. They'll be out filming you on the mound later in the day.''

"Are we going to be on television?" Zach asked eagerly as he followed Kitty though the flower-bedecked tables toward the one Button had indicated for them.

"I sure hope not," Kitty answered. "I've got to whip out a prince and an old witch today and get on with some blocking. Besides, who wants to be charming at seven in the morning?''

"I do," Zach answered, so distracted watching the interview with Craig Stuart and Kevin that he bumped into Paul Feneau's chair.

"Careful there, Hollywood," Paul Feneau kidded him. "You'll get your turn."

"Do you think they'll talk to us like they're doing to them?" Zach grasped Kitty's arm and kept up with her.

"Hopefully not until I finish my juice and a cup of decaf.''

"Come on, Mom. I mean it. Will they be talking just to us?''

"Maybe they'll interview me," Kitty conceded, finally easing into a wide-armed wicker chair with very large cushions that felt heavenly. "I'm not trying to play the hotshot, but I wouldn't get your hopes up that you'll be on camera. I think they'll be more apt to stick just to the team members. They were doing a lot of shooting of Rapunzel's Tower yesterday while the scaffolding was being lifted off. Then I heard Stuart and Kevin took some of them up there for a closer look later in the evening, after we all quit for the day. So they may want to talk to me about the tower.''

"But you don't think they'll want to talk to me." Zach guessed precisely where her conversation was heading. His mouth set in a firm, downward turn.

"I'm only speculating," Kitty replied. "Depends on what kind of a story they're doing. I'd rather they stick to the work itself. I don't particularly like the idea of having my family and my personal life brought into this."

"Why not?" Zach stiffened, eyeing her with an unusual stormy darkness in his sea blue eyes.

"Because I like my privacy," Kitty said simply. "I like *our* privacy." Then she nodded to the waiter who was passing from table to table with a steaming pot of decaffeinated coffee. "Thanks, I needed this." She sighed in relief as he filled her cup. "We would like a couple of large orange juices, too," she added. "Or are we still doing breakfast buffet style?" With all the equipment that had been brought out on the deck, the service tables were nowhere in sight.

"Either way," the young fellow answered. "You can give me your order, or you can slip around these tables and go through the other door. Frankly I think you'd be more pleased choosing from the buffet. There are a lot of really fine pastries this morning. And the fruit selection is great."

"I'm going inside," Zach blurted out, still disgruntled over the interview discussion.

"I think we both will," Kitty studied Zach's expression. "Maybe you would like to go ahead and start while I drink my coffee."

"So you can be on television while I'm gone?" Zach countered accusingly. His lips were squeezed into a convincing pout.

"No. So we can avoid a battle," Kitty said calmly. "I'm not awake enough for a head-on confrontation this morning. And we both would be wise to save our energy for the more productive things we've got to do today."

"Being on TV is productive," Zach argued.

"Perhaps. But there's no sense getting worked up over something that may not happen at all. Until we know what they want, there no reason to get upset. Wind down. How about going in there and pick out what you want for breakfast?"

"You won't let them do it without me, will you? If they want to talk to you while I'm gone, will you make them wait?"

"I'll ask them to hold off," Kitty promised. "But that still doesn't mean you're going to be part of any interview. It means you can watch."

"But what if they ask me something," Zach protested, still unwilling to leave quite yet.

"We'll handle that if and when it arises. Not now." Kitty tapped her finger on the tabletop for emphasis. "Now is a good time for you to smile politely and head for the buffet."

For a few seconds Zach sat there without moving, studying her expression, well aware that she was annoyed. "All right." He stood up. "But don't let them do anything without me."

Kitty drew in a long, steadying breath.

"All right, I'm going." Zach flashed a deliberately ingratiating smile and strode away, glancing back only once to see if she was watching his grand exit. Without comment but with astute timing, the waiter came by and refilled her cup.

"Good morning. Are we having fun yet?" Vince asked guardedly as he hesitated by the unclaimed chair next to her. "And is it safe to sit down?"

Kitty gave him a slow, barely amused look. "Sit. Just don't talk."

"You and Zach having a little domestic tension?" Vince teased.

"He wants to be on television."

"So?"

"I don't like the idea."

"Why not?"

"I'd rather not draw attention to him."

"Why not?"

Kitty leveled her gaze at Vince. "Because we don't need it. He's a little different, and he's a little behind in school. I don't want that brought out in any way that affects him. He's been doing very well this year. And he's having a great time here. I just don't want any reporter picking him out for some human-interest angle. You should hear Paul Feneau talk about how they martyred him for his leukemia. They even mentioned how the chemotherapy affected his pubic hairs. I don't want Zach exploited."

"I see."

"I know. I'm overprotective," Kitty muttered. "But he's so vulnerable. . . ."

"You've got no argument from me," Vince insisted. "I gather Zach wasn't convinced."

"I couldn't quite put it to him that way. What could I say? You're a little slow, son, and I don't want anyone getting media mileage out that? I doubt he'd appreciated hearing that from me."

"So what did you tell him?"

"I told him I like my privacy. And that applies to my family as well."

"Sounds reasonable."

"To us. But not to him."

"We'll see. His disposition may improve with some food. Same with yours. You look a little tired." Vince reached over and rubbed her shoulder, diplomatically changing the subject. "I gather you spent a large part of

the wee hours creatively stewing,'' he guessed. Their
poolside brainstorming session the previous night with
Sandy Huff, Kevin, Stuart, and Paul Feneau had been an
open affair. Anyone who had suggestions about possible
fairy tales was invited to come along and speak up. But
when Jack Button joined them, the event became unex-
pectedly entertaining. Button very rapidly became the
unofficial narrator, recounting from memory one tale after another in a flamboyant, melodramatic style. Occasionally he would slip into a magic routine to the delight
of Zach and the other children, who ultimately abandoned the pool for the impromptu story hour.

A consummate teller of tales, Button had the audience
of sculptors, guests, and children circled around him, all
gazing raptly at him as he gave his rendition of ''The
Master Thief'' who would not steal unless the task involved incredible danger, cunning, and dexterity. Pretending to be the thief disguised as an old woman, Button
passed by the kids in front-row seats, squirting imaginary wine laced with an imaginary sleeping potion into
the mouths of imaginary guards who then fell asleep
while he stole the imaginary horse they were protecting.
But to the children watching his halting step and hearing
his old crone voice, it all seemed real.

When Craig Stuart saw that Button had brought along
the frizzy-haired fellow with the video camera and the
guy was off to one side filming, he'd nudged Vince.
''Look at that. Button is one shrewd dude. Not only does
he come off like Mother Goose, but look at the footage
he's getting.''

''Talk about a pitch man . . .'' Kevin had observed,
smiling broadly as he studied the mesmerized faces of
the kids. ''The guy has the gift of gab, all right.''

"And one hell of a memory," Vince chimed in. "I'd bet he's been staying up nights cribbing out of Grimms'."

"He may have," Stuart said, nodding. "He sure came up with a lot of good suggestions when we started planning this thing."

"I have to hand it to him, he's a real showman." Kevin beamed, listening intently to the tale in progress. The two others sat smiling politely as Button recounted the exploits of a devoted servant called "Faithful John."

Later, when the audience dispersed and team members reconvened, the schematic of the triple mound was spread out on the table. The newer, untitled molds, already inked in, were tagged, with the Master Thief and Faithful John among them. "Thumbelina" gave Myron Hansen and his art students an entire expanse to fill with one tiny person and multitudes of huge, fantastic flowers. Sandy Huff's suggestion of "The Twelve Dancing Princesses" was another unanimous choice. And there was a dragon. Sandy had found a tale called "The Four Skillful Brothers," which not only had a flying dragon but a great sailing ship.

"Big and nonhuman," Sandy had whispered to Kitty, pleased that she had found a tale that spread out the labor. Kevin and Paul Feneau inherited that set of figures. But Vince was right on target. When Kitty finally got to bed and closed her eyes, she'd slept fitfully, surrounded by a host of shapeless images, all begging for faces full of character, each one unique. And when she awoke that morning, she could still feel them tugging at her, begging to exist.

"I'll be in a better mood when some of the ideas in my head are out there in the sand," Kitty promised. She nodded gratefully when the waiter bringing coffee for Vince also brought some more decaf. "I just hope this interview business doesn't take too long. I was looking forward to a pleasant, quiet breakfast with my son, then tripping off to the mound while it's still cool.''

"Would you prefer including or excluding me in that pleasant breakfast?'' Vince hesitated.

"You definitely are included. Besides, we may need a referee.'' Kitty really smiled for the first time that morning. "Plus I need moral support. The impeccably coiffed and groomed folk with the cute little mikes get me edgy.''

"Just pretend they're all dressed in something totally ludicrous,'' Vince suggested. "How do I put this tastefully.'' He stalled, pausing for effect. "Let me just pass on to you this tidbit of art history. Salvador Dali imagined chapeaus of excrement on the head of anyone who intimidated him,'' he said quietly. "I'd say that would be a pretty effective equalizer. Or if that's too crude, how about imaging them naked, maybe with argyle socks and a bow tie or knee-highs and pearls?''

"I could handle that.'' Kitty chuckled, glancing at the blond woman across the room.

"You'd better start,'' Vince cautioned her, following her line of vision. "It looks like that impeccably groomed one is speaking with Button about you.'' The blond was now following Button's directions and was on her way toward them, a few technicians in her wake.

"Unfortunate timing. Here comes Zach,'' Kitty observed warily, spotting the curly-haired figure diligently balancing a tray and a glass of juice as he edged between the chairs. "I hope he doesn't take any of this too seriously.''

"Good morning. We'd like to talk with you a few minutes,'' the reporter introduced herself. "I'm Sylvia Kent, Miss Westberg.''

"Just Kitty is fine."

"Okay, Kitty. While the fellows set up their cameras and clip a mike on you, I'll just give you a general idea of the areas we'll be covering." She pulled over a chair and explained the procedure. "Jerry will give us a signal when we're ready to start taping. I'm especially interested in finding out how you became so involved with sandsculpting. I'll ask you about any art experience you have had. And since you're the only woman on the core crew, I'm very interested with how you're handling the strenuous routine." She clearly wasn't interested in rehearsing the answers, only in outlining areas of discussion. "We'll wind up with the tower you finished yesterday and what it's like working that high up and on scaffolding. And you're a single parent, is that right?" She looked over notes, glanced up, and smiled at Zach as he eased in at the table, trying to appear nonchalant.

"Yes. This is Zach." Kitty introduced him, while the technician clipped a tiny microphone to her shirt collar.

"Zach." Sylvia Kent reached out her hand. "Nice to meet you, Zach.'

"Nice to meet you." Zach shook her hand.

"And this is Vince Ammons," Kitty added.

"Yes, another of the team members," Sylvia recalled. "You're the architect. As long as you're already here with us, I'd like to ask you a few things, too. I'll be speaking in greater depth with you later. I want to do some close-ups on the castle and the town you're working on." Vince inched his chair closer to Kitty. "Wire him, too," Sylvia requested. She jotted something in her notes then turned her attention back to Zach.

"I was wondering if you are interested in sandsculpting like your mom is?" Sylvia asked.

"I like it, but I'm not real good at it," Zach answered,

sitting a bit stiff and trying to see if the cameras were filming him. They hadn't given him a microphone, so he wasn't sure in which direction he should be speaking.

"What kind of things do you like to make?" Sylvia asked, smiling fleetingly while her hazel eyes checked the status of the technician's progress in the background.

Zach looked about nervously, then swallowed and shrugged. "Is any of this stuff working right now?" he asked in a hushed voice. Behind Sylvia and Kitty, a fellow with a headset was signaling for her to keep talking so he could check the sound.

"Oh, no . . . we're just having an off-the-record chat," Sylvia told him reassuringly. "I wouldn't put you on the spot like that without warning."

"Oh," Zach responded, clearly disappointed.

"But if you'd like an on-camera conversation, it could be arranged," she added amiably. "You could give us a kid's-eye view and tell us what it's like to be a part of this spectacle."

"What's a spectacle?" Zach narrowed one eye and looked at Kitty uncertainly.

"A big show," Kitty explained. "A huge event like this is."

"I'm part of one, aren't I?" Zach frowned, unclear about what he should say.

"You're part of everything here," Kitty said, trying to get off the subject gracefully. "But unless you start in on that breakfast, you'll be late to class."

"You've got to leave here and go to school?" Sylvia questioned him.

"We have a tutor here. We have to do schoolwork part of the day," Zach said dully, poking at his melon balls and strawberries.

"And what else do you get to do?" Sylvia seemed genuinely interested.

"We swim and take out the boats and watch movies. We play videogames. We learned about the statues and stuff around the hotel. We hike on the Nature Trail." Zach recited the list, uncomfortable that none of it sounded very important.

"Will you eventually get to help on the sandsculptures?" Sylvia asked.

"There's a minimum age of sixteen," Vince interrupted. "Because of the height of the structure and the equipment involved, no younger kids will be allowed on the mound."

"That's a shame," Sylvia replied, somewhat distracted. Behind Zach, the sound man indicated they were ready. Efficiently, Sylvia Kent introduced Kitty and Vince and swung right into the interview. "We have here two of the remarkable talents whose work is already visible on the sandstructure. Kitty Westberg . . ."

While interviewing with Kitty and Vince proceeded, Zach, out of camera range, watched sulkily and occasionally poked food into his mouth. They were filming over his shoulder, right past him.

"If you're finished here, I have another fellow who'd like to talk with you." Button stepped near enough to get Kitty's attention. "He's already set up over here." Kitty nodded and eased past Vince to an area where another crew had stationed their equipment. "This is Kitty Westberg, the only woman among the master sculptors." The reporter introduced her to his would-be audience. "Tell me, how long have you been at this . . . ?" Kitty smiled a bit stiffly, but answered with as much enthusiasm as she could muster.

When she finished with that one, she headed back to

the table. "I've had it. I want to get to work. I don't have time for chitchat," she grumbled.

"See what a little camera time does for you," Vince confided in Zach playfully. "Makes you grumpy."

"It makes my toes curl," Kitty replied, grimacing. "Look how nice and overcast it is this morning. Imagine how cool and pretty it is up there on the mound. That's where I'd like to be."

"So we'll grab you some food on the way through and get out there," Vince replied. "You've done your bit for the news folk. Let's get moving."

"And how about you?" Kitty aimed the question at Zach. "Can you head over to the classroom now. You've got about five minutes to make it."

"I'd rather go with you guys."

"That's not the agreement," Kitty reminded him. "Look, Friday is the start of spring break. Then you have no school at all for a few days. Just picnics and movies and field trips. You have two days to endure till then. Come on, give me a hug and take off. I'll meet you back here for lunch. How about it?"

Zach didn't budge.

"I'll walk part of the way with you while your mom gets her food," Vince suggested. "Come on. Somewhere there's a felucca waiting for you. Or Chris, or Corey, or Melissa. How about if I'll tell you about some Egyptian stuff while we go. How about the guy with the dog's head. The one in the men's john . . ." Zach looked up, shrugged, then got up and followed Vince.

Kitty mouthed a silent "thank you." Then she pointed to the far door where she would meet him.

"The guy's name was Anubis." Vince nodded and kept on talking. "He invented the funeral rites, all that neat embalming stuff." Zach was staying right in step with him, but he was watching the cameras all the while.

Kitty went off in the opposite direction.

"What happened? Did you make it there and back already?" she asked when she returned to found him waiting. Vince gave her a sheepish look. "Well?"

"Well, that guy, the second reporter you talked to, he intercepted us. He asked if he could interview Zach. I told him he'd have to wait for you. They're over there." He tilted his head to a couple of wicker chairs overlooking the gardens. The reporter was in one. Zach, already wired for sound, was in the other.

"Oh boy," Kitty groaned. She squared her shoulders and move in. "Hi again. I'm afraid you'll have to pass on this one," she told the reporter and crew point-blank as she stepped between them. "Zach is already late for his class, and I'd feel better if he was checked in with his tutor before I left to work on the mound."

"Could I check him in for you after we do a short interview?" the reporter asked.

"I'd rather take him over there myself," Kitty replied, still trying to be tactful.

"Well, could we set this up for some other time? I'll be here off and on all week."

Kitty looked at Zach and shook her head. "I really don't think so. I'd prefer to keep my private life just that, private."

"Sure, I can understand that," the fellow admitted. "Whatever you say. Sorry, buddy," the guy apologized, bending closer to disconnect the mini-microphone from Zach's shirt. Without a word, Zach burst past Kitty and cut across the deck of the café, straight for the exit.

"Whoa, Zach. Hold up." Vince loped across diagonally and headed him off. "Easy now."

"She won't let me do anything!' Zach tried to yank away from Vince's grasp. ''I was all ready to be on television, and she butts in.''

"Zach, let's have a little talk." Kitty caught up to them. "Please hold this for me." She handed her plate to Vince as she grabbed Zach with the other hand. "Let's go." She marched him right through the café exit into the hallway. "First of all, you're late for class. And second, you know I don't like the idea of dragging you into all this publicity."

"Why not?"

"Because I don't want anyone making a big deal out of our private affairs. You and I have worked through a lot in the past couple of years. Newspeople ask a lot of questions because they need a hook for a story, something a little different. They're looking for easy labels. You heard them. I'm 'the only woman' or I'm 'divorced' or a 'single parent.' They'll be looking for labels for you, too. And I'm not sure I want anyone labeling you on television or anywhere else.'' She rested her hands on his shoulders and bent down, meeting his angry stare. "I love you. And I'm concerned about you."

"You're afraid I'll say something stupid. You think I'll embarrass you."

"That's not it," Kitty argued. "I'm concerned that they'll say something that may make you uncomfortable."

"Like what. Like saying I'm retarded?" His blue eyes flashed and drilled into hers.

"Perhaps." Kitty didn't waver. "That's an old label. An easy label. We both know it doesn't fit anymore. I don't think it ever really did. But it might come up. And if it did, people who treat you just fine now and people who have yet to meet you may treat you differently. And neither one of us would like that. You're a neat kid. You don't need to be on television to prove that.''

He yielded grudgingly. "I suppose not. But I'd like it. It would be fun.''

"Maybe something will work out later. For now, just do me a favor. Please don't get into any conversations with reporters, not without me being there.''

"I'll try.'' Zach chewed on his lower lip and stared at the floor.

"Come on. Let's get you to class. If you still feel bad, we'll talk it over tonight.''

"Sure. But they won't be here tonight.''

"There'll be reporters here from now on. And each of them will be looking for a special story. I don't want either of us to be singled out.''

"I understand. I'm sorry.'' Zach glanced up at her. "Are you mad at me?''

"No. I'm a bit angry at the guy who cornered you. And I'm not too thrilled that Vince let him do it. But I'm not mad at you.'' She tugged him against her and gave him a big hug. "I love you. And I know it sounded pretty good at first. Now. Go to class. And I'll still check in with you before lunch and see if we can get together.''

"Is Vince going to be mad at me?''

"No. He'll be fine.''

"Tell him I'm sorry about acting up in there.''

"I'll tell him. But he understands. He loves you.''

"Yeah, well, tell him I'm sorry anyway.''

"Class. Go. See you later.'' Kitty pointed him down the hallway toward the temporary classroom. Then she stood watching him meander along, trying not to look impatient if he glanced back. Which he did. Twice. Then he knocked on the door, Corey came out to greet him, and both of them waved in her direction. "Patience . . .

patience . . ." Kitty muttered as she waited for the door to close, then turned and walked away.

"Robbie. Robbie James, answer me. Robbie . . ."
Slightly balding, and with pale spindly legs sticking down from the wide cuffs of his new Bermuda shorts, the fellow wearing a Dunesfest souvenir visor wove his way through the scattered flow of onlookers. "Robbie . . ." he called louder, oblivious to the curious looks he was drawing.

"Could you help me find my son?" He approached the teal-and-tan-clad young woman patrolling the Port-o-let area. "He came over here a while ago to go to the bathroom and he hasn't come back."

"Sure, we'll find him," the woman answered. "Give me his name and a description and I'll send word out to the others."

"Robert Earl James, Jr. Robbie, for short. He's nine. Blond straight hair, trimmed short at the sides, and combed back on top." The man's eyes continually scanned the passing flow of spectators as they spoke. Every time a door to one of the portables opened, he looked at the individual exiting. "Four-foot-one. He was wearing red and blue OP shorts and a red T-shirt with 'Riverside Little League' on it." He licked his dry lips nervously.

"That should make it real easy," the guard said confidently, cupping her hand over her earphone while she called in the description to communications center. "They're notifying the other security people. Let's start back this way," she suggested, accompanying the man on another circuit of the bathroom facilities.

"No luck so far." The reports came in over the next half hour from each of the main quadrants around the mound. Nothing in the parking area. Even the gate guard and the internal security at the Grand Nile Hotel had been alerted. No one recalled seeing a child matching the description of Robbie James.

"Let's get together at the communications tent," Bo Shepherd suggested. This was their first extended search since Dunesfest began, and he wanted it completed rapidly. Already the sun was sinking low in the sky. The after-dinner browsers and the night crowd was increasing as folks who'd been working all day drove to the area to stroll around, eat ice cream, and watch the lights go on. Before it actually got dark, he wanted Robbie James, Jr. found.

"We're going to take the bullhorn and go around in the cart making spot announcements," Bo told the day shift. "There are some replacement security and traffic folks coming in, but I don't want any of you leaving in the midst of this. Just get out there, be conspicuous, look confident, and enlist the cooperation of everyone you can. They may remember something that will help. Talk to them." He looked up at the darkening sky. "We're fighting time here. We're going to get everyone we can helping on this. Someone had to have seen him. I'll have traffic check every kid and every car trunk leaving the grounds." He narrowed his eyes and looked around the group. "Don't get all uptight. This may be nothing more than a kid off prowling around on some adventure. Look everywhere a kid could explore. He may have crawled in some nook or cranny and fallen asleep. It happens. Take flashlights, just in case. And call immediately if you get any information."

The crew dispersed while Bo grabbed the bullhorn.

"Good evening, folks. Welcome to Dunesfest. We have a little problem we would like your help with. We have a missing child. . . ." Bo Shepherd repeated the message at intervals around the mound then circled farther out with the speaker, announcing it all over again.

By the time the lights on the mound were turned on, Button had arrived and agreed to call in the Crystal Springs K-9 patrol. Robert James, Sr., now pale, frantic, and hollow-eyed, supplied them with a pair of tennis shoes left behind by the boy. The K-9 officer began circling the bathroom area letting the dog lead the way. Then because the grounds inside the fringe of trees had been tracked across by so many people already, the officer moved the dog father out, hoping to determine whether Robbie left the area on foot. In the perimeter of low shrubs well beyond the Port-o-lets, the dog finally picked up the trail of Robbie James.

"He must have bypassed the johns and come out here to take a leak," the officer guessed. He shone his wide-beamed flashlight on the ground. There were visible bare footprints in the soft soil leading back to a clump of palmetto shrubs that would have screened the boy and given him some privacy. But the dog was straining at the lead, heading deeper into the snarl of branches and vines beyond. He lunged ahead, with the officer and Bo Shepherd after him, then circled excitedly inside a small, cleared out area, almost like a burrow, where the kid had apparently wandered. Then the dog sniffed around, yanking at the leash, eager to work its way into the woods beyond that.

"Okay, keep back," the officer told the few others who had come this far with him and Bo Shepherd. "It looks like this has been some kind of hideout. This has been here awhile. I don't think we should disturb anything until we get a lab team out here."

"Look at the bushes." Shepherd pointed to the broken

branches and trampled leaves where something had pushed its way deeper into the woods. There were large recognizable footprints all over the clearing, but only partials. A few farther out that Shepherd spotted with his light were clearer and deep.

"From the looks of these prints, I'd say it was a pretty big guy," the cop noted. "Probably someone was hiding back here and grabbed the kid. From the way the dog's acting, I'd bet that someone picked him up and carried him out of here." The animal was sniffing the air now, unable to find the boy's footprints on the ground among the larger ones.

"The dog can follow that guy's track, can't it?" Bo Shepherd asked.

"Sure can." The cop strafed the woods with his light. "There's bound to be snakes out there. I think I'll grab my boots and leather jacket before I head in. Incidentally, the highway patrol has a helicopter they could send over. They might use their lights and spot something from the air."

"Worth a try," Bo Shepherd agreed. "Give me a few minutes to get up a couple of search parties." He started back immediately, herding the others along ahead of him and firing off directions. "We're going on after him as soon as we're ready. Call communications. I want lights, some machetes, and a couple of men with shotguns. I'll get my stuff from the truck. Meet you back here." He went to the tent to find Button and the senior Robert James.

"No helicopter." Jack Button rubbed his beard then announced his decision. "I don't want all that commotion around the resort at night. We've got all kinds of media folk staying here. I don't want them playing this up. Let's just stick to what we know. The boy wandered off into the woods," he stated succinctly, looking a bit strained. He'd already stood by when Robert Sr. called his wife farther south in Port Richey and told her that their father-and-son evening out had turned sour. Despite Button's suggestion that she just stay put until the security staff finished their search, she was having a neighbor driver her up to the Dunes. Button had arranged for her to check in at the gate so she could be taken to the hotel security office instead of coming out to the site. He didn't want a hysterical woman near the crowd. Now he wanted the rest of the search conducted inconspicuously.

"Saying he went off into the brush justifies a search effort, but not a helicopter assault," Button declared, his brown eyes hard and expressionless. "Let's keep it simple. I don't think we should make any other information public until any speculations are confirmed. We don't need to go scaring folks."

"Suit yourself," Bo said grimly. "I don't care how you handle it. I'm going after the kid. But I think we'll have to do something about that woods access. Robbie James wasn't doing anything any other kid wouldn't do. He was just poking around in the goonies. It could happen again."

"Tomorrow we're putting in a playground and some wading pools with sprinklers on the north end to keep the little kids occupied. I'll have it fenced and put a few Port-o-lets inside the area so they won't have to come down here at all."

"They'll still wander. . . ." Bo persisted.

"Then I'll have a six-foot chain-link put up around the whole place. I'll have it patrolled. Whatever it takes," Button shot back. "Let's just handle this quietly tonight," he insisted.

Bo shrugged again, tugged on his boots, and went out to meet the others.

"Whoever he is, he's driving the dog nuts," the officer leading the patrol muttered as the dog backtracked and looped around a clump of trees they'd already been around before. He's been everywhere. A lot of these look like real old tracks."

Bo Shepherd shook his head, thoroughly befuddled. For hours they'd done nothing but fight the mosquitoes, crawl though the underbrush, and sweat. There were pockets where the air didn't stir at all. "Let's just fan out, wide as we can get and still stay in sight of each other, then we'll head toward the big creek. There's one about ten-foot across. It's back a ways." Bo remembered it from several aerial maps of the terrain. In between there were smaller creeks and breaks in the vegetation where the terrain changed from flatlands to sloughs to sloping hammocks then to bog, but the wide creek was a clear boundary beyond which he didn't plan to venture. "Call the other squad and have them do the same thing. If nothing shows up, then we'll all link up at the creek, swing west, and get the hell out of this jungle. We'll let the cops come in tomorrow with a whole pack of dogs and see what they can do." It was already midnight, so he radioed back to Button at communications to tell him what was going on. One of the security officers answered. Button had set the Jameses up in a room in the hotel, and he'd gone back to his townhouse, leaving one of his assistants to do the hand-holding while he got a few hours sleep.

"We'll be there when we get there," Bo said grimly. "But it doesn't look promising. We haven't seen any sign of the kid."

They were on their way back from the big creek when

they found him propped against the stump of a tree. He'd been gagged and tied with his own T-shirt, which had been ripped into strips to make the bindings. Robbie James, Jr., was half-naked and covered in mud, but alive.

"Take it easy, son." Bo Shepherd knelt down and hugged the slim child while the officer untied him. Ungagged, the kid let out a high, hiccuping wail.

"I want my mom. . . ." Robbie shrieked, trembling and clutching Bo's neck desperately. "I want my dad. . . ." Then he broke off into a series of racking sobs. "Don't let him get me. . . ."

Bo lifted the lad and wrapped him in a shirt one of the searchers offered him. He'd been left with nothing other than the shredded bits of shirt and a pair of ripped jockey shorts.

"I'm going to mark off this area," the officer told the others. "Try not to disturb anything. We'll come back here later." Now, exhausted and relieved, he just wanted to get the kid back to civilization.

"We're bringing him in. He's scuffed up pretty bad, and he's real scared. But he's safe," Bo radioed in the news.

Haggard and anxious, Robbie James, Sr., and his wife were waiting with Jack Button and two security officers in the staff communications tent by the mound when the search party came out of the underwoods. The lights illuminating the mound were still on, but the area around it, closed to the public since ten o'clock, was vacated except for the few security workers who had been left on guard and Button and the Jameses, who'd come out to meet the search party as soon as the message was forwarded to them.

The moment the parents saw the boy's pale hair they

ran to him. While they wept and held the sobbing child, Bo Shepherd and the officer signaled Button aside.

"Looks like we have a real problem out there." The officer spoke quietly, jerking his thumb toward the dark woods behind them. "May have been a onetime hit-and-run thing with some transient or a whacko on the loose. Or it may be some freak who's been camped out there for a while. But whoever he is, he's dangerous. The kid wasn't just abducted. He's been sexually molested."

White-faced, Button listened.

"The boy is really freaked out over this." Bo Shepherd shook his head wearily as he spoke. "He said some dirty man with big hard hands jumped out of the bushes and grabbed him. Tied him up and gagged him. Part of the time he was blindfolded, but it slipped down. He said the guy ran all over the place with him, sticking him up in trees and shoving him in rotted stumps, then leaving him there, going off, and coming back again. He calls the guy a monster because he was so ugly and dirty. He had lots of hair and a beard. Said what he could see of his face was painted with something dark. He's so strung out, it's hard to tell how much of it is real."

"Apparently the kid saw our lights far off a couple of times," the officer reported, "but I guess the guy would stash him somewhere then take off in another direction, making prints leading the dog away from there. He said the guy acted afraid of the lights."

"We're going to have to bring in more dogs tomorrow, when it's light enough to see," Bo Shepherd declared. "If he's still in the area, we have to get this guy."

Button looked at his watch. It was 4:00 A.M. and the sky was still dark, but dawn was only hours away. "Yes. He must be caught," Button said stiffly. "I'll personally put up a reward for any information leading to his apprehension. I'm sure the Dunes will do the same. In the morning, I'll call in the press and issue a news release. I'm sure they can be enlisted to handle this tragedy with a fair amount of restraint." He pursed his lips thoughtfully. "I'll take care of it. We do want an all-out effort to track this transient."

"I only said he *might* be a transient," the officer interrupted.

"He must be," Button countered stonily. "He certainly doesn't belong around here. That should be obvious."

"He probably heard about the castle and came snooping around," the other security guard commented.

"Then we'll make sure he doesn't come back," Button responded. "I'll have that fence up by tomorrow at nightfall, and you put on extra security," he told Bo. "Call in whatever law-enforcement agencies we need to track him," he told the officer. "The national guard, if necessary. We're going to make this fellow sorry he ever set foot on the Dunes property. Nothing is going to spoil this event. Nothing and no one." Button stuffed his hands in his pockets and strode off.

Chapter 4

TOMMY SQUATTED CHIN-DEEP IN THE COOL MARSH WA-
ter, surrounded by the whispering expanse of maidencane grass and rushes, listening. He could hear nothing
except the flat, dull grunt of the bulls and the higher
intermittent trilling of the cricket frogs. If the men with
lights followed the serpentine meandering of the big
creek and came this way after him, he figured they'd give
up when they saw how the waterway opened out into the
marsh. The freshwater marsh spread for acres, its perimeter guarded by spikes of tall marshgrass and its dark
interior surface carpeted with floating lilies and broad-
leafed spatterdocks. Without a flatboat, no civilized man
would venture out into the area, especially at night. This
was the haunt of snakes, water rats, and gators, and it
was the one place Tommy knew he'd be safe.

He crouched there for hours, chewing on the sweet

grass, straining to hear any sound that might indicate they had come this way. On the opposite shore, a series of three-level houses stood unlighted and silent, their angular roof lines standing out like jagged tree trunks against the night sky. With the gray dawn came the first waterfowl. Tommy watched them circle, drift in, and start their foraging. Then he knew the men were long gone.

Cold and dripping, he waded and half swam back along a waterway to the creek, following it until he found a place where the low limbs reached down close enough to grab and were strong enough to support his weight. Then, hand over hand, he climbed out, and swung from tree to tree, until he was far enough back to risk touching ground again.

Even then, he took a roundabout route back to the cave. He backtracked a few times, partly to confuse anyone trying to pick up a trail, but mostly to stall before he went home to face Lon. Tommy had been gone since afternoon the day before. And he'd been drunk when he left. Then he stayed away all night. Sometimes they did that. Sometimes they took off on their own for days. But this time he'd left with work undone. They had gotten the shovels. And that meant they could start digging through the rubble of the great cave. They could find whatever remained of the others and give them a proper burial. Lon would have expected him to help. He would want to know what he'd been doing instead. Tommy had no intention of telling him the truth.

Tommy didn't dare say that he'd gone back where they stole the shovels. Lon wouldn't understand why he'd gone off and holed up in the woods again and watched the people who had come to see the mountain of sand. Not since they had the shovels they needed and it was heavy upon them to honor their dead.

He wouldn't understand that Tommy had to be there. This had been their wetland, long before the men in flying machines and trucks came. And it was still his land to roam. He wasn't afraid of them. They couldn't chase him off. His chest had thudded with excitement when he saw how many more there were than before. Herds of people. All clean and white and beautiful. And so many children. Then Tommy had noticed that one boy child moving apart from the others, coming in his direction. It was a silky, pretty thing with hair of pale gold that glistened in the afternoon sun. He was so smooth and soft looking that Tommy couldn't tear his eyes from him. And the boy kept coming right out there toward him, as if he could sense Tommy's hunger.

It had been a long time since Tommy had a sweet love pet to fondle and kiss and caress. Their last one, the breeder's brother, had died in the Great Blast, and since then, there had been no love pet at all. Since all the plowing and building started and the men with the trucks kept coming and going, he and Lon had been too cautious to go off in search of another boy child. There had just been the breeder, sullen and silent and dull-eyed. She couldn't even feed or clean herself anymore. But mounting her was no better than mounting a stump in the swamp. If Tommy get real loose with the likker and if he hurried, he could make do with her, but it left him hung over and uneasy and foul-tempered.

And Lon wasn't like the other wetlanders had been. Over the years, the men in the clan, the Trapper and the healer and the elder and Tommy and others before them, would turn to each other when the need was there. There were times when some other want existed that one of the breeders or whatever boy they had could not satisfy. Then they accommodated their kind. These male-to-male encounters were a different kind of contact altogether. Stronger. Darker. Primal. One that came upon them from time to time and seemed to sustain a certain bond among them. The elder taught that this contact had always been part of their brotherhood. It took away the edginess that crept into the cave with them after a while and sometimes erupted into fistfights or shoving contests.

Sometimes when they knew it was time, they would sit and smoke the dried leaves of the stinkweed and drink the elder's likker brew. Then they would smile and laugh and paw each other, roughhousing like clumsy bear cubs. But they would recognize it in each other's eyes, and feel it in the groin, and they would go off into a darker chamber together.

Sometimes it happened without any preliminaries at all. Like when they swam together naked in the springs and started wrestling in the shallows. Sometimes just the brush of skin on skin and the firmness of muscles could start the blood racing. Then it was quick and easy and uncomplicated.

But for Lon it was not like that. He didn't seem driven by the same kind of sexual hunger that made the others almost ravenous at times. He could hold out for months, going off into the woods alone when Tommy or one of the others satisfied himself with the breeders or the boy. And when he did take his turn, he spent the whole day working up to it. He would make a place off in one of the far caverns. He would whittle, cutting away at little figures, tiny totems that he'd give as a present. He would bring berries or flowers. And he would hunt and cook fish or game, and set aside a portion just for the two of them. Then he'd burn scented wood and fill the air with its aroma. And he always bathed before and again after. He would never talk about it. He never made jokes.

Only once in a while, with his senses numbed by stink-weed or some other concoction the healer had made, Lon would join in with the others in naked games where they toyed with each other and made a show over who could make it spurt first. Only once, when they were mourning after the Great Blast, had he let Tommy touch him in that way. Even then, he had gone off and kept to himself for days afterward.

Lon wouldn't understand how it happened with Tommy and this boy. At first, Tommy thought he'd simply watch the kid. Then he felt it in his blood. And he had to have him. So he hid until the boy was so far back in the underwoods that no one could see them. Then he clamped his huge hand over the kid's mouth to keep him quiet.

Tommy was so excited, he could hardly walk. But once he had the kid, he knew he had to take him far away. Someone would come looking. So he started circling and weaving through the undergrowth. Once he had the kid far enough in to stop and tie and gag him, deciding when and where to do it became as much of a game as confusing his would-be searchers. He would leave the kid and gallop around, making false trails and dead ends. He would touch and fondle and rub against the bound captive. Then he would run off again, tantalizing himself all the while with thoughts of what it would be like the next time he touched him. By the time he heard the dog and saw the lights, Tommy was twitching with excitement and the blood was really pumping. He knew he was showing them all what fools they were.

He also knew that he wasn't going to share his prize according to the custom of the clan. Except for Lon, all the others were dead. The old order was gone. He wasn't going to let Lon coddle the plaything and win him over like he had the other one. Lon turned him soft by giving him presents and special treats. Tommy wouldn't play up to any pet. This one was his alone. Almost in a frenzy of defiance, he took him. Even with the search parties scouring the underwoods around them, he abandoned all pretense of playfulness and claimed the boy, ferociously. He could see the distant gleam of the lights in the trees as he did, and he had to bite his lip to keep from screaming in triumph as the rush swept through him and the release came. Right under their noses. The boy moaned and whimpered, but no one heard.

If they'd been on the other side of the big creek, closer to the part of the bog that was still moist and gooey, he would have set the boy down in the dark mud and given him over to the swamp. But he didn't have time to do it right. The few times before, he'd brought someone to the wetlands in secret and had chosen to hide what he'd done from the others. Once, a long time back, he'd snatched a kid right off the tail of an old pickup truck at the fishing camp. That time he'd been prowling around, looking for anything left behind by the few stragglers who came out there in the winter. He'd seen the kid crawl under a tarp in the back and fall asleep. There were two men with him, both drinking and talking loud. By the time it was getting dark, they were reeling. They checked that the kid was in the back, opened themselves another bottle, turned on the radio full blast, and started down the narrow dirt road that eventually led to the highway.

Tommy had followed them. He loped along after the truck as it wove and lurched along. Then the driver stopped altogether and got out to take a leak. By the time he got himself situated again, Tommy was under the tarp with the sleeping kid. The next time the truck slowed, Tommy grabbed his prize and was out before the kid had blinked his eyes awake.

That one hadn't been soft or pretty. And he had fought like a tailed bobcat. So Tommy held him tighter, keeping one hand clamped over the kid's mouth while he scurried through the woods. In all the struggling, Tommy finally must have snapped his neck. He just stopped squirming. But Tommy finished with him anyway and carried the body to the edge of the bog. And he sank it. Just like they gave up their dead to the swamp. Only he didn't wrap the kid in cloth or tuck any food or whittled dream sticks or totems in with him like he would if the kid had been one of the clan. He just weighted it, then took a pole and set it down deep, making sure it stuck fast under some roots.

He would have done the same to this one. But giving it over took time and they were getting too close. So he tied the kid to a tree and headed off the other way so they'd follow him north. Now he was heading back south, hoping that Lon had slept through it all and had not heard anything in the night that would have made him suspicious. Tired as he was, Tommy figured he'd grab the shovel, head for the old cave site, and pretend nothing was wrong.

Jack Button paused a moment before he took off his sunglasses as he faced the press Thursday morning. Above the trim beard and mustache, puffy reddened eyes gave his baby face a worn, soulful look. He took out a clean linen handkerchief and dabbed his forehead then the back of his neck.

"Please, if you want pictures, don't take ones of me," he requested. "Take some of the dedicated security people out on the grounds. This tragedy has touched us all deeply," he said in a voice etched in weariness. "But I wouldn't want the perpetrator to feel any sense of tri-

umph. Right now, I look whipped. I'm exhausted. So are
a lot of others. I'd rather he not have the satisfaction of
knowing that. I'd prefer to stay in the background and
let the police officials have the spotlight.'' He put the
sunglasses on again, dabbed his throat and forehead, and
turned to his notes.

"First, I want to thank you for coming here so early,"
he greeted the assemblage. "The Dunes has appreciated
the attention and fine coverage your various newspapers
and television and radio stations have already given this
event. Now we're asking your continued support in handling this tragedy. I'm sure you can spare the Jameses
any unnecessary further distress by using your discretion.
The little fellow has been through enough.'' His voice
wavered slightly. Then he cleared his throat. "But there
is someone out there who deserves no mercy.'' He wiped
his hands then touched his handkerchief to his temples.

Bo Shepherd, coffee mug in hand, moved along from
the back of the room, inching past cables, technicians,
reporters, and chairs toward the front, where Button was
standing. He still hadn't had a break since the search
began the night before. But he'd agreed to brief the press
before going home, and he'd managed a quick shave in
the security-office bathroom. Button glanced at him,
nodded, then continued.

"I want to suggest in advance that we focus on tracking the assailant and alerting those in other communities
that he may be moving their way. He obviously knows
we're after him, and he surely won't find it safe around
here. That places the danger somewhere else.'' Button
already had rousted someone from the local fence company. As soon as the work crew arrived, they'd be in-
stalling a six-foot chain-link fence beyond the rest rooms
and fencing in a separate playground area. He'd also had

Bo Shepherd double the number of adjunct security workers and had added one officer to patrol the fence line with a guard dog. A police lab team and two K-9 units had been in the woods with Shepherd since shortly after dawn, collecting physical evidence and trying to pick up a trail.

"We have posted a reward for any information that leads to an arrest," Button added for those reporters who were just piecing together the story. "The total is now fifteen thousand."

"Mr. Button, is it true you personally put up a portion of that?" one reporter asked.

"Please, I'd like you to keep me out of this," Button said gently but with a firmness that was almost a reproach. "After all, there are people out there doing the actual investigating. And there are folks who were out most of the night searching for the boy. If you want a hero, pick one of them. I'm just a quiet man who hopes that a reward might accomplish something that I personally cannot." He pursed his lips pensivefully then managed a weak smile. "Just say that part of the reward came from employees of the Dunes. Make it plural, please. Keep the emphasis where it belongs, and that is on apprehending this transient. Our security chief, Bo Shepherd, will take over now and give you further details." Button mopped his brow and throat again as he surrendered the podium.

Button's next audience was down the hall, the group of sandsculptors having breakfast in the Felucca Café. Word of the lost child and the search had circulated around the hotel late into the night. Most of them had gone to bed not knowing that the boy had been abducted. Word had only come in about three that morning that Robbie James had been found.

* *–*

"Let me give you a brief rundown of what happened last night, and put aside any rumors that may have been circulating," Button began. Sandy Huff had already told him that Kitty Westberg and two other sandsculptors with children in the Dunes program had called the information desk repeatedly during the night, asking for information about the boy and the search. On Button's orders, they said that the child had simply wandered off. But by morning, news of the abduction and rescue had spread throughout the hotel from the front desk to the grounds-keepers. When Kitty and some others called Sandy for confirmation, Sandy had stalled them, again on Button's orders, until Button finished briefing the reporters and could meet with the sandsculpting team at 7:30. He wanted to handle this group himself.

Button got right to the point. "First of all, there is no reason to worry about the safety of any of your children. Your children are closely supervised at all times. They are with Corey or Melissa and they've been paired up in a buddy system that never has them going anywhere, not even to the rest room, alone. I hate to sound accusatory," he went on, shrugging slightly, "but the young man abducted last night was off by himself. He was not being watched by his parent at the time. He went to the Port-o-lets alone, bypassed them, then roamed into the woods. The abductor was hiding back there and seized the child. In other words, there were several contributing factors involved here."

Again Button shrugged, then leaned forward, tapping his fingertips on the tabletop. "This may not have happened at all if the boy had not wandered into the wrong place at the wrong time. Regardless, we are not taking any chances with anyone's children," he stressed in a carefully controlled voice. "Yours, or those of our visitors. We've taken additional precautions and added more security to keep the children safe. Spring break for most schools starts this weekend. Easter holidays come along next week. The week after, all this will be completed, and the mound will be open for tours and light shows. This is a time for rejoicing. We're not going to let one transient ruin a marvelous event for all of us and for all of those visitors, but particularly not for the children." Unable to hold back any longer, he drew out his already damp handkerchief and wiped the perspiration from his face and neck.

"What exactly did this guy do to the kid?" The point-blank question came from a short, dark-haired sand-sculptor named Rich who ran a jet-ski shop on St. Pete Beach. His ten-year-old daughter was staying with him at the Dunes.

A second sculptor raised his hand. "Yeah, I heard something about the boy being taken off to the hospital. Was the kid hurt?" About the room, anxious eyes scanned Button's face.

Button raised one hand, stilling further questions momentarily. "Let me just say a few things. Rumors have a way of making things seem worse than they are," he proceeded calmly. "Taking the victim to the hospital is just standard police procedure. The boy was mosquito-bitten, scratched, dirty, a bit bruised from being hauled about in the bushes. He had also been sexually abused." He had rehearsed all this on the short drive over from his town house. He kept the details simple, the delivery matter-of-fact, and his expression concerned but not alarmed. Plus, before he left home, he'd fortified himself with a double shot of scotch, a dose of Maalox, a Percodan for his headache, and a mouthful of breath freshener. "The victim was treated and will be released once he's had a good sound sleep." He deliberately avoided the graphic details. Tissue damage, internal bleeding, semen samples, antibiotics, and sedation were matters he didn't have the stomach to discuss. He'd tried to cut Shepherd off when he'd called earlier to tell him about it. But Shepherd fired off the list without stopping. Button wasn't about to repeat it.

Kitty Westberg raised her hand. "What makes you think that this guy won't come back?"

"The police assure me that this kind of hit-and-run attack is the act of someone who is basically a coward," Button replied, smoothing his trimmed mustache with a deliberately casual movement and determined to ignore the sweat trailing down under his shirt. "Obviously, he was a stranger here. He was frightened enough to run into that god-awful swamp and brush area east of here. Then he turned north toward the marsh. No one with any knowledge of the area would go that way. Maybe he's on the run from a hospital or a prison. The police are checking into all of that. But whoever he is, he must have torn himself up real good on the branches and thorns. If he didn't meet up with a gator or a snake, he's probably miles away now, still running, and licking his wounds as he goes." His dark eyes narrowed contemptuously. "Vermin like that don't come back, certainly not to a place like the Dunes. But if he should come snooping around, he'll find a whole new ballgame this time."

Kitty looked at him, still visibly uneasy. She'd spent most of the night calling the desk, hoping that the child was safe and the worried parents had their son returned to them. When she crossed paths with Craig Stuart in the coffee shop at 6:30 that morning and heard from the waitress that the boy had been abducted and molested, she'd decided to pack up and leave. Zach didn't need to hear about any of this, much less be exposed to any danger. But Vince had persuaded her to hold off until they heard the whole story from Button.

"I guarantee you, your kids are in good hands," Button reiterated. "And we'll all be doubly careful now. Please don't inadvertently punish yourselves or your children by depriving them of a wonderful time here." He addressed his comments to the other parents as well as to Kitty. "They are having a great time. Lots of fun, lots of exercise, neat things to do, and they're keeping up with their schoolwork as well. This is an event they will remember all their lives. And so will you folks. Trust us to take care of everything," he said with quiet assurance. "We won't let you down." He made a quick swipe at the perspiration beading up on his forehead.

There was a moment of near silence. Then Button flashed his genial smile. "Let's do what we can do and get on with this magnificent work out there," he suggested, replaying a theme that Kevin had first mentioned, but one Button particularly liked. "We can do something positive here." He looked at the intent, now familiar faces. "We can create something beautiful. How about it. Have some breakfast. Another cup of coffee or whatever. Then let's get on with this." He had them. And he knew it. But he went over to say a few words to Kitty and Vince anyhow, just to smooth out any wrinkles that might remain.

"Don't worry," he said softly, resting his hand on her arm. "We'll keep a special eye on Zach. He's such a fine kid." Button could tell by the softening in her jaw that he'd won her over. Then he left them all to enjoy their breakfast while he headed for the office.

Only after he was in the service elevator, riding alone

to the main-office floor, did Jack Button let the tension he'd been holding inside spill over. Both meetings had gone well, but his stomach was burning, his eyes felt as if they'd been scrubbed with steel wool, and his whole body trembled from lack of sleep. His whole system was off. He couldn't stop sweating.

"Son of a bitch . . ." Button snarled, slamming his fist again and again against the cool metal wall panels. "Why the hell did the son of a bitch have to pick here? This is my place. This is my show. Why did the fucker have to come and do this here. Damn him." He almost wept with frustration. "Damn him to hell."

By the time the elevator halted, Button was composed again, still perspiring and a little red in the face and short of breath, but he strode out, icy calm. He kept his hands, stinging and red from pounding, out of sight. " 'Morning, Jean." He passed the receptionist. He went straight to his desk and took a vial of Valium out of his drawer. "I'm going into the suite upstairs and get a few hours sleep if I can," he told the secretary. "Try not to disturb me until eleven. Then book me an appointment at the Men's Room at 11:30. Tell Barry I need resurrecting. We're doing some filming this afternoon and I have to look human."

"Will do," the woman replied, nodding sympathetically as Button stepped back in the elevator and disappeared behind the whisper of bronzed doors.

"We're going to close off the upper plateaus of the center and north peaks today," Craig Stuart announced when he'd gathered all the team members by the base of the south mound for a Thursday-morning update before they went off in their separate directions. "The work up top is almost completed. I want it finished off and everyone off by noon. Button sent word that we have some kind of press coming out after lunch. So let's have something to show off. Besides, old Mother Nature may have a surprise in store for us.'' He'd been eyeing the sky off toward the Gulf and didn't look too happy.

''In case you haven't heard the weather reports, there's some kind of storm brewing off toward Texas,'' Stuart informed them. ''If it drifts this way, we may have to have Crockett help us put back some of the scaffolding and try to tent and buffer the main pieces. Then again, the storm may turn or dissipate and leave us alone. Just to be on the careful side, I'll be taking the electricians up top today to finish their installations. Then we'll give it one final spray and hope for the best. Regardless, the heights will be off limits by shut-down today. Ready or not, we all shift down. So as you finish up, get everything down from there. Buckets. Hoses, Shovels. Whatever. We're going to rake the area, make it pretty, roll out the paths for tours, then rope it off and let it all sit for a few days.''

''Meanwhile,'' Kevin started in, equally anxious to get everyone back on track, ''we need to have the mound ready for the influx of people. This thing is going to snowball. Spring break starts this weekend and that means we'll be surrounded by spectators and swamped with volunteers. A lot of these folks will be willing to put in a full week's work if we let 'em. We can cover a lot of territory if we train them and use them well.''

''But that means we have to know where to work them in,'' Stuart stated. ''Roseanne Petty and Sandy Huff will both be coordinating the volunteers. They have to have an up-to-date progress report. And they have to know exactly where and how many volunteers are needed. We don't want anyone wandering around aimlessly.''

"I assume you're exempting the press," someone wisecracked from the sidelines. There had already been a few mishaps with cameramen stepping on portions of completed work or otherwise getting in the way. One female magazine photographer backed off one slope and slid down thirty feet on her stomach. She wasn't hurt, but was extremely embarrassed. A lot of cameras caught her in unflattering positions during her unplanned descent. But the prevailing rumor was that she'd clumsily knocked into one of south-mound sculptures and damaged it, and later, when she asked the sculptor to pose, he kept inching forward deliberately so she would keep stepping back to keep him in focus. Chris Jones only shrugged and insisted he'd only been trying to be cooperative. Then he rebuilt the damaged piece.

"Occasionally we have a few klutzes." Stuart retained his good humor. "There are some things we have to learn to live with. Most of these folks are trying to be as careful and unobtrusive as possible. They don't always succeed."

"Just keep your sense of humor and be patient," Kevin stressed. "We're getting a lot of fine coverage, and that's what helps draw the crowd that pays the overhead," he reminded them. "It's all part of the game."

Stuart took charge again. "Let's get on with this. Today we need to line up specific jobs. We need a lot of places to put these folks to work. Get the settings, all the cottages and sheds, the gardens and hedges blocked out and ready. There are a lot of simple buildings that volunteers can detail for us. The Three Little Pigs. Hansel and Gretel. Goldilocks. Little Red Riding Hood," he read off some site names, inclining his head toward Stuart and Kitty, who were in charge of that list on the center mound. "Saturday and Sunday we'll need to pull some of you folks off the mounds to run some training sessions. I'll need a couple of you in the workshop area to train volunteers for architectural detail work. Thatching roofs. Framing in windows. Making shutters. Building steps. That kind of thing.'' He looked at Vince expectantly. "How are things coming on your end? Will you be able to run a couple of these workshops?''

"By the weekend, I'll make time," Vince promised. "If we hustle, we'll have Prince Charming's castle and the upper part of the town done today." He stared at his schematic of the south mound as he gave his progress report, mentally adjusting his schedule as he spoke. "I can leave Chris finishing the pumpkin carriage, and if Kitty can give me hand with Cindy and her prince, we'll make it. I just need some fine tuning there. Then we can spray and rope it off. By tomorrow we'll have the Snow White scene underway on the back side, the farm for Jack and the Beanstalk on the front, and the bedroom setup with the twenty mattresses for the Princess and the Pea on the far side. I've already got some folks working with me who can take over supervising each of those areas. So, barring disasters, by Saturday, I can break away and teach some.''

"What about the Pied Piper idea. Did it get worked out?'' Stuart asked, making notations on his own clipboard. Two days before, when they were filling blank areas, they had poured a few vertical columns designated for the Piper and some children in the sloping area where the south mound and the center one ran together. But Stuart hadn't checked on it since.

"Jaisen is taking a group with trowels and landscaping all that hillside today. He's got another crew digging out the mountain cave and the river. All I need is for Kitty to whip the Piper and the kids into shape, then bring on the rats.''

"Rats. How about rats? Where's our beastmaster.'' Kevin raised his voice slightly.

"Here,'' Paul Feneau answered from the sidelines.

"The man needs rats for the Pied Piper,'' Kevin relayed the message.

"He'll get plenty of rats,'' Paul Feneau promised. "I've got a real nice old lady who showed up yesterday and asked to help. I started her on ducks, but she caught on like you wouldn't believe. She can whip you out rats and squirrels and swans. You name it.''

"Just rats . . .'' Vince laughed. "Big ones. Maybe eighteen inches tall sitting on their haunches.''

"She can handle it. No problem.''

"Wait. I heard ducks and swans. Who is this woman? We'll need some ducks and swans later,'' Kitty called out. "What did you say her name is and how long is she going to be around?''

"Elizabeth. Elizabeth Frye. And she'll probably be around forever,'' Feneau joked. "She's eighty-four and said she'd be here every day after she popped off her nine holes of golf. But don't mind if she breaks from 2:30 to three. She's Canadian. That's her time for tea.''

"I'll look her up,'' Kitty promised, smiling as she jotted down the woman's name on her schematic next to the Ugly Duckling pond and the Frog Prince's fountain. "Please tell her I need to see her.''

"Let's get back to the subject of workshops,'' Stuart took over again, pacing as he spoke. "What about the time, Vince? Saturday and Sunday morning. Eight till nine?''

"That's good for me,'' Vince answered.

"And I guess we'd better do some small-animal workshops. Can you do some? Eight to nine?'' He aimed his question at Paul Feneau.

''Well, since Elizabeth cannot be here until eleven,'' Feneau said with warm and gentle humor, ''I guess I'll have to do it. Unless I can persuade her that we need her for the next week more than her ladies' foursome does.''

''Maybe you should ask them all to come,'' Kitty suggested. ''Never underestimate the talent of our silver-haired citizens.''

There was genuine amusement in the eyes that met Kitty's evenly. ''Elizabeth isn't white-haired. She's a red-head. Mahogany, to be more precise,'' Feneau corrected her.

''At eighty-four . . . ?''

''I didn't say it was natural.''

''Regardless . . . come on, you guys,'' Stuart said, laughing despite his impatience. ''That's a yes from Paul on the small animals, so we're set for weekend workshops. Now unless anyone has something to add, we can get on up there and get to work.'' The sculptors stood and started gathering their tool bags or belts before heading off toward the wide pathway that led up the south mound.

''Don't forget to keep your headsets on in case you're needed,'' Sandy Huff called out to them before the group broke up. ''I'll keep you posted on the weather.''

''And please, folks, be careful with those hoses,'' Stuart reminded them. ''Turn them off when you're drawn whatever water you need. We don't want any spillover on the mounds. The sand up top is drying fast. If you wet one of the lower levels, it will leach into the sand and start drawing away. Then we'll have whole sections shearing off. Look at this beauty,'' he boasted, turning and waving his clipboard toward the peaks. ''We've got

Rapunzel's Tower completed. If the rain leaves us alone, we have the world's record for both height and mass. All we have to do now to make it official is cover every square inch that's left with something artsy. And I mean every square inch. So get with it. Be careful. See you at lunch.''

"Don't forget to grease down with sunscreen," Sandy Huff called. "You can burn really bad on these overcast days.''

"You sound like my mother," Chris Jones called back, teasing her.

"She doesn't look like your mother," Jaisen Crockett said quietly, brushing his sun-bleached hair back and tugging a Dunes visor low over his eyes.

"You've got a point." Jones chuckled, regarding the tall young woman with sun-streaked hair approvingly. "What would you guess she is . . . eighteen, twenty?''

"Twenty-one. Junior. Business major," Jaisen answered, unrolling his sketch of the Piper's cavern as he followed the others along.

"Hey. How'd you know that?" Jones nudged him.

Jaisen smiled noncommittally and kept walking.

"She's too old for you." Jones walked faster, his long, lanky form towering over that of his friend. "And she's too tall. Man, she must be five-ten," Jones insisted.

"She's five-nine," Jaisen responded with that same slightly lopsided smiled. "And she seems to have no trouble looking eye to eye.''

"I saw her first. I was just looking for the right time to make my move.''

"He who hesitates . . . ?" Jaisen replied good-naturedly.

"Are you telling me that you've been seeing her?" Chris quizzed him as they reached the top. "Have you?''

"Father, retired air force. Mother sells real estate. Two older sisters named Lisa and Amy, both married . . ." Jaisen said casually. "She likes vinegar on her french fries and she's pretty good at miniature golf."

"You rat . . ." Chris grinned back. "I can't believe it. Here I am flexing my muscles and giving this girl my irresistible routine, and you—"

"I just happened to sit next to her at lunch and ask her a couple of questions. What can I say?" Jaisen shrugged his shoulders in mock resignation. "She likes me for my mind."

"You rat . . ." Chris groaned, shaking his head and patting his buddy's shoulder. "Shoot." He gave him a sidelong look. "She's a cute girl," he said softly. "Real nice girl." With one final nudge, Jones left him standing there as he took off at an angle over the south mound toward the half-completed pumpkin carriage. "See if she's got a friend," he called back over his shoulder. "I promise not to hesitate next time."

Twisted and tilted at awkward, freakish angles, the tall oaks and pine trees still clung desperately to the uneven soil, refusing to fall. When the Great Blast came and the subterranean tremors collapsed the cave under them, the trees had all lurched in various directions from the force. Mutilated roots, snapped off and ragged, were exposed to the air, and dried and shriveled like old war wounds. The creek no longer flowed this way. But enough of the longer roots held and drew nourishment, and the trees survived. Now the canopy of their branches shaded Lon and Tommy while they worked.

They had started in at the sinkhole. The gaping wound in the midst of the brush-covered area, centuries past, had been a riverbed nourished by a working spring. But it had shriveled into a small creek long ago, and the great caverns beneath its path had many rooms that were dry and livable. The father of the elder had found this place and settled here before Tommy or Lon were born. As long as they could remember, that labyrinthine cave had been their sanctuary. Then the blasts ripped open its heart and brought mud and rock and water and roots thundering down on those sleeping below.

Tommy and Lon had been out gigging for fish at the time. A dark storm had moved in. The half brothers had felt restless holed up below. They liked being out in the woods surrounded by the sound and movement of wind and rain in the trees. They knew that big, lazy fish came near the surface then to catch the bugs impaled there by the raindrops. Then the first blast thundered across the wetlands. They had felt the heavy air press against their ears and the shock wave shake their innards, and they had looked at each other in alarm. Then the second unnatural blast sent a more ominous tremor through the underwoods, shaking the earth beneath their feet and sending them leaping homeward. A third blast stopped them at the entrance of the old cave, spewing out the frantic breeder and knocking them all sprawling with its force. The gaping cave opening snapped shut, closing off all passage to the rooms beyond. And the tall trees above did their grotesque dance of death.

But they had tools now. And they had come back with them to recover the remains so they could honor those they had lost.

Lon's hands were bloody already from digging with the shovel and from working his fingers between the shattered rocks and boulders that had once been the vaulted ceiling of the great cave. The heavy folds of flesh between his fingers were split and stung like fire. But they had uncovered very little. They'd found some sharp-toothed metal traps and a section of chain that had hung near the Trapper's ledge. They dragged out a few mud-caked pelts that had been his. But even with the tools, they found the rocks packed too tightly together and too heavy to lift aside. Then Tommy and Lon moved further down, trying to guess what part of the old cave was beneath them. They tried again, opening up their own wounds as they searched for their past.

"Elder . . ." Tommy held up the latest memento he found, the strip of deer tendon with the smooth, unbroken talisman still attached. Tommy caught it between his fingers when he forced his hand into a crevice where three slabs of rock had wedged together and left an open space below. The oval limestone pendant with the fossil etched into its side was indeed the scorpion totem that the elder, their father, had worn as long as Tommy could remember. Passed down from one generation to the next, it hung over the heart of the leader of the clan, the one who sat first at the campfire, first smoked the sweet grass, the one whose wisdom settled disputes. And when he slept, it hung over his bunk. It stayed with that leader until he was given over to the swamp after his death and a new leader took his place.

Finding it at last meant that the body of the elder was very near, buried below that broken barrier of limestone.

"Let me try," Lon insisted, crowding in close and trying to push Tommy away from the opening. But Tommy handed him the pendant then plunged his arm in the hole again, lying flatter and straining harder against the rough surface of the rocks. Anxiously he stabbed away with his outspread fingers, probing in the dark mud below the open space. Then he stopped as he dug into the ooze and grazed the stiff twiglike extensions that he knew instinctively formed a human hand.

"Here . . ." Tommy grunted. As he started to pull, the spongy flesh gave way, peeling upward with the motion of his hand. Tommy slid his grip down again, trying to get a more secure hold. He pulled again, then the whole thing gave way. Tommy lifted his arm from the narrow opening, still clutching the decaying forearm of the elder. Then the stench of death floated up with it. Tommy dropped the limb and wiped his hand on his pant leg. Lon staggered off, retching violently as he steadied himself against the tree trunks.

Determined to retrieve the rest of the elder, Lon broke off the handle of one shovel, trying to ram it into the opening then use it as a lever to pry the slabs of rock apart. Tommy went off in search of a sturdy tree limb and came back with one that fit into the hole. But it splintered under the weight of the two of them. Nothing moved. Furiously, they tore at the rocks with their hands. Dirty, bloody, and exhausted, they sat there, staring sullenly at the exposed arm, pale and unreal in the light.

Soon Tommy was openmouthed and sound asleep, slouched against a tree. But Lon still sat there, his arms crossed over his chest, staring at the arm. His weathered moon face, half-covered by his graying unkempt beard, was streaked with sweat, dirt, and tears.

At last Lon dragged himself to his feet and circled the area, kicking at the twisted roots of the trees. He pulled out his knife, cut off an exposed portion, then he scraped his blade over it, removing the outer surface and baring the knotted burl. Satisfied with the shape, he crouched a ways off, whittling away, his thick lips drawn into a glum downward line, his expression resigned. He'd almost completed the second figure before he spoke.

"Tommy. Get up." He waited. Tommy didn't move. Lon went over and nudged him with his foot. "Tommy. Get up. You bring leaves and clay," he said, prodding Tommy into action. "Go. Now."

Tommy grunted and rolled onto his side.

"Tommy. We must give them up. We need leaves and clay. Now." Lon grabbed Tommy's shoulder and yanked him up into a sitting position.

Tommy blinked his big frog eyes. He scratched his crotch. He dug his fingers in his sparse, bristly beard and scratched. Then he looked at the sharp-bladed knife and the face beginning to take shape on the root in Lon's hand. And he understood. Lon was making a second self, a likeness, for each of the ones he knew were trapped in the communal grave below. Each carefully chosen section of root became the body; its knot became their face. Finally they would all be there with them. The healer. The elder. The Trapper.

Somberly Tommy stood and disappeared into the underwoods. He would do his part.

Lon wept again when he made the fourth figure, more delicate and smaller than the rest. He wasn't really one of them, but Lon had loved the boy. He remembered how they played in the river and how he carried the boy on his shoulders when they went out after fruit or hunted small game. The boy would sing sometimes, his small thin voice repeating fragments of songs half remembered from that other world. He had been more cheerful than some of the others had been over the years. He and his sister, the breeder, were quick to learn that it was useless to cry and fight when one of the men of the clan chose to be with them. And it was futile to try to escape. So when it was time, they would submit. And their reward was that by day, the ankle chain the Trapper had made for them would be removed. They could move freely about the caves and they could go out with Lon or one of the others to fish or hunt or swim. Only at night were they chained. And it was because of those chains that Lon knew the boy was dead. No matter how quick or small he was, the night of the Great Blast, he'd been shackled next to the Trapper. Now, even without having the body, Lon would give him over with the proper care, like the others.

Later, they crouched over the row of wood-root figures, each with its face painted ashen with pale gray clay as a sign of death. Lon had rubbed each image with tree sap and sprinkled pungent root scrapings over top. And he had enfolded them in the broad leaves that Tommy had found. Instead of wrapping an outer layer of cloth like they would have done with the actual bodies, they peeled strips of rushes and wound them round, sealing them with sticky sap. He remembered that the elder had brewed a water potion with witch hazel and berries and some roots he did not recall, but he made do with what he and Tommy could find. Then he took a gourd poked full of holes and showered them with the brew.

"I don't know the words," Lon admitted when all the preparations were done.

"I don't know, too."

For a moment, they simply stood and hung their heads in silence. Then Lon lowered the figures one by one down into the open place, back where he'd already told Tommy to put the elder's arm. Then he poked in a layer of rocks to weight them down. He opened the sacks of swamp muck that Tommy had brought and poured the dark wet soil into the opening until the space was full. "Go to a place of water and birds and fish and game. Go where you can be with your brothers. One day, we meet there.

Go. Peace.'' Lon spoke haltingly, trying to remember how it went. Those hadn't been the words of power that the elder would have used. But they bore the same message. And he was too tired to care. Night was closing in and he wanted only to sleep.

"Good," Tommy grunted, nodding wearily.

"Good," Lon agreed. The sun had already dropped low behind the trees, and the cloudy sky that had hinted of rain and smelled like spring still hadn't growled or grumbled. There would be no storm tonight.

"Home now." Lon picked up his shovel.

"Home." Tommy put his arm around Lon's shoulder as they turned to leave.

Chapter 5

"THE FUCKING DESCRIPTION SOUNDS LIKE A CROSS BE-tween Quasimodo and Bigfoot," Bo Shepherd said under his breath as he read over the handout he'd been given Friday morning. "Get me copies and let's get them circulating." He xeroxed a duplicate for himself then handed the original printout to the secretary. "Follow me, Lieutenant," he said, signaling for the police officer who'd delivered the piece to follow him down the hall. "Hurry up with those, Ginny," Bo called back to the secretary. "We'll need about fifty of them right off for the meeting comin' up."

"I thought it was you, boss."

Shepherd stopped in surprise as the bruised and bandaged face of one of his regular staff poked out of a doorway. "How ya' doing, Buddy."

"I'm sore as hell," Prado said stiffly, trying not to move his jaw any more than necessary. "I got so bored sitting at home, I figured I could come in and ache here and have better scenery.''

"You serious? You think you should be up and around already?''

"I'd like to give it a try,'' Prado replied. "Daytime TV sucks. From what I've seen on the tube, you've got more interesting stuff going on around here.''

"You heard about Quasimodo,'' Button said dully. "Here's the description.'' He handed Prado the page. "Sound like anyone you know?'' Bo was only half kidding.

"Just the big and hairy part,'' Prado said quietly. "I didn't get any kind of a look at the two guys that decked me.''

"Well, this asshole probably only goes after little guys,'' Bo bit off the words. "Give him someone big enough to defend himself and he'd probably be crappin' eggrolls.''

"The James kid gave you this?'' Prado asked, turning to Lieutenant Rowe.

"Yeah. It took a while,'' he said grimly. "Poor kid was freaked out. We got this in bits and pieces. They have to keep him sedated. He's spooked by anything that moves. He can't sleep without having nightmares.''

"This guy is a nightmare,'' Bo stressed, taking back the printout copy. "Tell Buddy what the kid said about the hands.''

"I read he had callused hands,'' Prado recalled.

"Like I said, the kid was real upset,'' Rowe said, his typical-cop razored hair and trimmed mustache the blond counterpart to Buddy Prado's darker version. "He said the guy was like a monster. Besides looking like a damn hairy troll, the kid said he had webbed fingers. Calluses for sure. But he said the fingers were webbed between the knuckles. We didn't put that down on the official release. We figured that in the dark and with all the trauma he'd been through, the kid was more than a little hysterical. We couldn't put out a wanted sheet on some frogman. But we'll pass the word and keep it out of the press, just in case there could be something to it."

"Webbed fingers," Prado muttered.

"One of the personal-violence investigators suggested he could have been wearing some kind of gloves," Lieutenant Rowe added. "You know, the surgical kind. We had a rapist who did that to keep from leaving prints. If the gloves didn't fit right, maybe they would have looked webbed."

"Or maybe the kid was just so scared out there, he thought some creature from the Black Lagoon grabbed him," Bo offered. "Poor kid. He'll be whacked out for the rest of his life from this thing."

"Is it all right if I stay around and help out," Prado asked hopefully. "I could at least run relief at the communications tent. They're paying me anyhow."

"But you're so ugly," Bo teased. The older security officers had always kidded Prado about his good looks and the attention he drew from resort guests, little old ladies and teens in particular, but occasionally a gentleman. Besides the white hospital patch that covered the stitches over his cheekbone, the entire left side of Prado's face was stained deep purple and his eye was swollen almost shut. "You know all that company policy crap about keeping up our public image," Bo rubbed it in. "Putting our best face forward, and all that. Button calls it camera appeal. You ain't got it no more."

"I could wear a bag over my head," Prado countered, trying not to grin. "Come on. No one will be looking at me."

"Let me clear it with Button. I'll tell him that we really can use you," Bo promised. "Besides, he'll like getting a warm body for free. But if he says yes, just don't go pushing yourself too hard in all this heat. I don't want to have you on the disabled list any longer than necessary. When this is over and we start having a load more permanent occupants moving in here, we're going to have our hands full. So take it easy."

"I just want to be useful," Prado insisted.

"You just want to stare at all the women." Bo laughed accusingly. "Gotta go." He pointed down the hall to the room where the morning briefing was scheduled.

"Lookin' like this, I doubt I'll get lucky," Prado responded, falling in step behind Bo and Lieutenant Rowe.

"Unless someone is into maimed and magenta," Rowe commented softly. "We once had a case where a guy liked to rough up the woman before he raped her—"

"Please . . . not so close to breakfast," Pardo muttered.

"You're looking better today," Sandy Huff greeted Jack Button as he stepped out of the company golf cart next to the volunteer sign-in table. Wearing a Dunesfest visor, a new ivory and teal shirt with his name on the back, ivory shorts, amber-lensed glasses, and a streak of aqua sunblock on his nose, he looked rested, tanned, and very much like one of the pros on the team. Only he was carrying a telephoto-lens camera instead of a tool belt, and that set him apart from the sculptors.

"Amazing what a full night's sleep will do," Button answered spiritedly, loading the camera in the shade of the tent. "Bo said there was no trouble, no calls last night. How was the crowd?" He'd gone home late in the afternoon, suffering from a pulsing headache that took two Percodan to subdue. They put him under and he'd slept through the night. Sandy had stayed over at the resort and was to cover any administrative or PR issues that came up.

"About the same as the night before. A bunch of us came out here after dinner just to look around. It was a little weird." Sandy's expression shifted to show a certain disquiet. "I think there were a number of people who just wanted to see where Robbie was grabbed. Kinda morbid."

"It was strange," Roseanne Petty agreed, wrinkling her nose. "Sort of like people wandering around the scene of an accident looking for tire tracks and body parts."

"Everyone was quiet and sort of remote," Sandy added, watching Button as he adjusted the lens on his camera then aimed it at the heights. Stuart, Kitty Westberg, and a few of the other pros were already up there, apparently mapping out the day's strategy. Again the sky was overcast, but the Texas-oriented storm brewing in the Gulf hadn't intensified enough to send out storm warnings.

"Well, that was last night." Button spoke while he focused on the completed pumpkin carriage with Cinderella nearby. He fired off a shot. "Tonight, if the weather holds, we're bringing in a couple of bands. A jazz group and a soft rock. It won't be quiet," he guaranteed. "This whole incident with the boy was a definite setback, but we're not going to let it get blown out of proportion. It's history. Yesterday I contacted that couple from Gainesville who'd asked about getting married here. I told them we've changed policies and offered them a suite for the weekend. So they agreed to move up the wedding. They're driving down here today to have the ceremony performed up there by Prince Charming's castle. They're letting the media photograph and tape the whole thing. I've got it set up just before sunset, after everyone is off the mound for the night. So when Dunesfest hits the late news tonight, we'll have a whole new story.''

''I thought you said no weddings up there until the whole thing is finished—'' Roseanne looked at him, slightly bewildered.

''We needed this now,'' Button cut her off with a reassuring pat on the shoulder. ''And I may schedule in a couple more next week. There's enough done to look good. Besides, we need positive press. Weddings. Music. We'll make the most of it. And we'll hope the news folks do the same. Give them a good story, and they'll run with it.''

Smaller and darker than Sandy, Roseanne Petty was the quieter of the two, and older by a few years. She'd coordinated special events for several hotels before coming to the Grand Nile resort. Weddings were relatively simple productions to organize, and they were sentimetal and showy. But she didn't like Button's sudden shift in policy. ''I guess that makes sense,'' she said, shrugging, but the look she gave her friend held a clear message of disapproval.

Sandy offered her a guarded, noncommittal smile in return. ''I guess we'd better get back to the armbands and sign-in sheets,'' she suggested diplomatically. ''Here they come.'' She looked toward the group of volunteers heading her way. Button and his traffic-control aide Otto Breshears had instituted some additional changes. Only those team members and volunteers already registered and issued armbands earlier in the week were allowed inside the chain-link fence that Button now had ordered extended to the approach area. No longer allowed to enter the construction area as soon as they arrived, all the early birds had been directed to wait in the north parking lot until eight o'clock. Spectators who simply came to sit and watch would not be admitted to the grounds until nine, after the training sessions for volunteers had begun. That let all the team members and their crews get situated before the crowds converged. Besides that, Button had a horseshoe-shaped moat bulldozed around the base of the mound then added posts and cord to keep the observers from moving in too close. With lines and gates and waiting areas, the entry procedure was becoming increasingly regimented, but as Button insisted, if it worked at Disney World, it would work at the Dunes.

"I guess I'd better start getting some shots for our own files," he remarked, aiming the camera at Sandy and Roseanne Petty behind the registration desk. "Smile, this is for posterity," he called out to them. "Or perhaps for a company brochure. Or a slide show around the time of the quarterly salary reviews," he added enticingly. "Come on, look like you're enjoying this," he said with a definite edge of reproach. Both women glanced at each other then flashed big smiles, smiles that faded considerably once Button had his picture and turned his back.

"I expect him to bring on the clowns and elephants next," Roseanne whispered under her breath.

"Easy," Sandy hushed her. "He's just doing his job."

"Yeah, but you have to admit, he's cold-blooded. Hustling up a wedding just to make things seem better here . . ."

"It's a festival. So he's making it festive," Sandy reminded her, not really comfortable being Button's advocate. "Let's get to work." She nudged her friend as the first of the new volunteers strode up to the table.

"Welcome to Dunesfest." Sandy lifted her bright blue eyes and assessed the first fellow to reach the tent. "We're delighted to have each of you folks here to give us a hand. And a strong back," she added a bit louder, her smile broadening naturally as she looked at the variety of shapes and sizes and ages of those lining up, willing to sweat and sizzle just to be a part of the occasion.

"You will be given armbands that will indicate the type of work you are assigned to do . . ." Roseanne Petty began the explanation while Sandy checked driver's licenses and signatures.

"My cow collapsed," Paul Feneau muttered forlornly as he sat next to Kitty on the shuttle in to lunch at the hotel. Instead of the usual sandwich-and-cold-drinks setup in a tent on the site, Button had arranged a casual affair in the air-conditioned comfort of the board room, but he'd limited the guest list. Besides Sandy Huff and Roseanne Petty and six representatives of the sandsculpting team, he'd invited several of the top people from each of the sponsoring businesses, and the message implicit was for the staff and sculptors to charm the backers. For an hour.

Earlier Button had taken the executives on a shuttle circuit of the mound. The skyline pieces were almost completed. The moat was being pumped full. The wading ponds on the shady north end had been installed and equipped with fountains and separate Port-o-lets. Already children were splashing in the pools, and mothers held small babies and let them dangle their feet in the water or reach small hands under the fountains' spray. Sets of swings installed the day before were now cemented in place, and aqua-shirted Dunes security adjuncts acted as supervisors, pushing swings and refereeing disputes over whose turn was next. The sponsors had agreed that the play area was a wise precaution. Button had their firms listed as contributors on a neat billboard on the playground fence. Then he'd deposited the groups at the entrance of the Grand Nile. On the return trip, the shuttle picked up Sandy and Roseanne and the six sculptors. The remaining sixteen team leaders would supervise on the mound.

"Sorry your cow collapsed. Can you salvage anything?" Vince leaned forward, looking past Kitty at Feneau's somber face.

"What else is in Jack and the Beanstalk besides Jack and his mother and a cow?" Feneau asked. The mother and Jack were already completed and sprayed with fixative. But there had been a vein of dry sand in the cow form and it had simply split apart.

"There's a goose that laid golden eggs, a magic harp that sings, and a bag of gold," Sandy Huff chimed in from the seat behind them.

"Those come later," Roseanne added in a matter-of-fact tone. "If I recall, this is a pre-climbing-the-beanstalk scene. The thing was just starting to grow."

Kitty, caught in the midst of them, started grinning at the seriousness of the discussion.

"So how about a pig or a goat?" Vince suggested.

"Jack was poor," Sandy countered. "The cow was all they had."

By now Kitty was laughing. "I think the sun has gotten to all of you. You'd think we were at a summit conference."

"Mr. Button insisted on authenticity," Sandy Huff declared. "So I researched all this stuff."

"Besides, we don't want to lose our credibility with

the kids,'' Roseanne insisted. "I have two preschoolers who would file a complaint if we don't stick to the story word for word. Little kids aren't into poetic license,'' she said with a gleam of amusement in her eyes. "I can imagine Amy now if she spotted a pig in Jack's possession.'' She put her hands on her hips and scrunched up her face. " 'Mama. Jack didn't have a piggy . . .' '' She mimicked her four-year-old's delivery.

"I get the point,'' Vince surrendered. "No piggy. I guess we'll just put up a new mold and rebuild the cow.''

"With udders,'' Roseanne reminded him, prompting a few amused looks from the sculptors. "It said she gave milk in the story. Amy will expect to see udders.''

"Udders . . .'' Paul Feneau moaned, rolling his eyes and grinning. "I hadn't got that far when she collapsed. I won't forget her udders.''

"Mr. Button said we're striving for verisimilitude,'' Sandy kidded him as the shuttle pulled up to the rear entrance of hotel.

"I thought he was just inviting us in for lunch.'' Jaisen Crockett, silent until now, spoke up. There was a pale blue gleam of mischief beneath his long lashes.

"Did someone say that cow's name was Vera Similtood?'' Chris Jones joined him in further confusing the issue.

"I'd have expected something more pastoral, like Clover or Rosebud,'' Jaisen said solemnly.

"Or Bossie. Or Bessie . . .''

"Stop it, you two,'' Sandy pleaded. "Behave.''

Button was there to greet them, smiling and cordial as he escorted them to the executive elevator. "These folks have a considerable investment out there,'' he reminded them. "We need to make them feel that they're appreciated and that they're an integral part of the event.''

"Maybe we should have brought them each a personalized shovel," Chris Jones whispered.

"We all may need a shovel by the time this is over," Craig Stuart commented dryly.

"I didn't see our logo in there anywhere," one of the corporate officers from the Tampa brewery quizzed Vince over lobster salad and iced tea. "I thought they were going to be sculpted in sand somewhere."

"They're coming," Vince assured him. "We're going to use the sand from the training areas for the logos," he explained. "Once we've got a few more working days under our belts and we've trained enough skilled returnees to suspend the demonstrations, we'll set up the logos. We'll scrape up all the sand in the training areas, load them into molds set up in front of the mound, and put some of our people to work on the designs. Paul here is going to do your eagle."

"I'll be glad to to something really dramatic," Feneau spoke up. "I've spent the morning working on a cow. For Jack and the Beanstalk," he added quickly when he saw the man's slightly bewildered look.

"Ah, I remember the beanstalk part." The brewery executive nodded. "I saw a fellow working on a big column with leaves."

"That was Hansen. He's doing all the exotic plants including the beanstalk," Craig Stuart explained. "But what you saw were the brambles that go up the wall of Sleeping Beauty's castle."

"Is Hansen doing our logo?" the female president of BloominGail's Nursery asked him. Slim, dark-haired, tanned, and tall, and dressed in a T-shirt and slacks, she looked more like one of the team members than a corporate officer.

"That's going to be a joint project," Stuart told her.

"Kitty is dong the head and face part. Hansen will take over and do the surrounding flowers."

"It should be beautiful," Sandy Huff piped in, recalling the art nouveau design of that company logo, the head of a female with windblown, streaming hair of flowers and leaves.

"Right, like Mother Nature, only younger," Roseanne joked.

Jack Button concluded the luncheon with an enthusiastic review of the attendance to date. His boss, Stan Jacobson, sat a bit stiffly through it all, nodding and smiling, but slightly uncomfortable in his suit and tie. All the others had taken Button's "casual" classification literally and had come in sport shirts and jackets. They were clearly pleased with the progress of Dunesfest, and Jacobson assured them that the momentum was growing. "This is going to be news worldwide," he declared. "It's going to exceed all our expectations."

"I appreciate your coming to join us," Button thanked the sculptors, precisely on the hour. Button, Jacobson, and the officers would linger over coffee while Craig Stuart, Kitty, and the others excused themselves.

"We've got a cow to rebuild and a lot of territory to cover," Stuart said, somewhat relieved to be heading back to work. "Come out and see us anytime." He issued the invitation to the sponsors, holding the door while Kitty led the small procession out. "I hope you'll pass the word to all your employees that this is a sight well worth seeing firsthand," Stuart added sincerely. "It's going to be a real beauty." With a casual wave, he closed the door behind him and jogged down the meet the others at the elevator.

"I felt so guilty sitting there all cool and clean, sucking back that lobster, while all the other folks are out there slaving away on the mound.'' Feneau smiled as he spoke. "Every once in a while I had the urge to carve the butter patties into little critters.''

"I think that's udder sublimation,'' Roseanne murmured, winking at him. "We all know what you really want to get your hands on.''

"Bossie's bosom . . .'' Chris guessed.

"Right now all I want is a mold about eight feet long,'' Feneau replied, laughing. "And about two hours of uninterrupted time to work on it.''

"To work on her,'' Sandy Huff corrected him. "Cow. Udders. Female.''

"Right—Bessie,'' Chris insisted.

"I thought you said her name was Vera . . .''

"And I bet she has a mole on her right shoulder,'' Vince suggested from behind them.

"Actually she just has a collar and a bell,'' Sandy replied, maintaining a deadpan expression. "But a mole would be nice. . . .''

"Fine. I'll give her a mole,'' Feneau promised, smiling slyly as the elevator doors opened and they all stepped in. "Just let's get on with it.''

In the late afternoon, Jack Button took his camera and strolled through the crowd, stopping to take pictures and talk with visitors along the way. He'd finished four rolls of film already, concentrating mainly on the children, but he'd occasionally take a shot of one of the sculptors at work or a Dunes employee amid the crowd. His efforts had drawn nothing but smiles. Even when he took almost an entire roll of two young prepubescent girls, less self-conscious than most of their peers, playing topless in the dappled sunlit area in the playground beneath the oaks, no one regarded him with any suspicion. His camera was professional caliber, his outfit clearly associated with Dunesfest, and his name tag indicated he was an official of sorts. He simply looked like a staff member doing a job. If anything, the parents were pleased if he singled out their child to be photographed.

"Mister. Is that Runtzelstilkin?" The little fellow stopped him, floundering over the pronunciation as he pointed to the tower up top. Bare-chested and russet-haired, the lad looked like a mischievous elf. But it was his older brother, a slim lad of ten or so with the same autumn coloring, that Button had been trying to get an angle on. Button knew right off where he could send that one once he'd had prints made. There was a pen pal in Seattle who was very fond of redheads and would weave some very personal fantasies around this attractive lad.

"No. I think Rumpelstiltskin will eventually go farther down the other side," Button stalled, talking to the younger one. "They have to work on the sand mound from the top down. They finish one layer, then they move down to the next. That way they don't knock any sand on the next level." The smaller child wasn't really impressed, but the older boy was listening, nodding thoughtfully. Button smiled at him, determined not to rush him.

"Then who's that," the younger brother asked.

Patiently Button crouched down beside him. "That's Rapunzel with her long hair dangling down. And that's the wicked witch peeking out from the bushes next to it. And the fellow standing at the bottom is the handsome prince who comes to visit." Poised on one knee with his arm resting on the boy's shoulder, Button held the child spellbound while he identified the characters and the tale. An elderly couple, delighted and amused, stopped and looked from Button to the mound, listening just as attentively as the child did. Other visitors stopped. The older brother moved a few steps away, easing into the side-lines.

"Do you remember how the mean old witch made Rapunzel stay up there all by herself?" Button asked the younger lad. The boy shook his head shyly. "And do you remember how Rapunzel braided her long hair and dropped it down so the witch could come to visit her?" This time a nod.

"Then one day, a handsome prince heard the witch calling to Rapunzel. . . ." Even without looking up, Button could tell he was gathering a crowd. Other pass-ersby stopped to listen, enchanted both by the storytell-ing and the quiet, intense way the little red-haired boy stared into Button's face then shifted wide, soft brown eyes to the scene on the center mound then to Button again. Button was aware all the while that the autumn child, the boy man, was still there, watching.

When he reached the part where the unfortunate suitor, blinded by the evil witch, had his sight restored by Ra-punzel's salt tears, Button grinned with satisfaction as several tentative, relieved smiles replaced the anxious looks on the faces of youngsters who were crowded around him, entranced. "And they lived happily ever after. . . ." he concluded. "And that's the end of the tale."

Some of the kids grabbed his hand and thanked him. Some begged for another story.

"You're really good at that," one parent said to But-ton. "Thank you." Others simply applauded.

"You sure have a way with kids," a grateful mother thanked him. "That's the first time he's stopped whining since we got here."

"I enjoy kids," Button declared pleasantly. "That's

what this event is all about." He continued fielding comments while the older brother retrieved the younger one and began leading him away. Then the boys paused and stared up at the castle. Button checked his camera. He had two shots left. By the time he looked up again, the boys had slipped away into the crowd. Button hid his disappointment behind his tight, public smile.

"You should put that story on tape and play it over the speakers," one father suggested while the audience still milled about. "Or maybe you could print it out and give out copies. But your telling of it is really good. I may be just a big kid myself," he added, "but it sure made all this come to life."

"Mister. Tell me about that one." A youngster pushed closer, catching Button's sleeve. "Tell another story," he pleaded.

"Another one?" Button replied dramatically, kidding with the little boy as he bent down and lifted him up to eye level. "I'll tell you what," he suggested, picking up on that father's idea. "Let's try making this a little more organized. We'll have a kids' storytime. I'll get the PA system set up and we'll try doing another story, loud enough so lots of folks can listen. We'll do Cinderella. Just give me a few minutes," he said, then strode off toward the communications tent. "Got a new idea," Button told Sandy Huff. "I'm going to have a technician set up the PA over near the south mound. We announce a story time for kids. Let's see what kind of response we get. If it works out, we'll figure a way to work some story times into the schedule during the next couple of weeks. "Get Mike down here to film this," he added. "Could be nice footage with the castle and all right behind us."

Roseanne Petty simply looked up, raising her dark eyebrows.

"You got it," Sandy answered him, putting in the call to the office.

By the time Mike arrived with the camera, the sun had moved lower in the sky, and Button was set up in the shadow of the south mound hoping his young audience would be cool as well as attentive.

"Okay, boys and girls," he began, his rich voice coming over the speaker like liquid honey. "It's Storytime at the Dunes." He paused while a few more latecomers skidded in and settled in a semicircle on the sand in front of him. "Once upon a time . . ." he began. Instantly the murmur of voices faded. Even some of the workers carving away on the east face of the mound behind him stopped to listen. Gradually a stillness settled over the crowd as Button's clear voice, electronically amplified, drifted over them.

Button told them the older version, from the Grimms' tale in which the two evil, conniving stepsisters chop off their toes and heels to get the slipper to fit. For a while, each one fools him, but some doves warn him of their trickery. Those same sisters have their eyes plucked out by the birds when they come to Cinderella's wedding at the end. The children grimaced, enjoying the grisly parts. And the camera clicked. Besides the videocameraman, there were other photographers, amateur and otherwise, circling the area, capturing Button and his audience on film.

Button squeezed his own eyes shut as he reached the part about the eyes, stressing that in the old tales, the bad guys, especially evil stepsisters, didn't get off lightly. "And that's the way it happened, once upon a time. . . ." His last words reverberated slightly. Button bowed from the waist, waving his arm melodramatically like he did years ago when he did his magic shows.

The kids started cheering.

"Thank you, thank you," he repeated, continuing the same flamboyant bow. "That's all for now, folks," he called out.

"Encore . . ." several teenagers called back. Then the younger kids joined in.

"Not today. Maybe later, over the weekend . . ." he replied. Then he saw the fellow from the Channel 8 remote unit moving in on him with microphone and cameras. It was the same reporter who had been at the briefing the morning after the assault.

"Nice job. You're quite a versatile showman," the reporter commented. "How about a short interview? You're the one who posted part of the reward in the abduction case, aren't you?"

With the visor shading his eyes, the sunblock on his nose, and the dark beard covering the lower part of his face, Button looked almost comical, considerably less official then he had that morning at the briefing with Bo Shepherd and Lieutenant Row. "Yes. I am," he replied.

"How about the interview? This fairy-story business was great."

"Okay," Button agreed. "Just let me clean up a bit." He cut across to the staff communications tent and borrowed Sandy's mirror. Hastily he wiped off the sunblock, combed his hair, and left the visor behind.

"You sure have a nice way with kids," the reporter said, nodding to his backup team to start shooting. "Let me just put together a lead-in." He hesitated, gathering his thoughts. "Okay. I've got it." He moved closer to Button and held the microphone between them.

He stared into the camera. "Good evening, this is Jeff

Wise. Two nights ago, an unfortunate incident involving a child happened here at the Dunes. But this evening as the sun set, the children here enjoyed a wonderful, magical experience.''

Button beamed, anticipating the impact this story would have on anyone considering whether to bring a child here after the James abduction. He couldn't have written a better script himself. Then it was Button's turn.

He talked of the added security measures, the wading pools and playground, and the magnificent scenes taking shape before their eyes. "And in about thirty minutes, we're having a sunset wedding," Button added, determined not to miss an angle. "Right up there by Prince Charming's castle.''

The reporter promised his audience wedding pictures on the late-night news. Button smiled into the camera for all of Florida. The few remaining sandsculptors gathered up their tools and started working their way down for the the day.

The technician who'd set up the PA system moved the microphone setup back into the communications tent. "Jack says to start playing that baroque tape," the technician told Sandy. "Something about putting everyone in the mood for the wedding.''

"I would have guessed he was planning more along the lines of 'There's No Business Like Show Business' or 'Hail to the Chief,' '' Roseanne Petty observed with a smirk. She'd been watching him work the crowd and the reporters and found something about Button's ever-present smile more than a little synthetic. "I'll tell you, that Button is a trip in himself. I think it must be time for me to go home and wash diapers and cook macaroni for my kids. I need a good dose of reality. . . .''

* * *

The fringed teal-blue-and-gold-striped canopy made the portable stage look like the setting for a pharaoh's throne. Illuminated by lights set underneath the rim of canvas, the group performing was surrounded by a golden glow. They seemed to be floating on a river of darkness. The music, gentle and free-flowing jazz, spilled out over the sea of onlookers, who had settled on blankets around the triple-ridged mountain of sand like a massive encampment of nomads. Picnic hampers, ice chests, wine bottles, and even an occasional candelabrum added to the pleasant, relaxed ambience.

"I could get used to this." Vince Ammons nuzzled Kitty's neck as he wrapped his arms around her. She settled back against him contentedly. After dinner, they had decided to come out and enjoy the free concert. Zach was stretched out on the blanket next to her, his head resting on her lap. His mouth was ringed in chocolate ice cream, the front of his shirt was streaked with drops that had escaped his licking, but he was blissfully asleep, lulled by the music and the cool soft breeze that swept overland and brought with it the scent of orange blossoms from some nearby grove.

"It's a good thing we're getting so much exercise during the day," Kitty noted. "Otherwise with all the good food and absolutely disgustingly irresistible desserts, we'd be getting roly-poly. We're going to be so spoiled when we get back to the real world."

"I'm glad we came," Vince said softly. "And I'm glad you decided to stay. Zach is having the time of his life."

"I think so," Kitty agreed. "He's got blisters on his hands from sailing that boat with his buddy, but he hasn't complained. At home, he'd insisted on having bandages up to his elbows."

"He's got a different image to maintain here," Vince

observed, smiling as he reached down and stroked Zach's pale hair. "Here he's just one of the kids. No one treats him like he's a little different. I think he'll come out of this feeling a lot better about himself."

"You're probably right."

"As long as you're so agreeable"—Vince broached his favorite subject again—"how about considering making this threesome official? Heck, if some off-the-wall outsiders can get married up there on our mound, so could we. When I said I could get used to this, I meant all of it. You, me, Zach. Even the part that comes next, whatever that is."

"I wouldn't want to get married up there in front of a lot of strangers," Kitty replied, sidestepping an answer. "I'm sure it was very romantic and picturesque, but that kind of thing isn't for me."

"What is for you?" Vince asked. "How about something small and intimate, maybe in one of the gardens. I'm not interested in the place, just in you. And the question is, are you interested in me? Permanently. Now this time I really want you to understand that I'm serious. Let's get married. I love seeing you over breakfast every day. I love going to bed with you at night. I just don't like the waking-up-in-separate-bedrooms part. I don't want to go back to driving across town every time I want to see you."

"This really has been very nice," Kitty admitted. "A little like living in paradise, though—"

"It's not the surroundings," Vince interrupted her. "Or the fringe benefits. We could be cooking burgers in the backyard and listening to Mozart on the CD. I'm not taken in by all the fancy stuff here. It's being with each other, being like a family, that feels more normal than at home."

"It does, doesn't it?" Kitty stared pensively at the light reflecting off Zach's pale hair.

"Does that mean yes?"

"It means maybe. No, more than maybe. It means I want to let the idea settle for a while." She looked at him, loving the familiar, faintly eager expression on his face. "I do love you, you know," she said gently. "I'm just a bit hung up on this independence thing."

"I've noticed," Vince murmured, lightly kissing the tip of her nose.

"And you know how I am about Zach. . . ."

"Like a mama tiger . . ." Vince kissed her again.

"But I do like this better than commuting. . . ."

"So that's a definite maybe," he said, smiling.

"At least." This time Kitty pressed her lips to his, caressing them more than kissing. Then Vince drew her closer, tracing a line of warm kisses from her lips to her earlobe then down toward the base of her throat. "Let's go back to the hotel," he murmured in a low, rich rumble.

"Mom . . ." Zach stirred. "I need to pee." He struggled to sit up, rubbing his eyes and blinking in the darkness.

"We're going back to the room," Kitty comforted him.

"I need to go now," Zach insisted.

"Okay. We'll detour to the portables," she agreed, standing then helping him to his feet.

"Ride me piggyback, Mom . . . please," Zach said sleepily.

"You're getting a little heavy for piggybacking," Kitty told him. But she sighed and looked down at his bare feet. "One of these days you're going to take off your darn shoes and lose them."

"I'm sorry."

"It's all right this time." She chuckled. "Climb aboard." She turned her back, bent down, and caught his bony knees with her arms as he held on. "Pitch me that towel?" she asked Vince. "I'll mop off the chocolate kid. How about you pick up this stuff and meet us over by the bathrooms?"

"I'll grab a couple of cups of coffee at the concession stand on the way."

"Coffee. I'd love some coffee." Kitty paused and stared down at him. "You are a real prince, Vince Ammons. I think we're moving well past maybe. . . ." She smiled then bumped Zach higher so his weight was on her hips. "But I don't think the place is here." She carried Zach off toward the row of portable units.

They weren't going to go near the place again. They'd agreed. But then the music started sometime in the afternoon. It filled the air and wound amid the trees and drifted over on the breeze. And even inside the cave, it pulsed in the air, barely audible, but tantalizing.

At first they only intended to get close enough to see what was happening there. The closer they came, the more the music surrounded them. Tommy made sure that they circled around, away from the place where he used to hide and watch. He didn't want to go back there, just in case someone was looking for him. So he took a different route all the way around the parking area, stopping every once in a while to observe. Then they moved on.

Lon spotted the fences first. Then the fence inside the fence where there were kids playing. Then they saw one fellow patrolling the area with the dog. So they broke off some leaves of the jimson and wild ginger and rubbed it over their bodies so the dog wouldn't pick up their scent. Then they crept farther around, downwind. They got there in time to see the females in pale dresses as fine as spiderwebs climb up to the top. There, the sand buildings stood with pointed towers aimed skyward like spears. The men in stiff gray suits and tight collars were already up there waiting. And the music changed and swelled as the female with the most spiderwebs came to join them. Then they stood there like statues, while a man with a wide ribbon over his shoulders moved his mouth. The sun sank lower, making the dresses transparent and turning everything to gold. The people stood awhile longer. Then one stiff-suited man took the female by the shoulders and kissed her. The music changed. The crowd below applauded. Some of the lights went on up top. And everyone came down the sloping road.

Colored bubbles and ribbons decorated the low cart that was waiting for them at the bottom. Everyone got in, and the one in front drove them around the mound. And they waved. The people applauded. Then the cart took them away, off toward the high-stepped building that had once again turned amber in the sunset.

Lon and Tommy waited after that, half expecting something else to happen. But it didn't. Only the music changed. No more pale-skinned ladies in dresses that floated in air came forward. There were many other people, far more than before, who came with chairs and blankets, and sat gazing up at the mountain while the music floated all around. The sun slipped below the horizon and finally was gone. Huge lights went on before the last glow left the sky.

Some men set up a platform and put a cover over it. They set out huge dark boxes with long wires like snakes trailing across the ground. Then new men in far different suits came, carrying boxes from which they took gleaming tools with strange shapes. When they lifted those tools, the old music stopped. New music, louder and pulsing and wonderful, boomed throughout the clearing. More people came to listen. Lon and Tommy understood that the new music came from the dark boxes and was made by the shiny tools they now could see the men strike and blow and push with their hands. And when some of the others who had gathered around stood and swayed and clapped and danced to the music, something stirred deep in the wetlanders' memory. There had been a time when their kind had made music and danced.

Gradually the entire area was cloaked in twilight, and Lon and Tommy sat a ways apart, each caught up watching the beautiful pale clean people move in and out of the lighted areas. And there were so many children. They had never before seen so many lovely creatures.

Lon was fascinated by the row of boxes where occasionally people would stand in line. Then a door would open, and the one who had been inside the box would come out again. Someone different would take his place. Only when the wind shifted and he caught the acrid odor, ever so faint, on the sweet night air, did he guess what they were doing inside there. Then it fascinated him even more. His kind had always used the woods, returning everything to nature.

Off to the side of the boxes, there were some pipes pointing up from the ground. The people would stop and push a handle and the water would flow out. The women came there, bringing small children. Low watched the women pour the water into their hands and scoop it to the small one's face, washing away the dirt or streaks of food there. Huddled in the dark, he found it strangely comforting. And more memories stirred.

He remembered the breeder woman back when she still had the light in her eyes, before the Great Blast.

She had often led her brother by the hand like these women did. She would bathe him in the springs, or pour water from a jug in the cave and rinse the boy clean. But the memory went far beyond this last breeder. Lon rubbed his hands together and remembered.

Even in the dark, he could tell they were stained with juices from the leaves and dirt from scavenging in the woods all day. He wished to hold out his hands and have one of the pale females rinse them clean. But his hands were like Tommy's and the elder's. Folds of skin between his knuckles held the dirt and made the stubby fingers look far different from the others'.

Suddenly he knew there had been a female once, someone who had washed and groomed him and held him close. He couldn't quite remember who she was, but some sense of her was still with him. She had been there. Back in the time when there was music and someone danced at night around the fire. Back before the elder and the others feuded and some part of their family went away south, away from the groves, following the retreat of the great crocodiles. Lon held his head and rocked to and fro, trying to remember, but his round dark eyes remained fixed on the creatures of the light.

The tall woman with hair of gold stood out from the rest. Her skin was darker tanned than most. Her body lean and harder. And she was strong. She carried the boy partway on her back, his slim arms grasping her around the shoulders, and his weight seemed not too great for her strength. Yet when the child stood down and leaned against her, his arm wrapped around her waist, she stroked the ivory hair of the boy with a gentleness that made Lon's chest grow tight. That gesture was familiar. He had stroked their boy like that. He had borne the boy on his shoulders. But in a time long before that memory, he knew that someone once held him. Someone had stroked his head. And he had been beautiful to her. And he sighed, this time for whatever he'd lost that made him no longer beautiful to anyone.

Lon watched and the woman waited while the boy disappeared into the box. Then he came out again and went right over to her. The woman took the boy with the moonlight hair, stopped by the upright pipe, and ran water over the cloth she carried. Then she wiped the dark streaks from the boy's face, smiling while she scrubbed him clean. She made him catch some water to wash his hands and use a part of the cloth to dry them. While she turned and let him climb upon her back again, the towel fell onto the ground. They walked off without it. And as her tall form wove through the crowd then finally disappeared into the darkness, Lon looked after her, forlorn. Some part of him longed to be closer to them, to pass among them as his kind once had done. The other part trembled at the thought.

When he could see neither the woman nor the child, he crossed his arms over his chest in a gesture of comfort, silently mourning things lost and things half-remembered. But he could not leave.

The two finally started home together when the music makers stopped and the crowd rapidly thinned. They circled around the lake like they had come, each silent, each drawn inward by his own thoughts. When they reached home, Tommy went in ahead and grabbed the breeder and took her to his bunk.

Lon was sickened by the prospect of having to listen, so he turned back toward the creek and sat there, cooling his feet in the dark water. Then he bent forward and saw the face that was reflected back at him by the moonlight-polished surface. The hair was long and wild, the beard matted. Even when they lived with their kinsmen in the great cave, he never looked like this. The breeder would use the shears to cut their hair and trim their beard. The elder showed them how to take the blade and scrape away the face hairs if they chose. And they would bathe while the breeder washed their clothes and hung them on the tree limbs to dry. They had not done any of that since the blasts. Now there was little he recognized in that reflection. Nothing he would want the child of moonlight to see.

In the stillness of the night, Lon started back to the place alone. This time he went straight to it. The man with the dog was still there, or perhaps it was another man and another dog. Lon only knew that he must not be seen. When they were well past, he climbed a tree next to the fence and leaped over. Crouched low and smelling of leaves and ginger root, he hurried toward the upright pipe and ran his hand through the grass and dirt next it. The cloth was gone. Still huddled close to the ground, he crept farther out. Finally he found it lying in the dark grass. It smelled of something delicious and sweet. Clutching his memento, Lon went straight to the white box where the boy had been. Silently he opened the door and stepped in and closed it behind him. He sat there a long time, stroking the sweet towel, sniffing the exotic odors, and remembering the pale, clean, beautiful people. He stayed there until he heard the man and the dog pass on their rounds.

The next target was the tent where he'd seen the people stop and write on the paper that the women had. Usually one would unroll a strip of colored ribbon and cut it then fasten it to their arm. The ribbons were different colors, but Lon knew that no one went onto the mound without wearing one. But it was the shears he remembered glinting in the sunshine. He wanted them.

Huddled among the boxes at the back of the staff communications tent, Lon waited until the man and the dog passed by one more time. He had found the box of ribbon, heavy plastic strips of red, white, yellow, blue, and green. And he found the shears, two pairs of them. So he cut an arm's length of each color to take home with him. Then he placed the ribbons and one pair of shears in the center of the boy's towel and rolled it up so he could tuck it in his shirt. He wanted his hands free, so when the guard passed, he could run toward the fence and vault over it.

The moon was high when Lon reached a crescent-shaped curve of the spring-fed lake that the men had made behind the colony of new buildings. The low area had once been a slough through which the heavy summer rains would drain when the wetland was inundated. But the men had dredged the marsh area to make it deeper. They had blasted and set up dams of their own. Now that curved slough was filled with crystal water year round and formed the most distant point of the system of waterways in which he'd seen them sail the sleek small boats with pointed sails. Lon generally avoided this part of the territory by day, but now its surface caught the moonlight and no trees obscured his view.

Lon peeled off his clothes one piece at a time, then he slipped into the water and wet himself. Standing waist-deep, he scrubbed each garment again and again, holding it up and letting the water trickle over his palm until it ran clear. Then he squeezed and twisted them and waded onto shore and hung each piece separately on the nearby bushes while he proceeded.

He waited until the surface of the inlet stilled so he

could crouch over it and see himself. It took him a few tries to get the shears to work. He practiced first on the low grass along the water's edge. Then he ran his fingers through his wet hair and clipped away the matted ends. When he had shortened it all over, he stuck his head underwater, then smoothed it down. But it bristled. So he started over, trimming it closer this time, carefully avoiding his ears as he clipped around them. Then he pressed the shears close against his chin and clipped his face hairs, as short as he could get them. He'd seen a few men like that in the crowd, their jaws covered in smooth dark hair, shiny hair, like the panther. Even in the cool evening air, he was sweating and his hands would tremble as he strained to hold the shears just so. He stopped from time to time and slid into the water to calm himself, then he come out and crouched, motionless, until the ripples subsided and he could see himself again.

When he cut off the ledge of hair that hung over his lips, he had to smile at the image looking up at him. Men like that came to the fishing camp with caps pushed back on their head. Men like that had driven the trucks and bulldozers that cleared the land. He had seen men like that.

He knew he could pass among them.

Lon walked naked back to the cave, carrying his damp clothes over his shoulder and his towel and ribbons and shears in a tight bundle against his chest. His heavy body hair glistened in the moonlight and his skin felt tight. Outside the cave, he hooked his clothes onto tree limbs so they would wave and dry in the breeze. Then he listened. Other than the sound of breathing, there was no noise inside. Soundlessly Lon crept into the dark interior and felt his way to his bunk, clutching his bundle like a pillow beneath his cheek. And the sweet smell of the child with moonlight hair filled his senses. Smiling still, he fell asleep.

Just before dawn, Tommy rolled onto his stomach then groaned. It hurt again. It hurt bad enough before he fell asleep, but now it throbbed. He eased over on his side, scratching himself carefully. He'd almost rubbed it raw last night, humping away again and again on the breeder. But she smelled of stale food and sweat and urine, and he kept losing it. Even if he held his breath and tried to think of the beautiful children, it would still get soft and he'd have to stop. Then he'd shove her aside and try to doze off, but the smooth bodies would drift into his dreams, delicious and ripe and tight, and he'd feel it stiffen again. Then he'd roll her over and try to pound away to get some release. But it hadn't worked.

Tommy held it and pissed on the floor of the cave where the breeder was sleeping. The sharp, irregular pains made him wince. It jerked and spat erratically and sent warm liquid down her backside. His smell this time. She didn't even move. Her flaccid rump caught the faint light of morning from the entrance, and what little stiffness was there diminished in his hand. Tommy looked at her then stuffed it back in his pants. He knew what he needed.

Tommy took the logboat most of the way, lying almost flat in it so his head wouldn't touch the low branches where the snakes liked to spread out in the morning in ambush for birds and mice coming down to drink. The current was strong enough to move him swiftly downstream; coming back, he'd have to row. But he'd feel better then.

Tommy left the boat wedged up into the overgrown section where the creek narrowed and turned southeast.

Then he walked overland through the swamp hardwoods bordering the stream, weaving through cypress and tupelo, cinnamon fern and wild pine, until the ground beneath them stopped feeling so spongy and he knew he'd come near the ridge where the railroad tracks once were. He followed the old track bed, planning to follow it until he hit the strip of asphalt road that ended in the campground.

There were trailers there year round now, not just in the summer when they came to swim or the winter when the deer were out and hunting was good. Since the groves died in the frost and the men began clearing ground downriver and cutting in roads, several of the old fishing camps had turned into colonies of metal homes on wheels. There were always kids playing around the place. He'd come this way before and stopped, remembering the place just in case he needed it one day. It was still early. Cars and trucks were parked alongside all the metal homes. Bicycles and swings stood empty. There was no aroma of food cooking. Tommy figured he'd have to wait a while.

But someone else was up early, too. Tommy backed into the bushes and crouched low when he saw the kid. Hair still rumpled from sleep, he was wearing nothing but swim trunks and tennis shoes, and he was eating a slice of cheese. Fishing pole in hand, the boy carried a bucket and line and was heading back toward the creekside, ready to try his hand in the brackish water where the bloodlike swirls of tannin seeped from tree roots and turned the clear spring water golden brown.

Tommy had come in the back route deliberately, partly because he didn't like swimming in the brackish water. The other reason was that too many windows faced that way, overlooking the view of the creek and a small swimming area and boat dock set in there. Anyone inside those metal homes could be watching. But now the kid with the fishing pole was heading down there in plain view of the whole circle of trailers. Tommy waited to see where he stopped.

Just as he neared the water's edge, the kid turned left, keeping parallel to the water, but moving farther upstream purposefully, off in the direction where Tommy had stowed his boat. Tommy gave the kid a headstart, watching the trailers and sniffing the air for any suggestion of activity. Somewhere to the right, he heard water swoosh. Then a door shut. Then silence. Glancing at the sky, he could see the sun already streaming through the trees and he knew he'd better make it quick.

Hastily he retraced his steps along the track bed then cut back through the bushes toward the creek, ahead of the boy. He stayed back from the edge, listened, then moved on, closing in on him. With his fishing pole propped under his arm, the boy was preoccupied, unwrapping a slice of cheese when Tommy grabbed him. The pole fell forward and caught on a root. But Tommy's chest was pounding and his face felt hot, and all he wanted to do was have his release. With one hand clamped over the kid's mouth and his other around the small body, he dragged him back against a fallen tree, intoxicated by the scent and the softness and pure excitement of what he was doing. Then he slammed the kid facedown over it, knocking out whatever air he was holding in. Tommy ripped the boy's bathing trunks off. And this time, it didn't take long at all.

When it was over, Tommy took the fishing pole. He left the kid, still alive, draped over the tree. He knew he had to hurry. It was getting on into the morning. He'd have a long trip back upriver, and Lon would be waiting. Somewhere along the way he'd figure out a story that would do.

Chapter 6

"WILL YOU LOOK AT THE CROWD DOWN THERE."

Two hours into work Saturday morning, Vince Ammons had brought his levels and measuring tape all the way across to the north mound to recheck the proportions on the Sleeping Beauty castle. More block-shaped and Romanesque than his delicate, multispired one for Prince Charming on the north mound, this one was set lower against the skyline, and the contrast in styles was deliberate. Vince had patterned this one after the castle of Rummell Hissar, built by Mohammed II to guard the Turkish Straits. In keeping with the north mound's nautical theme, eventually a huge sailing ship, waves, sea creatures, and even Pinocchio's whale would be crafted below.

Like the masses of throned brambles clinging to the castle walls, the overall effect was wild and strange and exciting. This castle wasn't intended to be pretty or tall, just formidable. Its crenellated upper edges and part of the rounded tower formed a plateau around the uppermost ridge of the northern peak where the enormous winged dragon sat poised, as if it had just touched down. The dragon had taken Kevin and his crew most of the week to complete. He'd taught his volunteers to press and polish its serpentine surface with trowels until the textured wings and sinuous body were totally covered with burnished scales that caught and bounced back the light and gleamed like a coat of armor.

Myron Hansen had adapted his talent with plant design to the construction of the dragon's free-flowing fiery breath, half the length again of the beast itself. It spilled out in ominous rolling clouds and spread over the castle walls, ending in pointed tongues, pale flames of sand. Compared with the elegant, civilized town scenes that were set at various levels down Vince's north mound, the south mound was dramatic, primitive, and bursting with energy. But when everyone vacated the mound the night before and had a chance to look at the progress from a different perspective, the cannon just didn't look right. Ten cannons set into the wall openings, giving the fortress a warlike appearance, looked too large for the structure. And the cannon balls carved in stacks next to them were larger still. All ten cannons had been beautifully done by a trio of volunteers the day before. Now the team leaders had called Vince in to confer over the weapons' fate.

Vince measured them against the other architectural details of the buildings set at a similar height. No matter how they rationalized, the guns were oversized. They had to go.

"Sorry fellas," Kevin had said, shrugging, when he

broke the news. "I know how much work you put in on these. I should have been more on top of this." He'd been working on the back side of both the center and south peaks on Friday and was too engrossed in blocking in the Beast for Beauty and the Bears for Goldilocks to catch the error in scale on the cannons. He'd just been glad that the three volunteers were as talented as they were. Now they had to be talented on a lesser scale. "This is when art becomes a character-building experience," Kevin said philosophically, rubbing his reddish beard and eyeing the smooth barrel of the first cannon with a dark, regretful look. The mouth of each cannon was hollowed out deep enough to hold a strong shadow and give the illusion that the opening ran clear down the barrel. The other nine were equally realistic, and the workmanship was simply beautiful.

"Just frame them in, wet them down. Carefully . . ." Vince stressed. "Then reduce the scale." He even had several two-by-two standards cut and labeled so the volunteers who had built the ten cannons would be able to produce consistent-sized replacements. "Just be very careful," he warned them. They were going to be working above and among some already finished pieces. There was a real danger that the hoses or merely the movement on the parapets would start a wall crumbling or kick off a minor landslide below.

"Let's get right on this," Kevin directed, trying not to sound as glum as he felt. "This is all part of the game," he said, reminding himself as well as the others. Then with the three volunteer sculptors and a couple of standby shovelers, he began helping them reconstruct the wooden molds and start over.

Vince had headed back, taking a meandering route so he could troubleshoot any other areas that might be out of scale. He'd stopped and had been watching Kitty working on Hansel and Gretel's witch when he finally turned and noticed that the area around the base of the mound, beyond the roped-off moat, was totally covered with umbrellas, chairs, blankets, and lots of people. "Kitty. Take a look. We figured it would pick up this weekend, but this is really something."

"If it keeps getting thicker down there, we may be trapped by the end of the week," Kitty responded, wiping the sand from her spatula against the leg of her light cotton baggy pants. Now that the Texas storm had fizzled and the overcast sky was clear, she'd started wearing the long pants to protect herself from windburn as well as the sun. "Maybe they'll have to lift us out of here by helicopter like they did the big molds."

"We'll have a problem with Paul Feneau, then," Vince noted. "He doesn't fly."

"He may have to adapt . . ." Kitty was staring down at the mass of people and the bright striped canopies that marked the sites of the concession stands. One for souvenirs and T-shirts had been added next to the staff communications tent. Hundreds of aqua shirts and visors dotted the scene below. "This is really staggering," she said quietly, her sea blue eyes narrowed against the glare of the midmorning sun. "I know crowds get bigger on the weekends, but we didn't have attendance like this at the other castles, not until they were nearly finished. There are so many people down there, and we've still got a whole week to go. Next Saturday when they hold the opening ceremonies, the crowd will be unbelievable."

"Button was right on target with this idea," Vince remarked. "He tapped a ready audience, a bigger one than he projected. I guess the other castles helped create an interest. Folks who missed Bluebeard or Atlantis are making sure they don't miss this one. And the ones who worked on the smaller castles or just went to see them sure don't want to pass up a chance to check out this big baby. Besides, the coverage has been really well orchestrated. Button does a real good job with the media.'' The night before, both the six o'clock and eleven o'clock newscasts, had aired clips of Button's storytelling. On the later show, they'd interspersed clips of the sunset wedding with Button's telling of Cinderella, and the juxtaposition had been very romantic and highly effective.

"Now that he's got them here, I just wonder what he's going to do with all these people," Kitty said, still gazing downward at the crowd. "The parking lots are already full." No longer visible as black patches beyond the surrounding ring of trees, the north lot and an area further east were lined with vehicles. Like giant caterpillars, the two shuttles now each pulled two additional cars, continuously ferrying people in and out of the parking areas.

"They're talking about taking the dozers off to cut in a couple of additional lots this weekend. They're even thinking of running a second road behind us out to the highway so they can make that section one way." He pointed to the fork just inside the entrance where the road separated at the foot of the Great Sphinx. Cars were lined up bumper to bumper while somewhere below, Otto Breshears and his traffic staff searched for spaces to park them.

"I can't imagine all these people just sitting here all day in the sun." Kitty shook her head. "At least when we did the castles at the beach, they could go swimming or take a walk and look around the shops. Most of them are too big for the wading pool and the lake isn't ready for swimmers.''

"I was down to the communications tent a little while ago. Button's been working on entertainment. He's got everything from bands to storytelling to fashion shows to dance troupes to tours of the Dunes layout. And we've got another sunset wedding,'' he added pointedly. "Only this one is costing someone's papa a cool thousand to rent the site for thirty minutes.''

Kitty looked up at him. "A thousand? He's started charging . . . ?''

"I don't' know if it's Button's idea or his boss Jacobson's or if it simply came from the Dunes powers-that-be, but that's the latest. We're talking the law of supply and demand here,'' Vince said solemnly. "There are only so many sunsets and one castle. There are folks willing to put out big bucks to have this as a backdrop in their wedding albums. He could up the price and still book them solid.''

"I think that's getting a bit into the crass and commercial bracket,'' Kitty muttered.

"Accommodating a crowd like this raises the overhead. I have a feeling the marketing end of it is only going to get worse,'' Vince cautioned her. "It may be a good thing that we're a little out of it up here. I think our artistic sensibilities would get a bit bruised on ground level. We don't even have to listen to all the announcements.''

"What announcements?'' Kitty had heard only the soft-rock sounds on her headset all morning while she blocked out figures, finished the faces, then left the next stage to red- and blue-banded volunteers, trained carvers and apprentices. Later in the day, she'd circle back, putting in the finishing touches or whatever accent details were needed before the crew of sprayers came to hold it all in place.

"Wait until lunch. You'll hear enough then. Button's been doing some Dunes promos. They're pulling in extra trolleys to shuttle folks out to the model homes and condos for tours. You pay two bucks a head for the tour, but the hotel will credit that toward lunch or dinner in one of their dining rooms."

Kitty gave him a long deliberate look. "Does that mean the hotel restaurants will be packed? Maybe we should order in pizza tonight. Avoid the crowds. Besides, I'm tired of dressing up and going to restaurants."

"How about having a picnic," Vince suggested. "Remember how Zach said there were all kinds of gazebos and pavilions out on that Nature Trail? He said he and Chris stop at a big one when they take off in the feluccas. Maybe we could have the kitchen do us up a picnic dinner and go out there for a while. We could watch the sunset from the wilds."

"I could go for that," Kitty agreed. "Just have them throw in a couple of flashlights and a can of bug spray. Between the gators and the mosquitoes, it could be miserable. I want to *have* dinner, not *be* it."

"I'll have Sandy Huff see what she can do for us," Vince promised. Then he stopped, listening intently to the call coming in over the headset.

"Shit . . ." he muttered under his breath. "Someone left the hose run too long on one of Kevin's cannons. "A hunk of wall collapsed. I've got to go over there to help them improvise."

"You want me to come with you?"

"I don't think so. You keep on with what you're doing."

"If you need a hand, call me. See you at lunch." Kitty

watched him alk off, then went back to deepening the lines in the wizened face of her witch.

"Ladies and gentlemen . . . welcome to the Dunes and to the construction of the world's biggest sandcastle. . . ." Jack Button stood on a raised platform backing the central mound and spoke over the public-address system, sounding like P. T. Barnum hawking his sideshow of marvels and curiosities. Beneath his official visor, his brown eyes, glassy and hard, assessed the crowd. The head count was awesome.

"We've got a lot of entertainment lined up for you this afternoon," he promised, "but first I want to introduce a few members of the Flordel Corporation who are responsible for bringing this fabulous event to you." Button hadn't really wanted to do any of this corporate hype until the the official opening ceremonies the next weekend when the storybook sandcastle would be finished and open for public tours. But Stan Jacobson had seen the excellent media coverage, generally with Jack Button featured, and he had suggested a few informal presentations over the pre-Easter weekend might please the executive board. He'd even requested complimentary T-shirts for the board members, so if they chose to drop by that Saturday or Sunday, they could look more like part of the Dunesfest event.

Only three of the seven executives were there for the midday Saturday greeting. Stan Jacobson was one of them. Jacobson was wearing a panama hat to cover his baldness, the aqua tee, and white shorts, but his legs, spindly and pale, made Button smile. "This is our director of expansion. . . ." Button introduced him, then went on to present Burns the comptroller and Graham, director of sales. There was a polite round of applause, then Button went into his monologue about Flordel making "this paradise, in the middle of nowhere, accessible to everything."

"For those of you interested in a guided tour of those parts of the resort already completed, there will be shuttles scheduled every hour. Seating will be limited. The trip takes forty minutes. The price is two dollars, refundable in any of the dining facilities at the Grand Nile Hotel. We have a wildlife refuge area, a championship caliber golf course, housing and business areas, a shopping area, and fabulous gardens and waterways. Of course, you will be required to remain seated in the shuttle to assure that the current residents are not inconvenienced in any way by these tours. They've already purchased their part of paradise. . . ." he added, smiling broadly. "If you would like more in-depth information after the shuttle ride, Mr. Graham here has a staff on hand who will gladly give personal tours through the models to qualified investors." Graham had insisted on inserting last phrase, just to keep out the "riffraff." He didn't want his salespeople wasting their time and efforts on anyone who could not afford the Dunes' prices.

"There are also brochures and maps of the grounds at the communications tent," Button noted, sweeping one hand in that direction with a showmanlike flourish. "And as you will see from the artist's renderings posted there, the future plans for the Dunes are very comprehensive and very exciting. Cafés, schools, recreation facilities, theaters, and an Olympic-size pool and gym area will all be spread over these beautiful surroundings. Anyone interested in the ride, please sign up at the tent and you will be given a departure time." He completed that portion of the midday greeting ceremony and moved on.

Graham, Burns, and Jacobson stood beaming in the background.

Afterward, a taped musical filler played over the PA system while a live three-piece combo set up on stage. Button and his colleagues took a brief tour of the mound, stopping occasionally while the Dunes' official cameraman, Mike Izor, videotaped their progress. Graham and Burns each took a turn shoveling. Jacobson mopped his brow with a linen handkerchief and posed behind them, rubbing his pale manicured hands protectively. Then, hot and sweating, they walked down again and sat in the shade of the communications tent, sipping lemonade with some of the sandsculptors who'd come out of the heat for a break. By then, the combo had been playing for half an hour and was ready for an intermission. Button checked his watch and headed toward the stage.

"We'll be having a storytime for youngsters of all ages," Button announced as the band members left the platform. He lifted the hand mike from the pole and strolled casually across the stage.

"Here at the Dunes, we believe in bringing fantasy to life," he began, sending his silky voice out over the crowd. "Twice a day we set aside time to tell one of the tales that are being sculpted on the hillside behind us. So, if you will send the kids up front and let the taller folks gather around behind them, we'll begin our tale in a few minutes." Button smiled down at the group of little ones already pushing their way to the foot of the platform. "Now let's all take it easy and be very polite to each other." He bent forward and coaxed them into place. "Just spread out your blanket," he told one child gently, all the while speaking into the microphone. "That's right, son. Great. Now how about letting that little fellow sit right next to you. We're going to be doing

'The Pied Piper' and you may like to have a friend near.''
He looked closely at the second child, a dark-eyed fellow
of eight or nine with caramel-colored skin and carved
features, androgynous and exotic, like an Egyptian
sculpture. For an instant, his good-humored public smile
softened.

The lad blinked up at Button thankfully, shyly, and
Button knew he had to get that boy's picture for himself.
Whatever ethnic blend had produced him, the boy was
elegant and beautiful and brimming with the innocent
sexuality that only a child possessed. But Button could
teach him to explore all his possibilities. Long lashes cast
shadows on the lad's cheekbones, and his slender body,
just beginning to show the muscular understructure of
youth, was smooth and bare. And soft. Button rubbed
his fingertips unconsciously. He could imagine how soft
he would feel. And he was painfully shy, like Button had
been when he was a boy. But this one was on his territory, too close to home. And Button wasn't about to make
a mistake now. He'd come too far. He'd been too careful.
He'd changed too much. But he could get a picture. And
in the solitude of his condo, he could imagine.

"Okay, folks, gather 'round." Button stood, resuming
his carnival-barker mien. "Come on, boys and girls, let's
hear the tale of the Piper who came with his magic pipe
to rid the city of rats." He pointed to the valley where
the southern, city peak flowed into the central, country
ridge. There two young village children, carved from a
single mold, hung back watching as the caped Piper stood
beside a curving river, playing his pipes. Behind him was
a horde of large, plump rats, all courtesy of Paul Feneau,
eighty-four-year-old volunteer Elizabeth Frye, and their
sculpting trainees.

The rats were enormous. Some were scurrying. Some

were perched up on their back feet. Some of them were already shown in the water, nothing but their chubby feet and open mouths poking out of the river of sand. One playful fellow floated on his back. But beyond the bridge that the Piper would eventually cross was a gaping cave, convincingly crafted, which would swallow up and close over the children that the cheated Piper would lead away. The children in the audience nudged each other excitedly, anxious for Button to begin.

That was when he saw him. Standing back a ways among the teenagers and adults to the rear of the group of seated youngsters, a young man, maybe eighteen, was watching him, expressionless, chewing gum patiently as if he knew that sooner or later Button would look his way.

The arms were tanned and muscular, hands propped on his hips. The open-necked sports shirt was unbuttoned, showing off a bare, hairless chest, but even there the muscle definition was clear. The razor-cut hair, clean and sandy gold, caught the light. The youth himself was like a statue, slim-hipped, athletic, not as tall as Button, and motionless. Except for the relentless rhythm of the gum chewing.

Button didn't let his eyes linger on the youth. He ripped them away the second he felt that first tremor of recognition. Then he focused his attention in a safe zone, above the heads of the crowd, hoping he was mistaken. But even if he wasn't, he knew how to handle it. He would not offer any kind of confirmation, any acknowledgment.

Without losing his relaxed demeanor, Button pulled out his amber-lensed glasses, deliberately masking his eyes so the quick furtive glances that he darted in the young man's direction were not noticeable. Besides, the

glasses made him look almost handsome, and with the
beard, definitely more sophisticated. He was a new man,
slimmer, more dapper, more imposing. Button's palms
were beginning to sweat, and his stomach knotted. But
the public smile and the easy banter with the youngsters
at the platform drop-off continued unchanged while his
mind raced, trying to place the face that he was certain
was much younger when the two had last met.

He hated it when he saw them grown up. All the softness was gone, from their bodies and from their eyes.
He liked them the way they were in his pictures, shy,
trusting, gentle, unquestioning. He dreaded the time
when the resistance crept into those eyes like glacial ice.
That's when he let them go. He'd make up one story or
another, about him changing jobs or moving or having
some peculiar illness, whatever fabrication would work
best with that particular kid. Regardless, once he saw the
turning point approaching, he'd break it off. And he'd go
cold turkey for a while.

But there was always another child on the fringe. A
lonely, shy child, anxious to be loved, desperate to
please, easy to win over. And the pictures always worked.
He'd start out with innocent ones, with the kid fully
clothed. And he'd hug him. Maybe get him laughing with
a few magic tricks. Then they'd play with the camera and
take pictures of each other. Then Button would set the
automatic timer and get some of them together, just
clowning around. But they'd be hugging and touching.
Sometimes it took weeks to get to that point. But it was
groundwork that paid off later.

Soon the old pictures would get boring. Button would
pull out some of his special pictures of boys in the shower
together or swimming or in a bath. Naked. He'd wait for
just the right moment and tell the kid he looked better

than those others, and he'd get him to take his shirt off, then his pants. He always came up with the right words. Eventually he'd get the boy to pose naked, usually in the shower with water streaming over him. And then he'd help the boy dry off, praising him all the while, telling him how much better he was than those ''amateurs'' in the other pictures, admiring his smooth, bare body. And touching clean damp skin.

That part always gave Button a hard-on. Even through his clothes, it would be obvious. And that was exactly what he wanted. While he dried the kid off, he'd joke about it with the boy. ''Look at this, Boy, it feels like a piece of pipe. Go ahead, feel it. Does yours do that? Let me show you how to make it do it. Come on, I bet yours is really beautiful when it's hard.'' He'd show the kid pictures of other little boys with hard-ons, convincing the kid that there was nothing wrong with what they were doing. He'd get the kid to admit how good it felt.

That was a turning point of a different sort. After that, sex and play and friendship all got wound up together, and they never took a backward step. There would always be more touching, more showing off, and more pictures. Sometimes of the boy. Sometimes of them together. Sometimes ones from Button's special collection showing people doing what he wanted this boy to do next. And because it was always there in pictures, it was somehow acceptable. Then they'd do it and it would become real.

That's when he threw in the clincher, whichever lecture he figured would work with this particular kid. Button would make it clear that he and the boy shared a secret that could cause trouble. ''Other people wouldn't understand. They haven't learned to be free like you and me. They could even put me in jail if you told anyone. Then we couldn't go places together anymore. I couldn't be your friend." That was one angle Button took, especially if the kid's family wasn't well off, and the boy had grown accustomed to the things Button could buy him.

Then there was another tack. "If anyone found out, they'd blame your parents. They'd put your name and their names in the paper. Everyone would know. All the kids at school would tease you. Your parents would be humiliated. They'd hate you. You'd be all alone."

Sometimes another kind of fear worked better. "You know when you took that watch and then did me off? If the cops found out about it, they'd call that hustling. Look at these photos. Look what you're doing. The pictures never lie. They'd say you were trading sex for money. That's a crime." He'd always assure the boy that he'd never tell. Then he'd lead him one step further along a tightrope that had no net waiting to catch him. And he'd tell himself that he loved the boy; it was not the sex.

But the boys grew up. And everything would change. Sometimes it was because their body was developing and the differences made Button uncomfortable. Sometimes it was that shift in their eyes. But it would happen. Button would have to let them go. Sometimes he would mourn awhile. Often he was more relieved than sad. Then he would find someone younger, someone to make it all new again. Someone shy, and trusting, and lonely.

The eyes following his movements across the platform were not shy at all. They were remote, unfathomable, and Button found them strangely exhilarating. He was a new man. More important than ever before. No kid from the past could intimidate him. Certainly not here where he was the one in charge.

"Once upon a time in Germany, there was a little town called Hamlin, nested between the hills." Button launched into his storytelling, prancing, posturing, and altering his voice as he acted out all the parts. The narrowed eyes remained locked onto him like radar, but Jack Button kept his own eyes on the faces of the children or somewhere out there in the safe zone.

"All the citizens were horrified when suddenly there were ugly rats everywhere. What can we do?" Button asked rhetorically.

"How about traps?" he suggested in a deep bass voice.

"No. It would take too many traps for all these rats," he answered himself.

"How about bringing in cats?" he suggested.

"The cats all ran away. They're afraid of these big rats," Button responded in a falsetto voice that made the children giggle.

"Then what shall we do?" Button paused, looked at the small upturned faces, then held the microphone out to them, inviting them to answer.

"Get Robocop." Button rolled his eyes at that kid.

"Dirty Harry." He shook his head.

"Rambo."

"Call the Pied Piper," one little boy yelled out.

"Call the Pied Piper. . . ." Button crowed approvingly, really getting into the performance. A few people cheered good-humoredly. The kid that called out the correct answer turned beet red. Button could tell the crowd was with him. And he knew that the youth out there was watching him, witnessing how he could hold an audience. Button would really give him a show.

Then Button described how the Piper agreed to play a particular tune, since he had a special magic one for every living creature. The strange haunting tune coaxed the rats out of town. Delirious from the music, they danced along the narrow, winding road out of town and threw themselves into the river and were drowned.

"Every single one . . ." Button assured the wide-eyed children. "But when the Piper went to collect his money, the mayor of the town refused to pay. He weasled out of the bargain. He claimed that since the rats had drowned themselves, they owed the Piper nothing."

"Nothing . . . ?" Button said, walking slowly across the stage. "Nothing?" Then in a low voice, continued. "So that very day the Piper played a different tune in Hamlin town. A softer, more enchanting tune. And this time it was the children who followed him when he took the narrow, winding road out of town." Button paused. "When the Piper got to the river, he crossed over the bridge," he said, gliding his hand in an arc toward the bridge high up on the sand mound. Believing eyes saw what his words conjured up.

"The children crossed over the bridge. They danced off after the Piper into a great cave that opened in the side of the mountain. Only one child, a little lame boy with a crutch, couldn't keep up with the others. And when the great mouth of the cave closed all the others inside, he was the only one left behind."

Button came closer to the front edge of the platform. "And for many years in Hamlin, the little lame boy was without playmates. No children laughed or jumped rope in the streets. There was only silence and sorrow." The smaller children sat openmouthed, looking at Button. The two he'd persuaded to share a blanket held hands and sat close. He crooked his finger at the kid who'd called out the answer about the Piper, and that child obediently stood up and moved closer. "And that's why we always have to keep our promises and remember to pay the Piper." He reached down one hand and plucked a nickel from behind the child's ear. He placed it in the delighted child's palm. Then he produced another nickel from the other ear.

"Here's a souvenir for helping me out up here," Button said, handing the lad a child-sized Dunesfest T-shirt.

"Wow . . ." The kid took it and turned, grinning, to show his folks.

"Me too, mister," some of the other kids pleaded. The spell of the story was broken, and the other children scrambled to their feet and clustered around him, each begging to have a shirt. "Sorry." He shrugged, empty-handed. Button deliberately didn't bring any more T-shirts. He figured this would happen. There were plenty of them on sale at the souvenir tent he'd had set up next to the staff communications tent. The free one was just to whet their appetites. Once they saw this kid with one, all the others would get after their folks to buy them one, too. He knew kids.

"Sorry, I don't have any more shirts with me. But I might find another nickel," he said calmly, plucking another coin from another child's nose this time. The parents laughed and applauded. They took pictures. They thanked him and reminded their youngsters to thank him, too. And when Button looked up, his audience was dwindling away, and the young man whose silent presence had haunted him throughout his recital was gone.

"That was excellent. Mike got the whole thing on video," Sandy Huff informed him when Button stepped into the shade of the staff communications tent. "And the sound man got a separate tape of it like you asked, so if we're ever in a pinch, we've got one on file." Button nodded and got himself a cool drink.

"That was real good," Buddy Pardo congratulated him. "I have a little nephew who'd have eaten that stuff up. When's the next show?"

"Tonight. Six o'clock." Sandy Huff answered for him while Button took a deep drink of lemonade.

"I think I'll get my sister to bring him out here. This is really great." Pardo kept nodding. "Sure wouldn't want him to miss out on a show like that."

"Everyone seems to enjoy it," Button replied, standing slightly behind Pardo and scanning the passing crowd. He couldn't see the somber young man anywhere, but there was a cluster of kids crowding around the adjacent tent holding up official Dunesfest T-shirts while their folks checked them for size. A lot of parents had their wallets out. Sales would be good. Button glanced at his copy of the day's schedule then looked at his watch. "I think I'll run over to the hotel for a while. I'll be back about 1:30," he announced.

When Button took the golf cart and made a circuit of the mound before doing the six o'clock story session, Bo Shepherd rode with him. "Everything looks pretty good so far," Bo reported. "No one's spotted Quasimodo. No one's reported anything lost or stolen. We've had nothing other than a few fools who drank more than they should, and a few others who got overheated needed a shot of oxygen or a whiff of ammonia and time out of the sun to cool off."

Button nodded, relieved. The weekend crowd had been a little more boisterous and generally a lot younger than those who were out there during the past week. The clothing had become decidedly more casual and there was less of it. Even without a swim area available for adults, bathing suits were everywhere, some little more than swatches of fabric, strategically placed. The booth dispensing suntan-lotion samples had been busy all day, and they'd had to keep restocking supplies of the larger-sized products they had for sale. Dunesfest visors were selling at a record rate. The lines at the concession stands stayed six deep.

"Wait until the sun drops." Button eyed the acres of blankets with sun-reddened bodies. "They'll get cool quick. Then we let the aroma of chili dogs and french fries get to them. They have to pass the T-shirts to get to the food. One way or another, we'll warm them up again, for a price."

"I'll tell you one thing I don't like about those shirts they're selling." Bo narrowed his steely eyes. "They sure make everyone look an awful lot alike. If someone does get out of line or turns up missing, I sure hope the description doesn't include wearing a Dunesfest shirt."

"At ten bucks a pop for tees and twenty for sweat-shirts, they're pulling in a lot of money," Button responded.

Bo said nothing. He simply scanned the wading pools and playground area and frowned. There were an awful lot of kids wearing Dunesfest shirts. All the same color.

"Welcome to an evening at Dunesfest." At six o'clock on the dot, Button greeted the crowd from center stage on the canopied platform. Tanned, slimmer than he'd been in years, he assumed his master-of-ceremonies pose and began announcing the upcoming program, working the crowd. "How many of you are from Pasco County?" he asked. The locals cheered. "And how many of you are from Orange County?" He went on, choosing increasingly distant locations. "Any from Georgia?" Each time he returned their shout with a hearty "Welcome to the Dunes." But the loud exchange did precisely what he expected it to do. It brought the spectators.

Then he saw the face again, and the unreadable eyes. The youth was standing there, staring. This time he had his shirt off. And then Button realized why he hadn't

spotted the fellow in the crowd when he'd driven around
the mound that afternoon. He was banded. Red. Apprentice sculptor. Button knew the system. You didn't start
out red. You started out white, with a shovel. The young
fellow would already have put in some time shoveling to
be promoted to red. And the reds were the ones up top
working on the tricky stuff where Button wouldn't even
think to look. For a fleeting second, their eyes met. The
youth almost smiled. Then he turned and walked away,
his golden shoulders swaying with each unhurried stride.

After nightfall, the illuminated upper portion of the
mound appeared almost disconnected from the darker
world below. The Gothic spires and turrets and grand
stairways of Prince Charming's castle, lighted from below, became even more splendid, framed against the full
moon. And it seemed at any minute that the other prince
would climb the braided hair and join Rapunzel in contemplating the stars, oblivious to the stream of admirers
strolling around the base of the sand mountain. Even
Kevin's dragon appeared more benign in the moonlight
as the shadows played across his scaly skin and made
him seem to breathe.

Lon had waited until nightfall to move closer. Then he
fell in with the flow of people walking from the new
parking area toward the entrance. All day the dozers had
been pushing away tree roots and grading the area so
more cars could line up where laurel and oak and pines
had been. Lon had watched them. And all the while his
chest had hammered as he built his courage. Then finally
it was night. The lot filled with cars. And it was time for
him to try.

It had been years since one of them had tried to pass
among them. Except for the few trips to the fish camp to

trade pelts and gator skins, they stayed to themselves. But Lon had felt a need he could not resist. Some part of him wanted to be with them, simply be near them, and to see their lovely skin and smell their scent up close. At least being among them might ease the longing he felt for the child with moonlight hair.

For a long time, Lon watched the people. All of them were different. Some of them were built thick like him. Some wore pants as worn and boots as heavy as his. He'd even pulled on a wide-brimmed hat that he'd lifted from one of the trucks that had brought blocks in to one of the construction sites months before. The boots he'd taken from another truck were too tight, but he forced his feet into them anyhow. There were other men in jeans and boots and hats like his. And as he fell in with them, no one even seemed to notice him. But he was ready to race for the woods if they turned on him. He clutched the scorpion pendant in his palm to give him strength, and he kept his hands stuffed deep in his pockets. His were so ugly, partially webbed like Tommy's, and he couldn't let them show. They were wet, too, damp from the excitement.

Talking and laughing, the others just moved along, with Lon pacing himself so he could keep in step with them. The music got louder as he followed them through the gate and more people came from other directions. Suddenly there were people all around him, their voices loud, their speech fast and unintelligible, their bodies reeking of odors Lon could not recognize. A few were a head or more taller than he was and some were far heavier, and they brushed against him when they moved past, trying to get up to booths with striped canopies where other people handed them drinks and food to eat. The stench of the cooked food sickened him, and Lon had to fight the urge to bolt and run.

Desperately he focused on one person amid the congestion and followed her and the man with her through the confusing mass out into the open space beyond. For a moment, he just stood there, willing himself to breathe. Before him, the people moved freely. Some sat in groups. But they weren't pressing in any one direction. Lon picked out some who were walking toward the base of the mound, and he did what they did. He stepped around the obstacles. He walked slowly. He paused and looked up from time to time. Then he moved further around.

Soon he didn't need to copy them. He didn't need them to show him where to look. There were wondrous things everywhere, each drawing his attention and causing him to stop and marvel. Until now, Lon hadn't been close enough to see the detailed work they'd done. There were carved people, all with different faces, and animals who smiled or frowned like creatures of the wetlands never did. And he'd never seen anything like the gigantic winged serpent with the coils spilling from its mouth. And it amazed him that the rounded hills and ugly wooden frames that he and Tommy had climbed had been transformed into this wonderland.

Lon moved all the way around the sand structure, staring blissfully at each surprise. There was a frog wearing a crown. And three plump pigs, each with a house of his own. There was a boy in a cage with a humpbacked woman watching over him. And there was a lovely female, gently bending over the body of a man with the head of a wild boar. Lon didn't understand. But he could feel her sadness and see her tears of sand.

"Look, Mom . . ." he heard the children exclaiming as they pointed to the figures on the mound and squeezed in against the waist-high rope with colored ribbons trailing down. The barrier kept the onlookers from getting too close to the moat or the mound inside it. And Lon would pretend to keep looking at some detail, but he would know the child was next to him, and he would glance down from time to time. And always, when their hair was light, it would make his breath catch for an instant as he hoped it would be the child with moonlight hair. But it would be some other face, and he would turn away.

Once he smelled that sweet dark smell that he had clung to in the night, the delicious scent that had been on the towel he'd found. It came from a soft, glistening ball of food that a woman near him was licking. Then he saw another and another and sighed, grieving that he had filled his dreams with a scent that was not the boy's alone. Lon moved a little back from the rope this time and began another circuit of the mound, this time looking at the children and watching how they stopped and took such joy in the sand creatures bathed in the light.

He saw the woman first, walking along ahead of him where he'd already been. Her golden hair was pulled back. She wasn't carrying the boy, but Lon recognized her right away because she was tall and fair-haired and moved with grace. She was not alone. There was a man with dark hair with her, holding her hand like some of the others walking in pairs. And he wanted to run after her and push the man away and hold her hand instead. His fingers tingled for wanting that hand to hold. He moved a little quicker and fell in step behind them, pausing when they did, then moving on when they advanced. He squeezed his fingers to keep them still, and he rubbed the scorpion pendant and wished and wished again that his lovely moonchild would appear.

"Mom. Vince. Here's the change." The voice cut through him before he even saw the flash of color coming past him.

"Good for you," Kitty answered, putting her arm out and drawing the boy near. He was eating one of those dark and drippy things, but his was on a wooden stick. It had that same delicious smell. Lon squeezed his hands tighter, delirious with joy. And he knew because the old magic was still with him. He had rubbed the scorpion pendant over his mementos in the night and he had wished. And he had been in a state of grace then because he had not forgotten to honor his dead. He had given them over with due respect. Now that they were at peace, this moonchild had been returned to him. Just as he had wished.

"Zach, how about taking the change and getting your Mom and me some coffee," Vince asked him. They had dropped all the picnic gear back at the hotel after enjoying their secluded dinner out on the nature trail. But Zach had begged for ice cream and a trip around the mound, so they had strolled out for a look. Despite the crowd and the continuous music, the view was tranquil and impressive. But the night air was cool, and Vince had wisely grabbed his ivory team shirt and let Zach pull it on. It dangled almost to his knees, but it was enough to cut the breeze. And Zach had enjoyed the attention it drew as he strolled along. Vince figured coffee for the grown-ups would be fair compensation.

"You think I have enough?" Zach opened his hand and counted the change.

"Why don't you go check the price and see what you can work out." Vince knew Zach had plenty to cover the cost of two coffees, but he wanted him to find that out himself. "Do you remember what goes in them?"

Zach gave him a patronizing look. "I can handle it."

* * *

Lon watched closely as he walked away.

"Zach," Kitty called after him. "We'll meet you down the end by the dragon. I want to see how they fixed part of the wall that fell."

"Okay." Zach nodded. "North end," he said matter-of-factly. "No problem."

"Now where did he get that 'no problem' business," Kitty said softly, smiling as she watched him cut through the flow of onlookers.

"Probably one of his buddies from the group," Vince guessed. "Your little fellow is growing up, Mom," he kidded her.

"Yeah, he sure is," Kitty responded with a certain wistfulness.

Lon waited until they'd turned away before he started moving off in the direction the boy had gone. The boots hurt his feet, and he favored one foot slightly when he walked. That slowed him down. But it was better to stay back a bit so he could watch the boy carefully, absorbing every movement to remember later. Zach paused by the concession stand, finished his ice cream, and dropped the stick in the garbage. Then he stood there licking his fingers and comparing the change in his hand to the price posted for coffee. "Two coffees please," he said clearly, making his voice sound a bit lower than it did naturally. "One cream and sweetener. One black."

Lon inched closer to the garbage can and peered inside the open container. The stick was lying there on top of a soft-drink cup. His fingers twitched. He wanted that memento to make the magic stronger, but he didn't want anyone to see his ugly hands. Anxiously he lingered there, afraid that if he didn't grab it, someone else would pitch in some trash and knock the stick out of his reach. Lon tightened his jaw and looked around. Then a young woman threw a Styrofoam cup at the open mouth of the receptacle and missed. Lon waited until she was gone, then he bent down and scooped up her cup, careful to keep his fingers close together. And in one movement, he lowered the cup into the can and left it there, snatching up the stick on the way back. He plunged his hand back in the pocket immediately. The stick was still wet and tacky and it was rich with the special scent. Lon's heart raced.

Zach had the coffees now. One in each hand. He carried them carefully toward the north mound, dodging around the occasional stationary spectator in his path. Lon followed, always keeping far enough back so he was simply part of the crowd. "Zach . . ." he whispered the name softly to himself. "Zach . . ." He didn't even have to move his lips.

Later, when the crowd thinned and the threesome started to move toward the exit, Lon trailed along after them, squeezing the wooden stick and inwardly begging them to stay. But they didn't turn toward the parking area. Instead, they cut across the roadway and into the gardens where the statue of the man-faced beast crouched. Beyond that was the tall, gleaming building that towered above lands that once the wetlanders called their own. Lon watched them until they disappeared along the pathway. He didn't dare follow them, not there where all the lights sparkled and there was no crowd around. But he knew the shirt Zach wore, the one with the letters and number on the back, was different from the ones that the onlookers had. That pale-colored shirt meant that one of them went up the mountain and made miracles out of sand. It also meant they would be back there to work again the next day.

"Is this where you wait for the shuttle?"

Lon heard the question twice before he realized the elderly woman and her companion were talking to him. It had been so long since he he'd spoken to anyone but Tommy, he wasn't even sure how he would sound to one of them. He turned and looked into her face, afraid to make a noise for fear he'd frighten her. Besides, he didn't have the remotest idea what she said. She used some words he didn't know. He simply turned the corners of his mouth up a bit and shrugged. Then he walked out the way he'd come, toward the new parking area, so he could slip into the woods and work his way back home.

Once he was in the underbrush, Lon pulled off the boots that pinched his toes. He yanked out the stick and sniffed it.

"Zach, Zach, Zach . . ." He chanted the name out loud as he trudged along. "Zach, Zach . . ." He leaped and hopped and twirled, laughing in the moonlight. Near the mouth of the cave, he stopped and went to sit with his feet in the cool creek water while he drew out his knife. First he'd whittle a dream stick, trying to get a pleasing likeness of the slim young boy named Zach. And since the boy had touched and licked the wood himself, it would already have his spirit upon it. But he'd been given a sign. The boy was still there. He had time to draw the moonchild to him, and time to stalk the woman with the golden hair.

Silently Lon crept into the cave. He took out the scorpion pendant and rubbed it over the carved dream stick. Then he unwrapped his bundle and slipped the sweet-scented dream stick in with the other mementos he'd collected. This time he'd need stronger magic, and in the morning he'd have to scour the woods for special herbs to burn to make the power grow. But tonight, he would simply dream on it, and wish again, and since the magic was with him, he could sleep in peace.

His name was Mark Zimmerman. It was written in Button's neat block print across the back of the picture. He had been a pretty child. But that was eight years ago when Button worked in Lakeland. He guessed the boy was nine or ten then. That year Button had met Benjy and no one else mattered until Benjy's father got some kind of promotion and the family moved away.

"Mark . . . Mark Zimmerman," Button said the name, hoping it would stir some memories. But over the years, all the others drifted in with them and all the solitary fantasies swirled around until the stories and the faces were very much the same.

There were only a few pictures of Mark Zimmerman. All were mainly preliminary ones. And all the ones that may have had Button in them were gone. He had burned them all in a fit of disgust when he relocated and started to diet in earnest. After losing twenty pounds, he vowed to keep dieting until he hit one-seventy. That was thirty pounds ago. He was big-boned and still had ten more pounds to lose. But the old "fatty" pictures repulsed him, and one night when he'd been drinking, he took them out and burned them all. Now he only had the boys and the fantasies and memories well edited by time.

Maybe this one didn't go too far. Button stared at the picture, trying to link it to the more mature Mark Zimmerman he had seen today. Trying to decipher the youth's enigmatic expression had tantalized him all evening. Maybe he was going to smile out of affection. Maybe he remembers just the fun and the closeness and the magic tricks. Button could hardly remember the child Zimmerman at all. In his fantasies, he had done everything with all of them. All was possible in the privacy within his walls. They all became Benjy eventually.

Button closed his eyes. He'd taken another Percodan to ease the tension in his shoulders. Then he'd poured a short scotch, more out of habit than desire. And the two together were turning his limbs liquid. But looking at the boys had another effect on him. He'd settled into a warm tub to soak and drift and let the water play with him. "Go ahead, touch it and feel how nice it gets." He imagined warm fingers where the ripples moved. Then it was his own hand under the surface touching just the right way, the way that he liked to touch them. "Sweet dreams . . ." he murmured as he'd whispered to them. "Close your eyes and let it happen." He had taught them very well.

It was almost four in the morning when Button awoke, cold and cramped and uncomfortable, and still in the tub. The chilly water lapped against him and ran over onto the floor when he sloshed about, suddenly realizing where he was. Shivering, he climbed out of the tub, wrapped a towel around him, and hurried off into the bedroom. Climbing naked under the sheet, he cursed and thrashed about. Then he got out and grabbed his old heavy bathrobe from the closet. Like a huge blanket, the robe that had barely covered him in his fat days, wrapped a third again around him. Despite the cold, he stood before the mirror a moment. He liked seeing the difference. He was new man. And new men had no past.

Chapter 7

"I THINK YOU'D BETTER COME IN ON THIS, LIEUTEN-ant." Terry Rowe was still in his jogging shorts, coated with perspiration, when on Sunday morning they called him in to the station in Crystal Springs. "I think that guy from the Dunes case is still in the area. From the sound of it, he's been at it again," the sergeant informed him. "This time Quasimodo hit a trailer park about six miles southwest of the Dunes. We're trying to get the mother to let the kid go to the hospital. She's real skitterish. Just take it easy."

"How old's the kid?" Rowe asked, pulling on a sweat-shirt and smoothing down his hair as he followed the sergeant down the corridor.

"Nine."

"My son's nine."

"That's one of the reasons I called you in." The sergeant hesitated by the office door before going in. "So far, she's done most of the talking. He nods. But we need to get the details from him and we need to get him to a doctor for a thorough check. The mother said he's had a couple of baths, so that pretty well kills any chance of physical evidence. He's got some facial bruises and finger marks on his forearms, and who knows what else. I'd suspect he's torn up a bit on the inside, but he's a tough little dude and apparently planned to grit it out. Until she saw the finger marks. Then he cried a lot. Don't take it out on the mother. He first told her he fell."

"What's the problem in getting him to a hospital?"

"Her husband is a bad drinker. He got pulled in once for hitting on her and the kid. I doubt it was an isolated incident. She's afraid he might get blamed for this."

"Let's talk to the kid."

The pale, washed-out face of the woman appeared cadaverous under the fluorescent lights. Next to her, the boy sat in silence, staring at his clenched hands. "Mary Ann, Paulie, this is Terry Rowe. He's real interested in cases involving kids. He's got a boy Paulie's age. I'd like you to talk with him a few minutes about what happened." The sergeant took his desk chair. Rowe settled cross-legged on the floor closer to the boy, deliberately diminishing his size and eliminating any illusions about formality. The kid only had to shift his eyes slightly to look down at him.

Mary Ann Kirby licked her lips. Her skinny hands smoothed the faded fabric of her skirt. "This isn't what it looks like. Bobbie never hit the boy. I didn't neither. He just came in like this Saturday morning. Actu'ly I didn't see him till lunchtime. We all slep' late. Paulie had been out early then snuck back in and went back to bed. Didn't wanna come out for lunch. Said he was out in the woods climbing trees and fell and hurt hisself. He goes out in the woods a lot.'' Her eyes kept shifting from the sergeant to Rowe then back again. "He stayed in bed for most of the day. Jus' got up to shower off.''

"But you don't think now that he fell?'' Rowe led her gently.

"Nope. This mornin' when I peeked in, he'd yanked the covers back in his sleep and I saw them handprints. Ain't no tree did that to him. He was jus' afraid to talk 'bout it. But he kept havin' these bad dreams. So when I got him to tell me about it, he told me about this guy. He grabbed Paulie when he went out fishin'. He ain't s'posed to go out fishin' without tellin' us first. The boy can't swim. We don't like 'im going near that creek without someone along with 'im. He didn't wan' us to find out he took that pole and went fishin', so he made up that story about fallin' outta a tree.''

"You were pretty scared, weren't you, son . . . ?'' Rowe spoke to the boy.

The head nodded.

"You want to tell me about it?''

Hazel eyes, country hard and squinting slightly, cut at him then darted away. Thin lips stayed pressed together.

"Best I can tell, the fella raped him,'' the mother answered for him. "I guess that's what you call it when a man does it like that, you know, to another fella.'' Mary Ann Kirby's chin trembled as she steadied herself. "Found his pj's with little patches of blood on 'em. I brought them in.'' She patted a wrinkled brown paper bag next to her.

"Maybe Paulie would feel better if you let him talk about this while you wait outside,'' Rowe suggested. "One of the guys can get you a cup of coffee or a Coke or something. You just relax for a few minutes. I know

this is real rough on both of you," he said sympathetically. "You did the right thing in coming here. Just let
us talk to Paulie a little while."

"I don't know. . . ." She eyed the boy uneasily. "I
don't know what kind of questions you're gonna ask
him."

"We're only interested in this one incident," Rowe
assured her. "Go ahead. Take a break. Let us guys have
a little private time to talk."

"I'll have one of the officers get you something." The
sergeant stood, moving toward the door; clearly he expected her to follow.

She did.

"You want a Coke, too?" the sergeant asked the boy.

He nodded.

"Be right back."

Rowe didn't jump in immediately. "Just in case you're
worried about people finding out about this and giving
you a hard time, that won't happen," he explained. Dubious eyes skittered over his face then locked back on
the hands. "We keep the victim's name private." He
held off on the questions until the sergeant came back
and handed the kid the can of soda.

"Okay. Now go ahead and tell us what happened yesterday. Just take your time. We're going to put it all down
on tape, so you just tell it any way you want," Rowe
told him.

Paulie looked at Rowe apprehensively. He glanced at
the recorder on the sergeant's desk. He took a sip of
Coke. This time when he looked back, his eyes were
rimmed in tears, and his chin trembled like his mother's
had.

"I knowed I was doin somethin' bad. I got up early.
Ev'ryone else was sleepin'. An' I took my stepdad's

fishin' pole and went down to the crik,'' the boy began.
''I had my line in. Then some big guy came up back a'
me and grabbed me. Put one hand over my mouth so's I
couldn't yell. Then he slammed me 'gainst an ol' tree
that had fell over. You know,'' he said, moving his drink
can horizontally, ''it was sidewise.''

Rowe nodded.

''Hit my belly 'gainst the tree so hard, I couldn't
breathe. Then I started to slide off, so's he grabbed me
and slammed me 'gainst it again. That's when I got
these.'' He pushed back his mop of straight dull brown
hair and gave Rowe a clearer look at the purplish bruise
and the darkened scrape marks down one side of his face.
Paulie stopped, took a drink, then swallowed hard.

''All's I had on was my swim trunks.'' He stopped
again. ''He tore 'em right off. Then he spit. I heard him
spit a couple of times. Then he just stuck it in me.''

''We need to get the details clear so there won't be any
misunderstanding. Just tell me if this is what you mean.
The man used his penis. He inserted it into your anus.
Your rear end?'' The sergeant clarified for the record.

Paulie nodded. His chin trembled. He took a few slow,
ragged breaths. ''Tha's what he did. It hurt real bad,''
Paulie said as the tears he struggled to contain slowly
trailed down his cheeks. ''I woulda fought 'im. But he
was real big.'' More tears.

''You're doing fine, son,'' Rowe said gently. ''You're
doing just fine.'' He turned to the sergeant and reached
out his hand. The sergeant passed him a fistful of
Kleenex.

Paulie sniffed and wiped his face. Then he took a few
breaths. ''He made awful sounds. I jus' closed my eyes
and didn't move. You know, I played possum. Like I was
konked out. I figured I was gonna be dead if I moved.

He was so big. And he held my arms real hard.'' He pushed up the sleeves of his shirt so the dark handprints on his upper arms showed. "I thought I was gonna throw up." He locked his eyes onto a spot on the floor and was staring down at it. "Later, when he was gone, I did. I couldn't stop." Big tears trickled down his face and dripped onto his shirt. Paulie didn't move to wipe them. "I couldn't find the fishin' pole. I tried to poke around in the water in case it fell in. Got in up to my neck and felt around with my feet. But I was scared. Can't swim. I couldn't find it anywheres. It was my stepdad's. Mom hasn't told him yet. I made her promise not to. He ain't gonna like this."

Rowe reached out and rested his hand on the kid's forearm, hoping that Paulie wouldn't recoil from the contact. "I'll help you straighten things out with your stepdad," he promised. "You just help us to get the guy who did this to you. This is tough on you, I know. You're doing a good job remembering all this. Just take it easy." His own voice quavered as he fought the impulse to hug the little fellow. But he had made contact, and he left his hand there as reassurance.

"Did you ever get a good look at this fellow?" the sergeant asked.

Paulie shook his head. "Nope. Like I said, he jumped up in back a' me and grabbed me. I got a peek at the back a' 'im before he took off. He went down to the crik. I guess that's when he stole my stepdad's pole. Musta took it with 'im. He was big. Big ol' beard and bushy hair. Didn't have no shirt on, just old jeans. He had hair all down his arms and on his back. Even had hair on his hands and the back of his fingers. I could see them when he was holdin' on to me. They was real funny. They looked like regular hands but his had big ol' thick skin between the fingers. Went way up to here." He held his own fingers outspread and pointed at the larger finger joint. Rowe and the sergeant looked at each other. They'd thought the James boy's remark about webbed fingers was the creation of a hysterical, frightened child. But Paulie Kirby wasn't hysterical.

"Anything else you remember about him?" the sergeant pressed.

"He was real dirty. Smelled bad. And he was all gritty, like you get at the beach. You know, all sandy and rough. I washed it off when I was in the crik looking for the pole. Made me feel dirty." He squirmed and rubbed one forearm distractedly.

"And you've bathed since that time?" The sergeant deliberately kept his voice and his facial expression noncommittal.

"Coupla times. I jus' don't feel clean," the boy said softly. The sergeant nodded, then his eyes met and held Rowe's. Frequent bathing was a typical post-assault reaction, but they knew the cleansing wiped out any trace of pubic hair or body fluids that could help identify the assailant or match him to the evidence in the James' assault.

"And what about the blood spots that your mom mentioned. Did you hurt bad down there?"

The boy lowered his eyes. He nodded. The two men exchanged a dark look.

"Have you been able to go to the bathroom since then?" The sergeant covered essential territory.

The boy shook his head. "Jus' to pee."

"Sometimes things like this can hurt the inside of your body," Rowe explained, keeping it as simple as possible. "When something like this happens, it's best that a doctor check you. He'll have some medicine to make it hurt less, and he'll give you something to make sure you don't have any kind of infection. What that guy did to you was bad enough. You don't want to keep on suffering or have any other problems with your body because of him.'' Rowe gave him a few seconds to let that sink in. Rowe knew the doctors would test for sexually transmitted diseases as well. All the poor little kid needed was a dose of VD or something worse.

"How about I go with you and your mom. We'll take you over to the hospital. It will all be very private,'' Rowe stressed. "We'll have them take real good care of you. You've been hurt enough. You've been very brave. But it's time to let someone else help you.''

As small as he was, Paulie Kirby seemed to shrink even more, as if the last breath of resistance had drained out of him. "I really hurt,'' he said in a small, scared voice. Rowe reached up and wrapped his strong arms about the boy, hugging him against his chest.

"I know you do, son.'' He stroked the hard little shoulders and felt them tremble. Silently at first, Paulie wept. "You're gonna get better. You're not gonna let the creep mess you up. Come on, let it out, son. We'll get you all fixed up.'' Rowe's own eyes now brimmed with tears. The boy he held could have been his own, slim, bony, innocent, and no match for a grown man.

"I'll go check on Mrs. Kirby and call the hospital so they'll be expecting you,'' the sergeant said, patting Rowe on the shoulder then adding another for the sobbing boy before he left. "You two come out when you're ready.''

"What's it look like, Sarge?''

"We got another one for Quasimodo?'' The officers in the corridor slowed his progress.

"Looks like the same scumbag, all right.'' His words

shot out in spurts as the fury he'd concealed erupted. "Filthy bastard. Webbed fingers even," he added grimly. "Covered in grit. We got us a Sandman. A fuckin' Sandman. Only this asshole ain't givin' any little kids sweet dreams. Just fuckin' nightmares." He moved off, stone-faced, in search of Mary Ann Kirby.

Jack Button needed these occasional Sunday-morning drives. He'd put on a sports shirt and slacks, grab the unopened newspaper, then take off. He'd drive thirty miles south into the next county, have coffee at the Hernando City McDonald's, read the paper, then go to the post office to pick up his correspondence. Once little more than a truck stop and a refueling point for travelers, Hernando City was a country town in a state of transition. Tracks for motorcycle racing and demolition-car derbies had expanded to include truck and tractor competitions. The development of area pulpwood manufacture, gravel pits, and the cement industry had brought in block houses for the workers. Farther south, former citrus groves have been subdivided into "country estates," attracting commuters from the urban areas nearby who wanted to keep a couple of horses or have enough acreage to be weekend farmers. But unlike the Dunes area, there was no master plan and no growth control, and the result was an ugly succession of strip shopping centers, gas stations, fast-food places, auto-repair garages, and country bars. Outside of a four-square-block core of old department stores, city buildings, and a medical clinic, surrounded by back streets with a couple of schools, a few fine old houses that had been converted into office spaces, two churches, a fire station, and a library, there was no center, no organization, no neighborhoods. And

Button chose the place precisely because of the anonymity he could maintain there.

After he finished reading the Sunday paper, Button would order a couple of burgers and a Diet Coke to go.

There was hill sloping down to a small lake and a park behind the library. Surrounded by oaks and willows, it was overrun by squirrels and ducks, was otherwise quiet. There were a few benches in shady areas under the trees. Kids coming home from Sunday school generally passed by, hurrying home to Sunday dinner, a few of them stopping to feed the ducks. Some of them took a few sweeps on the gray metal swing sets or a couple of turns on the old metal roundabout that generally had traces of water lying in the rutted track worn down around it. They'd bypass the bathrooms in the two dull green-painted wood buildings with peeling labels reading "Men" and "Ladies." The park, like most of the town, was old and outdated and generally ignored by everyone else. Especially on Sundays.

Button liked to take his special mail there. He'd leave his car parked by the post office, sling his camera bag over his shoulder, and walk the block downhill to the park. Usually he'd have three or four tightly rolled magazines or brochures waiting for him in his P.O. box. Often more if he'd missed making a pickup for several weeks. It was always safer to get these things past the authorities wrapped inside something innocuous. Between the pages, there would be a few letters and an assortment of pictures from his correspondents. He usually threw out the cover magazine. Then right out there in the open, he'd read the letters, leisurely rereading certain details that caused a particular twinge of delight. And if there were kids around the park, he'd watch them and listen to their voices and draw them into the fantasy to get himself even more excited. But he never rushed. Not on his Sunday outings. He'd save the pictures until he got home. That way, he could think about them and imagine what they would be like all the way back. When he got inside his own place and could spread them all out together, he'd really be ready.

This time, Button had a hard time settling into the routine. Even in the middle of a paragraph, he'd stop and stare off into space. Mark Zimmerman. The puzzling smile had haunted him all night. He'd awakened repeatedly from uneasy dreams, had even gone out into the darkened living room once, switched on the light, opened the book, and looked at the slim boy, frozen in time. And he'd let his fingers glide over the cool plastic page cover, trying to remember how the warm flesh had felt, trying to dredge up the recollection and separate what was real from the fantasies he'd woven over the years. He kept replaying the smile, the turn, the way the way the caramel shoulders swayed when the grown-up Mark walked away. Each time, it would make his palms sweat.

That's why he knew he needed to get away. Everything was building up, like steam in a pressure cooker. He'd been under too much stress juggling the finances and manpower and special events that the Dunesfest required. The assault case had settled into a none-too-optimistic investigation and had ceased to be news, but now the Zimmerman kid only added another kind of pressure, one still unfocused. Even with the sandsculpting activities scheduled all day, Button knew the next weekend, the grand opening and Easter Sunday, would be worse, so he squeezed in this Sunday morning out of town.

Button took a sip of the Coke and looked around the small park. A mother duck and her four mottled brown babies were poking around in the uneven grass under a nearby willow. Near the opposite bank, the kid on the old roundabout was one he recognized from previous Sundays. He'd seen him hang around the park, pitching pebbles in the water, floating makeshift vessels of twigs and leaves. Stalling. Button had even said "hi" to him once or twice in passing. The faded jeans legs were getting shorter, the tennis shoes were worn, the shirt faded from many launderings. And the kid was alone.

Deliberately, Button picked up his camera, set the zoom, and aimed it across the way. Then the kid yanked off his shirt and shoes, rolled his pant legs up, and waded into the edge of the pond. In the morning sun, his tanned skin looked like velvet, and Button sat and stared. He couldn't keep his eyes from following the contours of his shoulders and the shadowy outline of his spine as it dipped beneath the dark waistband of his jeans. It was all so familiar, yet all so new. And time and place and caution all became irrelevant. Button tucked everything except the magazines and camera into the bag and began working his way around the pond.

"Hope you don't mind," Button said apologetically when the kid stopped pitching pebbles long enough to notice his picture was being taken. He had waded out again and was standing on the grassy bank. "I'm an artist, I like to shoot folks in different locations then go back to my studio and rework them in pastels. There are some real nice lights and shadows around here. I like the way those ripples change your reflection." He kept talking and pointing at the widening circles upon circles spreading out from where the last pebble hit. "You make a darn good model. Say, you wouldn't happen to be hungry, would you?" he asked, smoothly keeping the one-sided flow of conversation going. "I picked these up at

McDonald's and haven't even unwrapped them." He grabbed the bag with the two burgers and held it out to the kid. From the looks of the kid's clothes, he figured food and money were safe negotiating tools. He'd kept a lots of kids calm and cooperative by feeding them.

Until now, the kid hadn't thrown another pebble. He'd just stood there with a walnut-sized rock in his hand, eyeing Button from head to toe. He took it all in, the dark razor-cut hair, shiny aviator sunglasses, trimmed beard, nice clothes, shined shoes. He looked at the expensive camera then at Button's long-fingered graceful hands. "Here." Button reached out and plucked a quarter from behind the kid's ear. "Call McDonald's. Ask 'em if I wasn't just there. Buddy Butler," he introduced himself, deliberately using a name he'd used with kids before.

The kid took the quarter. Then he took the bag with the two burgers.

"Let me take a shot of you sitting there eating one of those," Button suggested. "Maybe if you pitch a little of the bun into the water, you could get those ducks to come over here. They'd be interesting in the background." He held up the camera and aimed it at the kid, moving from side to side after different angles. Across the way, the mother duck and her entourage made a V pattern on the water. Button fired off a shot. "How about it. Try to get those ducks over here," he urged the kid, trying to establish a pattern of following directions. Almost grudgingly the boy pinched off a section of the bun and tossed it out onto the surface. The ducks promptly shifted directions, zeroing in on the tidbit. "Great. Do it again," Button urged him. The kid did, this time with a little more enthusiasm. Button took another shot then let the kid sit there and finish the first burger.

"Man, it's getting hot." Button sighed. "Say, would you mind leaning back against that tree there. Pretend like you're daydreaming in the middle of a lazy summery day? I know it's not summer, but I need an illustration for a calendar. That would be perfect." He could tell the kid was thinking it over. "Look, I'll give you ten bucks to model and I'll send you a couple of calendars for your folks. How about it. Lazy summer days . . ." he coaxed the kid.

"Ten bucks . . . ?"

"Sure. Come on. I'll tell you what to do." Button stood and walked toward one particular willow tree that trailed its branches barely above the water's edge. When he turned around, the boy was right behind him. He was real close. The kid glanced up and almost smiled. And Button's palms turned damp. There was something enticing in that fleeting expression, an eagerness to please that echoed the seductive beauty of another boy, another time.

Button could feel his body responding. His pulse accelerated. Then the boy stepped under the branches, just where Button pointed. Shadows danced across his bare torso, making kaleidescopic patterns on his velvet skin. Button's hands were trembling. He steadied himself and took several quick shots. "Great. You're picking up some great shadows. You're really excellent at this." He kept up a continual stream of praise.

Then he gave the kid the ten. "Worth every cent," he insisted. "I just wish we could get some really dramatic shots with some light-and-dark patterns over your whole body. You'd look like one of those high-class sculptures. Photos like that would be real art. I'd give you twenty bucks if you could do one like that. But you sure couldn't slip off those pants out here in the open." He glanced around, frowning, succeeding in looking very professional.

"I suppose we could go in there," Button said as if he were merely thinking aloud, tilting his head toward the green men's room. There's a couple of windows. I bet we could catch some unusual angular light patterns in there. How about it? Twenty bucks. Just to pretend you're a statue?"

The boy hadn't yet stuffed the ten-dollar bill in his jeans. Button peeled off a twenty and held it by his side, tapping it against his pant leg. "All you have to do is stand there. No clothes. But I'd want you to turn your back to me. That way the patterns will be smoother. It's nothing personal. No one will get to see your face."

The kid was sliding the ten between his thumb and fingers, looking from Button to the green rest room, then back at the bill.

"Look, I wish I had time to let you think this over. Maybe talk it over with someone. Lots of artists hire nude models. There's no big deal involved. But I've got an appointment in an hour. I have to hit the road if I'm going to make it on time. I wish I knew when I'd be through here again. But you know how artists are, we don't have regular schedules like other folks." He shrugged and looked at his watch. "I just think you're a natural talent. If you could use the cash, I sure would like to try a few shots."

The small fingers still rubbed the ten-dollar bill. Then the kid shrugged and walked toward the rest room. Button pursed his lips. He looked around the park. No one was there, except for the ducks. And a few squirrels.

Lon lay sprawled out on his stomach in the underbrush, watching the woman with the wide-brimmed hat.

He was there when she came out in the cool of the morning. Her long golden legs were bare then. He watched her step off the shuttle and walk over to the tent where he'd found the pretty colored strips of plastic and the shears. She spoke to the people there, then she walked alone around the entire mound. When she came back, the dark-haired man was there with the others. But there was no Zach. There were no children out there at all.

Then the man with the dark hair handed her a shirt, the same color as his. When she pulled it on, Lon understood that she was not just one of those who came to watch. She was one of them, one of the people who made those marvelous figures of sand. And he wanted to be near her, to watch how her hands worked, to try to understand the meaning of the things he saw created here. But he also knew that if he followed her, the female that Zach called Mom, eventually she would lead him to the boy.

But for the morning, he had been content to lie still and watch everything. He saw the mom and the others in the light-colored shirts, almost the color of the sand, climb to the midlevel plateaus and survey their work. Then a group of other workers came in through the gates, all of these banded in certain colors. Some picked up shovels and work gloves. They were banded in white. Some carried shiny small hand tools and were banded in red and blue. The ones banded in yellow carried containers of liquid up the mound and set them up in shaded places where the others came to drink. The ones that kept pointing at the figures and looking into dark boxes and those who stood in front of other boxes while they smiled and talked into sticks they held in their hands, they were banded in green. They only talked and walked from place to place and pointed. They seemed important but they did not touch the sand.

Then a new group of people were admitted. These went to the long table under the tend and made marks on paper. They held out a card. Then they were given a shovel and work gloves. The female at the table then pointed to a place on the mound. That worker made his way up there and joined the others laboring on that section.

Finally, once the early-comers were banded and on their way up the mound, the gates were opened wide to admit all those gathering in the parking areas. These were the ones who only came to watch. They carried chairs, blankets, umbrellas, and ice chests and settled in for the day.

It all made sense once Lon watched for a while. Even the orange-banded ones who had containers that sent out a spray had a specific job. Lon watched them move from place to place, gently misting a figure, then coming back later to mist it again. They were always the last ones called in, after the others had finished. The craftsmanship that made the figures emerge was beautiful to watch, and Lon especially marveled at the artistry of the woman that his Zach had called Mom.

Mom was among the most gifted in whittling the sand, like the elder had been with wood, for she could take a shapeless mound, dig out quick wedges, and make the image of a person appear. It would be a rough shape at first, but the body would have a definite energy in its pose and she'd give it a distinct head and face. Then, like the elder, she would take time with the others to help them learn; she'd call in some red or blue bands and talk awhile. Then she'd leave them to complete the body and go on to another formless lump and begin her magic again. But she'd come back from time to time and define or accentuate a line or straighten a lopsided shape, then encourage them to go on working.

Midway through the morning, Mom came down and washed the sand off her arms and legs with the rubber hose near the tent. Then she pulled on loose-legged pants and went back up the mound again. Lon watched her. Even under the cover of the trees and brush, he'd felt the heat of the sun. He understood it would be brutally hot where she was. But the pants would protect her from becoming red-skinned like so many others had become, and he noted her wisdom.

In the afternoon, she was up there for hours without stopping. Sometimes she would be poised on a ladderlike structure, only her hand and arm moving as she whittled the features, flicking unneeded scoops of sand like sawdust in the air. Sometimes she cupped her hand over one ear and seemed to speak into the dark wire attached to the headband, then she'd walk purposefully off.

Even when she did not immediately proceed on to some new piece to whittle, she was constantly involved in some kind of work. Everything interested her. She would take a shovel and labor side by side with the white-banded men. She would line up with the others and help lift away the sides of the wooden boxes to reveal the working surface within. She would carry buckets. Sometimes her graceful hands would draw pictures in the air when she spoke in earnest with the others. But what made Lon feel that strange tightness in his chest was when she rested her hand on someone's shoulder, smiling down at them and nodding at their efforts. He wanted to be that someone. He wanted to bask in the brilliance of her approving smile and feel the touch of that marvelous hand.

If he could be close to her . . . Lon wished it over and

over. If he were close to her, he might able to get close
to her boy, the child with the moonlight hair. He had
already passed among the ones who watched. Studying
the workers, he could imagine himself there, among
them. He could shovel. He was very strong. It was the
business at the long table he had to avoid. So he decided
he'd have to come again at night. He already had a shovel.
He had plastic for the armband. He could pass if he had
those heavy work gloves to hide his ugly, webbed hands.
For the rest of the afternoon, Lon settled down in earnest, analyzing every detail about the white-banded shovelers whose hands never showed.

Late in the day, Lon watched the men with wheeled
pushcarts unloading metal kegs from the long-backed
truck. They had parked the trailer end of it just inside
the fence and set up a canopied booth with a rectangular
box counter in front of it. Then the people had started
lining up, exchanging coins and paper currency for a
paper cup full of the foam-topped liquid that squired out
of shiny pipes on the counter. Some called it beer and
others called it Bud. And the aroma that drifted on the
afternoon breeze reminded Lon of the brew the Trapper
brought them sometimes when he sneaked into a camp-
site and came away with things to share. It had been a
long time since any of the wetlanders had tasted beer.
And Lon felt his mouth grow wet.

The lines at the concession continued on into the night,
long after the workers and Zach's mom came down and
went away. Lon was too far away to follow, and the crowd
was very large. But he stayed there in his leafy hideout,
hoping she would come back, this time bringing Zach.

At sunset, there was another parade up to the top with
men in tight clothes and women in pale dresses. The

female in the longest dress with a trailing spiderweb of white came last. The same music played. Then everyone cheered. They all came down again and rode off toward the tall building filled with lights. The crowd cheered again. Then it was over. Then the music changed, and the flow of people increased, and the lights went on. Lon waited, hoping that the tall mom and her Zach would come out with the others into the night. But they didn't.

Finally the music in the air stopped altogether. The people gradually went away. The ones in uniform and those under the canopied areas went last. Men in overalls scoured the grounds carrying plastic bags and spearing papers and cups with a metal-pointed stick. Lon watched the two who'd carried the metal kegs back and forth all day set aside the ones they had used. He watched the cloud of pale cold smoke pour out as they slid up the end of the truck bed and put the last two kegs back inside again. Then they wiped off all the pipes and handles and left.

One by one the canopied areas turned dark. Still he watched and waited. Finally there was only one man remaining, the one with the dog. The guard and the animal walked the entire perimeter slowly, then they settled down in the long tent where the workers gathered from time to time during the day. Other than Lon, he was the only one there now, and only night sounds floated in on the breeze. The huge fairyland in sand stood lifeless and magnificently illuminated against the dark surroundings.

Lon rubbed himself as he had before with fresh wild ginger leaves. Then silently he scaled the fence behind the truck bed, using it for a screen. On hands and knees, he crept between the wheels into the canopied space where the beer kegs were lined up. He shook one. It was empty. Another. Empty. Another. He took a stack of cups and slid them inside his shirt. Finally he crawled around to the back of the truck and braced his hands against the heavy door. Carefully he pushed it up, a little at a time, while the rigid current of air wheezed out around him. Then he climbed into the dark void, bracing the door with his knee so it wouldn't close completely while he reached out, groping in the unnatural cold. He felt a heavy keg. He slid it toward him, then clutched it against his chest while he pushed the door up high enough so he could scramble out under it. Still holding the keg under one arm, he scaled the fence again, then crept back into the bushes and hid it there. Chuckling to himself, he rubbed his hands to drive out the chill. Tonight, when he went back to the cave, he would take it there. He hadn't been home all day, or most of the night before. There was much to tell. He would be like the Trapper and take home beer for him and Tommy to share.

But there was something else he had to get. Lon stayed under the cover of the trees and worked his way to the larger tent. Then he crouched there, waiting. Finally the guard and the dog stood and began another circuit. Lon inched closer to the fence. When they passed out of sight, he vaulted over and raced for the tent. Work gloves. He shoved them inside his shirt. Then he scurried to the next tent and grabbed a visor and the tube of white goo that he'd seen them put on their nose and lips. He reached under the counter, picking up and shaking out one T-shirt then another until he found one that looked large enough for him. Stuffing all his treasures in with the gloves, he looped across the shadowy strip toward the fence and tugged himself over it. "Zach, Zach, Zach . . ." He chortled, singing triumphantly as he grabbed the keg then ducked into the underbrush and headed home.

"Tommy." Lon nudged him in the darkness of the cave. "Tommy. Come see what we got." He tugged at Tommy's arm. "Good stuff. Real likker." Tommy rolled up on one elbow and squinted at him in the dark. Grunting, Tommy stumbled from his bunk and followed.

"Where you been?" Once they stepped out into the moonlight, Tommy reached out and ran his hand over Lon's short-cropped hair. "What you do?" He rubbed Lon's chin, feeling the bristles instead of the familiar matted beard. "What you do?" he demanded, his voice edged in anger.

"Come here. Likker," Lon persisted, then turned and led the way toward their sitting place by the creek. He'd put the keg in the cool water, anchoring it with a stout rope. Now, ceremoniously, he dragged it out. "Likker," he said proudly.

"Where?" Tommy demanded.

"Out there." Lon thrust his thumb in the direction of the sand mound. Tommy's frog eyes blinked then narrowed into slits. "Here." Lon slid the keg higher up the bank. Then he held out a slightly dented paper cup and turned the spigot. Cool beer filled the cup. He gave it to Tommy. Then he drew another for himself.

Silently they drank it down, just the two of them, standing together.

Tommy licked his lips and wiped the foam from the stringy fringe of hair that hung down over his mouth. The frog eyes blinked at the shiny keg then shifted to the strangely barbered version of Lon. Tommy sniffed and poked him, snickering at the shorn hair and beard. Then he poured himself another cupful. "Good." He settled down on the grass beside the keg and downed the second cup so rapidly that rivulets ran down his beard hairs and onto his chest. "More . . ." He thrust it out for Lon to refill. Then he belched.

Hot and tired and hungry, Lon drank a few cups in quick succession. Gradually the thirst subsided and the softening effect seeped into his limbs.

Tommy kept refilling and emptying his cup, until his heavy eyelids drooped and his broad mouth hung open in a loose grin. "Good," he rumbled, snorting happily as he lolled against the bank. Then he stretched out his toes and poked the bulge in Lon's shirt. "You got sumthin'?" he questioned him.

"More. See." Lon reached inside his shirt and pulled out the plastic visor. He tugged it on, letting it rest above his eyebrows.

Tommy's slightly unfocused eyes widened, then the shapeless grin spread into a broad, dark-toothed opening. "Stupid . . ." He pointed at him, gasping and grunting as he laughed.

Lon turned away and leaned over the water, trying to see his reflection there. Tommy placed his foot on Lon's buttocks and gave him a quick shove, headfirst into the creek. Sputtering and cold, Lon surfaced, flopping wildly to rescue the visor before it was swept away by the current.

"You got sumthin' good?" Tommy challenged him to show what else he'd picked up.

Lon stood waist-deep in the water with his arms crossed defiantly across his chest. "No."

"Come on. . . ." Tommy insisted.

"No . . ."

"You see what I got," Tommy growled at him, staggering and swaying toward the cave. Lon had waded to shore and was standing, dripping on the bank when he returned. "See this," Tommy boasted, holding up the fishing pole he'd brought home from his wanderings. "This is real good." He shook it above his head like a spear.

Lon shrugged, pretending not to be impressed. Then he picked up another paper cup and poured himself more beer.

"Come on," Tommy coaxed him. "Show me." He jabbed a stubby finger at the wet lump under Lon's shirt. Lon simply shook his head and turned away. Tommy would never understand about the pale-haired boy or the woman who walked with the grace of a deer. Tommy wouldn't feel his awe for the ones who whittle in sand. Tommy wouldn't understand any of it. Lon sighed, then he settled down on a root, dangling his feet into the water.

"You mad?"

Lon looked at his half brother standing there, bleary-eyed, with his clenched fists on his hips. Tommy was drunk and spoiling for a fight. A cold, dark silence hung between them.

"Have more," Lon said at last. As an act of conciliation, he handed Tommy his cup of beer and got himself a replacement.

"Good . . ." Tommy took the cup and drained it.

"Real good," Lon mimicked Tommy as he held the cup of beer up in a mock salute.

Tommy stared at him. He snorted and rubbed his crotch. "Mine real good," he sniffed triumphantly. Fishing pole in hand, he went back toward the opening of the cave. "My woman . . ." he bellowed for Lon's benefit. Tommy was loose and feeling smug. If he couldn't work up a good fight, he wanted someone to mount. "Woman . . ." Tommy muttered as he disappeared inside. His humorless chuckle indicated he had found the pregnant breeder woman somewhere in the dark interior.

Lon didn't stay around to listen. He picked up his cache of secret mementos, ones he'd hidden in the twisted knot of the cypress, then he took off into the underbrush to sleep out underneath the canopy of trees. "Zach, Zach, Zach . . ." he changed, rosy with the beer. "Mom, Mom, Mom . . ." he alternated the refrain.

Carefully he spread out his own clothes and the stolen T-shirt to dry in the gentle breeze. Then he patted down a bed of cool ferns and sprawled out over them. Above in the darkness of the overhanging branches, an owl hooted. Lon hugged his mementos against his chest and rolled onto his side. Tomorrow he would rise with the birds. He would be there before anyone else.

Chapter 8

"If you feel for the moment that we're leading you through the galleries of Egyptian art at the Metropolitan or the Smithsonian or perhaps a reprise of the exhibit of the Treasures of Tutankhamen, you're in for a surprise. We're filming today at the fabulous Grand Nile Hotel in the Dunes resort community in west-central Florida. . . ." The reporter's voiceover continued as the on-screen picture cut from the main corridor with the artworks and artifacts in plexiglas display cases, to the lush indoor gardens with tall clumps of papyrus and ponds with floating lilies, to the granite falcon-headed statues guarding the entrance. Next an aerial shot panned from the seventeen-story stepped hotel to a view of the Great Sphinx, and beyond the surrounding trees to the pale sands of the great sandsculpture. "The largest sandsculpture in the world is being completed this week. . . ."

"Mom, come see this." Zach called through the bathroom door. "It's 'Good Morning America' and they're showing the hotel and the mound and everything. Hurry . . ."

"This one-hundred-thousand-ton sandpile with its uppermost towers nearly seven stories tall is already the tallest and largest ever built. All that remains to secure the record is for hundreds of workers to decorate the entire surface with creatures, buildings, landscaping, and storybook characters. . . ." The shot picked up Prince Charming's castle and Cinderella's pumpkin carriage.

"Mom . . ." Zach yelled.

"Take it easy. They're going to be here all week." Kitty emerged, draped in a large towel. "Jack Button said they'll be running some kind of spot each morning. We're all supposed to be interviewed sometime over the next few days."

"Look, I can see you." Zach thrust a finger at the ivory-shirted figure on the screen. Perched atop a six-foot section of scaffolding, Kitty was helping Paul Feneau with the Frog Prince on the west face of the central mound. The camera panned over to Rapunzel's Tower, zoomed in on the princess, then panned again off toward the country club, passing over the steadily growing spring lake and the expansive system of waterways with a few white-sailed feluccas sailing along.

"I guess they shot all this yesterday." Kitty stepped closer to the TV. "Is that you? Were you guys out sailing?"

"I was probably swimming. There were so many people here that the boats were all booked up. I'm never in the right place." Zach bristled with indignation.

"Next Saturday they're filming the opening ceremonies. You can come up with us and get your smiling face on TV then."

Zach didn't say anything. He just frowned and kept watching until they shifted to a commercial.

"Come on. Let's go to breakfast. Get dressed."

"Can't I just stay here and watch TV today?" He flung himself across the bed and buried his face in a pillow.

"I think you'd have a better time with Corey and Melissa and the bunch. Didn't I hear that you folks were going on a field trip today. Something about glass-bottomed boats and a live reptile show?"

Zach stiffened. "Today's Monday?"

"All day."

"I'll get dressed."

"Mornin' everyone." The security guard in The Dunes tan safari uniform greeted the steady stream of volunteers as they arrived Monday morning. "If you've already registered, just go on and check in. Those of you who haven't already been issued your armbands and T-shirts, just hold back awhile until we get things set up. There'll be plenty of work for everyone, so don't get anxious," he added good-naturedly.

Jack Button stood in the shade of the staff tent, ostensibly studying the day's agenda. But his dark eyes, masked by the Dunes visor and his amber-lensed sunglassed, skimmed the procession of banded workers as they entered through the gate. The moment Mark Zimmerman stepped into the clearing beyond the north parking lot, Button locked onto him. Except for a calico headband and the red sculptors' armband, Mark was naked to the waist, and his hair, still damp from his morning shower, looked darker than Button remembered. But the sway of the shoulders and the color of his skin were unmistakable. He carried the pale aqua Dunesfest T-shirt in his hand. What mattered was that he was back.

Button busied himself making notes, deliberately positioning himself well behind Sandy Huff and Roseanne Petty, but Zimmerman never even glanced his way. Like the others who had worked the mound before, he simply gave his name to Sandy or Roseanne then pick up his tools and climb the walkway to the plateau where he'd be needed today. With a peculiar blend of anxiety and relief, Button watched the youth's solitary progress until he disappeared around the south end.

Mark Zimmerman hadn't been there at all on Sunday. When Button came back from Hernando City, he had gone right out to the staff tent and got things rolling on schedule. For the first hour, he moved almost mechanically from one post to another, introducing the board members and sponsors present, bringing on the first band, getting the sound setup ready for his storytelling stint, and keeping the press representatives briefed. All the while he kept smiling, despite the cold knot in his stomach and the cottony dryness in his mouth. He'd screwed up. Simple as that. He'd slipped out of control and screwed up royally in that rest room in the park in Hernando City.

He'd rushed it. Maybe it was the heat and the closeness in that pathetic little green building, or maybe he'd misread the kid's expression in the strange light, or maybe having Zimmerman show up the day before had stirred up too many old memories and secret desires. Or maybe it was just that it had been so long since he'd actually been that close to a beautiful child alone. It had been over a year since he'd touched such soft skin.

"Stand over there, just a little to the right." Almost

involuntarily he'd started fondling himself when the kid turned his back and dropped his pants to pose for the photo. Then Button had reached out, only intending to move the kid into a better lighting position. The kid glanced over his shoulder at him. Button was sure he smiled. Just like Benjy. He let his hand slide from the boy's shoulder, down along the curve of the slender arms. There was something electric in the contact, and something overpowering in that transitory smile. Button lost control.

"I won't hurt you. Please. Just be quiet. Let me do this. I won't hurt you." Button's face turned hot with embarrassment, remembering how he whined as he knelt down and grabbed the kid, pinning his arms against his sides. Button had pressed his face into the hollow of the boy's back, breathing in shallow, rasping breaths, while he masturbated with the other hand. His lips grazed the velvet skin; his chin rested on the rise of the boy's firm buttocks. He couldn't stop himself. The boy simply stood there, rigid.

Afterward, Button wept. He told the kid he was sorry. He made up a story about having been divorced and separated from his family and how seeing the kid there in the dim light looking so beautiful got him all confused. He said that he ached so desperately for his kids and for sex with his wife that everything got so churned up he couldn't help himself.

"I didn't hurt you. I would never hurt you. You are so beautiful. I sure am sorry," he'd apologized tearfully. But his large frame still blocked the narrow passage to the door. Then he gave the kid the twenty he'd promised, and an extra ten, begging him not to be afraid and not to tell anyone. "I don't want anyone to know how lonely and foolish I am. I'd be so embarrassed. I try to cover up being lonely. . . .'' He knew that would get to him. The kid was a loner, too. A poor country hick who drifted on the fringe even in a little town like Hernando City. And the terrified kid had stared at him stonily in the distorted light of the putrid green rest room, and gradually his expression shifted from fear to disgust to pity.

Button kept talking until he could tell the kid really felt sorry for him. Then he calmed down himself, and he talked awhile longer. Finally he and the kid went outside and Button thanked the boy for being so understanding. And he fired off a couple of pictures. Button figured that sealed their bargain of silence, and it gave him leverage if he ever came back and wanted to pick up the kid again. Those ''after'' shots were always powerful tools. They shifted him from victim to accomplice. They confirmed a state of compliance. However outraged or disgusted the kid may feel or have felt over what transpired, because he allowed these ''after'' pictures to be taken, Button could use them. He could show him an indisputable visual image, tangible proof that he obviously had come through it and made his peace with Button afterward. They said it hadn't been so bad. The pictures didn't lie.

But Jack Button had no intention of going near that Hernando City kid again. Not any kid. Not now. He remembered that feeling of desperation when he touched the kid and started sinking to his knees. He was terrified that it might happen again. So far he'd been lucky. Never once had one of his special kids turned on him. None had told. Now he was about to make a quantum leap in his career, and he couldn't take any risks. Not with a minor.

But Mark Zimmerman was no child. Button had looked

for him on Sunday, as if he were some kind of loose end that needed to be neatly tied. He had scoured the volunteer list for his name but there was no check beside it, then he searched the mound anyway in case Zimmerman had somehow missed signing in. But he never showed. Button had gone through the scheduled events without a hitch, then went home to his Percodan and turned off the world.

Monday, Zimmerman was back.

"Mr. Button? Do you remember that Lieutenant Rowe from the Robbie James case?" Sandy Huff called over Button's headset about midmorning. Button was leading a trio of bay-area news photographers, all banded in green, across the already completed upper plateaus for close-up shots. The television crew had made the same circuit an hour before, again with Button leading the way.

"Sure." Button stood absolutely still, staring down at the staff tent where Sandy was sitting.

"Well, he just called here. He'd like to see you and Mr. Shepherd down here in about thirty minutes. It seems there has been another assault on a child." Button's stomach knotted.

"I'll be down shortly," he responded, struggling to keep his voice steady. He checked his watch. It was eleven o'clock. As far as he knew, other than the general overview on the morning show, there had been no TV coverage of Dunesfest during the day. And since so many photographers were out, he'd worn sunglasses and the visor all day Sunday, efficiently diverting any press coverage toward the sculptors and the fairy-tale characters. He intended to stay out of the media for a while, just in case the Hernando City kid might make a connection.

Now Button wiped his brow, determined not to panic. Repeatedly he assured himself that he'd covered himself with the kid. He'd given him the Buddy Butler routine, with a false name, a false hometown, an esoteric tale about the kind of work he did. Then he'd concocted that bullshit story about being lonely. He was real convincing. And when it was over, he'd even checked that the kid was nowhere in sight when he got into his car. Rowe's call was just a coincidence, Button told himself.

Then he saw Zimmerman. And like the shifting patterns in a kaleidoscope, there were a whole new set of possibilities. The youth was standing two levels below him, partially screened by an umbrella shading the cold-drink break station. Like Button, he was wearing dark sunglasses. But he was watching.

"I've got to go back down in a few minutes," Button told the three photographers. "Is there anything else in particular you'd like to see before we retrace our route?" It came out smooth and genial enough, but Jack Button could feel his mind racing. There had to be a statute of limitations.

"Sorry to have to inconvenience you both," Terry Rowe greeted Button and Bo Shepherd in the security office in the Grand Nile Hotel. Showered and dressed in street clothes, Rowe looked young and somber and less official than Button expected. Button had left a message at the gate for him to meet them in the security office. Whatever crime Rowe was here to discuss, Button wanted to have the details in private.

As soon as Shepherd closed the door, Rowe got to the point. "We just picked up another child assault case with the same general MO and the same description as the perpetrator in the Robbie James case. Right down to the webbed fingers." Rowe handed both of them duplicates of the description Paulie Kirby gave. "The boy went fishing early Saturday morning about six miles from here. . . .''

"Saturday . . ." Button stood staring at the paper Rowe had given him. His hands trembled. Cold sweat trickled down his back. This assault wasn't in Hernando City. It had nothing to do with him. He let out a slow, silent breath.

"The guy threw him against a stump. Scraped him up. Assaulted him. Then took off. They waited to report it and the kid bathed and all before he was examined by a doctor. We don't have any solid medical proof, but from the description, we know it was the same guy. He was gritty and hairy. Down at the station, they're calling him Sandman.'' Rowe's words sounded distant and hollow and vaguely inconsequential until he said Sandman.

Button's head snapped up. "Wait a minute."

"Sandman . . ." Bo Shepherd arched his eyebrows. "Oh, that's real cute."

"I know. That's why I came right over here. It's a grabber. Especially with the castle and the Dunes and all. But I want you folks to be prepared.''

"The Dunes wasn't connected with this incident in any way," Button countered.

"True," Rowe agreed. "But he is staying close to the area. He seems to know the backwoods enough to cover his tracks. The K-9 went out to this location and he did the same thing. The trail starts and ends with the creek. Only this time, there were indications of a boat of some sort being beached there. Could be we've got some sort of hermit character hiding out in the woods.''

"We sure have a lot of waterways around here," Bo Shepherd noted. "If the guy has a boat with a shallow draft, he could show up anywhere. Back at the family condos, or the country club, or right on the steps of the hotel.''

''We don't want to start a panic,'' Button cut him off sharply. ''This guy hit here once, I doubt if he'd be stupid enough to come back.''

''The point is that he may be smart enough to come back,'' Rowe said quietly. ''I think your guests should be advised to take precautions. Children should not be allowed to wander off alone. Your security staff needs to be briefed.''

''And what do we do out at the mound,'' Button asked, ''make hourly announcements that some hairy, web-fingered monster may at any minute grab a kid and drag him off into the woods?''

''I'm not saying he's a monster. We don't know what to make of the webbed-finger bit. But we've got two pretty consistent descriptions. And they're both from kids that he did grab and drag off into the woods''

''Sandman's a-comin' and he's gonna' get you. . . .'' Bo Shepherd made the childlike singsong comment unnervingly ominous.

''The children are safe here.'' Button issued the declaration amid a crosscurrent of dark sensations.

''That's probably what Paulie Kirby's mama thought about their trailer park.'' Rowe's grim expression tightened. ''And I bet Robbie James's dad thought his kid was safe here. But this Sandman thought otherwise.''

''Stop calling him that.'' Button's lips thinned in annoyance.

''Look, I don't care what you call him. I just came here to give you some advance warning. I'm not even on duty today. But I think we've got a problem here. And I think we'd better make some serious plans to be sure the children are safe." There was a perceptible tremor in the muscle above Rowe's jawline.

Button lowered his round eyes and calmed himself. "You're right. You're absolutely right." He shrugged, shifting, chameleonlike, into a more diplomatic stance. "I'd like to handle this as quietly as possible. I'll have a security staff meeting scheduled for this afternoon. But I'd like to keep this Sandman name out of the headlines. Stick to calling him a hermit or a derelict or whatever. Just not Sandman." His familiar, efficient mask descended once again. "I want a chance to meet with the sculptors later on in the evening and give them the details as smoothly as possible. We've got the manpower to keep everything under control."

"What about the boats? You want me to have Buddy do a check and see if any of the feluccas are missing?" Bo Shepherd suggested. "Maybe we should suspend any sailing until this guy is caught. He could be out there somewhere waiting in ambush."

"First make sure the boats are all accounted for." Button tried to slow the pace. "We'll discuss the next step later."

"It may be a good idea to keep any kids from taking out boats unless there's an adult along," Bo persisted. "Some of those back waterways are real picturesque, but they're out in the middle of nowhere. Just a lot of bushes and some wildlife. We just don't know how wild. . . ." he added pointedly.

"We don't need to take chances," Button acknowledged. "Have that handled through the boat checkout. Just have the dock hands be real subtle about it. Don't make any general announcements. Let's keep the hysteria level down. I still think he wouldn't dare come back around here."

"He may never have left," Rowe stated.

"Well, if he does come around," Bo said slowly, checking over the description, "he should stick out like a sore thumb with all that hair and those damned fingers. Must be some kind of birth defect or something. Sandman. We'll get the word out on him."

Button gave him a hard look. "I wish you'd watch your terminology," he said in a voice that was firm, final. But even he knew how futile it was The name fit. Dark, hairy, covered in grit. Creeping around between twilight and dawn. Sandman. It would be dynamite in print.

"We're going to rebox the forms for the sails and mast over here," Kevin Walters told the crew assembled on the lower plateaus of the north mound. The magnificent thirty-foot-long fire-breathing dragon still commanded the heights, but below the fortress walls, portions of the lower sections were collapsing.

"The sand has dried out too much to get clean cuts unless we wet it down, so we'll have to pull in the hoses and backtrack a bit. Just keep in mind that wetting the sand at this point can get risky. Even with the lower forms still in place, we may have some breakaways. So keep alert. We may have to jump clear if the top shifts." Kevin's dark olive eyes studied the upper plateaus and the billowing dragon's breath. "I sure hope we can keep this under control," he murmured softly.

The lower plateaus were still supported by a series of wood-framed tiers, waiting for the crews to work their way down and remove them. Some levels had additional smaller boxed molds stacked up on them, designated for individual figures. But the sand spillover from the dry upper plateaus had half-buried some of those smaller molds. Kevin had called for a lower-mound "face-lift."

Once the workers repaired the largest, steplike forms that had been pulled off the day before, the spillover could be loaded into hoppers and lifted back up the mound.

"The northwest section needs to be reboxed for Pinocchio and the whale. North central we can simply level it off then let it set awhile. We planned to fill it in with waves, mermaids, and dolphins anyway. We can use small molds for them, but we have to get these big displays resurrected first." Craig Stuart stood on a ledge slightly above Kevin and the rest the group, pointing out the work areas on the schematic he and Kevin had revised that morning. Vince and Kitty had joined the two of them earlier, checking and rechecking the condition of the sand. Throughout the night much of the detail work they'd finished the previous day on the north mound had been sliding away. The final consensus was that the only way to prevent further erosion and save the front end of the dragon and the Turkish fortress was to reframe and rewet the entire area.

"Upper northeast has to be re-formed to make the sails for the ship of the Four Skillful Brothers," Craig continued. "Midnortheast is all right. It's still in molds for the Twelve Princesses. We'll simply rewet them and try not to pull too much sand down around them." While the workers crowded around, Craig pointed ot the trouble spots and directed the activity.

"For those of you who missed the glamour of shoveling and stomping wet sand last week, Mother Nature has offered you a second opportunity," Kevin declared, grinning his lopsided smile. He looked out over the group of about thirty-five volunteers and six crew members. Because of the somewhat precarious condition of the north mound, everyone else had been restricted to the south and central mounds until the face-lift was completed.

The crane with its hopper basket had been brought in to straddle the moat, close to the base. "Just don't try to prove how tough you are. You can contribute more with a steady succession of three-quarter shovel loads than you can if you throw your back out with a few overloaded ones. We can't rush this or we'll end up making mistakes." He picked up a shovel and demonstrated, his body swaying with the power and grace of a man long accustomed to heavy labor.

"The trickiest part of this procedure is regulating the water," Craig Stuart stressed. "I want only the crew chiefs operating those hoses. So let's get to it and please be careful. Kevin and I will try to run interference with the equipment."

The crew leaders split off, each taking a contingent of shovelers to one of the designated locations. Kitty and Vince went back to their mound, both of which were drying at a slower pace.

"What's your agenda?" Vince asked her, knowing the reconstruction would disrupt any setup work she'd anticipated on the north end.

"Trolls."

"Trolls? Where does it call for trolls?"

"It doesn't. But I've got a load of volunteers ready to work. We have some vacant space between Hansel and Gretel and the Ugly Duckling," Kitty said, waving one hand to show the area intended for the duck pond. On the level below, low molds were set up for an exotic garden Myron Hansen would do with large flowers, small fairies, birds, butterflies, and Tom Thumb and Thumbelina. "I want everyone to feel useful. So I'm improvising."

"And obviously that means trolls." Vince shrugged accommodatingly.

"Don't you remember any fairy tales about trolls living in the hillsides?" Kitty asked. "Sandy Huff loaned me her books and I tracked down a couple of good ones about how the earth sometimes opens up to reveal the trolls' secret kingdom. I think I can turn that ridge into a split in the earth and work in some neat dwarfish faces." She made a horizontal sweep. "It will look like they're all huddled together, peeking out, like a bunch of kids ready to get into mischief."

"I thought trolls were foul-tempered little fellows who hid under bridges and kidnapped girls and boys."

"And billy goats and fair young maids and innocent travelers," Kitty added simply, remembering the tales. "But those are the bad trolls. Mine are nicer." She was looking at the blank plateau of sand, but Vince knew there were already faces looking back at her in her mind, and apparently none of them were malevolent.

"Yours are nicer. . . ." Vince grinned, clearly amused.

"Right. Until they get that area cleared for the Twelve Princesses and their dancing partners, I'm sort of at a standstill anyhow. This will keep some of my folks busy without making too big a mess. So while Jaisen and part of my crew do their thing with the duck pond and Elizabeth Frye and her brigade go ahead with ducks and swans, I figured I'd take some people and work in some trolls."

"That's perfectly logical to me," Vince said, straight-faced. "But don't you think that after a week of this, between all the Egyptian stuff at the hotel and the fairy tales out here, we're all sounding like we stepped into a Spielberg movie?" he kidded her.

"My only reading material lately has been Hans Christian Andersen and the Grimms," Kitty agreed, shaking her head slightly. "What part of never-never land are you doing today?"

"Paul Feneau and I are whipping together a street scene and an inn for old Puss 'n Boots and the four critters for the Bremen Town Musicians. Then I'm coming off the mound totally to start framing up the sponsors' logos."

"You have everything else done?" Kitty shaded her eyes and looked over the surface of the sound mound. There were over a hundred volunteers there, laboring on cobblestone streets or diligently putting tile roofs, a multitude of windows, flower boxes, protruding gables, or stairways on a hillside crowded with churches, shops, and quaint old houses.

"I've delegated most of the work. I don't need to do anything but check the scale occasionally. I've got a lot of good carvers who can improvise, too. Button says the sponsors are pretty anxious. They want their logos done. Can't say I blame them. There's a lot of good press coverage slipping by."

"I guess that's right," Kitty admitted, frowning as she looked thoughtfully down at the tent Button had installed that morning to accommodate the increasing number of photographers and film crews. He'd even had electric ceiling fans installed to keep them more comfortable. Several news services had sent people to cover the event. "I suppose I could pull off the mound and work on the Bloomingail's head if you need me."

"Just take your time with your trolls for now," Vince reassured her. "When we have something for you to carve on, I'll come and get you. But it won't be today," he declared.

"Okay, but I'll be here if you need me," Kitty told him.

"A fair maid among the trolls." Vince chuckled. "Just don't let them carry you off."

"I told you, mine are nice ones. They don't do things like that." A light smile played across her lips.

"I'll see you at lunch then," Vince said in parting. "I'd be glad to grab you and carry you off. Maybe for an artichoke and avocado salad in the Courtyard?"

"I'll surrender without a fight."

"Meet me at the tent at twelve, I'll try to get Button's golf cart and we'll ride off together." He turned and followed the pathway onto the construction area on the south mound, bypassing the Pied Piper and his rodent followers.

"Okay, guys, I need this edge cut out along here," Kitty summoned the shovelers who were assigned to help her. "Take it back about a foot and square it off. See if we hit any sand that has some moisture in it." She walked the twenty-foot stretch of sloping sand, watching the shovelers lift away the drier, outer sand and toss it into a pile farther down. Using a metal spatula, she stepped between them from time to time and cut a few vertical bands in the newly exposed surface. All told, she guessed she could get the head and shoulders of fourteen trolls there. "It's still pretty dry. Take it back about six more inches." This time the surface held her cuts.

"I want most of you to go down to the next level and help Jaisen with the pond and whatever else he needs. Or you can scrape up the loose sand and help Elizabeth mold ducks. Elizabeth is the one with the peach-colored picture hat." She pointed out the sprightly old woman below. Then Kitty blocked out the general shape of the first of the fourteen dwarfish figures, with lumps left on for squat hats, frizzy hair, big ears, puffy beards, and bulbous noses.

"How about the rest of you grabbing some cutting tools and clearing out between these figures. Just cut in about six inches. Anyone who feels ready can start in on a face. Leave the lower edges sticking out so we can have their hands and arms protruding. And if anyone isn't busy, we need some buckets of water up here." Almost eagerly, she dropped down onto her knees and began doing the farthest face in more detail. Barely glancing at the four who remained to help, she crafted one chubby, impudent face and moved on to the next. "Someone can give this fellow clothes," she called another carver into action.

One red-banded carver started at the midpoint, crouching so he was working at eye level like Kitty. A young woman, banded in shovelers' white, decided to try her hand carving and moved farther down. One shoveler in a straw hat, souvenir T-shirt, and overalls put a half-filled bucket of water behind each of them.

"That's good," Kitty commented on a gnomelike face emerging from the sketchy outline she'd started earlier. The young male carver with the calico headband smiled, paused to watch her cutting away on her troll, then went back to his own. The young woman looked from one to the other apprehensively. Then she started in again. For a few moments they all worked in silence. Then Kitty got up and walked behind them, looking over their shoulders to see how they were doing.

"Let me give you a little more to work with," she said to the young woman. With deep, sure cuts, she realigned the eyes, nose, ears, and chin. "Go ahead. Finish it. Don't be timid. Cut into it. See how it goes. I'll be here to bail you out if you have trouble." The young woman gave her a grateful but dubious look.

The young man in the center was moving along on his

own. "You can backcut the nose and eyes a little more," Kitty coached him, using one of her half-finished faces to show him how to backcut. She took the smaller carving blade and cut along the facial features to give the illusion of depth. "Even a little crevice makes a nice dark shadow. Close up it may look strange, but from a distance it works great."

The fellow cut a similar slice on his troll deepening the shade line around the nose. Suddenly the nose appeared more prominent. "I get it," he murmured. He sliced a deeper opening between the lips.

"We'll get the sprayer to come over as soon as we've done each one. I love those eyes. . . ." She paused and leaned back, grinning at the puffy, froglike eyes he'd cut out above the snoutlike sweet-potato nose. "This guy has real personality. Is he someone you've met?" she joked.

"You might say that. I used to play Dungeons and Dragons," the young carver replied. "There was a time I knew all the monsters by name, rank, and special abilities. They all had distinct powers and personality traits, and I could probably still quote their vital statistics. Back then, I took the game a little too seriously, but this is fun. This one looks like a cross between an orc and a gnome, except the gnomes wore armor and orcs are a little more animal-faced."

"I don't care what he's called, I really like him. That face is exceptionally good. We definitely need your kind of imagination. What's your name?"

"Mark. Mark Zimmerman," the fellow answered.

"I'm Kitty Westberg. If you're going to be around, I can sure use you the rest of the week. There's an old crone or two we'll tackle once they get the north mound ready. Then there's all kinds of leprechauns and fairies or anything else you can dream up. And if you can do handsome as well as you do ugly, we can team up for twelve very lovely princesses and their escorts."

"I'll be here the rest of the week. I'd be glad to work with you," Mark said quietly. "I've been watching you for a couple of days. I'm learning a lot."

"Believe me, we're all learning a lot. I've never even heard of an orc before or about gnomes wearing armor," Kitty noted. "But it's never too late to pick up some valuable pointers."

Zimmerman looked at her a bit defensively. Her bemused expression made it clear that she wasn't being the least bit sarcastic.

"I'll be back in a little while to see your next creation." She went back to her end of the lineup and left both volunteers engrossed in their work.

"How about getting a small shovel and digging out all that background." Kitty turned to the remaining shoveler. He'd been following her along, lifting away all the loose sand she and the others cut away and routinely replenishing the water supply. He stood there uncertainly.

"Here, take this." She grabbed a three-inch shovel from her tool belt and demonstrated. "Like this . . ." With fast and efficient jabs, she cut away the extra sand on the space of wall between two of her trolls. "Just clear it back about this deep," she stressed, stopping when she'd reached the depth she wanted. Then she handed the small shovel to the man. He took it in his gloved hand. Then he stood there a moment longer.

"Come on. I know you're signed on as a shoveler, but right now I need you to shovel on a smaller scale. You won't hurt anything," she encouraged him. "Just lift out the excess and pitch it behind you. We'll pick it up later."

Carefully Lon placed his long-handled shovel aside.

Then he knelt down on his knees, face-to-face with a troll, like the three others were crouching. And just as she showed him, he lifted out the unnecessary sand between the figures, so each one stood out in high relief.

He couldn't bring himself to look directly at her this close up. He was afraid he'd panic if she caught him staring right at her. So he dug away neatly like she'd told him, aware every second of her movements. Whenever she moved over and started crafting a figure farther down, he shifted on to the next space, too. Each time he almost caught up with her, he'd get too nervous to keep his hands steady. He'd stop, get up and take the long handled shovel, and clear away the sand behind her. Then he'd fill up the water buckets. Once Kitty had moved on a bit and the thundering of his heartbeat had subsided, he'd put the large shovel aside and take out her smaller one, and go back to work.

"I sure think we're doing something right," Kitty exclaimed, stepping away for a moment to scan the lineup. "We're moving right along. Mark, your little men are great." Each of his three completed figures was delightfully grotesque and individualized. The latest fellow had one eye closed, staring out suspiciously, and was smoking a large briar pipe. "And you . . ."

"Susan . . ." the girl responded.

"Susan, you're doing much better. Don't worry about making every detail perfectly symmetrical. We're after dramatic. Make your cuts a little deeper around the features. Be brave," she encouraged her.

Then Kitty walked over behind Lon, who was on his knees, digging away silently. "I can't thank you enough for the way you're keeping this area neat. You're doing a great job with this part, clearing out the background, but it sure helps that you're also keeping the rest of the ledge picked up," she said, standing behind him and resting her hand on his shoulder. "What is your name?"

He shook his head. The wide brim of his straw hat shaded his entire face. Kitty bent down and saw the uncertainly in his expression.

"Can you tell me your name?" she asked softly. He pouted out his lips, heavily coated with white zinc oxide, and hung his head. His pulse was suddenly thundering in his ears.

"Can you talk at all?" They had been working together for almost two hours, and Kitty realized that the heavyset fellow who looked like a farm worker hadn't said a word. He'd followed directions precisely and had not been idle for a moment. She knew he could hear. Now she studied his moonlike face, covered in rough stubble, and saw the peculiar mixture of petulance and embarrassment there. It was an expression she'd seen occasionally on Zach when he was confronted by an awkward situation that would make him self-conscious about being slow.

"I know this is uncomfortable for you, but it's all right if you don't like to talk much. I'm really pleased that you're working with us, and I want you to keep at it. I just want to be able to say your name when we talk. You can talk a little, can't you?

He nodded. He could talk.

"I thought so. I'm Kitty. Please, tell me your name."

Lon ground his teeth anxiously, dreading that he might make a sound that would offend her.

"Try . . ." Kitty coaxed him. "You've done such a good job here. Mark and Susan and I have been real fortunate to have you as our backup man. Please. Don't be shy."

Lon shrugged. Then he tried to move his tongue. It

felt dry and swollen, and he knew it was because she was so close to him. She was so beautiful. He could smell the scent of her body and feel the pressure of her hand on his shoulder.

"Lo-on." It came out in two syllables. With a nervous swallow in the middle. He was burning with a heat that didn't come from the sun.

"That's good. Could you say it once more."

He had to exert a conscious effort to draw in a breath. He felt his throat constrict. "Lon. My name is Lon." It came out hushed and hoarse, barely a whisper. But she understood.

"Okay, Lon. Is that it? Lon?"

He nodded.

"Lon. Fine." She looked sympathetically at his sweat-streaked face, a bit more ashen now. "You are one heck of a good worker, Lon. This is Susan and next to you is Mark. Meet Lon."

Mark Zimmerman had not stopped work, but he'd been close enough to listen. He hadn't wanted to make the situation more tense for the big fellow by gaping at him. Now he turned and reached out a sandy hand. "Nice to meet you." Lon stared at the proffered hand, then he looked down at his own, enclosed in heavy work gloves. "No problem," Mark grabbed it, glove and all, and shook it. Startled by the contact, Lon simply stayed immobile until Zimmerman let it go.

Kitty glanced at her watch. It was almost noon. "Look, time for a break. Why don't you all go on down and get some cold drinks and a hot dog or something. Get out of the midday sun for a while. How about meeting me back here in half an hour?"

Zimmerman looked at his watch and nodded. Lon didn't move. He wasn't ready to go down. At dawn, he'd hurdled the fence and crept into the compound. He'd hidden on the west side of the mound, away from the tents and cold-drink stands. He'd lain there, behind the wooden forms, before anyone arrived. Then he'd waited, watching the people pass by, until there were so many banded volunteers on the heights that he could slip out and move in among them, shovel in hand, without being noticed at all. Getting up the mound and passing himself off as a worker had been an ordeal. He'd had to squeeze the shovel handle until his hands were numb to keep himself from shrieking and running away. But finally he had seen her, in her loose sand-colored pants and pale T-shirt, with a lace-patterned sun hat casting shadows like butterflies over her shoulders. He had simply followed her and waited until she began work, then he joined in.

Working so near to the one Zach called Mom had alternately thrilled and terrified him. Watching up close the magic she did with her hands and a few unlikely tools made him want to weep. Smelling her body scents stirred something else in him. And her voice, soft and low and calming, was sweeter than the wind. Then she had touched him. She had said his name, and he had dared only a quick glimpse into her strange blue eyes. There was nothing submissive, none of the breeder's acquiescence in those eyes. That disturbed him. She looked at him straight on, like an equal, but without any combativeness. And as she talked, he began to feel the panic subside and a thousand other sensations began to tantalize him. Having to leave her now and go down the mound made him want to bellow in frustration.

"Come on, Lon. Let's get a cool one," Zimmerman urged him. "I've been through this before. I'll show you the ropes." He'd untied his headband and rinsed it in the water bucket, wrung it out, then mopped his face and neck. He rinsed it a second time and hung it from his jeans waistband. "Half an hour." He nodded to Kitty. "We'll be here."

"Go on now." Kitty shooed Lon along. "You've been working hard. These fellows can wait." She tilted her head at the eight completed trolls and the six others, only vague outlines in the sand. Lon looked from her to the trolls uncertainly. Then she smiled. That strange quick glimmer of light in her eyes caught him by surprise, and he realized that she was making a game.

"You wait," he repeated, pointing his gloved finger at them. "Stay here." He stretched his mouth into a line so she'd know he could make games, too. Then he followed the man named Mark without looking back.

"What's the meeting all about?" Vince asked Roseanne Petty on the bumpy ride into the Grand Nile Hotel for lunch. Button and his golf cart had already left for the hotel when Vince came down at lunchtime, so he'd planned on using the shuttle. Then Button had sent Roseanne Petty in the cart back to the staff tent for a list of all the volunteers, and she'd offered Vince and Kitty a ride. From the solemn expression on her face, Vince knew something was wrong.

"I'm not supposed to say," Roseanne glanced at Vince and Kitty, then she let out a quick burst of air. "I'm not into the secrecy stuff," she admitted. "Lieutenant Rowe was decent enough to tell me that there's been another assault on a child. Near here. Security is being upped, and the police are going over all employee and volunteer records checking for previous criminal records. I called my sitter and told her to keep the door locked. Apparently that creep who attacked the James boy is still in the vicinity.''

Vince could see Kitty stiffen. Her sea blue eyes iced over.

"Easy now. Zach's well supervised. Notice that the guy did not come back around here," Vince cautioned her.

"I want to go to that meeting." Kitty's jaw set.

"Kitty, it's just for the security staff," Roseanne explained apologetically. "I really shouldn't have mentioned it at all. Mr. Button plans to have a special meeting with the sandsculptors this evening. He'll tell you everything then."

"I want to hear what he's telling them, not what he tells us," Kitty insisted. "I don't want the sugarcoated version."

"I doubt if he'd be too pleased about this. I think Bo Shepherd is the one in charge. He and Lieutenant Rowe."

"Where's the meeting?"

"Second floor. But they'll shoot me if they find out I told you about it."

"They won't. Kitty sat back, thin-lipped. "I just want to get the straight story. I don't like the idea of some Neanderthal lurking around here when I've got Zach with me." For a few seconds, no one spoke.

"They think he might be some kind of hermit," Roseanne added uneasily. "Lieutenant Rowe thinks he may have been hiding out in the woods somewhere around here, perhaps for quite a while."

"That's not very reassuring," Kitty said tersely.

"Sounds like my jokes about trolls weren't so funny after all," Vince muttered glumly. "Apparently all the monsters in the neighborhood aren't ones in fairy tales."

Roseanne Petty looked at him, with a dark and troubled expression. "They're calling this one Sandman. . . ." She bit her lip nervously. "Not officially, of course. The description matches the other one, all hairy and wild. Only this kid remembers that the guy was all gritty. Of course, Mr. Button is upset because it makes it sound like this guy might be connected to Dunesfest, you know, with all the sand. That's why they're checking these lists. They're running the names through a computer." She kept her eyes straight ahead as she guided the golf cart along it route, but her voice had a hollow sound. "I just find it all really spooky. Sandman. I don't like the name at all."

"I don't like any of it," Kitty said quietly. "Not at all."

Jack Button was courteous but a bit stiff when Kitty and Vince approached him in the hallway outside the security meeting. He and Rowe were looking at the lists Roseanne Petty had just handed them.

"I don't have time to waste churning over rumors," Kitty said simply, sidestepping Button's inquiry about how she happened to find out about the meeting. "I can deal with the facts a whole lot better. Before I feel comfortable about going back out and leaving Zach for the afternoon, I want to hear what's going on. We'd like to sit in the back and listen. You don't mind if we sit in for a while." She asked Lieutenant Rowe first.

"Fine with me."

Roseanne Petty said nothing. She just stood off behind Button, looking relieved.

"I figure you folks would understand," Kitty said, glancing only fleetingly at Button. "You know how mothers are. . . ." Kitty and Vince left Button standing there, assuming that somehow they must have heard about this latest assault from the spectators or perhaps other workers on the mound. She didn't give him a chance to object to her request.

"We're going to continue like we've been doing, only we'll add a few more staff each shift," Bo Shepherd told the group of adjunct security people. "We are going to curtail some activities involving youngsters at the hotel particularly. No more unsupervised walks along the Nature Trail or backwater adventures in the feluccas. It seems that his fellow has a flatboat of some sort. We don't want any kid running into him."

"But didn't Lieutenant Rowe say that he comes out mostly at night or real early in the morning? No one uses the feluccas then," one of the security personnel noted.

"We only know what he's done so far. First time was early evening. Last time, he hit early in the morning. We're stopping the kids from going out in the feluccas alone or deep into the trail just in case he tries an afternoon attack. We'd rather not make it easy for him."

"Zach isn't going to like this," Kitty muttered. "He loves taking the boats out."

"They'll let him go if a counselor or one of us has to go with him."

"I rather he stay away from the waterways completely," Kitty whispered. "Maybe we can give him something else to do."

Vince looked at her curiously. "Like what?"

"We could have him come out to work with us," Kitty said thoughtfully. "I know they said no kids on the mound. But as long as you're coming down to work the logos, maybe you could use him as a ground-level assistant. Zach would love it. He's been itching to be involved with this thing. We're down to the last few days. I'd feel better having him near one of us."

Vince kept his voice low. "Button would have heart

failure. There's probably something in the small print on the insurance about not having a kid working at all.''

"I can understand keeping him off the mound. But on the ground . . .'' She shook her head. ''The logos aren't terribly complicated. You said yourself, Zach's pretty good at small details.''

"He is.''

"So . . . ?''

"So I'll ask Button at our meeting tonight,'' Vince promised, hushing her while Bo Shepherd continued talking.

"If he refuses . . .''

"I'll try to make sure he doesn't,'' Vince said succinctly. ''I'd feel better having Zach around a little more myself.'' The details of the second assault had gotten to him.

"Good.''

Mark Zimmerman was the first to greet her when Kitty returned to the mound half an hour later than scheduled. ''Say, what happened to you? We waited, then we figured we'd better go on without you.'' He and Lon had finished two more trolls. The worker named Susan was nowhere in sight. ''I think she fizzled.'' Mark thumbed toward the uncompleted face that Susan had been doing before their break. ''She didn't come back after lunch.''

"That happens,'' Kitty said. ''Sorry I'm late, but I went to a meeting.''

"I think your friend there was worried.'' Mark leaned closer so Lon wouldn't hear. ''He's been working all alone, but he's been watching out for you.''

"Well, I'm back. You guys have been doing very nicely without my help,'' she said, raising her voice a bit so Lon could hear. He was busying himself farther along the ledge, but she could tell he was listening. ''Sorry I was delayed, Lon," she apologized. "But I saw you two up here slaving away, and I brought you something. She opened her ditty bag and held out two foil-wrapped ice-cream Fudgicles. "Hurry before they melt."

She handed one to Mark. Lon looked at the thing she offered him doubtfully.

"I hope you like chocolate." Kitty ripped back the paper and folded it around the stick. Then she held it out again. Careful not to drop it, Lon took it in his gloved fist. The smell was wonderful. "My son loves these things," Kitty said, reaching in the bag for a third one. "I guess Susan loses out," she said, claiming the last one for herself.

"This is great. Thanks." Mark Zimmerman caught a piece of sliding chocolate with his tongue.

"Hurry," Kitty coaxed Lon. "Or all you'll have is a puddle." She bit into hers.

Lon watched them both, then he took a bite. He stood still, letting the cold delicious substance glide over his tongue. Then he saw that Mark had almost finished his, so he took more bites. Then suddenly, it was gone. All he had was a thin wooden stick and that heavenly scent on his gloves.

"Okay, let's get through with these guys," Kitty said, licking her fingers then rinsing her hand before backing up to study the faces already done.

"Something wrong?" Mark came and stood next to her, bewildered by the strange and disquieting look on her face. "Did we mess up somehow?"

Kitty stared from one ragged bearded face to the next, haunted by Lieutenant Rowe's description of the assailant. Vince had been right, the jokes about trolls weren't so funny anymore. The impudent troll faces had been transformed. The bulging eyes and grimacing mouths framed in wild, bushy hair were no long innocent. A maniacal grin and a half wink became a evil leer. They all looked like the one called Sandman. They all reminded her of the horrible things he had done. They were no longer her or Mark's creations. They were monsters.

"Kitty?" Mark's voice seemed to tug at her. "Are you all right?"

Slowly she turned. "I'm all right. I guess I'm a little more upset than I knew I was," she said quietly.

"Is there anything I can do?"

Mark was shifting from side to side in front of her, and she could tell that Lon was standing watching her. She felt foolish. "No . . . I'll be fine," Kitty said, wishing she could turn off a switch and stop the details of the assault from echoing through her head. Gritty. Gritty. The thought of the terrified child remembering that grit made her skin crawl. "I'll be better once I get back to work," she insisted.

"Well, pick your place."

Kitty tied on her tool belt and knelt down again. Without having to ask, she noticed a water bucket appear next to her, delivered by a gloved hand.

At the end of the day, Lon didn't want to leave. But when the sun settled low in the sky, Kitty said she was winding it up for the day. She carefully rinsed all her tools and tucked them into her ditty bag. "See you tomorrow," she told him. And she smiled and patted his shoulder and thanked him for his good work. Everyone else was coming down off the mound.

Lon stayed behind and picked up the area, poking Kitty's discarded Popsicle stick and wrapper in his pocket. Then patting the pocket holding his new memento, he left his shovel up top near the place they would begin the next morning and walked down alone.

Kitty waved at him once more before she went out the gate. She had stopped at the base of the mound by the big boxes newly filled with sand. She was with the dark-haired man Lon had seen her with before. The two of them were talking and looking up at the line of trolls. Then Kitty had bent her head against the man's neck, and he had draped an arm around her. Their faces were not happy. They had looked up at the row of trolls again, then they went off together toward the tall building. Lon didn't understand what their strange, comforting gestures meant. But seeing them touch each other like that made him feel peculiar. He had stared up at the trolls like they had, trying to comprehend what troubled them up there. All he saw were funny, almost familiar faces. They were all crowded together, like it had been in the great cave when there were many of them and they sat and drank and made jokes. He saw old friends, wetlanders. He saw kinsmen now buried and gone. And it made him both happy and sad.

Jack Button faced the roomful of sculptors. He'd called this cocktail-hour get-together an "information session." Most of the ones attending were team members and their dates or wives, but others who had signed on for the duration of the event were there, too. The majority of them were college kids, home for the spring break, but there were a few housewives and businessmen, retirees and professionals, all drawn into the fantasy and committed to see it through. Mark Zimmerman was among them. His sun-lightened hair and even tan were no more distinctive than the appearances of the fifty or so volunteers who had expanded the sculptors' ranks. Wearing a pale plaid sports shirt and gray shorts, Zimmerman had obviously showered and changed. Button found himself wondering where he'd gone in the interim and and where he stayed each night.

"We're holding this meeting to update you, not to alarm you," Bo Shepherd began with his clipped, military delivery. "We're doing it to assure you that the Dunes has everything under control. But we may get some unwanted publicity because of a crime that occurred within a few miles of here." He turned the podium over to Lieutenant Rowe, whose smooth, soft southern delivery contrasted with the hard-edged facts he had to present.

"There has been another assault on a child," Rowe began, his face a bit haggard despite his blond good looks. "We have a male perpetrator who abducts and rapes male children. He's between five-seven and six feet tall. His victims are small, so their perception of his height may be imprecise. But the rest of the description fits the guy that took the James boy from these grounds five days ago. He has a full beard, long hair. . . ."

Button kept his expression impassive as he listened the second time that day to Rowe's presentation. The description of the actual assault was less graphic than at the midday security staff meeting. Button felt his stomach tighten involuntarily as images of his encounter in Hernando City played off against the horror story Rowe was telling of the Paulie Kirby attack. But he didn't dare show any emotion, and he didn't dare leave. Standing off to the right with his shoulder against the wall in a deliberately casual stance, Button occasionally glanced over the group of sculptors. Even without looking directly at Zimmerman, he could tell the youth was watching him. So he stayed, appeared concerned, and kept his composure.

"We're safeguarding all the youngsters," Bo Shepherd was saying, "but that involves adult supervision at all times. There's no cause for alarm," he assured them. "We'll have plenty of security on duty twenty-four hours a day. We're not taking any chances. Just relax and be confident that we're around and your children are safe."

Button let him conclude, then took over. He told them that the buzzword in the press just might be Sandman. "You may have already heard rumors to that effect. Reporters try to be cute and clever and they are bound to play it up," he said, shrugging it off. "Sandman does have a rather dark ring to it. But it will pass. Just keep in mind that we've checked out all our people. Don't let some loose nut or some thoughtless verbiage in the newspaper get to any of you. Keep on doing what you're doing. Keep making something wonderful. As Kevin said early on, 'Do it for the sheer beauty of it.' I hope you continue to enjoy your stay at the Dunes." He thanked the full-time volunteers. He had Craig Stuart and Kitty give a brief summary of progress on the mound, and he invited them all to refill their glasses and enjoy the hors d'oeuvres. Then he mingled, making sure he never lost track of Zimmerman and that he targeted his next conversation partner before leaving the one he was with.

"I understand you're starting the eagle logo." He cornered Paul Feneau. "How long should it take to get the whole piece done?"

Zimmerman stayed essentially on the fringe. Even without looking, Button could sense his presence. Time after time, he'd glance over a shoulder and find himself momentarily locked to Zimmerman's serene and contemplative dark eyes. Button would smile a bit more affably at his conversation partner and laugh a little louder and look as if he were totally at ease. Then sometime later

Zimmerman simply wasn't there. Button made a slow circuit of the meeting room, easing through the guests, half expecting to see him again at some turn. But he was gone.

"I need to talk to you," Vince Ammons intercepted Button as he headed for the door.

"Sure. Is there something I can help you with." Button managed a quick smile, but his eyes tracked anyone who stepped toward the doorway or anyone who came in.

"I know Zack has some free time in the afternoon. Now that the feluccas are off limits, Kitty and I would like to have him help out on the logos. He's a pretty good carver, and he could stick with me. I'll make sure he keeps on ground level."

Button bit his lip impatiently. "That might cause some problems," he ventured. "There are other sculptors with kids who may want to get in on the act."

"Then let them," Vince said evenly. "They probably know as much about what's needed as half the adult volunteers. It wouldn't hurt to have a few kids out there showing that they can help."

The last comment hit home. Button pursed his lips. Then he leveled a sharp and assessing look at Vince. He nodded. "You're right. At this point, it wouldn't hurt. It would show youngsters making a positive contribution." Button liked the images that brought to him. Intense young faces glowing with enthusiasm. Active involvement. Children front and center at the Dunes. Good visual material. "Let's try it on a limited basis. I can't make an exception of Zach, so I'll have Corey ask for volunteers. Zach simply has to express an interest. If the other kids want to work, we'll try it like an apprentice system. Each one will be assigned to an adult worker.

And they can only help out on ground level.'' Button knew that letting kids pitch in would draw new interest from the press. ''We may need to scrape up a pile of sand somewhere down there for the spectators' kids to play around in. We might find some budding Michelangelos,'' he quipped.

''We could really use more the Walt Disney type,'' Vince said softly. But this time Button wasn't really paying attention, and Vince didn't really care. He just wanted to tell Kitty that he'd made the deal, and it came off a lot easier than he'd expected it to.

Once he'd left the meeting, Button headed straight for the desk clerk. ''Is there a Mark Zimmerman on the computer?''

''No, sir. He's not registered here.''

Button hesitated a moment then looked around the foyer of the hotel. The musicians on the raised platform had begun to fill the cavernous garden area with their soft sounds. Early diners were drifting into the the bars and pool areas while those dining later descended in the glass-walled elevators. No one hurried. Button glanced around, still wondering if Mark Zimmerman were around there somewhere, deliberately trying to stir up something.

''If you should need me, I'll be out at my place,'' Button called in the message to security. His neck was tight. He was tired of smiling. He wanted to get off stage.

''Yes, sir. Have a good evening, sir.''

Button walked out into the employees parking area. He paused to speak briefly to the uniformed guard. Then he strolled over to his parking place and unlocked the car. Tucked under the wiper was a sheet of hotel stationery. Button picked it up and tilted it to one side so he could read the message there.

The letters were blocklike and well formed. Almost like calligraphy.

Hope the Sandman brings you sweet dreams.

It wasn't signed.

The breeder woman was huddled just inside the cave entrance when Lon came home. She'd soiled herself.

"Tommy," he called into the dim interior. "Tom-mmeeee . . ." There was no response.

Lon guessed right off when he saw that the new pole was gone that his half brother had gone fishing. Tommy hadn't even taken the time to feed the breeder or give her water. While it was still light, Lon carried her down to the spring. He pulled off her breeches and rinsed them in the water, then carefully waded in, lifted her into the shallow part, and let her sit submerged up to her neck while he scooped up handfuls of water and washed her face. Her loose shirt drifted up, pulled along by the current, and her breasts and belly, swollen with child, looked like large ugly opalescent melons. Lon tried to pull the fabric down to cover her, but it only drifted up again.

The breeder never changed her expression. She never resisted. She never helped. She just blinked her eyes and stared at nothing.

Lon spoon-fed her the vegetable mush that Tommy had left. He gave her water until she stopped drinking and it dribbled down her face. He wiped off the overflow, led her to a grassy place under some oaks, and set her there until her clothes dried on her body.

Lon got out the gig next. He went a short distance upstream, scattered some food scraps in the water, then moved back down the creek a little ways and waited, hunched over and spear raised, for fish. It didn't take him long to get two. He built a small fire, quickly gutted the fish, sprinkled them with crushed leaves, impaled them with a stick, and propped them over the heat to cook. Then he lined some plump agave spears next to the hot firewood, where they would swell and bake, making a juicy addition to the fish. While he and the breeder sat there, hearing only the forest sounds as night began to settle over the wetlands, Lon took out his knife and started whittling the sweet-scented Popsicle stick.

Lon knew he wouldn't be able get her face right. Even while he worked that day with Kitty, every time he glanced over, he saw something new. Sometimes she looked so serious, he'd worry that she was angry. Sometimes she bit her lip in thought. And then something would please her and a smile would soften her lips and she would be so beautiful that Lon hardly dared to breathe. The face was constantly amazing to him. So instead of laboring on the face, he whittled the sun hat atop the slender body with the strong legs that made such long strides when she walked. Gradually the dream stick became a passable likeness. Lon gathered the leaves and roots and scraped cypress shavings to put on the fire after the fish were done so he could season the dream stick with the herbal smoke to make the magic work.

Tommy chewed on the wad of sweetflag root and lay on his stomach watching Lon from the underbrush across the creek. He'd been doing that all day, lying in the shade, watching Lon. In the morning, he'd tracked Lon all the way to that mound of sand, expecting to find him hiding out under the bushes. But Lon's trail led to the fence, so Tommy knew he'd climbed over.

Tommy had finally spotted him. He'd recognized the lumbering stride as Lon came down the walkway with a tall young man. They'd gone to a tent where a woman handed them food and drink. Then Tommy had watched, fascinated, as Lon ate, then walked back up the mound. All afternoon he shoveled and carried buckets and acted just like one of them. He even looked liked one of them.

Then afterward, Tommy had followed him back toward home. He saw Lon stop and take off his shirt and jeans and hat and put on a change of clothes he'd hidden away in a hollowed place at the base of a tree. Then Lon tucked the clothes, his hat, the work gloves, and some other things back in the secret place. Tommy reached in after Lon had gone on ahead and felt the bundle. But he didn't have time to pull it out. He'd hurried on to see what Lon would do next. But all Lon did was clean up the breeder, then catch some fish, then he sat there, whittling, like he often did at nightfall, while the aroma of cooking food drifted on the air.

Tommy's stomach grumbled. He was hungry. He moved back in the brush and circled around the creek. He'd come in empty-handed just as everything came off the fire. Lon would share.

Jack Button opened the sliding-glass doors and let the cool breeze from the marsh sweep the air-conditioned staleness from the room. Dressed in only his thin silk robe, he strolled onto the balcony and looked out over the moonlit grasses and the silver slashes of water.

"Sandman . . ." He whispered the word, pursing his lips slightly as the Percodan started to take effect. His neck muscles felt like tight springs, and the tension headache pulsed behind his eyes ferociously. Lying down was out of the question. Button knew the whole head would feel like it was coming off if he tried that. All he needed to do was wait, wait for the Percodan to ease everything. It had been one hell of a day.

He hadn't needed that damn note. *Sweet dreams . . .*

The words were his own. The Zimmerman kid was playing with him. It was bad enough that the youth was spooking around after something. But now he'd been clever enough to pick up on this Sandman thing and turn it all into a nasty little joke just to taunt him. Button didn't need the aggravation.

"Come on . . . damn it . . . ease up." Button slowly rolled his head first to one side, then to the other, trying to unknot the taut muscles. Then he poured himself a small scotch, just to calm his nerves while he waited for the Percodan. "Fuck him. . . ." he muttered, unable to shake the enigmatic image of Mark Zimmerman. The man-boy was getting under his skin. Button downed the drink in one gulp. Then he pushed the release and waited as the cabinet opened. Button tucked the book of photos under his arm and walked over to the glass doors. "Fuck you, too," he muttered to whatever hairy creature might be lurking out there on his waterways, contaminating the Dunes with his presence. "Fuck all of you."

Button closed the glass doors and switched the air-conditioning back on. He settled down on the sofa near the light. Gradually the space around him grew hazy, the cocoon of cool air enclosed him, and the beautiful young faces blurred before his eyes. "Sweet dreams . . ." Button nodded, jerking his head suddenly as he caught himself drifting off to sleep. Groggily, he closed the book and set it aside. He inched forward deliberately and leaned heavily on the armrest, pushing himself to his feet. Without stopping to switch off the lights, he ambled off into the bedroom and slid, stomach down, on top of the spread. Almost instantly his breathing became deep and regular.

Outside, the gentle wind over the marsh had the maidencane swaying. With his backside comfortably wedged between two branches of the tall sprawling branches of the oak, Mark Zimmerman took a bite of his Snickers bar and leaned back, waiting for Button to come back into view. But he didn't. Zimmerman aimed the binoculars at the hallway into which Jack Button had disappeared. He waited. He ate a small box of raisins. Button still didn't return.

Zimmerman sat there for a long time, staring at the illuminated living room, almost level with it. He had watched Button leafing through the photo album. It was still there, in plain view. And he wondered what was keeping Jack Button. After an hour, Zimmerman climbed down. Keeping close to the ground, he crept up to the building and pressed his ear against the wall. The only sound was the steady hum of the central-air unit.

But he'd found the place. And he'd watched the man. And he knew he could find him again anytime he wanted.

"Sweet dreams, you son of a bitch," Zimmerman whispered. Then he walked away.

Chapter 9

"I WON'T GET IN THE WAY OR ANYTHING," ZACH promised for the seventh or eighth time as he rode the shuttle from the hotel out to the mound after lunch to work with Vince. "I'll stick right by you. I won't be any trouble."

Vince rested his hand on the boy's shoulder, gently calming him. "Hey, I'm on your side, partner. I know you'll do just fine. Don't forget what your mom said about using sunscreen. Layer it on. You get burned out here, and your career as a sandsculptor is over."

While the shuttle bumped along, bypassing the steady pedestrian traffic between the Dunes and the mound, Zach uncapped the sunblock and rubbed some on, then pulled on one of Vince's spare team shirts, and coated his lips and nose with white zinc oxide.

"If we need a model for Pinocchio, I'll volunteer

you,'' Vince kidded him. "I think you overdid it a bit."
He smoothed the clot of white ointment on Zach's nose.
"Come on, partner. Let's get to work." Vince paused
long enough to relay a message through his headset to
Sandy Huff. "There'll be two of me out here this after-
noon, Sandy. So if you're reading shirt labels, the short
Vince is Zach. I'll be the other one."

"Got it," she replied, winking at Zach in his almost
knee-length official shirt. "Here's a visor." Behind him,
Vince was belting on his battery pack and adjusting his
headset.

"And tell Kitty that we're here," Vince added. "Ask
her to come down and visit when she gets a break."

"Will do," Sandy answered.

"Do I get one of those?" Zach kept in step with him,
eyeing the communications paraphernalia.

"I think having one of us wired is good enough. I may
let you try it out later. I doubt if you'll like the music,
though, I'm tuned in to classical today." Vince scanned
the progress on the three peaks as they passed along,
troubleshooting for any discrepancies in scale. "There's
your mom." He pointed to the north end. Kitty obviously had received his message and was looking for them.
Once she spotted them from her position on the lower
north mound where they'd just popped the molds on the
first three figures of the Twelve Dancing Princesses, she
waved vigorously and gave them the thumbs-up sign.
Then all three men surrounding Kitty turned and looked
down at them.

"I think your mom's showing you off to her buddies.
I guess you'd better wave." Vince nudged the boy. Zach
obliged. Then one by one the men waved back. The
heavy one, the one holding the shovel, hesitated the longest. Then he lifted a gloved hand in a shy, awkward sa-

lute. "That's Kevin on the left. I guess the guy with the headband is that carver she mentioned, Mark something. And I'd bet the fellow in the straw hat is the one who doesn't talk much."

Zach stared back at the men. Then he locked onto the shadowy face with the big white lips, and he grinned. "Yeah. That must be Lon. Mom said he was painted up so he kinda looks like a clown."

"So do you, sport," Vince reminded him, tapping his finger on Zach's ointment-covered nose. "Now let's show these folks what you can do." He picked up his tool belt and handed Zach a stainless four-by-twelve trowel and a small spatula. "I'm starting you off with lettering. I'll finish the sun emblem and the bathers, you'll spell out the company name along here." He made an arc with his hand beneath the larger-than-life tubes of tanning lotion and a couple, both in sunglasses, leaning back, using the tubes as beach chairs as they basked in the sun. The stylized sun in the background was the one used in the company trademark. "I want you to burnish this area with the trowel. Press hard. Glide that trowel over it. Get it real smooth and pretty. Then I'll sketch in the shape of the letters and you carve out between them and back-cut them so they stand out."

"I just get to do letters?" Zach questioned him.

"Let's look at it this way." Vince kept his voice low, conspiratorial. "There are seven separate logo displays set up across the front of the mound. All of them have to be lettered. Right?"

Zach shrugged.

"When they're almost finished with the big mound, along the base of it we'll need 'Once Upon a Time . . .' written in fancy script like it starts out in a storybook. Complete with little dots. Get the picture?"

Zach nodded.

"You pull this first title off nicely," Vince continued, "and you'll be front and center on our official label-making squad for the rest of the week. That should get you some flash on the old airwaves."

"You think so? Just doing lettering?"

"The sponsors will love you. The press will love you. And Jack Button will make sure you get coverage because you're so good-looking. Just play it cool. First, you do some nice work here," Vince stressed. "The glamour will come in its own good time."

Zach stared at the space thoughtfully, then he looked at the portion of the big mound where "Once Upon a Time . . ." would go. The labels and whoever worked on them would indeed be front and center. Then he arched his eyebrows and gave a tight nod and started in. Letters he could handle with no problem.

Zach had been working for almost an hour without stopping when Kitty's voice came from behind him. "That's coming along nicely."

He hadn't seen her approach. His right arm ached from pressing and sliding the big trowel over the sand to get the smooth, burnished look Vince had wanted. Now Vince had blocked in the word "Coppertone" just as it appeared on the products, and Zach had the "COP" part standing out in high relief. The rest still needed to be dug out and detailed. "You want to stop for a Coke break?" Kitty asked.

He glanced over his shoulder and saw there were drinks already in her hands. The sides of the cups were dripping with glistening drops. "Sure." Zach inched backward carefully until he was clear of the lettering before he stood up. "Thanks, Mom." He wiped his sandy hand on the leg of his shorts.

"Where's Vince? I had one for him, too."

"Someone called for him. He went off to help with the construction-company logo. He's down there." Zach pointed past Paul Feneau's eagle for the brewery and the flowery head that Kitty and Hansen had started for Bloomingail's Plants.

"How's it been going?"

"Okay, I guess." He stood next to her, sipping his soda while they stood back and looked at the letters he'd done so far. There'd been a marked decrease in attendance since the weekend, and Zach was vaguely disappointed that the excitement and attention he'd expected just hadn't materialized. People had passed by and occasionally commented, but essentially he'd worked undisturbed and unheralded. "Nice clean job," Kitty commended him. Zach nodded.

"Are you getting tired?" He was rubbing his upper arm unconsciously.

Zach shook his head. "Not really. I guess I'm out of practice," he admitted uneasily.

"It's tough adjusting the the first day on the job," she conceded.

"I'll be all right," Zach answered, self-conscious about making any complaints. "I'm not tired or anything. You don't happen to have a smaller trowel, do you? I could switch off once in a while. Like when I get to certain parts of the letters."

"I don't have a smaller one, but I can check around up there. I think switching off would be a good idea. I'll see what I can come up with."

"It's okay if I have to keep using this one," Zach said halfheartedly. "Am I doing all right, really?" He glanced up at her with anxious eyes. "The letters so far really look okay?"

"You're doing great," Kitty said patiently. "They're so smooth, they look like they're carved out of marble. You're doing a great job."

"You're sure?"

Kitty put her arm around his shoulders and hugged him against her. "Yes, I'm sure. I'm very proud of you."

"You are."

"Yes, I are," she said, laughing.

"Are you two going to stand around and chitchat all day?" Vince strolled up, grinning as they both turned toward him.

"I can chitchat with my son if I want to. Hey, I'm the one who ate a hot dog on the run while you went into the hotel for lunch," Kitty countered accusingly. "I'm also the one who brought you this delicious icy-cold drink."

"Excuses, excuses . . ." Vince sighed with mock exasperation. "But thanks for the drink," he said, gratefully accepting the Coke. "How's the sand up there today?" He shaded his eyes while he studied the plateau where she'd been working.

"Except for the parts that were wet down yesterday, it's still pretty powdery. Kevin had to make some big changes on the ship to get it to come out at all. He tried burnishing the area for the sails, but patches of sand were dropping off. So he cut it back and settled for the rough look." Vince was nodding as she updated him. Elsewhere on the mound there had been similar complaints about the dry sand conditions.

"What about the whale on the other side?"

"It's coming along. There's a whole group burnishing the surface. It's turning out smooth and really beautiful. The tail is finished. Kevin had trouble with one of the front flippers breaking away, but they fixed it. He's cutting open the mouth now. In a while, I'll block in Pinocchio inside the jaws, then they can finish around it.''

''What about your princesses? How are they coming?''
The area around them had been vacated. Only some scaffolding and tools remained. ''Where is everybody?''

''We're all on a break right now. I've blocked in half the faces. I've got Mark doing the detail. After he gets back, Hansen's high-school kids are coming over to start the gowns and suits. They've been on the west side in the shade all morning finishing Snow White and the Dwarfs. Now the sun's on that side, and I'm bringing them over here to keep cool.''

''Clever . . .'' Vince nodded. ''Maybe tomorrow Zach and I can switch over to the lettering on the mound in the afternoon. If Hansen and Elizabeth and whoever else is working on the pond and the flower garden there can maneuver around us, we'd be in the shade a good part of the day. I think I'll check into it.''

''And I think I'll work on Bloomingail's face for a while then I'll check out the princesses. I'll either be at the logo or with the princesses or over by the whale.''

''Eclectic company you keep,'' Vince commented with a wry smile. He picked up his sculpting tools and started on the logo figures.

''Comes with the job,'' Kitty said, shrugging as she turned to leave. ''I'll check on the spare trowel. Meanwhile, back to work . . .'' She directed her parting comment to Zach.

Zach grinned. ''If you don't find one, I'll be fine,'' he said casually, resuming his place on hands and knees in front of the remaining letters. ''Thanks for the Coke, Mom.''

''Yeah, thanks for the Coke, Mom,'' Vince echoed his words from somewhere behind the giant sun.

Kitty stopped by the staff tent on the way back. "I'll be going up top in a few minutes," she told Zimmerman and Lon, who were standing well back in the shade, eating hot dogs and drinking sodas. "Give me a call when you two finish lunch."

"No problem," Zimmerman replied.

"Sandy, do me a favor and make a general request around to the guys," Kitty asked. "Zach is using a real big trowel that Vince had. It's about twelve by four. See if anyone up there has a smaller one they aren't using. I'm sure this big one is too much for him. If a smaller one turns up anywhere, give me a call. I'm going over to work on the logo for a while and give Hansen a break."

"I'll check with the rest of the crew," Sandy promised.

"But don't say anything about it being for Zach," Kitty cautioned her. "I don't want him to get the idea that I think he can't handle the one he's got."

"I won't."

Lon waited until Kitty had started on the exquisite floral-haired head logo by the base of the south mound before he made his move. He'd been waiting all morning for some sign that the magic was still with him and for some sign as to what to do next. He had stopped and reached in his pocket and touched the scorpion pendant again and again. The elder said that once the magic starts to grow, things all fall in place. You just had to pay attention and read the signs. This one was clear as spring water.

Zach needed a trowel.

Tommy and he had a small trowel in their tool cache. He didn't comprehend exactly what size Kitty had been talking about. He didn't understand "twelve by four." But he could tell by looking over at the place where Zach was working that the one lying on the sand next to him was bigger and duller than the shiny new one he and Tommy had picked up from the building site months before. It would fit Zach better. It would fit him perfectly.

Slowly Lon strolled off in the direction of the Port-o-lets, just like the others did when they had to relieve themselves. But he kept on going around the end of the mound, past the bank of the spring lake, then he made an abrupt turn past the north end and started walking faster through the clusters of incoming spectators until he was at the gate. He simply walked out, knowing that the guard there would recognize him by the shirt and the armband and would let him back in again.

At the end of the parking area, where the trees crowded close, Lon cut into the woods, then broke into a run, ducking low branches and leaping over roots as he raced for the wetlands. Bobbing and dancing, he laughed out loud for sheer joy. He took out the scorpion pendant and pressed it to his lips. The magic was growing. He knew it. He had something for this boy, something just for Zach. His heart was pounding and his breath came in short, rasping spurts as he reached the creek. Then he stopped and began circling in around the clearing near the cave area, trying to avoid any kind of confrontation with Tommy. He didn't want to explain where he'd been or why he was taking the shiny trowel. He didn't want Tommy to know where he was going each day. He only wanted to get to the smaller cavern they used to store their tool cache, grab the trowel, and get it back to Zach.

Zach had finished three more letters before he noticed the large shadow that had fallen across him as he worked. He was used to people passing by or pausing for a few moments to look at them working on the Coppertone logo display, but this one was standing closer than most.

This one made no comment at all. This one stayed. Zach had the feeling the observer could have been standing there a long time before he looked up and noticed him.

"Oh, it's you." Zach peered up into a shaded face framed by the bright sun. The big man didn't move. Zach shielded his eyes so he could get a better look. "You're my mom's helper Lon, aren't you?" he asked a bit shyly.

The sun glinted on Lon's white-ointmented lips. His chest was pounding. Every breath was difficult for him. Inside his work glove, he had slipped the pendant and he clutched it tight. All he could do was stare at the halo of sunlit hair and marvel over the slimness of the body. The blue eyes so pure and clear had him spellbound. Finally, the big man nodded.

"Mom said you sure are a neat worker. She said you're like a butler or a maid, always picking up after everybody." Zach remembered her words.

The big man nodded again. Then he held out his large gloved hand. The shiny metal blade gleamed in the sunlight.

"You brought me a trowel. Gee, thanks." Zach scrambled to his feet. Then he glanced over the other side of the logo. Vince was gone again. "I sure like this one better," he declared, flourishing the smaller trowel in the air. "My arm is so tired from working with that big thing. It's too heavy."

Lon pulled his mouth into a smile and nodded.

"Oh, I'm Zach." He thrust out his hand, remembering his manners.

Lon lifted his gloved hand and took Zach's, then held it. Zach gave it a brief up-and-down shake and pulled back. Lon still held his out a few seconds more, then let it drop to his side.

"Mom said you were called Lon. Is that right?"

Lon nodded.

"You don't talk much."

Lon shrugged and willfully widened his smile like he'd seen the others do. It wasn't comfortable, but he could make himself do it and he knew it made them more gentle.

"You know you really do look like a clown," Zach observed.

Lon didn't know the word "clown." In fact he didn't understand most of what the boy was saying. But it didn't matter. All he cared about was that he was there with his boy. Lon simply stared at him, slightly bewildered.

"I mean you look funny. Not funny like I'm making fun of you." Zach floundered, trying not to hurt the fellow's feelings. "I mean you look like someone who makes jokes and acts silly."

Lon still look perplexed.

"Looking like a clown is good," Zach insisted, distressed by the blank expression on Lon's face. "Vince said I look like a clown, too. That's because of all the goo on my face." He poked out his lips and traced an oval in the air in front of them. His small grin wavered uncertainly. For a moment Lon continued to stare placidly. Then he tilted his head thoughtfully, mimicking a gesture he remembered from one of the other workers. He poked out his lips and pointed at them like Zach had done.

Zach expelled a quick burst of air that was almost a laugh. "You're not angry 'cause I called you a clown?" Unconsciously Zach shook head as he asked, hoping for a "no" answer.

Lon shook his head like Zach was doing, only in broader sweeps.

"Good. I sometimes don't get the words right when

I'm trying to say something," Zach confessed. "I hate when it comes out sounding stupid."

Lon shrugged.

"Do you ever do that? Is that why you don't talk much? Do you think you sound stupid sometimes?"

Lon watched the boy's eyes, trying to guess what he wanted in answer. This time Lon's nod was barely perceptible.

"I sometimes talk too much," Zach said quietly. "But I'm not stupid. I'm just a little slow. My mom says I'm catching up. And I am. But sometimes I get kind of confused." He glanced sideward at the large fellow.

Lon was contentedly standing there, looking at him, listening intently.

"Are you a little slow sometimes?" Zach ventured.

Again came that slow smile, a sidelong look, and a slight nod.

Zach smiled, too. "I thought so." He didn't add that Kitty had voiced the same conclusion the night before when they'd talked over their about work on the mound that day and she'd mentioned her big, gentle, but generally silent backup man.

For a few moments they stood side by side, looking at the giant suntan lotion tubes and the sunbathers that Vince had almost completed. "I guess I'd better finish the letters on this," Zach finally spoke. "I suppose you have to get back up there and do your job, too. Back to work . . ."

"Back to work . . ." Lon recited the phrase he'd heard Kitty say, too.

"Wow. You talked. You sound funny." Zach blurted it out before he could stop himself.

Lon hung his head.

"I'm sorry." Zach flung his hands up in frustration,

then he reached over and grasped Lon's wrist anxiously. "I didn't mean you sound bad. Just different. Like you got a cold or something. I'm glad you talked to me. You're not angry, are you? I didn't mean to hurt your feelings." He was shifting from foot to foot, peering up into the big man's face. "Friends? Please?" He let go of the wrist and stuck out his hand for Lon to shake.

Lon made a sound like a sigh.

Lon wanted to take off the work glove. He wanted to fold his hand around the young boy's and feel the softness and smoothness he imagined. But he didn't. He simply grasped the hand and let the boy move it up and down like their kind liked to do. But he made a smile like the boy's and he understood that things were all right between them.

"Maybe you could come down again."

Lon nodded.

"Thanks for bringing me the trowel. Tell my mom I said thanks for finding it. Is it yours? Do I give it back to you when I finish with it? Mom gets on me for not giving things back like I should." He wasn't offering it back yet, but the way he held it out a bit while he spoke distressed Lon.

Lon's smile disappeared. He didn't want the trowel back.

"This. For you."

"I know you want me to use it. But whose is it?"

"This. For you," Lon repeated.

"You mean I can keep it?" Zach's sea blue eyes widened.

"For you. Keep it."

Zach drew it up near his chest and scrutinized the smooth-polished, apparently new trowel. "Gee, I don't know," Zach said slowly. "My mom doesn't let me take things." He looked at Lon's guarded, uncertain expression. He tried to figure out how to explain Kitty's admonition to avoid contact with strangers, especially ones offering gifts. No one had ever offered him anything before. "Mom wouldn't like me to take this." He held it out toward Lon.

Lon looked from Zach to the trowel. He made his mouth turn down at the corners. "Keep it. For you." His voice, edged in confusion, came out a little harsher than he realized.

"Don't be angry. I'm sorry," Zach said quickly. "I guess maybe it could be okay. I mean, my mom knows you. Maybe I should ask her if it's all right." He took a couple of steps around the tanning lotion logo, looking past it to see if he could spot Kitty anywhere on the mound.

Lon moved next to him. "For you." The boy had been talking too fast. Words were slipping right past him. He didn't understand what all of Zach's words meant. And he didn't want the boy to go away. All he wanted to do was to make the worried look on Zach's face stop. "For you." Lon wanted to run and hide. He didn't understand what was happening. He rubbed his forehead forlornly. He squeezed the pendant tighter.

"Don't be upset. Please." Zach looked up at the big man. "It's all right. I'll keep it. I don't have to say anything. Don't be sad. It's okay." He reached over and patted Lon's arm.

Lon looked at the boy's small hand. He understood the gesture of comfort. And he smiled again.

"Friends?" Zach ventured.

"Fends . . ." Lon did the best he could. Zach smiled.

"I gotta get back to work," Zach said quickly. "Only a couple of other kids volunteered to come here, and they're over there helping some old lady make ducks and birds. I'm kinda out front, so Vince wants me to make a good impression.''

Lon tilted his head to one side and shrugged. He didn't understand ''impression.''

''He just wants me to do a good job,'' Zach translated.

''Good job . . .'' Lon rasped out the words. He got that. He pointed where Zach had been working and nodded. ''Good job.''

''Yeah, well . . . I gotta get back to work.''

''Back to work.''

''See you later, Lon.'' Zach picked up the tools and tried to look industrious.

''See you, Zach.'' Lon turned and headed back up the pathway to the level where he was needed. At least he could see the boy from up there. At least the boy had spoken to him, and he knew that the next time, things would be easier.

Jack Button stood directly below the overhead paddle fan, sweating. On the far end of the same striped press tent, Sandy Huff passed out the information packets he'd had her put together. Button had just briefed the newest contingent of reporters, Sandy had banded them in green, and he was getting set to lead them out into the midday sun. This was the third excursion of the morning, and Button was running on willpower. Physically, he felt miserable, but the figures from the sales staff already showed that his efforts with Dunesfest were paying off big time. Already prime waterfront lots were selling at an unprecedented rate, many to northern interests who'd caught the coverage on television and wanted their piece of paradise. A number of Florida building contractors had bought up entire sections of land still not cleared.

Existing town houses and condos were sold out except for the few the Dunes held back as models, and stacks of contracts were being signed on proposed sites with an eight-to-eighteen-month estimated delay until occupancy. Advance men from two prominent northeastern corporations had come to assess the possibilities for moving their headquarters or expanding their facilities there because of both the Florida weather and the special amenities the Dunes had to offer. Despite the dubious publicity over the child assaults in the area, everything Button hoped to see was showing up on the sales charts.

"Are you feeling all right?" Sandy came over to ask him.

"I'm fine. I just must have picked the wrong antiperspirant." He tried to be flippant, despite the periodic dizzy spells and bouts of nausea he'd been experiencing all morning. "Next time, I'll be SURE," he said, mimicking the commercial in his faked radio announcer's voice.

"You really don't look good. Your color is a little grayish."

"I'll be all right," Button said brusquely, smiling tightly as he shrugged her off. He'd had some trouble getting up that morning. The medication he'd taken the night before had cured the tension headache, but he woke up feeling hung over. Except for an occasional sip of mineral water, he hadn't been able to hold anything down.

The heat while he gave the first few press tours during the morning had been oppressive enough. Beneath his beard, his face itched. But he didn't scratch. Then every time he turned around, the Zimmerman kid was there. Like some sort of persistent demon, tormenting him without making any direct contact, Zimmerman would be waiting for Button to glance his way, then he'd turn back to his work and become totally absorbed in sculpting, until the next time. Then from some other vantage point or on another walk-through with a new group of reporters, Button would glance over where he knew Zimmerman was working. It would happen all over again. The look. The turn. The air of preoccupation. Occasionally, a trace of that smile. Button knew it was a game, but he just couldn't figure out the rules, nor could he resist playing.

The worst part was that the Zimmerman kid was proving to be darn good at sandsculpting. More and more, his name was cropping up in conversations Button overheard and in comments by the press. Kitty Westberg had adopted him as her adjunct, assigning him some of the most difficult characters. Craig Stuart and Kevin called him on the headset when they needed some input about a character and Kitty wasn't available. In a group discussion, the young man made quiet, insightful comments, and when he worked, he had a peculiar air of isolation that Button found intriguing. And he was remarkably photogenic. One feature reporter with a penchant for allusions labeled the good-looking young man a contemporary Pygmalion. His staff photographer caught Zimmerman at a variety of dramatic angles creating the Twelve Princesses. Zimmerman displayed equal skill at crafting their male dancing partners, whose faces ranged from aristocratic and aquiline to pug-nosed and cherubic. Each one exuded a unique character and charm. He was good.

"I like the guy with the fez," one reporter commented. "They must have flown that one in on a carpet."

"I bet that's the youngest, the one that's the airhead," another one guessed, looking over the princesses.

"This looks like my ex. He was so stuck on himself, and he had sand between his ears, too."

Button had tried to deflect the attention that Zimmerman and his work was drawing. The kid was a nobody, and Button wanted it to stay that way. As long as he stayed a nobody, he wouldn't dare risk a confrontation. However, Button wasn't sure if a confrontation was what Zimmerman wanted. The end of the game was as uncertain as the rules.

"If you folks are all ready, we'll take a stroll up top," Button summoned his group of press representatives to assemble near the front of the tent. Already he could feel his blood pressure escalating, knowing Zimmerman would be out there and they'd play their game again.

"You have a general schematic of the tales represented." Button sounded very efficient. "South peak is primarily city-related scenes, the central peak is the countryside, and the north peak gets into wilder, more exotic territory and heads down to the sea. We'll eventually have crashing waves and some sea creatures off the north end. The moat is just temporary. Incidentally, there is a summary of each tale in your packet. If you have any questions about the displays, please feel free to ask me." He issued the same general directions as he did each time.

"Can we interview some of these folks as we go along?"

"Pictures, yes. Interviews, no. Not up there," Button stipulated. "Please try not to distract the sculptors while they're working. We're trying to finish this up by Friday afternoon, and they're all pushing to make that deadline. And, of course, stay on the pathways and try to move carefully from site to site. It's hot out there, as you well know, so we'll try to make this fairly quick. There will be complimentary ice-cold lemonade awaiting you on your return." He added that touch to make sure they wouldn't linger in any one place too long and would be eager to get off the structure by the time they reached the north plateau where Zimmerman was working. Button put on his sunglasses and safari hat, took a last sip of mineral water, forced a smile, and headed out into the sun.

After almost thirty minutes into the tour, Button realized Zimmerman wasn't even up there. With his press contingent trailing behind him, Button had trekked across the upper pathways, both dreading and anticipating his next glimpse of the tanned back, the streaked hair, and the smooth, gracefully muscular arms that haunted him. But Zimmerman wasn't working faces on the Twelve Princesses. Only the high-school kids were there, about ten of them, all intermingled with the dancers, engrossed in crafting ballgowns and necklaces, uniforms and dress swords. Button was drenched in perspiration by then, but he stood there, searching the area like a lighthouse beacon while the photographers in his group snapped off some shots.

"How about that lemonade, folks?" Button began hurrying them along. "We've still got the logos at the bottom. And there's a young kid down there, only eleven, who's trying his hand at this. His mother is Kitty Westberg, the one who did Rapunzel. She's the one in charge of all the faces." The press had already seen the production setup with the two other children who were helping Elizabeth Frye and her cohorts mold small birds and animals. However, Button knew Zach was good camera fodder, and he wanted them to move on. His head would explode if he didn't get out of the heat.

Mark Zimmerman was down at the staff tent, standing in the shade, watching, when Button and the others trailed past. Once Button caught sight of him, Zimmerman turned and walked lazily toward the concession stand. The movement was subtle and seductive, and Button felt foolish for having fallen for it again. Half-hidden behind Sandy Huff and a videotape production team, he moved into the shadowy interior of the press tent while Zimmerman bought a soda. Button gulped a glass of mineral water while the overhead fan sent the air gently swirling around him.

Zimmerman crossed back to the staff communications tent, leaning in profile against the tent post only a few yards away, speaking occasionally to one of the other crew members as he sipped his drink contentedly. He took a few pieces of ice from the cup and ran them over the back of his neck then down his throat and over the rise of of his chest. Wet and slick, his skin glistened.

Button couldn't tear his eyes away. Despite his attempt to short-circuit any reaction, he could feel his body responding. Then Zimmerman took another handful of ice and glided it from side to side over his abdomen. Button imagined rivulets trailing under the waistband, and the image excited him even more. Then Zimmerman turned suddenly and caught Button staring. This time the young man didn't turn away immediately. His deep brown eyes stayed locked onto Button's as he languidly popped a piece of ice into this mouth. Then he smiled, a definite secret smile, and sucking the crushed ice, he broke contact and strolled away.

Button knew he didn't dare react.

''I think I'm going up to the office. I've got some calls

to make," he said to Sandy Huff before leaving. "I'll be back in a couple of hours." His hands were shaking. He needed something to calm him. Valium. Percodan. A stiff drink. Anything. And he needed to lie down in the air-conditioning and let it all ease off.

"What if we have some new press folks show up? Do you want me to take them through?" Sandy had occasionally substituted for Button on the briefings, but she hadn't led a tour.

"Hold off until 5:30. Then we'll have a walk-through for all the stragglers. It will be easier then, since most of the crew and volunteers will be down." He didn't want another face-to-face with Zimmerman.

"You plan to lead them?"

"Sure. I'll be back by then," he assured her.

"Don't forget you're doing a storytime at six," she reminded him. "That only leaves thirty minutes for the tour."

"I'll make it," he snapped at her. Then he caught the startled expression on her face and fluttered one hand in the air apologetically. "Look. I'm sorry. I think you're right. I'm just not myself today. Let me take a break and I'll be back." He kept talking while he strode over to the golf cart. Without a backward glance, he drove off. His entire body was trembling on the inside. The cold sweats were turning his muscles to putty. And he knew it had nothing to do with the heat. "Fuck him," Button muttered, fighting off the urge to take one parting look at that north mount plateau. "Fuck the little bastard."

Tommy chuckled out loud when he saw Lon come down and sneak away from the mound. He had followed him there in the early hours, careful to stay far enough behind that Lon would not suspect. But he had sensed for days that Lon was up to something. Now he knew what it was. Lon had made himself look bare-faced and clean just so he could pass. Lon wasn't good at keeping secrets. But at least now Tommy knew what that secret was. Lon was passing. He was right out there among them like the elder spoke of doing from time to time. And that meant he could filch all kinds of things and bring them back.

Tommy had raced on ahead of Lon, determined to get home before him. He didn't want to spoil Lon's surprise. He figured that when Lon finally got back, he'd be waiting there, lolling around and acting bored, just like normal. Then he'd listen dutifully while Lon showed off whatever he had snatched and boasted about how he'd tricked them all. He'd probably tell him about more things he was going to swipe for them the next time. Tommy covered his loose-lipped mouth with his hands as he galloped along, hoping he wouldn't laugh then like he was doing now. He didn't want Lon to know that he'd been onto him all along. He'd let Lon have his show.

Tommy started his own performance sitting on the cypress roots over the creek. He even put his feet in the current for a while. But the longer he sat, the colder the water felt. The knotted tree roots became increasingly uncomfortable against his buttocks. So he moved to another place, grabbing some moss and setting it out under the low branches by the cave entrance. He leaned back with his eyes seemingly closed, just for effect, until his legs felt crampy and stiff. Then he got up and walked around the area, standing in various sites where he figured Lon might show up, looking back over the clearing for a place where he'd look real relaxed and uninterested. Just like normal.

But Lon didn't come. Tommy waited and waited. He

listened for sounds of movement in the undergrowth. There were none other than the usual skirmishing of squirrels and the flutter of birds. He even circled the area, making the broken hawk cries that usually brought an answer. There was no response. Finally he back-tracked all the way to the mound.

Lon was up there again, just like before. He hadn't come home at all. He was right up on that pile of sand, carrying buckets of water and shoveling. Hunched under the branches, Tommy inched closer. He was confused again. It was all going wrong. Lon should have come away first chance he had. He'd broken away and started for home. Now Tommy wondered what had turned him back. The Lon he'd grown up with wouldn't change di-rections in midroute. His Lon was always faithful to the clan. His Lon never sought the company of these others before.

Tommy studied the hulking shape of his half brother more closely, worried that some charm or spell had com-pelled him to stay on. He searched for some sign of ten-sion, some hint of resistance in Lon's expression. But Lon seemed to be perfectly content up there. He even stretched his mouth wide from time to time like they would do. None of this felt right. Whimpering and mut-tering to himself, Tommy spread out on his stomach and settled in, determined to make sense of it all.

At first it was almost funny, seeing Lon in his wide-brimmed hat, moving from place to place, setting things in order. Then once, twice, the woman in the loose-legged pants stepped back and rested her hand on Lon's shoulder as she spoke to him. And Lon would stand there then he'd go off and do whatever it was she'd told him. Soon he'd be back again, following her along, waiting for her next command. The whole thing gave Tommy an uneasy feeling deep in his gut.

''Kissin' ass . . . Kissin' ass like damn breeder . . .'' Tommy squinted as the revelation hit. Sure enough, Lon was shuffling around like a wetlander's breeder woman, doing the stupid work while the menfolk did what they damned well pleased. ''Watch it. She fuck you. . . .'' Tommy amused himself as he watched Lon bend over, buttocks raised, just as he'd often caught a breeder doing. Tommy loved to pop her when she was like that, bent over and not expecting it. He'd have the whole clan laughing over it. But most of the clan was dead now, and the one with the ass in air was his half brother, all he had left of his kind, and the one giving orders was a skinny woman in a T-shirt.

Tommy clenched his fists, first in frustration and incomprehension, then in anger when he could see nothing but Lon kissing ass.

The elder had said that women were like that. They'd use all kinds of spells and charms and temptations to make a man do for them. The elder said that women were troublemakers. They never were content with just one man. They'd wait till one was gone off somewhere, then they'd start in on another, turning brother against brother, kinsman against kinsman, just like in the old days. The elder said that the fighting over women reached such a point that his father, the great elder, had sent them off. He drove out the wetland women and the male wetlanders who had betrayed their brothers, and they had followed the path of the panthers south, moving far beyond the region of springs. And from then on, the only females allowed among the clansmen were captives, mere breeders, who were taken to serve them all and had no say, no spells, no charm, and no power. Until the Great

Blast there had been no more bitterness between kinsmen. Until now, Lon had kept no secrets, nor had he served anyone. Until now, Lon was free.

"Bad woman . . ." Tommy growled low in his throat. No woman was going to rule a wetlander again. The elder had warned them. And if Lon were somehow under her spell, Tommy would break her magic. He would break her spirit. He would show her how to serve. No one was going to be laughing when he'd had his fun with her.

From that moment on, Tommy watched her every movement, cataloging her sins. When she pointed, one of her menfolk would move to another place or go back over his work or change tools. Her words ruled them. She'd call for water, and someone, usually Lon, would bring a bucket. She'd wave a hand and whole clusters of workers would come or go at her command. She would instruct them all, then she'd go off to work alone while they labored on obediently. Whatever it was she requested, some man was there to provide it. Tommy even watched her send Lon with paper money to the tent where food was handed out. He would bring back dark brown stuff on sticks that they would lick until it was gone. Once Lon ate his in the shade of a tent, all the while watching a pale-haired boy working in the sand. Lon stood here for a long while. Then the boy say him there and made his mouth stretch and shook his metal tool in the air in some kind of salute. Lon nodded and went away.

Lon was still on the higher level, scraping sand, when the woman left. Tommy watched her stop at one group of workers then another group, smiling and pointing and still giving orders. Then she passed by the striped tent and handed over the headwire she had worn. But when she walked toward the pale-haired boy, Tommy began to piece it all together. This light-haired one was her child. This one was special to her.

Tommy covered his mouth and snickered softly. One way or another, he knew he could really show her now. But the glint of metal in the boy's hand as he finished up his work froze the grin on Tommy's face. He watched as the boy rinsed it in the bucket. He blinked his froglike eyes, waiting for a clear view. Then he felt the chill. He knew where Lon had gone when he left the mound. And he knew why Lon had not come to the cave at all that day. Lon had stolen a tool from their special hideaway. He had taken it and made it a gift to the boy. He was courting. He was courting the woman and the kid just like he sometimes had courted the breeder or her brother before the Great Blast. Lon gave them things. He treated them soft. He was gentle with them. He was weak.

"My tool," Tommy muttered, eyeing the trowel they had stolen together. "My tool . . ." he repeated in a strained voice, like an off-key chant. Tommy saw the boy quickly wrap it in a towel. Then he saw the woman signal to the boy, summoning him to join her farther on. Like the other males, he obeyed. "Breeder . . ." Tommy growled, staring at her as she stood near another carver, talking to him and watching him work. She touched him. Her hand rested on his shoulder and he turned his head and pressed his mouth to her fingertips. There was something extraordinary in the gesture and in the look they exchanged, something that made a place low in Tommy's stomach feel warm and quivery, then his loins itched. He could feel that it had stiffened. But then she moved on, and the anger came back. He pressed his crotch against the ground until it hurt and grew softer. Tommy would not respond. He would not be drawn under her power.

He would follow and watch and wait. Then he would find a way to carry her off and teach her that she had no domain over a wetlander.

Tommy couldn't help chuckling as he watched her move toward the gate with the boy walking a few steps off from her. Lon wasn't the only one with a secret. Now Tommy had secret, too. It had to do with his finding them a new breeder, someone to make things interesting. This one was lean, almost boyish in build. She looked strong and healthy, like the dummy breeder had once been, and like the dummy, this one came with a pretty love pet trailing along. Everything would be good again, like it used to be. Tommy snickered delightedly. Lon would be surprised when he showed up at the cave one day and found the two of them there, shackled and ready to train. He might even laugh. It would be like the old days.

This time when Lon came down from the sand mound and moved slowly through the onlookers then out into the parking area, Tommy watched but he didn't bother to try to head him off. He knew Lon was through for the day and was probably headed home. But Tommy had some prowling to do once the darkness settled in. Very carefully he backed deeper into the underbrush and wriggled until he'd made a comfortable hollow in the ground cover. If he was going stalk the woman and her boy, he would have to do what Lon had done. He'd have to pass. He'd have to cut and scrape off his beard and lop off his bushman's hair. He would have to find some clean clothes to wear, ones that were enough like theirs to allow him to mix with them unnoticed like Lon had done. Worst of all, he'd have to bathe. The prospect made his stomach ache. His head hurt from thinking. He closed his eyes.

It was the music that finally woke him. Tommy had

intended to nap only for a little while, until the night shade made it cooler and possible to move more freely around the compound without being seen. The pale mound, majestically illuminated, rose before his eyes, pointing its tall spires toward the velvet sky. The soft music that seemed to float everywhere on the wind with a pulsing rhythm had gently prodded him from a sound sleep. Just by smelling the night air, Tommy could tell he'd been asleep for a long time. Already the crowd around the mound was dwindling. The Dunes grounds-keepers in overalls and safari hats were crisscrossing the open space now nearly vacant, spearing away at cups and wrappers with pointed sticks. They each toted a large plastic bag in which they deposited all the litter. Lon couldn't imagine what they wanted all that stuff for or where they were taking it. None of it looked any good to him.

After a while, when the music stopped, the tents dispensing food and drink and T-shirts were closed and vacated, and the crowd was mostly gone, a trio of the cleanup men angled off from the rest, following the traffic pattern and moving out into the parking area. Like hunters on the prowl, they stabbed cups and papers all the while. Silently, Tommy followed, closely observing the actions of the one who was closest to his size, mimicking his movements. Tommy stayed back in the darkness of the surrounding foliage, but gradually the line of landscaped vegetation provided another screen, so he could close in nearer.

Suddenly the night sky darkened even more. Behind him, the main lights on the mount went out, leaving only enough illumination for the security guards to see by. The last few cars pulled out of the parking lot. A peculiar silence settled over the area. The stabbing and bagging of ground clutter continued, vaguely reminding Tommy of times past when he and his clan stood waist-deep in the spring waters and gigged for fish. At least they came out with something useful.

"When you finish here, work your way back along the service road toward the hotel. We're taking the main route and will do Delta Drive."

Tommy heard the words from the distant worker. He didn't understand many of them, but from the way he spoke, Tommy knew that was the boss man. The thickset fellow most like himself nodded and started moving across the lot, off toward the new roadway. The two others followed.

Tommy shuffled from side to side as the workers slipped away into the night. One of them had long hair pulled back at the nape of his neck. Tommy pushed his own stiff, matted hair back like that, but he couldn't make it stay. He watched until they were well ahead of him, then he crouched low and scuttled across the open parking area and ducked between the newly planted tiers of oleander, papyrus, and palms that lined the far side of the service road. Twice the heavy ropes that were connected to stakes and kept the palm upright caught him and threw him back. Then he learned to expect them. Rapidly he caught up to the workers, close enough to hear their comments and smell their scent on the breeze.

"I'm goin' to take a dunk," the one thick-built like him told the others as they reached the curve of the road where a path split off. He took the turn toward the lower outlying building where Tommy had seen them drive the riding grass cutters and the machines that spread foul-smelling brown spray. "Three cups of coffee tonight set me loose. I'll catch up." The fellow angled away from the others and followed the path toward the door. The man yanked it open. A slash of light spilled out on the ground then was bitten off as the door swung shut.

Tommy's chest was thumping as he inched up behind the squat box that hummed incessantly next to the outbuilding. He lay between the shrubs and the cool wall of the building, close to the door, listening, but the humming box obscured all other small sounds. After a while, the door swung open, the light leaped out, and the man in overalls came out. Tommy watched him move off down the pathway. He didn't go after him. Instead, he waited until the man was out of view, then he reached for the knob, crouching low. He yanked the door open, closing his thick hands into fists in case he might be challenged there, and ducked inside.

Tommy had to shade his eyes from the harsh artificial light. But gradually he adjusted to it, and he sniffed the air and listened. Then he saw the wall switch and flipped it up like he'd seen the others do when he dared to creep close to one of their dwellings and looked in through their windows. Just like he'd seen it happen with them, the switch moved and the light was gone.

In the dark hallway he could feel the unnatural waves of cool air coming down on him from little grids in the ceiling. There were doors off both sides of the long corridor. A few were open. Two cast blocks of light on the smooth, hard floor. Most of them were closed. At least for the moment, Tommy was inside, safe, and apparently alone.

Most of the rooms in this outbuilding had flat tables stacked with papers and a chair or two. One room had a larger table with many chairs all around it. That room also had padded benches and the box that sometimes made noise and had color shapes that moved. There were tall machines that he recognized from the fishing camp.

Men put their coins in them and pushed buttons, and food and cold drinks came out.

One after the other, Tommy peered into the remaining rooms. In the vast unlighted room at the end, he found a wondrous hoard of tools and pushcarts and riding grass cutters, all lined up where yellow paint outlined their place. The smaller room next to that had more treasures—an assortment of the bowllike hats of the workers; work gloves, like he'd seen Lon and the others with shovels wearing; overalls, some on hooks, others folded and stacked up; dark boots that were soft and stretchy.

Tommy tried on rubber boots until he found ones that fit him, then he picked out coveralls, work gloves, and a hat and pulled them on. He took two more pair of coveralls. Fully outfitted and carrying the extra gear, he went back in the tool room. He grabbed a shiny pair of hand shears from the silver hooks on a wallboard patterned with small holes. He stuffed them in the leg pocket. He took a spear and a fistful of plastic bags like he'd seen the others using and started back toward the door to the hallway. Then he heard the voices.

"Check the schedule. . . ."

"Who's turned the damn lights off . . . ?"

"Fucking double shifts . . ."

"Anyone want a donut . . . ?"

He could tell there were several of them. He ducked behind the riding machines, kneeling in the dark, alert and tense, clutching the spear. If they came in the same way he had, he was ready to charge. But the voices grew muffled.

"See ya' tomorrow . . ."

"You two want to stop at the bar . . . ?"

"Don't forget to sign out. . . ."

Then there was the scrape and shuffle of movement. And silence.

Tommy waited. He opened the hall door a crack. He opened it wider. The rubber boots squeaked against the floor with each step. He walked quickly. He heard the flush of water inside one room, and he stopped, pressing back against the wall in case someone came out. He heard the guy inside whistling, and he heard the water rush again. But the door didn't open. Then he heard the music, soft and smooth and sudden.

Tommy lowered his armful of booty. He inched forward, curious to see what was going on inside the lighted room. At first he couldn't see anyone, but he could tell the whistling and the music came from a smaller area beyond the first lighted room. He kept close to the wall and moved over behind the open door. He could see clothes and shoes set out on a flat bench. Tommy kept low and slipped inside. He picked them up and looked them over, but they were small and smelled peculiar.

The rush of water stopped. So did the whistling. But the soft music kept coming from the box on the counter.

Tommy stepped back behind the solid door. A pale-skinned man, naked and soaking wet, stepped out of one of the little boxlike rooms and rubbed himself with a big cloth then wrapped it around his lower parts. He opened a bag and spread the contents on the counter. Peering into the glass, he whistled again, then he started scraping his face. Tommy watched carefully, remembering when the elder used to scrape his face like that. And he knew the stick the pale man held was something he would need.

Tommy waited while the skinny man dressed. The fellow put everything back in his bag, even the strange can that hissed and sent a gray mist over his head. Then he turned the radio off. Tommy knew he had to act.

"I want that." Tommy stepped out of the darkness. The thin fellow jerked up and wheeled around, his eyes wide.

"Who the hell are you? And what the hell are you doing in here?" He drew himself up full height, slightly taller than Tommy, and puffed his chest up like a rooster. "And where the hell did you get those workclothes? Those don't belong to you." He stepped back, and his little bird eyes darted toward the other room.

"Want that." Tommy pointed to the bag of toiletries.

"Fuck you, you fuckin' hobo." The guy clenched his fists. "You get your ass out of those clothes. I'm callin' security. You're a damn thief."

Tommy shuffled and hunched down, not looking in the guy's eyes. The guy was getting really wound up now. But Tommy didn't wait to hear the rest. He waited till the sputtering bandy rooster glanced toward the door again, then he locked onto that little chicken neck with both hands and snapped it.

Tommy carefully tucked the bag with the razor inside his coveralls. He brought in one of his heavy bags from the hallway and stuffed the fellow and all his things, including the radio, into it. Then he slung it over his shoulder, like so much refuse, collected his booty and spear from the hallway, and proceeded down the hallway toward the door he'd come in.

With a grab and a lurch, he thrust the door open and was outside, surrounded instantly by the soft cover of night and the familiar scent of the outdoors. He chuckled as he slipped between the rows of neat hedges leading farther away from the tall gleaming building that stood out against the sky. He made sure he wasn't seen.

But in the morning or throughout the day, when no one would notice an extra worker on the grounds surrounding the tall building and the sand mound, he would make himself enough like the workmen to pass. He would be waiting for the woman and her pale-haired boy to come his way. Somehow, he would get close enough to grab one and then the other. And no one was going to stop him.

Humming tunelessly, Tommy followed the darkened trail that led off toward the wetlands. Somewhere, before he got too far in, he would find a boggy place, wet enough to sink the chicken neck deep down beneath some roots. Then he'd go home, hide his booty deep in the cave where Lon never liked to go, and he would sleep and wait for the dawn.

Like an image on a television set with the sound turned down, Jack Button moved back and forth across his lighted rectangle. Occasionally he could drift completely out of view, but then he'd come back again and Mark Zimmerman would raise the binoculars and sit forward, propping his elbows on the tree limb. The guy was wired all right. Button was bouncing around like a Ping Pong ball in play. He got a drink. He poked the buttons on his CD player, he sat down, he stood up again, he tried the television, he went into the kitchen, then he was off to the john. A couple of times he was on the phone, but mostly he prowled about, fidgeting with things in the room. Then he opened the lacquered cabinet and pushed the button that made part of it unfold. This time his backside wasn't in the way and Zimmerman could see exactly how he did it.

As soon as Button had the books out, he slowed down. But he'd already had two drinks straight up and whatever else he'd ingested off-screen. Zimmerman was beginning to see some pattern to the night ritual. Button tried to unwind, holding off as long as he could before he got out the books.

Zimmerman stood and twisted around an upright limb, trying to get a better angle on the pages, but all he could tell was that they were glossy and looked like more of Button's photo albums. "What the hell are you looking at, you scumbag?" he muttered softly.

He hadn't let up on Button all that day. He'd kept track of every move he'd made, including his hasty retreat into the Dunes during the afternoon. Wherever the baby-faced PR man made an appearance, Zimmerman kept showing up. Then he'd put on a show of his own, calculated for an audience of one.

Zimmerman knew that he had the man on edge, he just wasn't sure what he was going to do next. Everytime he looked at the baby-faced magician who had once held him so enthralled, he churned. One part of him wanted to bolt from Button's suffocating presence and the memories his smile evoked, another part wanted to smash a fist into that face. All the while, yet another part deep inside wailed in torment. It was that same childlike wail that haunted him since he was eleven, anytime he felt someone getting close. An innocent gesture, a hand on a shoulder or a hip brushing his in an elevator, could make his insides shrink into a cold knot. Sometimes it was a phrase caught in a passing conversation. Or a word. A name. Instantly, the years dropped away. Zimmerman knew there had to be something he could do to finally rid himself of the garbage Button had left with him. Somehow there had to be a way to put it all to rest.

"You and I have to talk. . . ." Zimmerman whispered. The leaves brushed against his bare arms. His chest hurt from pressing his full weight against the limb while he focused the binoculars. Just like the night before, the adjacent town houses were dark. They seemed to be furnished but unoccupied. There were no neighbors to disturb. Tomorrow he finally would say it out loud to Button. He'd wait until the man was through bouncing off the walls. Once he was well lubricated and sitting down with his picture books, then Zimmerman would show up on his doorstep. "We have to talk. . . ."

Button clutched the book under one arm as he stood and crossed the room. Suddenly the rectangular screen went dark. Zimmerman waited, straining his eyes for some sign of movement inside Button's town house. But the lights were out. The show was over, at least for the night.

"Sweet dreams . . ." Zimmerman formed the words with his lips, barely giving them breath. But he knew Button would be repeating the message as he tried to sleep. Yesterday he put it on the car. This time Zimmerman had printed it out and slipped it in the man's clipboard before he left for the day. It was all part of the game.

Chapter 10

Tommy waited until he heard Lon leave before he got up and made his own preparations for the day. He only pretended to be asleep when Lon crept out into the early-morning haze that hung over the wetlands. Lon had been asleep in the cave when Tommy had finally come home the previous night. The breeder was clean and snoring. Tommy knew that Lon had bathed and fed her. Tommy simply stepped over her curled-up form and hid his new clothes, the shaving kit and toiletries, the clippers, and the metal-tipped spear in the back, then crawled into his cot and closed his eyes.

As soon as Lon was out of earshot, Tommy got up. Bathing was the part he dreaded most. But he knew that to them he smelled bad, just like they smelled strange and unnatural to him. He knew he'd have to scrub the leaves and dirt out of his hair and beard before he could even get the clippers to work. He'd probably have to do it more than once.

He went downstream for the ordeal. He found a place where the roots were close enough to the water to hold the mirror propped up just like the chicken neck in the shower room had done. He put out the clippers and the razor and the soap along the same root, peeled off his clothes, and jumped in. The icy water swallowed him then splattered open. Hissing and sputtering, Tommy thrashed about, cursing the cold. "Shit, shit, shit . . ." he wheezed out through clenched teeth as he waded over and snatched up the bar of soap. It slipped from his thick hand and plopped into the crystal spring water, drifting down to the sandy and shell bottom. "Shit, shit, shit . . ." Open-eyed, he sank slowly this time, groped for it, and brought it back up.

By the time he'd scrubbed and dunked himself a couple of times, the morning sun had cut through the branches enough to warm the part of him that rose above water level. Hip-deep in the spring fed current, Tommy stood facing the mirror, clippers in hand. Then thick clumps of matted hair spread out on the shimmering surface of the water as the transformation began.

Shaved and shorn, Tommy inspected the unfamiliar countenance that stared back at him. The thick lips arched in a sneer. The frog eyes, drooping half-closed, gleamed with satisfaction. "Pretty . . ." Tommy wiped away the streaks of blood where he'd nicked himself.

Carrying the Dunes coveralls and armed with one unused plastic sack and the spear, he started off toward the hotel, following the fresh tracks that Lon had left. They abruptly made a detour toward the lesser cavern, the tool hideaway.

"My tools . . ." Tommy growled, stalking off to see

what Lon had taken this time. But the tools they had collected over the past months were still there. Groping about, making his inventory, Tommy was momentarily satisfied. Then he slid his hand behind the curve of the wall. The fishing pole he'd taken from the kid at the trailer park was gone. So was the smooth plastic tackle box he'd lifted from a camper's truck bed. "My stuff . . ." Tommy wailed, checking again that it hadn't gotten shuffled behind something when Lon went after the shiny trowel. He slammed the other tools out of the way. "My stuff . . ." He spat out the words repeatedly, his mouth twisted in fury. "Mine . . ." Breathing in deep guttural gasps, he lumbered off, stomping on Lon's earlier prints. "Mine . . ." he croaked out like a war chant.

He stopped cold at the second detour. Then he calmed himself while he took the time to follow the winding trail though the undergrowth back down toward the creek. He could tell by the way the ferns and grasses there were pressed flat and worn down that Lon had come there often. Probing in the open places where the old roots made pockets beneath their trunks, he finally touched cloth. He fingered the bundle then got a good hold and drew it out into the light. It was some of Lon's clothes. Not the clean ones he wore on the sand mound, but the old familiar ones that he wore in the woods.

Tommy unwrapped the bundle, eager to see what treasures Lon had stowed away. Some of it made no sense at all. A stinking piece of paper. Crushed dry leaves. Some brown-stained sticks. A section of cloth. Then he looked at the ones Lon had whittled. Dream sticks. And he bent low and inhaled the aroma of the leaves. Lon was using their magic. He was using the old ways to draw the woman and the boy away.

"Stupid . . ." Tommy shook his head. "Grab 'um.

Fuck 'um.'' His way was quicker and easier. His way didn't require any herbs or dream sticks or words of power. And it didn't take tools or fishing poles to get them. No ass kissing. ''Grab 'um. . . .'' he said again, rolling up the bundle so it looked somewhat like it had before. He was about to put it back in place, when he stopped. ''Fuck you, too. . . .'' He unzipped the front of his overalls. Then he peed on it. He zigzagged the warm stream back and forth over the fabric, watching the color turn darker.

Tommy put the bundle back in its hiding place. He wouldn't have to say a thing. When Lon found it, he would know. And when Tommy brought the woman and the boy back with him, Lon would be shamed. But Tommy would forgive him, like kinsmen should. And they'd have a good laugh, looking at each other's bare faces and the smelly bundle that was not good for anything at all.

''If you don't make it clear to him, then I will.'' Kitty faced Zach across the breakfast table, determined not to let him off the hook. Vince had discreetly gone off for another circuit of the buffet, absenting himself from the confontation.

''Go ahead. You talk to him,'' Zach said sulkily. ''He doesn't want it back.''

''Whether he wants it back or not isn't the issue here,'' Kitty stressed. ''It's your behavior I'm not pleased with. First you took it. If you explained the circumstances, I could have dealt with it then and there. But then you sneaked it into the room and hid it under the bed. That's how I know that you know you were doing something wrong.''

"I just didn't want you to made a big stink about it," Zach countered. "I didn't want you to hurt his feelings."

"And I don't want you sneaking things around and hiding them."

"I kinda got that point."

"Don't get smart with me, kiddo. I'm not in the mood for it."

"I got that point, too," he persisted stubbornly.

Kitty's fork stopped in midair over her bowl of fruit. "Well, how would you like to get this point?" She leveled the empty fork at him. "How would you like to stay in here with Corey and the others for the morning instead of working on the lettering? You could polish off a few of those assignments on the computer. Then maybe by lunchtime you can see your way clear to make some sort of apology to me for the sneaky stuff. Then we'll try to straighten the story out with Lon. I just don't think he's in any financial position to hand over a nice tool like that to a kid, and it's too fine a gift for you to accept permanently. Borrow yes. Keep no."

Zach kept his eyes riveted to his plate. "I'm supposed to start on the title today. Vince said so."

"And I said I didn't like the sneaky stuff."

"I heard you."

"And?"

Zach said nothing.

"I think you'd better plan on sitting it out in the classroom until you become a little more communicative. Finish eating, and I'll drop you off with Corey before I leave. I'll be back about eleven to see if you've got anything to say."

Zach clamped his jaw tight and stared at his half-eaten meal. The scrambled eggs were probably cold now, and the bowl of buttered grits had started to form a skin over the surface.

"Eat."

"I'm not hungry."

"Have it your way."

"I'd like to go to class now."

"Nobody's there yet. It's too early."

"Corey usually gets there early and sets things up. I could go and see if he's there."

"Sit. Eat."

"I don't want to."

Kitty leveled her sea blue eyes at him. She pressed her lips together, biting back the words that she knew would only make a bad situation worse. "Go ahead. See if he's there," she said quietly. "If he is, come back and tell me."

Without a word, Zach slid back his chair and walked away.

"Nice morning, isn't it?" Vince returned to his seat at the table. "I gather it's a stalemate," he observed quietly.

"Why can't he just say that he's sorry. Or that he won't do it again . . ." Kitty groaned.

"Probably because he's eleven—"

"And why can't I stop before I back both of us into a damn corner?" She watched Zach step through the café doors without so much as a backward glance.

"Because you're not eleven. You're the grown-up and you're supposed to do something. But the kid didn't come with an operating manual. Face it, you're merely human like the rest of us," he said matter-of-factly. "Gee, this is easy. Maybe I should give up architecture and become a shrink." He stopped poking at his strawberries and reached over to pat her arm. "Look, ease up on your-self. What did you do anyhow? Send the kid to Siberia?"

"I told him he had to stay in here with Corey and do schoolwork until he decided to apologize." She was already shaking her head. "I know. Lousy call."

"I don't know. He didn't look too devastated to me," Vince noted. "In fact, I'd say there was just a trace of relief in his face when I saw him head for the door."

Kitty stared at the exit thoughtfully. "Yeah?"

"Yeah. Like maybe he didn't really mind not being out there quite yet. Any clues?"

"I told him that if he didn't explain to Lon that he couldn't keep the trowel, I would."

"And that upset him?"

"He said he didn't want to hurt Lon's feelings."

"So he's going to let you do it instead." Vince arched his eyebrows. "Smart kid."

"Rats . . ." Kitty muttered. "I guess I blew it on both counts. If he apologized for hiding the damn trowel, he'd have to go out there and face Lon. Or face me facing Lon. He thought I'd make a big deal out of it and Lon would end up feeling bad. I guess Zach figured it was a no-win situation either way." She leaned her elbows on the table, pressing her hands against her temples. "Nice mature move, Westberg," she chastised herself.

"So what do we do now?"

Kitty looked at Vince and sighed, shaking her head. "He's supposed to come back and tell me if Corey is there. If he is, then he's going in early to help him set up or whatever."

"You think I could just wander over there and catch him on the way? Maybe if Zach didn't have to touch base with you quite yet, he'd feel a little less uncomfortable.

Some for you. It might give you both a little time to regroup.''

"I could use some regrouping. Am I dumb. . . .''

"Actually, no you're not," Vince insisted, leaning over as he stood and placing a quick kiss on her cheek. "In fact, you're almost perfect. I've found that a bit intimidating at times.'' She could tell by the gentle affection in his expression that he wasn't joking. "I'm sure Zach has found you a bit awesome at times, too. But then along comes one of these deliciously humbling moments when you don't have all the answers. Don't be too hard on yourself. I'll just tell Zach you both probably overreacted a bit and we'll schedule round two after a cooling-off period. How's that?''

"That would very chivalrous of you," Kitty acknowledged.

"Chivalrous? Me? I just want to get you into a good mood so I can take you out dancing under the stars tonight and squeeze certain portions of your anatomy.'' He spoke with only the faintest trace of a smile.

"Keep it up and you just might get lucky.'' Kitty grinned.

"Luck has nothing to do with it. It's persistence. Tenacity. That and irresistible charm.''

"Try your charm on my son," Kitty prodded him. "And thanks—''

"Nothing verbal, please," Vince interrupted her. "Just save some energy for a little intense nonverbal communication tonight. Eat.'' He pointed to her plate just as he'd seen her point to Zach's. "Build up your stamina. Think evil thoughts. See you in a while." With a wink, he turned and walked away.

"Thanks anyhow . . .'' Kitty whispered after him.

* * *

"Looks like the crowd is starting to build again." Bo Shepherd stood next to Button in the shade of the staff communications tent. Monday and Tuesday had been relatively light days, but with Easter weekend approaching and the sand structure nearing completion, attendance was again picking up. Clipboard in hand, Button was watching the flow of spectators, twisting and untwisting the end of his Cross pen as the overhead fan stirred the air. It was almost ten o'clock and the Zimmerman kid hadn't checked in yet. Button picked at the rough skin beside his thumbnail, finally succumbing to the urge to rid himself of the annoyance. He caught the hangnail between his teeth, then yanked. He knew better. His manicurist would be appalled. The hard skin tore irregularly, right down to the quick. Stung like a son of a bitch. "Shit . . ." he muttered, momentarily sucking the spot until he tasted blood.

"By the weekend, we should have 'em wall to wall," Bo speculated. "Good Friday comin' up. I guess all the churchgoers will be hung up in early services and won't out here till midmorning. But the heathens can slip in ahead of them and get all the closest parking places." Grinning as he eyed the crowd, Shepherd rocked slightly, hands locked behind his back.

Button stood motionless, like a commander reviewing his troops, still rotating his pen. "The believers will edge the heathens out on Sunday," Button commented dryly. There would be six denominations showing up for the Sunrise Services Easter morning. "I doubt they'll have much competition if we open the gates at five. They'll be all dressed up and streaming in for that one." Button had made sure that every radio and television station in the area would be covering the multidenominational service. "There has been a slight change in plans, however."

Shepherd glanced at him. "Change?"

"We're going to need extra men around the mound itself Saturday night," Button informed him. "After the fireworks, I want the grounds secured once all the spectators clear the area. We're flying three crosses up there. That's why those guys are up there getting ready to drill holes on the central mound." He pointed to the sloping area near Rapunzel's Tower, where the engineer Crockett was conferring with Craig Stuart, Kevin, and Vince Ammons. Next to them two muscular fellows were assembling a contraption that looked like an outboard motor. "Three twenty-foot crosses." Button took the pen and made an invisible arc in the air where they would stand against the sky. "Should be damned impressive Sunday when the morning sun hits them."

Shepherd's mouth set in a tight line. "Crosses." He'd heard something about some kind of last-minute construction. He'd heard grumbling about the possibility of the equipment causing cracks or slides. He'd heard the rumors that Button had authorized some kind of banners. He'd figured that if Button had banners to put up, he'd probably ordered ones with the Dunes logo on them, so they'd advertise continually as they flapped in the breeze. That would be his style. But crosses weren't what Shepherd had expected. "Good visual," he said evenly, parroting Button's catch phrase.

"That bit of information isn't for publication quite yet," Button told him. "I've got someone working on another angle, and if it breaks, we'll be holding a press conference later today to announce it. Until I give the word, don't say anything about the crosses. If this other deal comes off, I don't want the effect diminished." Button pursed his lips. "Regardless, we should have thou-, sands here Sunday. I want the whole procedure carried out with real dignity. Then right after the service, the crosses will be taken down."

"They're coming down Sunday morning?" Shepherd looked at him blankly.

"It's a matter of timing and propriety," Button said succinctly. "The crosses would look out of place when the crowd convenes and the reggae bands start in. Crosses and bikinis. Not a particularly suitable juxtaposition. We don't want to provoke any criticism about being disre- spectful. So when the services are over Sunday morning, we're replacing the crosses with some colored flags." Shepherd nodded. Now he understood where some of the rumors were rooted.

"That's why we're making it easy to take 'em down," Button explained. "They're setting a PVC collar in those holes. The crosses and the banner supports simply slip inside. Slick as can be." He glanced sideways at Shepherd. "But we don't want anything to go wrong dur- ing the fly-in or the switchover. Your men have to clear the area and close the gates while the copter gets the crosses safely up and away and the banners in place. It should be a simple exchange. The switchover should be completed by eight, before the regular crowd starts to gather."

"That's a lot of trouble for a couple of hours of—"

"Bo, that couple of hours should put the Dunes on the feature pages of every important religious publication in the country as well as get front-page color in the regular newspapers. We might make the Vatican daily." Button smile slightly. Behind the amber-tinted glasses, his eyes shifted restlessly from the passing pedestrians to the en- trance gate to the heights. "In case these religious publishers don't have their own photographers here, we're having our staff send out prints and a press release. Videotapes will be supplied to the religious channels. Believe me, the additional coverage will be worth the few hours of inconvenience.''

Shepherd's straight brows lifted a fraction of an inch. "I see."

"Have the extra people assigned. Keep the info about the crosses to yourself, unless you hear otherwise directly from me.''

"Will do.'' Shepherd hesitated. The scheduled update Button had him paged for was apparently over. He was dismissed. Button was still standing there, scanning the crowd when Shepherd turned away and left.

"Mr. Button," Sandy said from behind him. "There's a Dr. Cooley on the phone.''

Button snapped his head around.

"He said to tell you that he has confirmed that the man carrying the cross from St. Augustine will be bringing it here.'' She covered the mouthpiece with her hand and looked at him, obviously mystified. "Does any of this make any sense to you?" she whispered.

"Let me talk to him.'' Button stepped over and took the phone. "Dr. Cooley. Yes.'' He stood, amber glasses pushed back, daubing at the sweat that had beaded up on his forehead. "Absolutely fine. Thanks for the good news.'' He was silent while the man responded. Sandy Huff still looked bewildered.

"He'll make it Saturday for sure.'' Button's comment was more a confirmation than a question. "Where is Mr. Hernandez now? Good. I'll have one of my staff photographers come out there right away.'' He stood straight up now, bobbing his head. "Great. Now can you arrange to meet me here sometime this afternoon, say about

three? Great. We'll release the news to the media together.'' He listened a moment then nodded and jotted
a note on the pad on his clipboard. ''Yes. It will certainly
add to the celebration Easter morning. Thank you, sir.''
Button passed the the receiver back for Sandy to hang
up. ''Get me Mike.'' His polite, honeyed telephone voice
was gone.

Sandy put him through.

''I want you to take off and shoot some footage. Tape
and stills. There's a guy walking across the state coming
this way from New Smyrna. Enrico Hernandez. He's
dragging a crucifix. You got it, a crucifix. It's part of an
act of personal atonement or something religious like
that. It was on the news last night. He'd been convicted
of DWI, put a kid in the hospital, got a suspended sentence, then went through some kind of conversion. Anyway, he was heading for the coast with his cross. I asked
one of the pastors coming Sunday to intercede, and he's
convinced the guy to bring it here instead. He's on Highway 44. At the Wildwood intersection. Find the guy and
shoot some tape. Keep tabs on him over the next few
days so you can get him when he comes in the gates. He
has some people following in a RV. Have one report in
regularly on his progress. Give them phone money.''
Button listened. ''Yeah, it will look good edited into the
main piece. Let me know how it goes.''

Roseanne Petty arrived by shuttle and came in out of
the sun in time to hear part of the exchange. ''Is that the
guy from the east coast you're talking about?'' She's
caught the segment about Hernandez on the late news,
too.

''Yeah. He's going to be part of the the Sunday ceremonies. At least his cross is.'' He looked over at her and

stopped. Roseanne had a conspicuous dark smudge in the center of her forehead. "What's that?"

"Ash Wednesday. They're ashes. I went to church. That's why I'm late coming in."

"Ah . . . sure." Button smiled politely. "What exactly is that for?"

"Ashes to ashes, dust to dust. It's a symbol of mortality. It means we're thinking about and anticipating death. In this case, Christ's."

"Cheerful thought." Button's stiff smile arched slightly. "Do you have to wear it all day?"

"Supposed to." Roseanne began flipping through the volunteer roster. Button pursed his lips and watched her. Then he pulled them into another polite curve and turned. Just as he cleared the oasis of shade afforded by the tent, he stopped cold.

Zimmerman was standing less than ten feet away, directly between Button and the mound. His back was to the staff tent. His tool bag dangled from one hand.

Button's breath caught in his throat, then he let it out slowly. The game was on again. He guessed Zimmerman had spotted him on the phone and planted himself there so that whenever Button faced forward, he couldn't miss him. Zimmerman's shoulders, sloped casually to one side as he watched the action up top, were smooth and golden and looked soft as velvet. His hair glistened in the sunlight. The curve of his body was at once relaxed and seductive. In an instant, Button felt it happening again.

He'd tried convincing himself that the excitement came because he was drawn to the boy inside the man. But the night before, he had turned the pages of the photo albums, searching the faces there for the old magic. They stared back dully. Even the pictures of Benjy failed to reach through the day's numbness and touch him so he felt alive in his darkest, secret places.

He'd turned to Zimmerman's photos, still safe within plastic pages where age could not alter their perfection. But they were lifeless. Not like the man-child on the mound. Most of the evening, he'd moved about the town house restlessly, remembering that smile whenever their eyes locked. Day after day they had played their peculiar brand of hide-and-seek. He knew too well how his pulse accelerated, just anticipating that look.

"I'm not a fuckin' fag," Button had insisted, with no one but himself to hear. But it was not the Zimmerman in the book who haunted his thoughts and caused the familiar tingling sensation that Button craved. It was this one. The grown-up version. The one who seemed as intrigued by the peculiar chemistry between them as he was.

Last night when he went to bed and lay there, he had tried to work up an erection so he could do himself, just to ease the tension. But touching, alone in the dark, wasn't enough this time. Somehow he knew that the only thing that would satisfy that nameless hunger was the salty taste of sweat and the touch of sun-kissed skin. Zimmerman's skin. He'd finally given up and taken another Percodan, then willed himself to sleep with the promise that tomorrow he would make some move.

Zimmerman abruptly came toward him. "What's going on up there?" he asked simply. He didn't aim the question at Button, it was intended for Sandy Huff. Button half opened his mouth to speak, but Zimmerman stepped right past him into the shade of the tent. Button simply stood there, feeling the hot sun getting even hotter.

"They're doing some kind of drilling." Sandy began the official version she was allowed to give out.

Button's mouth was dry. "We're setting in some PVC supports that will be used in the weekend ceremonies." He forced the words out. The gasoline motor on the outboard apparatus on the mound sputtered and then revved into a high-pitched but steady roar. Zimmerman swiveled slowly around.

"We're having some standards set up there." Button spoke louder so the youth could hear him over the noise. The cottony stiffness in his mouth didn't seem to affect his enunciation. The motor stopped. The two men were face-to-face. Zimmerman had one of those smudges on his forehead. It was safer territory than the eyes, so Button focused on the spot then quickly shifted back in the direction of the drill.

"Aren't they afraid that noise and whatever vibrations that thing generates might shake something loose?" Zimmerman now stood close to him, shielding his eyes. Like Button, he was looking intently at the group, six men in all, assembled on the central heights well above the tiers of volunteers.

"They're not going to go very deep. Nothing dangerous is involved." Button licked his lips, moistening them. Zimmerman's arm grazed his as the youth peered upward.

Button glanced nervously over his shoulder. Sandy was busy on the phone. Roseanne Petty was talking to one of the volunteers. "I . . . uh . . ." Button licked his lips again. Zimmerman didn't move. He just stood there, looking perfectly calm. "I'd like to talk to you." Button didn't turn his head or shift his own gaze from the mound. He just moved his mouth slightly and said it quietly and quickly. For a few seconds, he wasn't sure if Zimmerman even heard him.

"Now?" Nothing that indicated surprise.

"No. Later. Alone. Somewhere private."

"Private."

"I just want to talk."

"Sure. I think we should talk."

The softness of Zimmerman's reply triggered a strange surge of relief and affection that eased the vise grip inside Button's chest. He drew in a steadying breath. "How about my town house. It's further back in the complex. I'll give you the address."

"When."

"After things slow down tonight. Maybe ten."

"What's the address."

Button stabbed his hand in his pocket, lifting out his business card. He flipped it over and wrote his address on the back. "Head northwest on Delta Drive. Where the road splits off."

"I'll find it." Zimmerman reached across his body and held out his hand. Button placed the card on his palm.

They never looked at each other. Zimmerman turned and walked away, leaving Button staring blindly straight ahead.

Kitty straddled the one corner of the low scaffolding, carving long ringlets over the shoulder of the last of the Twelve Princesses. Once in a while, she'd glance up to check on the drilling. Above, the gasoline motor growled then halted as they stopped to couple on another three-foot section of bit. Vince and Kevin shoveled up the sand that had been drawn out of the twelve-inch hole. Bucket load by bucket load, it was passed down the line of volunteers that was spread out along the walkway to the lower plateaus.

"So far, so good, I guess." Kitty bit her lip pensively, then flinched as the drill operator lined up the apparatus and the motor roared into action.

"I gather you weren't too enthused about the decision to drill." Zimmerman kept on working away on the princess's partner across the scaffolding from her.

"The sand is too hard and too dry to mess around with," Kitty answered, shaking her head regretfully. She had an artist's brush over one ear and the headwire poking out under her sun hat by the other ear. "Once Crockett took a look at it, even he wasn't sure he wanted to try this. But he was overruled just like the rest of us."

"By whom? Craig and Kevin?" Zimmerman asked.

"By Button. He simply said it had to be done."

"What if something comes crashing down? Isn't he worried about the *Guinness Book* and all that record-breaking hype?"

"The records are pretty well in the bag." Kitty took the paintbrush and whisked away the loose sand between the princess's curls. "All we have to do is finish up Friday and have the dimensions certified by an engineer. If the surface is completely worked, which it will be by then, this is the hands-down grande dame of all time. We could lose any one of the peaks, and as long as at least one of them still stands, we'll have the record for height as well as mass." Kitty's pale eyes drifted uneasily up toward Rapunzel's Tower. "I don't think Button is worried about records. I think he's just pushing this for all the publicity he can get."

"I'd hate to see any part of it damaged."

"So would I." Kitty paused, her spatula poised in midair. "All it takes is some kind of tremor to start a hairline crack. Then there's nothing to do but wait and see if it stays put, or collapses quickly, or just gradually slides away. I don't like the suspense. This whole drilling thing has my teeth on edge.''

"I kinda figured that might be what was bothering you."

"This has not been one of my more tranquil mornings," Kitty admitted. "I had a head-on with my son at breakfast, then this." She inclined her head toward the procedure up top.

"I noticed Zach wasn't down there working today. I was wondering what had happened."

"My error. He's back at the hotel." The roar of the drilling stopped once more. Kitty turned, standing to stretch her legs and look intently at the action around the drill site.

"I also noticed Lon wasn't here."

"My doing, too," Kitty answered. "I had a talk with him when we started work today. He'd given Zach a real nice trowel and I tried to explain that Zach couldn't keep it. That's just a safety precaution, no gifts from strangers. Then it finally dawned on me that I wasn't really getting through to him. Zach probably felt the same way. Lon has a good heart, but he just can't understand why Zach should give the trowel back. I could tell he was confused and I was just making him feel bad. So I changed tactics. I simply thanked him. Then I sent Lon in on the shuttle with a permission slip from me. He's supposed to give the note to the youth director and bail Zach out. Sort of a peacemaking mission from me to my son. They should be back here anytime." She looked down toward the gate where the caterpillarlike shuttle made its stops. There was a crowd of new arrivals, but Zach and Lon weren't among them.

"It's tough deciding when to bend the rules." Zimmerman's soft brown eyes followed hers.

"Sure is," Kitty conceded. "With this Sandman scare around here, I guess I'm a little paranoid. I haven't even been kindly disposed toward our trolls up there." She tilted her head toward the dwarfish faces peeking out from their subterranean hideout. "I've been around Lon enough to know he's really a gentle soul. It's a little tough to label someone a stranger after he's been shoveling up after me for days. Zach handled the situation as well as he could. I'm the one who overreacted. I have a tendency to do that from time to time. Like every hour on the hour." A self-deprecating smile flickered across her lips as she gave the gate crowd another cursory glance.

"Moms are like that," Zimmerman said good-naturedly.

"Well, this mom isn't too thrilled with herself right now." Kitty took the brush again and swept clean the last of the curls. "Okay. I'm ready to have this misted. How about you?" She craned her neck to see how Zimmerman's escort for the princess was coming.

"Just about done," he reported. "Bring on the spray."

Above them, the drill roared again. Kitty cupped one hand over her earpiece, blocking out the sound. "Sandy, this is Kitty. North mound. Princesses. Could you locate a sprayer for us. We're through up here."

"No problem," Sandy Huff replied.

"Have you seen any sign of Zach and Lon? I've been expecting them to show up anytime now."

"No sign. Want me to call into the hotel and check on them?"

"Please do," Kitty answered. "I sent Lon with a note to the front desk. He may have gotten lost. Let me know if he's made it that far at least."

"I'll get back to you," Sandy promised. "Meanwhile I'll have a sprayer up there right away."

"What's next after this?" Zimmerman asked. He rocked back on the bars on his side of the scaffolding and looked down at the hundreds of volunteers below. Some were working with Jaisen Crockett and his landscaping crew, making craggy caverns and grottoes where the cliff line would end and rolling waves begin. Others were nearer the central section with Hansen, filling Thumbelina's meadow area with huge flowers and leaves. In between them all, teams of carvers were working on individual molds, sculpting leprechauns and fairies, frogs and butterflies, sea sprites and mermaids, so no ledge would appear uninhabited. The area still unfinished was limited to the bottom fifteen or twenty feet, and the smoothed place midway on the central mound that Vince had reserved for the words "Once Upon a Time . . ."

"I'm going around to finish Pinocchio. Maybe you should check the west slope and see how everything is coming over there. If you're not needed there, you can go back to the ship and the Four Skillful Brothers." In an orderly spiral, descending level by level, all the other tableaux had been completed, sprayed, roped off, and declared off limits to everyone except Button and his scheduled walk-throughs with the press.

"Sounds good to me." Zimmerman slipped his tools into his pouch, slung it over his shoulder, and climbed down. Kitty's feet touched down about the same time. Up top Crockett was capping the first of the holes. The other men were setting up the drill for the second round.

"Maybe first we should go up there and take a quick look." Kitty said the words tentatively as if she were testing out the idea.

Zimmerman smiled. "Maybe we should."

Kitty stood slightly behind Vince, watching uneasily, while the large drill pulled the sand out of the second hole. She couldn't feel any actual movement in the hard-packed sand beneath her feet, but each time the motor revved, biting deeper into the mound, her jawline tensed and her pale eyes assessed the pile of white sand coiling out and spilling onto the ground like sawdust. They had finished the second hole and were drilling on the third when Kitty stepped over the ropes that marked off the tour pathways and made her circuit carefully around Rapunzel's Tower.

She'd inspected every block and returned to where she'd started when she saw it. She stepped closer to be sure it wasn't just a shadow. It started at the lower corner of the tower, on the inside of Rapunzel's thick braid of ivory sand and followed it upward, ending just below the corner of the balcony balustrade. "Vince . . ." The words were drowned out by the roar of the augur.

"Problem?" Craig Stuart stepped toward her the moment he saw the expression on her face. Vince and Kevin were shoveling up the last of the sand from the final hole and packing it into the remaining two buckets.

"We've got a crack."

"Shit."

"Where?"

"At the base of the tower." Kitty spread her hands and shrugged.

"How bad does it look?" Vince let the shovel drop.

"I don't know." Kitty exhaled with agitation. "Too soon to tell. It's on the northwest corner, right along the braid. It only goes partway up. Right to the balcony."

"Let's take a look at it," Craig said in short, clipped words, shaking his head as he had when Button first told him that the holes needed to be made.

"Maybe it will stop there," Vince said hopefully. "Let's see what can be done." He stepped over the remaining bucket and followed Kitty to the tower.

"It doesn't look too bad." Kevin crouched down near the base. "Let's try spraying a little fixative on it and sifting some sand into the spray. If we patch it over, that might keep the air out and stop the crack from widening."

"Better than nothing," Craig muttered. "I should have told that asshole flat out."

"Let's see if there are any other cracks in some of these other pieces." Vince Ammons tugged off his visor and headwire and shoved his hand through his hair. He'd buckled under just like the others when Button made his case for setting in the PVC sheaths. The fine creases at the corners of his eyes deepened as he squinted against the glare. "We might as well know what we're up against." He started over to Rapunzel's prince, standing just off to his right.

"I'll call Paul and have him take a look at the back side of the mound," Kevin offered. Paul Feneau would be quickest to spot any flaw in his Frog Prince or Beauty's Beast.

"I'll help you do the front side," Mark Zimmerman said, moving in next to Kitty. He started to put his arm around her shoulders, then let it drop to his side instead. "How about it?"

"I don't think I'm up to it." Kitty pressed her lips into a fine line. She kept her eyes lowered beneath her wide-brimmed hat, but Zimmerman caught the glimmer of tears building along her lower lash. "I think I'll go on up to the tent and see how Sandy's doing tracking down Zach and Lon. Maybe they've made it back." Her voice caught. "Sorry, guys, I'm just not doing too well with this."

"That makes two of us." Craig Stuart reached over and patted her shoulder sympathetically. "Go on down. Take your kid to lunch or something. We'll survey the damage and catch up with you later."

"You want me to come with you?" Vince asked.

"No need. I'll be all right." Kitty cleared her throat. "I'd just rather not be here if she drops anytime soon." She lifted her head with all the dignity she could muster and managed a quick look at the pensive Rapunzel. "I'll be back in a little while." She straightened her shoulders and walked off toward the regular pathway.

"Let's spread out." Craig Stuart took charge of the survey. "Mark, you go with Vince."

Kitty drew in a few deep unsteady breaths as she hurried away. "Damn," she muttered, embarrassed that the hairline crack had triggered such a strong reaction from her. "Rats . . ." She hadn't admitted, not even to herself, how much she had cared about this project or how possessive she'd become, particularly of Rapunzel's Tower. She loved the dreamy-eyed child-woman she had depicted, still secluded from the world and the adventures awaiting beyond her simple room. Rapunzel was her best piece there, by far the most beautiful. The lovely face radiated both promise and innocence, like any child on the threshold, so much like Zach even now, when she was just beginning to set him out on his own path in the world. Until the crack appeared, Rapunzel had been perfect and uniquely hers. She would have remained hers until the opening ceremonies when Kitty accepted her accolades and packed up and took Zach home. Then Rapunzel would be on her own.

"This is silly." Kitty brushed the solitary tear on her

cheek with the back of her hand, feeling increasingly foolish. The sculpture was just a piece of work. If it collapsed, the rubble could be reworked into something else, the wise, more resilient Kitty told her. But the other one, the one who was still a child inside, knew that without this fairy-tale dreamer, staring at the stars, "Once upon a time . . ." wouldn't be the same.

"Kitty, apparently Lon made it to the desk and one of the staff took him to get Zach." Sandy Huff called over the headwire. "Corey figures they left about thirty minutes ago."

"They should be out here somewhere then," Kitty answered, stopping abruptly to look down over the crowd from her privileged vantage point. "They might have been recruited to work somewhere else on the lower level. Put out a general call and ask if anyone has seen them. I'm on my way down anyhow. I'll check in with you in a couple of minutes."

"I'll call around," Sandy promised.

Kitty moved more briskly now, scanning the work parties as she passed. "Please, just let him be all right." She tried to calm herself as she hurried along. "Don't let anything be wrong."

Sandy was in the midst of a phone conversation when Kitty stepped into the tent to join her. "I gather the shrug means no luck in finding Zach," Kitty guessed. Sandy fluttered one hand then signaled for her to be patient. The erratic ripples of apprehension Kitty had been resisting were gradually building.

"That was the gate security," Sandy said the moment she was free. "Scotty there knows Lon and Zach on sight. He says he saw Lon leaving about an hour ago, but he hasn't come back through. Neither has Zach. They may have gotten sidetracked up at the hotel. I'm sure they'll show up soon," Sandy insisted.

"Well, I'm not waiting around to find out. I'm going up there." Kitty started to turn in her headset then reconsidered. "Call me if you hear anything. I'm going to check the room. He may have decided to change clothes or something." Despite the cold fear settling in the pit of her stomach, Kitty forced herself to appear composed. "If he's not there, I'll call you from the the security office." She smoothed her brow with the fingertips of both hands and managed a stiff smile. "This really hasn't been one of my better days."

"I'll keep trying to locate them," Sandy assured her, her own face clouding with uncertainty. "I'll relay the word to you as soon as I hear something."

Kitty nodded then disappeared quickly into the crowd packing into the area between the tents, the concession stands, and the gate.

Tommy knew that if he hurried to the site and watched and waited, he'd get his chance. He saw the woman boss with the sun hat almost immediately. She was on the ridge, higher than most. Lon was working below her, shoveling up the sand that fell away as she and the ones near her carved.

Tommy leaned forward, his frog eyes squinting with interest, when she touched Lon's shoulder and led him a short distance away from the others. Then she had stood there talking to Lon for a very long time. Her hands floated on the air. Lon shrugged. She looked up at him earnestly. He shuffled his feet and shook his head. Then she grew still. Tommy was puzzled. But then she went over to her work bag and took out a pen and made marks on paper. She handed the paper to Lon.

Tommy knew that it must have told a story. Just like in the old cave, there were marks that told the old ones' tales. And he knew that Lon would not be able to decipher this woman's dark lines, no more than they could read the ones left behind by their kinsmen before the Great Blast claimed it all. But it all meant something.

The woman rested her hand on Lon's shoulder and pointed to the gate. Lon was looking in that direction, shaking his head slowly from side to side. She kept on talking. Tommy saw the linked wagons carrying the people. The shuttle stopped by the gate where she was pointing. Many people climbed off and drifted toward the gate. A few, those who had been waiting there, climbed on. Then it carried them away, off toward the tall gleaming building beyond the hill shaped like a man-faced beast.

When Lon started toward the gate, Tommy lurched into motion. He had been watching them from the cool shade of a limb high in one oak tree on the southeast periphery. Now he swung down to the ground, grabbed his plastic bag and spear for paper, and hurried through the underbrush toward the fence. Swiftly, he moved parallel to the barrier, closing in on the gate where the linked wagons came and went.

Tommy was there first, pith helmet pulled down low over his forehead, a low circle of perspiration spreading across the back of his Dunes coveralls. He stayed back near the shrubbery, deliberately poking and stashing away the stray cups and wrappers in his sack when Lon came out through the gate and stood with the others awaiting the next shuttle.

Lon instinctively shifted back a bit while the linked wagons pulled up and emptied. Tommy saw him take something from his pocket and poke it down inside his glove. Then Lon closed his fist very tight and pressed it against his chest. Lon watched how the others grabbed the handrail, ducked under the wagon's canopy, and took a seat. He followed, sitting alone at one end of a bench. He held on tightly to the back of the seat just ahead on him, one gloved hand tense and unmoving, the other protectively locked over his breast.

Tommy kept his back to the vehicle until it pulled slowly away from the curb and began its scenic but ambling circuit back to the hotel. Then he crossed the roadway, angling diagonally through the gardens so he could round the man-faced beast and get close to the wagons before they stopped.

At the huge Grand Nile entranceway, flanked by monsters, this time hawk-faced warriors of gray stone, Lon got out with the others. They immediately went inside. He stood there, staring up at the monumental door guards. Totems. They reminded Lon of totems, just like the ones the elder used to carve beside the mouth of the cave. Anxiously he pressed the secret oval in his glove, hoping that his magic would strong enough to protect him against theirs.

"Can I help you sir?" The young man in safari garb strode out to greet him. Lon looked at the young man. Then he reached in his pocket and handed him the note. "Okay. I know where Corey's group meets. Come with me." Lon could tell by the way the young man paused that he was supposed to follow. With a cautious, sidelong look at the falcon-headed door custodians, he stepped past them.

Inside, the cool air embraced him, like the chilled waters of the spring often did when he plunged under its shining surface. Only this cool substance didn't blur his vision or cause him to hold his breath, and the myriad scents that drifted in its currents were ones that Lon had never breathed before. Sweet. Exotic. Pungent. Delicious. Underneath his thick-soled shoes, the carpet, bluer than any sky he'd ever seen, whispered as he walked along, hurrying to keep pace with his guide.

"Across the atrium and down the hallway to the right." The young man hesitated, then seeing the confusion on Lon's face, proceeded to lead him on. "Here. This is the classroom. Let me check inside and get Corey for you."

He left Lon alone in the corridor. Slowly Lon turned around, overwhelmed as he tried to take it all in. Behind him were glass walls, high as the stars. In the central area, there were ponds with lilies, delicate fountains, and giant trees made the color of the sun. Their majestic golden leaves spread out like the plumed tail of magnificent birds. And the brilliant jewel colors on the wall panels everywhere seemed to bite into his eyes.

"Hi. Zach's just putting his work away. He'll be right here." The one who led him there smiled and left.

The other one who spoke now stayed in the open doorway, glancing back inside. "He wasn't too happy about working in here today," Corey reported. "He really likes working out in that heat. You should have seen his face when Rob told him you were here for him."

Lon nodded. Inside his glove, he pressed the scorpion pendant against his palm. Despite the chill in the air, he could feel sweat trickling down his sides. He closed his fingers tighter. Zach. Zach. Zach. His heart pounded.

"You guys sure are doing a great job out there. It's really spectacular how it's coming along. You should be real proud."

Lon nodded again. Then he caught a glimpse of pale gold hair just behind the door and he knew the magic was with him.

"I thought it must be you." Zach poked his head

around the door and beamed up at him. "He said some big guy with a big hat and an armband brought the note. Mom sent you?"

Lon recognized the word "Mom." He nodded.

"I'm not in trouble, am I? Is this about something bad or good?" Zach's smile faltered. He paused next to the fellow who still stood there holding open the door.

"Good. Back to work." Lon recited what he remembered of Kitty's parting words.

"All right." Zach grinned.

"I guess you two can take it from here." Corey patted Zach on the shoulder. "Okay, bud, you're free to go."

"Great." Zach lunged into the hallway. "Come on. Let's go." He grabbed Lon's gloved hand and started tugging him along. Zach finally stopped outside on the steps where the shuttle would pick them up.

Lon looked out over the gardens beyond the covered entranceway and got his bearings. "Come. See. This for you." Now he moved off, leading Zach in the opposite direction from the mound.

"I thought Mom wanted me out there." Zach paused, reluctant to go on.

Lon shrugged. "For you." He curved his hand and pulled the air in a gesture that he had seen them make. "Come."

"Where are we going?" Zach asked.

"Come. For you," Lon said insistently.

"What is it you want to show me?" Zach demanded, wriggling his hand out of Lon's grasp. "There's nothing that way but the Nature Trail and some gazebos."

"For you. This for you." Lon walked off a few steps, turned, and waited.

"After we see this thing, you promise we'll go out to see Mom?"

"Back to work." Lon nodded.

For a few seconds, Zach didn't budge. "Okay. But this had better be good," he muttered.

"Good . . ." Lon held out his hand. Zach took it and fell in step with him.

Tommy stayed back from the main pathway so he wouldn't attract any attention. He had not risked going into the big building after Lon, but he'd busied himself along the walkway, picking up litter, and repeatedly glancing up over his shoulder at the grotesque creatures made of stone and the huge glass doors between them. When Lon came out with the boy, Tommy had almost cackled out loud. Once Lon and Zach started down the flower-lined pathway, he figured Lon was bringing the boy home. Apparently his half brother was smarter than he thought.

Tommy brought up the rear, keeping back so he wouldn't ruin Lon's surprise. But when Lon veered off toward the resort gardens instead of cutting across the stream and into the woods, the achy feeling in his stomach started up. It was going wrong again.

They passed by the first roofed area and went on to the next, one more secluded, before Lon stopped. This one projected out over the water, and the crystal stream made ripples and swirls around the outer pilings. Lon motioned for Zach to sit on the bench while he climbed under the gazebo and brought out his gifts.

Tommy trembled when he saw that there were two of them. The fishing pole was bad enough. That was Tommy's very own. But the tackle box was filled with shiny lures and feathered hooks and all kinds of wondrous things. They could have traded it off for plenty when the cold weather came again. Tommy clamped his hands about the spear, crouching behind the thick bushes.

"Wow. This is great." The kid bobbed up and down, almost dancing. He took one of the lures out of the box and tied it on the line, then he dangled it over the side. And all the while, Lon was right beside him, bobbing and grinning, too. Tommy clutched the spear, rocking from side to side, quivering with fury.

The kid reeled it in then sent it sailing out again. The lure cut into the surface with a gentle plunk and drifted downward.

"Stupid . . ." Tommy damned them both.

They kept it up. Bobbing. Grinning. Tommy inched nearer. He could almost feel the dull popping sensation it would make when he ran the sharp-edged spear through the pale-haired creature's chest. He would slam it into the boy and hold him high. Then he'd throw him at Lon's feet. And walk away.

"Hey . . ." The voice was loud but not angry. "Are you two Zach and Lon?" A dark-haired man in the Dunes safari uniform came down the pathway toward the gazebo. He had a black box in his hand and he talked into it. "Found 'em. Safe and sound."

Zach reeled in his line quickly.

"Your mom is up at the hotel looking for you," he told Zach. "Both of you had better hightail it back up there."

Lon looked anxiously from Zach to the uniformed man then back again. Zach was wide-eyed, biting his lip as he packed away the fishing gear. "My mom will shoot me," he whispered, fumbling with the trays in the tackle box.

Lon reached down and rested his gloved hand on the boy's arm. Then he carefully closed the box and took the pole. "For you . . ." he said quietly, pointing his finger downward at the floor.

"Come on, you two," the security man called out. He had started back down the path.

"We're coming," Zach answered. Then he nodded quickly as Lon rounded the building and put the pole and tackle box back under the gazebo supports where he'd stowed them earlier.

"Back to work . . ." Lon breathed a bit heavily as he caught up to the boy. Hand in hand they followed the security man along the winding trail.

"Where have you been?" Kitty tried to keep from sounding too shrill. She was waiting on the steps of the hotel. Once she saw the small procession led by the security man, the network of knots in her stomach eased. Then a countercurrent of emotions gripped her as she stepped out to meet them halfway across the drive. She had to quicken her step to get out of the way as the shuttle pulled in behind her.

"You scared the wits out of me," Kitty sputtered, realizing she was saying all the things she promised herself she wouldn't say.

Zach hung his head. Lon glanced down at him and hung his head, too.

"Do you have any idea—" Kitty stopped and took a deep breath. "I'm glad you're okay."

Zach decided it was safe to look up now. "I'm sorry. We just went out on the trail—"

"I heard. The guard called in. Not exactly where I expected you to be, but at least you're both all right."

"We did a dumb thing," Zach admitted.

Kitty arched her eyebrows. That edited out much of what she had planned to say net.

"I'm really sorry, Mom." Zach's anxious expression was mirrored by that of his taller, heavier companion.

"And I'm relieved." Kitty reached out and pulled the boy against her. Lon shuffled his feet self-consciously. He studied the gentle way her hand stroked the pale gold hair. He longed to stroke it, to be stroked. He stuffed his hands into his pockets.

"Look, I'll save the lecture," Kitty proposed. "Just don't do anything like that ever again, at least until you're twenty-eight."

Zach smiled. "I won't."

"Let's get some lunch. All of us." She took Lon's arm and started around the end of the parked shuttle toward the main entrance of the Grand Nile. "We'll eat. Then I have to go back to work."

"Can I still help?" Zach eyed her anxiously.

"That was the general idea all along." Kitty hesitated by the glass doors, distracted by another conversation. She cupped her hand over the earphone of the headset and raised a finger, signaling for silence. Her pale eyes narrowed as she listened. "I think we've got a problem out there. Sounds like something has broken away." She pressed her lips into a tight line, still listening. "I can't pick it all up," she reported. "Looks like lunch will have to be a burger on the run. I have to get out there. You guys come on." She grabbed Zach's arm this time and steered him toward the shuttle. "Come on, Lon. Hustle," she called out behind her. "Lon, now. They need help out there. Move it!" Lon lurched forward and bounded onto the seat next to her.

As they pulled away, the heavyset fellow in the grounds-keeper uniform stepped back behind the hedge.

"The score is two found, one lost," Roseanne Petty proclaimed when she saw Kitty approaching the staff tent with Lon and Zach close behind. "We heard that you tracked down those two. Unfortunately, while you were looking for them, we lost the Pied Piper.'' Roseanne pointed to the section just below the newly drilled holes where the mound was under repair. On the slope where the caped Piper had been, there was an upright cylinder almost six feet tall. ''He just sank, like someone deflated him,'' Roseanne said glumly. ''Craig has the guys putting that mold back up there. They're going to repack it, wet it down, and see if they can resurrect the thing.''

''Somewhat apropos, don't you think?'' Kevin Walters said quietly. ''Considering the season.'' His customary smile was gone, and he slouched in the shade of the staff tent, studying the notes Button had inadvertently left behind while he set up the podium for the three o'clock press conference. ''We may as well turn this into a real three-ring circus.'' He waved the clipboard then landed it on the table with a loud slap. ''We've got your repentant sinner dragging his cross across Florida. We've got airborne crucifixes. Why not throw in an extra resurrection on the side?'' His tanned face was expressionless, but his voice sliced with a sardonic edge.

''Kevin just found out about the crosses.'' Roseanne leaned forward confidentially.

''What crosses?'' Kitty stared at her, baffled.

''I forget who's allowed to know what around here,'' Roseanne muttered.

''It's supposed to be sort of a secret,'' Sandy Huff chimed in, fluttering her hands distractedly. ''But Mr. Button left this lying out here.'' She pointed to the notes on the clipboard Button had left near the phone.

''And I happened to be cosmically curious,'' Kevin interjected.

''In case you haven't heard,'' Roseanne elaborated, ''Button has scheduled a news conference this afternoon.

He and one of the pastors coming Sunday are announcing that some man who's carrying a cross across the state is ending up here. That cross and two others will go in those holes. Then after the Sunday service they come down and we're getting Dunes banners.''

"Sounds strangely irreverent, doesn't it, squeezing a little passion play in between the fireworks and the beach party," Kevin suggested mockingly. "But you can bet it will get a lot of play in the media."

"That's beginning to sound all too familiar," Kitty replied. "Every time we turn around, Button comes up with some other angle."

"That's his job," Sandy offered, trying to maintain a neutral ground.

"And we certainly must admit, he does it very well," Roseanne Petty drawled with distinct disapproval. "If Mother Teresa were up to it, he'd probably fly her in for the ribbon cutting."

"Wrong image," Kevin said with mock seriousness. "We're into tall, blond, and upwardly mobile here."

"Well, the only thing that's upwardly mobile right now is me. I'm going to see if I can help with the Piper." Kitty looked anxiously up at the group of workmen then farther up at Rapunzel's Tower, relieved that it was still intact. "Zach. Lon. You two get some lunch then get going on the letters up there." She sounded a bit impatient as she gave out directions. "We've all got work to do, too." She turned away without waiting for a reply.

"That's the tragic flaw in all of us," Kevin kept talking as he followed her through the crowd. "Tenacity. He hangs in there. Button knows how much we love doing this. So even if the SOB takes risks that cause disasters, he figures we'll be right back, busting our butts trying to make it all pretty again. And he's right."

"I just want to finish up and be out of here before the rest of the craziness begins this weekend," Kitty said wearily. "I can handle the work, but the ethics behind all this are beginning to get me down. Right after the opening ceremonies Saturday, we're taking off. I want to remember this project like it looks early in the morning or after closing at night, without the reporters, the music, the storytelling, the concession stands, the weddings, the tours, and all the other rubbish."

"When it simply is beautiful for itself." Kevin caught up with her.

"Right. And I sure won't be around when they bring in the bulldozers and flatten her," Kitty added. Vince had said he'd drive up with her after the week of tours concluded, but Kitty had declined. She had no interest in coming back up to the Dunes to see all their creations leveled and spread out along the shoreline of the spring lake.

"Right . . . leave on the creative upswing," Kevin was regaining his usual philosophical attitude. "I'll be in Vancouver planting trees by the time the downswing comes along."

"If corporate America is still functioning like it was when I used to play the game, Button will be having the title on his door redone about then," Kitty predicted.

"And we'll all live happily ever after. . . ." Kevin finally smiled that wild buccaneer smile.

"I doubt that. But I'd settle for getting back home and having everything return to normal. I even miss the moldy science projects in my refrigerator and the wet laundry Zach always forgets and leaves in the dryer. Normal, simple things that make sense to me."

"If Button stops coming up with these last-ditch efforts to reach yet another audience, we should all be through on time. I just hope the Pied Piper is the only casualty of this last escapade.''

''How's the crack look on the tower?'' Kitty asked. She'd glanced over at it repeatedly, half expecting to see parts sliding down the side at any moment.

''Not too bad. Vince and I spray-patched it.'' He kept pace with her long strides as the angle of their climb increased. ''We had a couple of others. There was a real noticeable split in the Grandma's house near Little Red and the Wolf. We patched it, too. Of course, the Piper didn't make it. All considered, we didn't do too badly, unless you count the couple of rats that got squashed while they were setting up the Piper mold. Elizabeth Frye said she'd whip up a few replacements.''

They were rounding the turn in the southwest walkway that opened onto the central mound. On the slope ahead, Kitty could see Vince and Craig Stuart shoveling the Piper rubble into buckets. Craig was passing them up to Zimmerman, who was using their scaffolding to reach the top. A bucket brigade of volunteers, all sweating and straining, were lined up in single file from the lower level, alternately passing up sand and the water to soak it all down. Beyond them, work parties were spread out over the lower ledges with hundreds of carvers and shovelers meticulously transforming sand to a storybook landscape.

''Ladies and gentlemen, boys and girls . . .'' Button's voice carried over the loud speakers and drifted up to them. ''In a few minutes we'll be having storytime.'' His words were distorted somewhat, but Kitty got the general idea. She could see children rushing toward the platform where Button held his storytelling shows.

Kitty paused and watched the activity. For a moment a certain wistfulness altered her expression. ''I may not like the way Button operates, but I have to hand it to him. He does know how to keep the crowd entertained. Look at them down there,'' she said softly. The rock music that had played incessantly for the past few hours faded as the lighter, bell-like tune that introduced storytime began. ''They're having a great time.''

''And then there's the rest of us.'' Kevin chuckled.

''I remember when I did this just for fun,'' Kitty remarked. ''We all did. And as far as I'm concerned, parts of it still are fun. I'm not going to let Button or anyone spoil that.'' She trudged forward, a determined look on her fine tanned features.

''Me neither,'' Kevin called out, loping across the sand after her. ''Here come the reserves.''

Tommy crouched for hours, waiting for them to come down and venture outside the gates again. But Lon and the boy stayed on the east slope of the center peak. And there were always ones around in uniforms like the one who made them come away from their fishing. They would stop and watch the boy. Often they'd speak into their black boxes and move on.

Once Lon and the boy took a break and went down for food and soft drinks. Lon never left the boy's side. Even then one of the ones in uniform stopped to speak to them. A female one walked behind them when they strolled all the way around the base of the structure, looking at all the others who were working. Then they got two more sodas and went back up. The woman spoke into her black box then went off the other way.

Even when the sun went behind the mound and sent a shadow over the slope where they worked, the two of them kept on, Lon shoveling while the kid was cutting lines, digging away between them, and patting it all with that shiny tool. "My tool . . ." Tommy said it softly but with a vehemence that sent the spittle flying. It took a long time before he calmed down and finally realized that the parts the boy made stand up smooth and flat above the surface were marks that meant something. But not to him.

The boss woman stayed up there, too. Never alone. When they lifted away the wooden form, she was the one who stepped forward first to cut at it. But there was a circle of others around her. She was the one who made the shape of a man appear then gave him a face and hands. A helper gave him clothes. Then someone came to get her. She left behind the one who had helped her and hurried off to another place. This time it was on the back side. Tommy moved around so he could watch her there. Like before, when she worked, she was protected. There was always a circle of others there.

Discouraged, Tommy finally retraced his steps so he could watch Lon and the boy, but by then his coveralls were soaked with perspiration and scuffed with dirt from scrambling through the underwoods. And his stomach growled. He could smell the food cooking in the tented areas and he saw those inside the fenced area devouring all kinds of aromatic treats. His mouth grew moist.

"Fuck it. . . ." Tommy growled, giving them all a long parting look. Lon and the boy still had lots of lines and spaces to go. There still was sun enough to see for a long time. Tommy guessed that if he hurried home and ate some food and brought back the other overalls, he would be back before they all came down for the night. Then they wouldn't have everyone watching them. In the dusk, he would look clean and neat and enough like them to pass.

The breeder woman was sprawled across the passageway well inside the mouth of the cave, sleeping, when Tommy lumbered inside. Before his eyes adjusted to the change, he stepped forward and caught his lead foot under her rump. Too soon for his reflexes to act, he teetered and lunged over her prone form, flinging out his arms to break the fall as he tried to straddle her. But she had soiled herself. The area around her was dark and slick and putrid with her filth. Tommy's feet slipped out from under him. He twisted to one side sharply, flailing one hand as he slammed headfirst into the stone outcropping that ran midway up one side. Then with a groan and a rush of air, he joined her on the cold, damp floor, and a darkness not at all like nightfall closed in.

Chapter 11

JACK BUTTON GLANCED AT HIS WATCH. THEN HE WALKED over to the VCR and read the time there. He poked the button on his CD unit and tapped his fingers on the shelf until the door slowly opened, exposing the disc. He removed it, inserted a replacement, and started it up again.

While the soft sounds flooded the room, he went into the bathroom again, looked at himself in the mirror, and took another swish of mouthwash. The antiseptic smell hung in the air. He took out the room spray and transformed it all to springtime. Nervously he unzipped his pants and tried to take a leak. But he couldn't. He zipped up again, washed his hands, used the towel to push back his cuticles, then looked at himself in the mirror again. Tiny beads of perspiration stood out on his forehead. If it weren't camouflaged by the mustache, he knew his upper lip would be shiny and wet, too. He could taste it.

Picking at his shirt with his fingertips, he walked back into the living room, turned down the thermostat, and stood directly below the air vent, trying to dry off and cool down. He'd already changed his shirt. Twice. He'd done it once just before ten. Zimmerman had been due then, and Button had worked himself into such a state that the top inch of his collar had changed color from the sweat rolling down his neck. At eleven, he'd changed shirts again. At quarter past eleven, he was still waiting and getting damper by the second.

When the doorbell finally rang at 11:20, Button had just finished a short scotch. Just enough to wash down the Percodan. He hurried into the bathroom once more to rinse the smell from his mouth. Then he took it slow and walked to door. He didn't want to appear too eager.

"Glad you could make it." Button was pleased with the ease of his delivery. "Come on in." Step back. Smooth gesture. Close door. He'd rehearsed it over and over again. "Can I get you something? Scotch. A beer? Soda?"

"Beer would be great."

Walk into living room. Let him look around. "Are you into art at all? That one with the palm trees is a Rubideaux. The other, the split image, is a Kronsnoble. They're both artists who work in the bay area." Pause. Get the drinks.

Zimmerman followed him from the slate-floored foyer into the ivory-carpeted living area, breathing in the cool, strangely scented air. Then he made a casual inventory of the room, studying up close the things he found familiar from his hours of surveillance. Gradually Button's surroundings lost their stage-set bleakness. Zimmerman liked the paintings. The Rubadoux was of pale trees and marshland. For a landscape it had a subtle energy and light and a certain drama that he hadn't expected. The other one had two heads, a man and a woman's in the first two sections. The third section was distinctly modern. It showed the torso of a kid in a thin shirt and underpants. He couldn't tell the sex. But he guessed the three sections together meant something.

From outside Button's place had looked bland. Even the pale carpet was deceptive. Up close it was rich and thick and elegant and gave way gently, cushioning each step. The austere-looking black leather chairs were soft and pliant, luxurious and inviting. Tranquil and understated, the decor suggested that in the years since he'd left Lakeland, Jack Button had been doing very well.

While Button got him a beer from the kitchen, Zimmerman stood pensively before the glass doors that opened onto the balcony. The view was awesome, but imperfect. Only the outermost branches of the oak on the water's edge were softly lighted by the moon, making it stand out full and dark against the sky. But its heart was black and unfathomable. Zimmerman been sitting out there for over an hour, stalling, watching Button slowly come apart.

"That's quite a view out there. Nothing like having nature right in your backyard. That's a wildlife refuge area. Lots of birds and raccoons. Sometimes a deer. Gators, too, but they pretty well stick to the water." Hand his guest the drink. Cross the room. Sit down. Button figured that by the time he got to that part, he would be able to breathe normally again. Almost.

"Here's your beer." Button gave him a tall frosted glass that Zimmerman knew must have been put in the freezer ahead of time. Button was careful about details like that.

"So . . ." Button sipped his scotch then expelled a slow breath.

Zimmerman took a long swallow of the beer. The taste was curiously reassuring, anchoring him to a reality beyond this room and this time and this man who'd changed his life.

"It's been a while," Zimmerman said evenly. He looked down at the pale head on his beer. Then he smiled, not so much out of nervousness, but at the irony that even now, he and Button had not spoken each other's name.

"Yes. Yes, it has. You've changed a lot. I guess we both have. . . ."

"Not enough," Zimmerman wanted to scream. But he just nodded.

"So are you in school? College? Or do you work?"

Zimmerman looked over at him. Button's face, polite, smiling, and curiously tense, stirred the dull ache of memory. He took another sip of beer. "I work. Sometimes I go to school."

"Is this vacation time, or did your company let you have time off to come and help out here?" Button could feel his cheek muscles quiver. What he wanted to ask was more basic.

"I'm not in school this session. My work hours are pretty flexible." Zimmerman eased back in the chair and deliberately stretched, like a cat quietly staking a claim on its territory.

Button's mouth went dry. He wasn't sure if Zimmerman was baiting him. "You did some nice pieces of sandsculpture out there. Are you some kind of artist?"

"I've taken a couple of art courses. I've had a little trouble focusing on what it is I really want to do." His soft brown eyes seemed to draw Button in.

"What are some of the things that interest you?" Button leaned forward in his seat, facing the youth. He looked as if he were conducting some kind of interview, but his main intent was to relieve the pressure on his inseam. It was happening again, and he didn't want Zimmerman to know how easily he could be moved.

Zimmerman lifted his glass and downed the last of the tawny liquid. "I'm interested in a lot of things." He stared at the empty glass and didn't elaborate.

"Would you like another?" Button held out his hand, ready to get him a refill.

"Sure. That was good." Zimmerman let his fingers graze the back of Button's as they made the exchange. For a second Button's eyes locked onto his. Then they darted away.

Button's entire arm tingled from the contact. In the kitchen, he grabbed a tea towel and mopped the perspiration from his face and neck. He put the cold beer out on the cabinet. The spare glass was still in the freezer. "Go ahead and take a look at the CDs. There might be something you'd like to hear. I'll be out in a couple of minutes," he called out. He hurt deep in his groin. He had to take a leak. This time it was for real. And it couldn't wait.

It was the stench that first penetrated the darkness. Then Tommy moved. His hand slid in the cold, foul substance coating the exposed limestone. For a long time he lay there, his cheek pressed against the coarse sand and shell, drifting in and out again. Then abruptly the details started slipping back into place. He opened his eyes and blinked until segments of the undifferentiated gray took distinct shapes. The breeder was still next to him, sleeping. The smell and the substance were hers. And the top of his head felt like it was coming off.

Tugging himself to an upright position, he slouched against the cave wall, gingerly feeling the fist-size knot on the top of his head. His hair tingled and felt like it was standing on end from the swelling. But he couldn't feel any blood.

Then he glanced down at the overalls, smeared and stinking from excrement. "Fuckin' dummy," he hissed, landing a hard kick at the breeder. Then he grabbed her by the hair and broke her neck. She didn't make a sound. Slowly, as he stood there peeling off his befouled clothes, he heard the air leak out of her body, and he knew she was dead.

"Fuckin' dummy," he kept muttering while he strode deeper into the cave and picked up the clean coveralls he'd stashed back there. "Fuckin' dummy," he growled, kicking the motionless lump. It was already dark. He could see the faraway glow in the sky that meant all the lights were on by the mound. And it meant they had all come down. Because of her, he'd missed them. They had all gone into that honeycomb building where they holed up all through the night. Unless they came out into the gardens.

Quivering as he submerged himself in the chilled creek water, Tommy sputtered out his rage. "Grab 'um. Fuck 'um." He was going in there again. Before he went, he was going to mess Lon's stash up real good. Fuck the magic shit. He wasn't coming back empty-handed. Even if he had to wait all night, even if he had to sneak inside, he would find someone. Anyone.

"Vince and I are going down for dinner now." Kitty had taken a long, leisurely bubble bath and sipped a glass of orange juice while Zach ate pepperoni and sausage pizza in front of the TV. Vince had it delivered along with two liters of root beer and a bucket of buttered popcorn as an outright bribe so Zach would settle in for the night and eat in the room. He and Kitty were dining out. Alone.

"Sure, Mom." Zach didn't take his eyes off the screen. He sat propped up in bed, like a potentate surrounded by the trappings of his feast.

"How do I look?" Kitty had pulled on smoky gray silk slacks and a shirt and slipped on the dangly pearl earrings Vince had given her for Valentine's Day.

"Good, Mom," Zach answered mechanically.

"Will you listen to me for a moment," Kitty insisted, stepping between Zach and the television. His mouth tightened in irritation and he leaned to side, trying to see around her. "Zach." He looked up, but only fleetingly. "You know the rules. No one in. No one out. If you need anything, call downstairs. We'll be in the Felucca Café. Then in the Oasis Lounge."

She'd inadvertently moved a little to the right, and Zach's eyes were leveled waist-high, soaking in whatever slice of action he could see.

"Zach . . ."

"I got it," he insisted. "You'll be downstairs. I stay here. No problem."

"I'll come up and check on you before we go to the lounge. I don't want you staying up watching television all night."

"I won't," he answered, still preoccupied.

"That's why I'm coming to check. I want to make sure you turn the TV off. You worked hard today. You need a good night's sleep."

"Right."

"See you later." She leaned down and kissed the top of his head. He didn't move.

"Yeah. 'Bye." He was still staring straight forward.

"Don't turn the dead bolt. If you go to sleep, I won't be able to get in."

"Right." He reached over and landed the bucket of popcorn between his outspread legs.

"I love you. See you later. Zach?"

"Sure. 'Bye."

Lon didn't want to go home. Not yet. He had spent the whole day with his boy. They had worked and laughed. They ate hot dogs. Zach had bought him "choklit" and sodas and they had walked all around the huge mound, looking at all the different figures while they ate and drank together. So when they all came down together, he only pretended to leave. Then he backtracked through the trees and brush. He climbed up into a huge moss-hung tree, wedged his rump between two limbs, and settled back. Just looking. And thinking about his day.

Gradually the sun that had edged the mound in crimson fire sank below the horizon, and only the topmost peaks glowed gold against the darkening sky. Far off the flash of lightning and the rumble that followed meant a storm was passing by. But Lon could sniff the air and feel the pressure of the breeze against his face and tell it wasn't close. There would be no rain. Just rumbling. Not like summer storms that came up suddenly and swept inland with a sudden rush of rain. This was all show.

Suddenly the clearing flooded with another kind of light as the multitude of spots around the mound went on simultaneously. Lon rocked forward, grabbing his crotch and grinning with childlike glee. High up, he wasn't conscious of the crowd that circled the mound. They were blocked of by the lower limbs and branches of surrounding trees. For the moment it was all for him. He could lean back, and look, and savor it, and think about this happiest of days.

Mark Zimmerman was standing by the black-lacquered liquor cabinet when Button finished in the bathroom and returned with the beer. His back was toward the hallway leading to the kitchen. Button had to take a few steps into the room to get far enough around to notice the scotch bottle was almost shoulder height. The center section of the cabinet had been elevated, and the serving table was folded forward.

"How did you do that? That's private," Button snapped. "Don't touch any of that." He expected Zimmerman to stop. Or put down whatever he was holding. Or at least seem startled. But the youth never even acknowledged his comment. He just kept leafing through the pages of the photo album he held.

"Let me have that." Button landed the beer on the raised top and reached for the book.

"Get your hand off that or I'll take out your eyeballs." Zimmerman was rigid, pale, and bit off the words with lethal calmness. "Back off, slime." Button was clutching the upper edge of the book. He looked from the open page to the cold, contemptuous eyes riveted to his. Neither man moved. Then Button let his grip loosen. He pulled his hand in toward his chest. He backed off.

"Are all these books full of pictures like these?" Zimmerman asked in a curious, hushed voice. "Are these all kids you've done?"

Button cleared his throat. "I don't know what you're

talking about. I'm a camera buff. Those are just regular photos. Please. Put them back.''

"Don't bullshit me." Zimmerman kept turning the pages, pausing to look at every face. "Sit down. Just shut up and sit down.''

"Why don't you just get out of here. Now. Before I call security." Button clenched his fists and straightened his spine. The song on the CD player ended. The disc had played out.

"Your phone has been disconnected," Zimmerman said simply. "And unless you sit down now, I'm going to hurt you.''

Button stood his ground, eyeing the youth and assessing the odds. Zimmerman was younger. He was slender, Button had him on both height and weight. But the kid was muscular. And there was something indefinable, something barely submerged in Zimmerman's angry eyes, something that threatened to surface. Zimmerman's hands trembled.

"Sit down.''

Button backed over the the leather armchair where he'd been sitting earlier. His breath seemed to have solidified like a rock in his chest. He was sweating again, only this time he felt cold all over. His mouth was dry. He could hardly pick up his scotch glass.

"Am I in one of these?" Zimmerman put aside the album he'd been scrutinizing. He pulled out a second one.

Button took a swallow of his drink. He didn't answer. He stared straight ahead, deliberately unresponsive.

Zimmerman realigned the books. He pulled out a couple of the videotapes and read the titles. Button though he saw the youth put one in his jacket. Or maybe the dark shape was one of the rolls of undeveloped film stacked up waiting to be mailed off. He didn't ask. Zimmerman took a third album and tucked it under his arm. He crossed over and sat in the chair facing Button. Carefully he leafed through the second book, one he'd already had open. Button watched his expressionless face as page after page paused in midair then turned.

"You don't know how bad you fucked me up," Zimmerman said at last, without even glancing up from the steady turn, pause, look, and turn sequence that had made the only sound in the room other than the gentle rush of air from the ceiling vents. "I spent years thinking I was a freak. I was the sick one. I thought I was evil and dirty and despicable. I even thought for a while that I was gay. If anyone touched me, or if anyone said something that you'd said, I was nothing. I was dead inside." He closed that album. He put it on the carpet beside his chair and opened the next one.

Button rubbed his hand over his mouth nervously. Zimmerman started turning the pages.

"I used to think somehow I was the guilty one. I hated my life. I hated myself." His voice was barely audible, as if it were struggling to get out from somewhere deep inside him. "I tried to kill myself. Got into some pills. It was like a dumb, bad joke. Turned out to be muscle relaxers. I couldn't move. Hardly could breathe. I crapped all over myself. It was really humiliating. But I didn't die. I figured maybe there was some reason for keeping me around."

The methodical turning of pages continued. Button's eyes shifted from Zimmerman's unreadable expression to the album pages then back. He liked his lips and glanced at the door.

"They stuck me in a hospital. Some counselor came to talk to me. She'd been molested by an uncle when she was a kid. She knew what it was like. She was smart. She asked the right questions. It almost killed me, but I told her. She's the only one who knows. Except for you and me. Since then, I've been trying to turn my life around." He stopped. He stared. The color drained from his face. He slumped forward slightly, drawing his forearm in against his midsection as if he were warding off a blow. Button knew he'd found the pictures of himself. He sat very still.

Zimmerman never said a word. He just stared. Then he inhaled, held it, and let it out. He started turning the pages again.

A few pages later, he froze. "Aw . . . no. God . . . no . . ." He looked up at Button, his dark eyes showing the pained dullness of disbelief. He reached down and touched the face on the page, hollow-eyed and momentarily speechless. "Jesus God . . . no . . ."

"No one ever sees them but me." Button started talking. "They're all I have. I have such an empty life. I don't have any family. I keep the pictures to remind me—"

"Shut up." The words were choked and tortured. He sat, shoulders sagging slightly, disoriented. In the tense chill silence, Button could hear his own breathing. He could smell his sweat.

Zimmerman finally looked at him again. His eyes brimmed with tears, but beyond them was a hard veil of contempt. "I sure never needed a picture to remember you," he hissed. "Every night when I lie down in my bed, I can see your smooth stupid-looking face with that shit-eating grin. And I can hear you saying 'sweet dreams' in that cutesy way you had. It still makes my skin crawl. You fucked me up bad. I thought you were my friend. I trusted you. And after you dropped me, couldn't understand what was wrong with me. I couldn't trust anyone. I turned into a damn recluse. At twelve. Until him. I trusted him.'' He pressed his fingertips almost reverently beneath the face in the book.

Button swallowed hard. He shook his head, totally confused.

Zimmerman spoke with a slight tremor in his voice. "There were lots of kids in my out-patient group. They were all kids who'd tried it. They'd all tried to kill themselves one way or another. But this one . . . this one was my friend." He placed his hand on the plastic page cover protectively. "Ben left town when we were in grade school, then his family moved back to Lakeland when we were both juniors. He tried an overdose and ended up in my therapy group. He was into everything—coke, crack, pills, booze. He just never said why. But now we know." Zimmerman's hard brown eyes fixed on Button. He turned the album around and held it out under Button's nose. "Ben. One of your boys. Ben is dead. He finally made it. Senior year. Said he couldn't take it anymore." Zimmerman looked down at the face. "I bet he didn't need a photo either."

Button stared bewilderedly at the familiar face in the photos on both pages. "Benjy . . ." He shook his head in confusion.

"Ben. Ben Hyland. He grew up, asshole. And he carried all your shit with him. He just couldn't handle it and he couldn't tell anyone."

"Benjy . . ." Button fingers dug into the soft leather of the armrests. Something beautiful and perfect was slipping away. "No . . ."

"Yes!" Suddenly Zimmerman was right in his face, clutching the open-necked shirt. He fumbled in his pocket, then he jammed Button's handgun up under his

chin. Zimmerman had found more than film and albums
in the enameled cabinet. "His name was Ben. Ben Hyland was seventeen when he died. You must have done a
real good job on him." He vibrated with barely checked
fury. Tears had started down his face. "Do the world a
favor. Take this. Blow your fuckin' brains out. You're
some kind of animal. You don't deserve to live." His
voice was becoming higher, more shrill. "You killed my
friend. You fucked us all up. All of us . . ." He took
the book and slammed it against the side of Button's
head, popping the pages from the binding and sending
photos flying around the room.

"Please. Don't hurt me. Please." Button clamped onto
Zimmerman's wrist, but he didn't try to pull the gun
away. Zimmerman's finger was on the trigger and his
other hand was back at Button's throat. Button could look
down and see into the barrel. He knew it was loaded.
"Please. I'll do anything." Zimmerman yanked him out
of the chair. Button slid onto his knees, and crouched
there, holding on to Zimmerman's arm. "Please . . ."

For a long time Zimmerman barely moved. He just
stood over him, gasping great breaths, and held him
there.

"Let go of my arm."

Button released his hold.

"Pick up all this stuff." Zimmerman backed away,
keeping the gun leveled at Button's head while he scrambled about picking up the pages and loose pictures. "Get
them all together. Everything . . ." Zimmerman jabbed
the barrel of the gun toward the liquor cabinet where the
rest of Button's collection remained intact. "Get a garbage bag. Put all this stuff where it belongs." Button got
up and hurried into the kitchen and came back with

ark heavy plastic bag. He stuffed all the tapes and al-
ums, loose pages, and rolls of film in it.

"We're going to take a ride. We need a garbage dump.
ake your car."

"Right . . ." Button picked the keys up off the shelf
y the television. "Whatever you say." At least there
vere people out there, people he could signal for help.
ate security surely would recognize him. He could make
is move then. He went ahead of Zimmerman, carrying
ne garbage bag downstairs into the enclosed garage. He
ot in the driver's side and Zimmerman moved in beside
im.

"Don't do anything stupid." Zimmerman leveled the
un at his midsection.

"Whatever you say. Just don't hurt me." Button trig-
ered the electronic door opener, then pulled out care-
ılly onto the street.

"Don't speed."

Button proceeded along to Delta Drive and turned.
head, the huge hotel stood out above the tree line,
eaming against the dark night sky. Farther east, the
iry-tale city spread along the horizon line, illuminated
w only by minimal security lights.

"Pull in there." Zimmerman stopped him before they
ached the parking area for the Grand Nile. He pointed
utton down the service road that ran down the lower
de of gardens toward the maintenance shed. Button
esitated. That section was dark and vacated for the
ght.

Zimmerman raised the gun up to his lower jaw. "This
where they dump trash." Button licked his lips. Then
pulled left onto the narrow, asphalt drive. "Get your
uff and get out." Zimmerman made Button exit first.

Then he came around the car, moved in behind him, and
directed him toward the boat docks and the Nature Trail

"Why not just put it in the dumpster?" Button stalled
uneasy about moving farther away from civilization.

"Someone might find it," Zimmerman replied, spac
ing out the words evenly. "Move it."

Button wiped his hand over his face, smoothing hi
mustache and beard. "Look. Isn't there something
else—"

"Move . . ." Zimmerman pointed the gun at the bacl
of Button's neck. "We're making a garbage run. Nov
walk."

It was the commercial on the TV that started it. Hi
movie had just ended on cable and he was holding dow
the remote-control button, changing channels when th
ad began. They were advertising beer. A bunch of guy
were having a great time fishing. They were laughing an
joking and showing off their catch. Big fish. Like th
ones Lon said were in the spring. Zach looked at thei
equipment. Then he started worrying. Kitty had unde
stood about the trowel. He wasn't sure if she'd unde
stand about the pole and tackle box. She might. But
was out there under the gazebo. It was out where some
one might find it and take it before he dared to ask.

"Zach, are you awake. It's us." Kitty's voice cam
from the hotel hallway. Then he heard the key in th
lock, and he swept the remnants of his popcorn off th
spread onto the floor between the double beds. "Time
shut the TV off. We're going down to the lounge for
while to listen to the music. You can turn on the F
station and play it while you go to sleep."

"I'm not really tired," Zach protested. "Can't I wat
another movie?"

"Nope. You'll have to settle for music. It's late, and you have to finish the letters first thing in the morning. Get some sleep." Kitty came and tucked him in, confiscated the remote control, and turned off all the lights except the one in the bathroom. "I'll be back in an hour or so. I'll even feel the top of the TV. It better not be warm."

Zach shrugged. She'd caught him a couple of times that way. "All right. I won't watch the movie." He reached over and tuned in the radio station.

"Good night again, sport." Vince had been waiting by the door; now he poked his head around the corner.

" 'Night, Vince. 'Night, Mom. Have a nice time." Zach rolled over on his side and tugged the cover up to his chin.

"Thanks." Kitty looked at him a second, then turned and left.

"That was almost too easy," she said warily as she joined Vince outside in the corridor.

"He's probably too tired to put up a fight. He worked his young buns off out there today. If you're not used to it, that sun really knocks the starch out you. He'll be out before we get to the elevator.

"I hope so. I don't want a round when we get in."

"Then don't feel the TV," Vince suggested with a wicked smile. "I have a lot of other warm places you can put your hands."

"One of the nicest things about you is the way you don't pussyfoot around." Kitty chuckled.

"Subtlety is what makes a lot of folks end up sleeping alone," Vince professed. "And living alone. I prefer the direct approach. How about thirty minutes of undulating to the music in the lounge then we'll retire to my room for a more intensive kind of communication."

"Let's take it one song at a time," Kitty suggested. Her voice was low and purposefully seductive. "I don't want to commit to thirty minutes. That can be a very long time."

"Maybe the band will stink," Vince joked as he pushed the button for the elevator. "Then we can come right back up and I'll hum. I'm one heck of a hummer."

"I'm getting breathless with anticipation."

"Does that mean we skip the lounge?"

"It means we go in, hold hands, dance a little while, then beat tracks back here. I like being breathless for a while."

"That makes two of us." Vince leaned over and kissed the curve of her neck as the elevator purred and stopped at their floor.

Zach had seen them do it on TV. He took the big pool towels from the bathroom and rolled them up. Then he took the extra pillow and blanket from the closet and made the body. He used the empty ice bucket for the head. He pulled the covers over it all and stepped back to check the effect. He figured to make it back well before the hour she'd estimated. But even if he didn't, he guessed she wouldn't come right in to sleep. She'd probably open the doors between the rooms and go over to see Vince. If all she did was glance at the figure in the bed, she wouldn't notice anything suspicious. But he planned to hurry and beat her back, just in case.

Outside, the hallway was empty. He didn't dare use the glass-walled elevators. There were too many people who knew him now. And wandering around alone at midnight, he was sure to be stopped. But down the end and to the right, the heavy doors opened onto the service elevator. Then he could cut along the second floor where the offices would be closed and use the stairs. He'd been that way on one of Corey's tours, showing them shortcuts through the building. Zach tucked his room key in his jeans pocket and took off that way. Within seconds he was in the stairwell and on the way down.

When the artificial lighting on the mound shifted from the overall floods to the few spots that stayed on all night, spreading an uneven glow over the area, Lon figured it was time to leave. Zach had said he'd meet him in the morning. They would work together again. Kitty said they did good work. Zach called them a team. All through the day, Lon could feel the magic between them getting stronger. Sometimes he'd reach into his pocket and slip the scorpion pendant in his glove for a while, and he would smile to himself, knowing that the power was with him. But he knew he should burn the herbs and hold the dream sticks through the night if he wanted to strengthen the bond even more. He had a new choklit stick of Zach's to add to the others. He'd just get his knife at home, start a small campfire, and whittle awhile before he went to sleep.

Lon made the first part of the trip in silence. Only the breeze in the palms and palmettos and the occasional crack of a twig underfoot interrupted his reverie as he wove along the now-familiar route into the wetlands. In the pale moonlight everything near the ground was spattered in crazy patterns of light and dark, but the cover overhead was edged in pure ivory.

Once he'd gotten beyond the first waterway, the owls and the frogs and crickets started in. Soon the far-off grunt of a gator punctuated the nocturnal serenade, and Lon began to whistle between his teeth one of the songs that he'd heard playing over and over around the mound.

He fell silent again when he got to the tree trunk where he usually undressed and bathed and hid his mementos away. He didn't want Tommy to know he was nearby. Quietly he slipped out of his T-shirt and overalls, rinsed the shirt in the creek, then hung it on a limb to dry overnight. Then he reached into the space in the trunk for his bundle.

He could tell it was wet the second his hand touched it. He could tell it was urine when he jerked back his hand and sniffed. But what sent the chill through him was the way it was wedged in there, tight and small. Still naked, he moved out into the clearing and unrolled the pack. It was all there, the dream sticks and the towel and his clothes, but the dream sticks were broken into fragments. Everything else was in shreds. And it all had been peed on. The stink permeated everything.

"Not funny . . ." Lon half growled and half wept as he rolled it back up into a bundle. He pulled on the overalls he'd worn all day then took the bundle and stalked off toward the cave. "Not funny . . ." He sniffed, his clenched hands shaking.

He found the breeder just inside the cave opening. He stopped and listened for her breathing or for some sound to indicate that Tommy was deeper inside. But the only breath he heard was his own. Lon bent down and touched her. She was stiff and strangely cool. Her head lolled grotesquely to one side when he reached under her. Her dull eyes, staring still, caught the moonlight from the opening and glistened. She smelled of excrement and death.

"Tommy?" Lon called into the darkness. The hollow sound brought no response. "Tommy . . . ?" He felt the lump of cloth just beyond the breeder's body. When he held it up, the long-legged garment, soiled with the breeder's waste, dangled before him. Lon carried it outside and looked at it more closely in the light of the moon. The patches sewn on it were familiar. He had seen the men in clothes like this continually crisscrossing the grounds, picking up the papers and straws and things that people dropped along the way. Sometimes they clipped the bushes or worked among the flowers. "Tommy?" Lon called out again, trying to put together the pieces.

He sniffed the workclothes. Besides the breeder's waste, he could pick up only one smell, the scent of Tommy's sweat. Then a cold uneasy sensation began to work its way down to the pit of his stomach as something clicked.

"Tommy . . . don't be mad. . . ." Lon wailed into the surrounding darkness. Frantically he raced for the tool cache. When he took the rod and tackle box, he'd moved everything very carefully. He'd been cautious to set all the tools back in order. Now they were strewn all over as if Tommy had rummaged though them then simply left. Lon pressed his hand against his head, the stinking garment still dangling from the other. "No . . . Tommy . . ." He rocked from side to side. Then he froze, as an oddly primitive warning sounded deep inside. "My boy . . ." Lon dropped the coveralls and grabbed a shovel. "My Zach." There had been one of those cleanup men on the Nature Trail where he and Zach had fished. And there had been one at the shuttle stop. They were all over, all during the day. And some were thick and squat and gloved, just like him. Just like his half brother. "Not my boy . . ." Lon lamented as he crashed through the underbrush. "No . . . Tommeeee . . ." he pleaded, clamping down on the shovel handle and thrusting the blade out before him like a shield.

* * *

Tommy squeezed between the tall flowering bushes directly facing the wide glass doors. He had circled the entire building, checking the doorways. Two smaller ones he tried were locked. The other ones opened into rooms with tables, where there were many people and sometimes music played. He stayed away from those and the ones near the pool or near the flat places with tables. Without going close, he could hear voices and laughter. So he came all the way back to the main doors, the ones with steps where he'd seen the guard lead Lon and the boy. The tall stone bird-faced sentinels towering on either side were lighted from below. They stared disinterestedly past him into the velvet shadows of the gardens. For a while, the train like the one that Lon had ridden on came and stopped, unloading a few people at a time, then it went away and didn't come back.

Tommy hunched down behind the shorter shrubs, studying the movement of the ones beyond the glass. One man in uniform, sometimes two, were always within sight of the door. There were not many of the others passing to and fro in the open space father in, but the uneven traffic kept him at bay. Once he broke away and followed a woman and her man off toward the parking area, but the lights there were bright, and there were others near, and the two were in their vehicle before Tommy could improvise a plan of attack.

He had just come back when he saw the boy, not at the main door, but at a smaller one farther down. At first he wasn't sure it was the right one. Tonight any boy, any female would do. But in the rectangle of light that framed the slender shape, he saw the hair and face and he knew it was him. The boy moved quickly from the exit across the driveway then started half running along the path, backtracking on the same route Tommy had followed him and Lon along earlier. Grinning, Tommy pushed his way back through to the dark side of the hedge and cut a parallel path toward the trail. He knew where the kid was going. And no matter who else was out there, Tommy was going to make his grab.

Zach didn't dare take his eyes off the path. His ears thundered and his heart raced, and he knew that if he stopped or looked up or glanced at the plants that lined the way, he'd be too frightened to go on. And he had to get there. Occasionally a pale glow from in-ground lights set among the bushes would tempt him to stop in the oasis and catch his breath. But he had to hurry. He had to get it and get back to the room.

There were only three small lights functioning under the gazebo balustrade. Two were near the bottom to mark the step up from the path to the stairs. The third was at the top. Its counterpart on the opposite end of the step had a bulb in it, but it was out. Zach kept one hand on the latticed underpinning as he stepped toward the waterside where Lon had ducked between the pilings and left the rod and tackle box. Grimacing as he stretched his arm into the inky darkness there and patted around blindly, hoping to make contact, Zach could feel the dark ooze give way as his shoes sank down under his weight. Then the cold, clammy mud closed in over his ankles. Now he knew he'd have something else to explain.

Zach leaned in further, wincing in dread of touching anything that might bite or sting or slither. Then his fingertips hit the upright pole, propped against one of the gazebo supports. Barely breathing, he passed it out to his other hand then groped for the box. Grabbing it by the handle, he eased out carefully. His tennis shoes made a dull sucking sound with each step.

In the dim light at the bottom of the stairs, Zach

crouched over and examined his shoes. They were black, melting ovals, completely covered with mud. He didn't dare walk into the hotel, not even through the service door he'd used, with feet like that. He lay the rod and box down by the steps, slid off the shoes, and started scraping the mud away by grating and thumping them against the wooden stair.

"Tommmeee . . . Nooooo . . ."

Zach flung himself back, landing on his backside on the path. Panicked, he turned toward the sound, the bellow from the darkness. But it was the movement from the other direction, the pounding of feet charging down at him along the Nature Trail that spun him around and froze the scream in his throat.

Zach could feel the concussion when the two bodies slammed into each other. The bare-chested one coming from the dock area, brandishing a gleaming giant blade above his head, cut right in front of the khaki-colored blur swooping down on him, spear in hand. The massive bodies collided with awesome force and plunged to the side, off the main path. They locked onto each other and rolled, grunting and growling, into the dark overgrown area beyond the hedge. Zach huddled immobile by the stairway while the repeated thud of fist on body and the crunch of bushes snapping and branches giving way resounded in the night. Finally he let out a tight, broken sound, more a moan than a cry for help, and all at once he could breathe.

Frantically Zach grabbed his shoes and scrambled to his feet. Then he started back up the path, moving unsteadily at first, then breaking into a full run. Behind him, the battle sounds came in explosive, violent bursts. He didn't look back. Panting and dripping with sweat, he raced right to the service door and grabbed the railing on the stairway leading up. He lunged two steps at a time up to the second floor then tore along the hall to the service elevator. Only when the doors swept closed behind him did he start to shudder uncontrollably, pressing his head against the cool metal walls and whimpering in agony. He hurt all over. His lungs burned. His bare feet felt as if the soles were on fire. His stomach was contracting and he could feel that strange saliva taste that meant he was going to throw up. Damp and chilled and weak, he swallowed again and again, trying to stop it. But it came up anyway. Even when he went into dry heaves, he could still hear the sound of fists and that terrible scream.

There was no one in the corridor when the elevator stopped. Zach stumbled out, searching his pocket for the room key on the way. The form he'd stuffed in his bed still lay there undiscovered. There was no sound of voices from Vince's room. Zach hurried into the bathroom and plopped his shoes in the tub. Then he grabbed a cloth and wet it and wiped his face. He blew his nose. It burned. Fragments of pizza and popcorn came out. He blew it again then took a glass of water and rinsed his mouth.

Quickly he peeled off his wet clothes and threw them in the sink. Shivering and choking back the sobs that came out high and incoherent, he crouched over the tub, scrubbing the shoes with a washcloth. "Jesus loves me . . . Jesus loves me. . . ." From somewhere buried in memory, the words came to him. "Jesus loves me, this I know . . ." Zach rocked back and forth as he scrubbed, tears streaming down his face and his slim body damp with sweat. It helped to keep his teeth from chattering if he sang. "For the Bible tells me so. . . ." He kept rocking and dunking the shoes under the faucet.

"Jesus loves me. . . ." Forlornly, he stared at the shoes. They were hopeless. He got up off his knees and flushed the blackened washcloth down the john. Shuddering in the air-conditioning, he carried the wet shoes back into the bedroom area and stuffed them between the mattress and the box springs. He raced over to the drawer, yanked on a T-shirt and pushed his fake body stuffings onto the floor as he slid into bed. Then he bolted upright, reached over, and tugged the blanket over his spread.

"Jesus loves me. . . ." Zach sang it over and over like an incantation to drive out the devils. But somehow, deep inside his rib cage, he could still feel the force of that collision. Even the song couldn't drown out the dreadful sounds of combat that echoed inside his head just like they'd come rumbling out from the dark beyond the hedge. Not even the extra blanket could still the trembling in his legs.

"Mama . . ." Zach lay there staring at the ceiling, sobbing, tears trickling down his face. And the demons danced before him every time he closed his eyes.

They were sprawled out side by side on the riverbank, scraped and bruised and panting from exhaustion when they heard the voices. Lon had a long jagged rip across his bare chest where Tommy had grazed him with the groundskeeper's spear. Tommy's foot was caked in mud and blood. Lon had brought the shovel down and sliced it open between his toes. But now, weapons shattered and lost along the way, they lay there under the stars, too drained to raise their arms or even move their heads.

"Look, couldn't we just dump these in a garbage can and drop a match on them?" The first voice was thin and tight. Like the annoying whine of a child.

"We're taking it far enough out here where no one will see." The second voice was cold and distant and emotionless. "Just keep moving." The flashlight he carried zigzagged on the ground slightly ahead of the one carrying the bag.

Lon reached out and put a hand on Tommy's arm and signaled not to make a sound. Sluggishly they both propped themselves up on their elbows and peered through the marshgrass and rushes toward the intruders. The two wetlanders had punched and chased and vaulted through the shrub bog, following the route of the old sough that the recent dams had turned into a waterway. They'd been within eyeshot of another of the wooden buildings set out over the water when they'd simply become too tired and sore to continue fighting.

"Take it up in there and dump it." The first voice spoke in a monotone.

"All right." The cow-faced one with the beard took a plastic bag like the one Tommy had carried, climbed the four steps, and dumped the contents onto the gazebo floor. The younger one switched off the flashlight and stuffed it in his belt, then circled around the pile, using his foot to push it into a tighter stack.

"Now get down on your knees."

Lon saw the glint of metal in the second one's hand.

"You want me to push it all together and light it?" Button asked. He hunched over the books, snapping open the rings that held the pages and lifting them free. The first one didn't answer. He just kept the gun leveled at the kneeling man's head.

"You aren't going to burn these . . . are you?" Button said dully when he looked up and guessed the verdict hidden in Zimmerman's eyes. "You're going to kill me," he whispered.

"Not me. You have to do it. You're the trash we have to get rid of." Zimmerman carefully wiped the gun with the tail of his shirt. He caught the other one by the wrist and shoved the gun, handle first, into the open palm. He closed his own hand tight over Button's. "You said it yourself, Button. We have to pay the piper. This is it. The payoff."

Lon could smell the fear from the first one. Tommy sat forward a bit more to get a clearer view.

"I won't do it. I won't do this. I don't care what you think I've done, you aren't going to get me to kill myself. And you don't want to do it yourself. You don't want to live with that kind of guilt." Button started in with a flood of words. "You aren't a killer. You've got all my pictures. You've cleaned me out. You've got what you came after. Just leave now before you do something that will ruin your life." He kept talking, trying to shake Zimmerman's deadly calm.

'Don't talk anymore," Zimmerman said in a quiet voice. "You talk too much. Talk is easy for you, but it doesn't mean a thing. Just shut up." He held the gun in Button's hand and gripped his wrist with the other. "Stick it here." He turned Button's wrist so the barrel was under his throat and pointed back and up toward the top of his head. "This will be over real quick. Just pull." His words were cold and exact and hard.

"God . . . no . . . please . . . no . . ." Button begged, and clutched at Zimmerman's arm with his free hand.

"It's over. This is the end. You've done enough."

"I won't do anything ever again. I'll turn myself in. I'll see a shrink. I'll get better. I'll do anything." He tried to wrench his arm away so the gun wasn't pointing at him, but Zimmerman was rigid. He was far more powerful than Button had imagined. "Please. I'm sorry. I'm not well. Please. Don't ruin your future because of me. I'll help you. I can see you have money enough to go to college. Please . . . no . . .'' he begged.

"You're amazing. You'd say anything. You always come up with just the right words. But not this time." Zimmerman's voice had a clipped and ominous quality. "You're slime." He tightened his hold on the gun and bent down, pushing it against Button's neck. "Do it. Maybe Ben is waiting for you. Maybe you can tell him how sorry you are."

"I can't do this. I'm Catholic. It's a mortal sin."

"You fucking liar. You aren't a Catholic, you bastard. You aren't anything. You'd do anything to save your ass. You're filth." Zimmerman's voice faded. "No more bullshit. Words can't change what you've done. End it. End it now."

"No . . .'' Button rolled his head to the side.

"Then I will." He crammed his finger over Button's and squeezed the trigger. "Sweet dreams."

"No . . .'' Button squealed and tried to struggle out of his grasp. But Zimmerman held fast. The chamber clicked. It didn't fire.

Button crouched there, unmoving.

"Now you know what it's like to think it's over, to get right to the edge, and find out you're wrong. I've been there. So had Ben. He made it all the way on the second try." Zimmerman kept an iron grip on his wrist. "So can you." He straightened up a bit. He licked his lips. "Now dismiss this servant, Lord. . . .''

This time the shot rang out. Quick, flat, dull. Button's head jerked back. He lifted off his knees slightly. Zimmerman held on to the hand with the gun still in it and guided him down. Button slumped on his side across the pile of pictures. A pool of dark blood began to spread beneath his head.

Neither Lon nor Tommy moved. They sat mesmerized, watching the extraordinary, serene ritual, far more deadly than their bloody free-for-all. They stared at the motionless body while the second one wiped his hands on his pant leg then turned and walked away off toward the service road. They didn't hear a car start, but they knew he was gone. They dragged themselves up and moved in closer.

Lon was the one who crept right up next to him and picked up the pictures. Tommy limped and moaned and sat on the steps holding his foot. Tilting them toward the moonlight, Lon stood puzzling over so many pretty faces. More than he ever imagined. But the grisly opening beneath Button's chin and the dark sticky blood kept drawing his long thoughtful looks. Lon knew something was over. He knew something terrible had happened tonight. He had almost killed his half brother. He had betrayed his kind and had taken things that were not his and he had given them away. He had turned his allegiance to an outsider. He'd cared more about the boy and the woman than he cared about his own blood. The elder had warned them. And he had forgotten.

Lon stood looking off to the southeast, toward the place where the fight had begun. Then he bent and placed the photos back beside the man.

"Wait here." He rested his hand on Tommy's shoulder to comfort him, then he strode off alone the way they had come. He found the fishing pole and tackle still on the lighted steps. Zach was gone. Lon picked them up, nodding his head sadly and sighing as he faced the hotel for a long moment. His eyes were already puffed and throbbing and half-closed from the blows that Tommy had landed. His lip was split and oozing blood. Slowly he made his way back through the bushes.

"Sorry . . ." Lon placed the rod and tackle box on the step by Tommy. In the moonlight Tommy's misshapen face was monstrous. His front teeth were broken off at the gum line. His upper lip protruded and curled up in a ludicrous sneer. His dirt-stained cheeks were so badly swollen that his nose almost disappeared between the bulging mounds on either side.

"Don't want . . ." Tommy shoved at it listlessly. Lon hung his head and blinked then glanced sidelong and focused on the heap in the gazebo. Solemnly he took the rod and tackle box and added them to the pile. Tommy studied the gesture, then he looked up at Lon and nodded. "Get dummy. . . ."

Lon shook his head, uncomprehending.

"Get dummy. Put dummy here."

"You get the dummy," Lon countered.

"Foot hurt." Tommy propped his damaged foot on his knee, cradling it with his hand and whimpering pathetically.

Lon didn't understand why Tommy wanted him to bring the breeder there. But he shrugged and set off into the dark again. It took him a long time to carry her back. He wrapped her in a blanket and hauled her, sacklike, over his back. He had to stuff his nostrils with wild ginger so her smell wouldn't make him retch. Then he rolled her out next to the man, just like Tommy wanted.

"Take Tommy home. . . ."

Lon crouched down and turned his back while Tommy hobbled closer. Then he boosted him up and caught his hands under Tommy's knees, supporting him. Tommy wrapped his arms around Lon's back. Moving slowly under the weight, Lon followed the waterway to a crossing point. He only looked back once at the tall, gleaming building that stood above the trees. Then he moved on in silence, careful not to sniff back or lick away the tears. They would be gone before Tommy saw his face again.

The day the bulldozers started in, Lon was out near the site alone. Their growling sound brought him there on a run. Except for the day after the battle when he and Tommy had lain low and soaked their wounds with cool water from the creek, he'd come out there every morning. But he only saw the boy briefly. And he kept out of sight because his face was bruised and both his eyes were ringed in purple. He could barely see out of the slits between the lids, but some place inside him ached, and he could not stay away.

Zach was standing next to Kitty on the level just below the letters they had worked on together. He looked small and tired, and he held her hand. All the others were there with them, lined up and facing the front. There were no tools around. No one was working. And the moat was filled with rows of potted green-leafed plants and flowers. The area beyond was packed with more people than Lon had ever seen, many with dark boxes aimed at the ones upon the slope. Sometimes the ones on the mound would raise their arms and wave.

Someone spoke over the speakers. Lon couldn't understand what he said. But everyone hung their head and became quiet. Then another person spoke and a woman with great shears came out and cut a pretty banner tied across the entrance to the walkway. The music came out louder then and everyone cheered. Clusters of brightly colored bubbles flew out from behind the castle and the tower and the long dragon and they floated up toward the clouds.

Lon had tried to make sense of it. He saw people streaming up the walkway, ones who had no colored ribbon on their arm to show what job they were to do. They walked and looked and pointed black boxes, but they didn't shovel or carry or carve. They just looked. Then they came down again and another stream started off on the same route. When the peculiar traffic pattern lost its fascination, Lon looked for Zach among the crowd. But he wasn't near the staff tent where he'd seen them heading. Lon went back and forth checking all the concession stands. He couldn't find him. The more he scanned the crowd, the more he realized that the ones who'd been up on the mound were gone. Kitty had disappeared, too.

He never saw them again.

If they'd come back, Lon would have spotted them. Every day he came to watch the people, scanning the crowd for the slender woman and the pale-haired boy. Every night he brought Tommy out to watch the strange beams of brilliant green light they made dance in the sky and form pictures on the sand. Then the bursts of sparkling fire would shoot into the air and spread out and fall gently downward like spring rain, and loud booms would echo through the night. The sounds were friendlier than the roar of the Great Blast, and the tremors these caused in his body were pleasing. There would be more bursts of fire and the people would cheer and clap. Then the sprays of light would multiply and fill the sky with strange-smelling clouds of gray. Then it would all abruptly stop. Until the next night.

Lon was there when the flying machine came and brought the three huge crossed sticks up to the top, he watched the women in floating clothes and the men in tight-fitting ones surround the mound, while the few up top spoke words that came together quickly and made no sense. He liked the happy sound of many voices all singing together. "He iz rizzin. . . ." They said it over and over and over but he didn't understand. The sun was barely up when they stopped singing and went away.

Then the flying machine came back and took the crossed sticks away. It brought back three more poles without crossbars. Instead, these had bright blue ribbons that fluttered in the breeze. The only singing this time came from the few people making music on a small platform at one end of the mound. The sound was loud and steady and went on all through the day.

No one worked on the mound again. The crowds remained steady until one afternoon when the far-off rumble sent dark clouds in over the spring lake and it rained. The next day there were only shapeless lumps over the great mound. A scattering of people walked around and looked. Two trucks came and took the green plants away. A work crew dismantled all the tents and concession stands, loaded all the pieces on a flatbed truck, and drove off. Other men pulled up the dark lines buried throughout the mound and packed away the boxes that made the brilliant light.

Then came the morning of the bulldozers. Lon stood on the lower branches of one of the taller oaks, bracing himself on the limbs above. He shifted feet and groaned and muttered as the machines pushed wide swatches of sand up over the top and down the far side. He'd thought they would pile it high again and they would all come back, all the carvers and diggers and bucket carriers, to make it beautiful again. But the dozer kept at it, gradually taking it down layer by layer and pushing it across the clearing and into the spring lake.

Lon was amazed at how big the lake had grown. It was

longer than the mound and it spread out across the bare place they had scraped away so long ago. The pale sand spread out along the edge farther and farther. They even pushed huge walls of sand out into the water. Men with rakes and shovels came and dragged and heaved it out until it settled below the surface.

They were still working near the lake when he brought Tommy out. He had to carry him everywhere now. They'd packed the foot in leaves that they'd heated in a pot over the fire. But Lon wasn't sure they were the right leaves. The healer always cooked the poultices and made the herb teas and potions, and the Great Blast claimed him before they learned his ways. So they had collected what they could, yarrow and healing blade and valerian. But the foot was oozing yellow. It had turned dark and had an evil smell. Tommy had to chew jimson root and plantain and bigroot to keep from screaming with pain.

"See, Tommy. . . ." Lon hoisted him onto a limb then climbed up next to him. Tommy's eyes, flat and impassive, followed the movement of one yellow machine as it deposited its load and went back for another. He ground away continually on his herbal chaw. Sometime the greenish spittle would run down his chin and Lon would always wipe it away.

The cool breeze ripped the leaves around them. Lon reached into his overall pocket for his knife and the stick he'd been working on. He'd been doing a lot of whittling lately, sitting by the cave opening, listening for Tommy to call. He'd bring him cool water or herbs or change the poultice or help him relieve himself. Then he'd whittle again. When it was time for Tommy to leave him, he'd need some dream sticks and some totems to wrap up with him when he gave him over. It wasn't fitting that he be given over alone. Lon kept telling Tommy that he was doing real good. But it wasn't true. So he whittled, night and day, and he tried not to think about the boy.

They waited until dark before they left. Lon loaded Tommy on his back and took the long route. There had been other machines lately that came and scraped away the shrubs and ground cover and left bare stretches exposed where they used to walk. So each time, it became more difficult and longer to find a route within the cover of trees. This one went past the stacked-up houses that all looked out over the marsh. It was pretty there and quiet and the water birds came and poked along its edge. There were more buildings now in that section than Lon remembered. Even the ones that had been there awhile had changed. Instead of hollow skeletons, these had roofs and windows and walls and driveways. Gardens and pools. And lights. Lights means people.

Tommy hung loosely on him, his head lowered onto Lon's wide shoulder. He was feverish again. His body gave off an ominous heat. "Grab 'um. Fuck 'um. . . ." Tommy stared up with glazed eyes at the houses that streamed light across the newly sodded lawns. "Grab 'um. . . ." he rambled on disjointedly.

But Lon had slowed his step. And he craned his neck for the glimpse of a toy or a bike or some small form cutting past a window or leaping into a pool. Soon there would be lights in all the stacked-up houses. More houses would stand up where the new drained land was plowed. There were more and more families coming. He could tell that every day. And somewhere there would be children. Soft and pretty ones. Surely among them, there would be one with moonlight hair.

WOMEN OF DARKNESS

THE BEST IN PSYCHOLOGICAL SUSPENSE

☐ 52722-4	LOWLAND RIDER by Chet Williamson	$3.95
☐ 52723-2		Canada $4.95
☐ 50009-2	MANTIS by K.W. Jeter	$3.95
☐ 52010-6		Canada $4.95
☐ 50070-9	THE NIGHT OF THE RIPPER by Robert Bloch	$3.50
☐ 50071-7		Canada $4.50
☐ 51778-4	NIGHTFALL by John Farris	$3.95
☐ 51779-2		Canada $4.95
☐ 51570-6	NIGHT-WORLD by Robert Bloch	$3.50
☐ 51571-4		Canada $4.50
☐ 50031-8	PSYCHO by Robert Bloch	$3.95
☐ 50032-6		Canada $4.95
☐ 50033-4	PSYCHO II by Robert Bloch	$3.95
☐ 50034-2		Canada $4.95
☐ 50253-1	THE SUITING by Kelley Wilde	$3.95
☐ 50524-X		Canada $4.95
☐ 51832-2	VALLEY OF LIGHTS by Stephen Gallagher	$3.95
☐ 51833-0		Canada $4.95

Buy them at your local bookstore or use this handy coupon:
Clip and mail this page with your order.

Publishers Book and Audio Mailing Service
P.O. Box 120159, Staten Island, NY 10312-0004

Please send me the book(s) I have checked above. I am enclosing $_____
(please add $1.25 for the first book, and $.25 for each additional book to
cover postage and handling. Send check or money order only—no CODs.)

Name _____

Address _____

City _____ State/Zip _____

Please allow six weeks for delivery. Prices subject to change without notice.

BESTSELLING BOOKS FROM TOR

BESTSELLING HORROR FICTION FROM TOR